DONALD BAYNE HOBART

TWO MYSTERIES

DONALD BAYNE HOBART

TWO MYSTERIES

The Clue of the
Leather Noose

The Cell
Murder Mystery

COACHWHIP PUBLICATIONS

Greenville, Ohio

Donald Bayne Hobart: Two Mysteries
© 2014 Coachwhip Publications
Donald Bayne Hobart, 1898-1970
No claims made on public domain material.
The Clue of the Leather Noose first published 1929.
The Cell Murder Mystery first published 1931.
Cover: Gecko © Liane Nothaft

ISBN 1-61646-253-1
ISBN-13 978-1-61646-253-6

CoachwhipBooks.com

CONTENTS

THE CLUE OF THE LEATHER NOOSE

THE CELL MURDER MYSTERY

THE CLUE OF THE LEATHER NOOSE

1
THE NOOSE

LARRY BENSON WALKED SWIFTLY along the Boardwalk. A frown creased his face, Now that his quarrel with Lannon Gordon was over, it began to dawn upon him that he had acted very foolishly. What right had he to object to her having an engagement with Watson Gregg? He had hurt her by the bitter, jealous things he had said. It was in the rather futile hope of finding her that he now strolled along the Boardwalk.

He did not like Watson Gregg. As he walked along he could think of no definite reason for his antipathy. Gregg was rich and elderly and said to be in poor health. Larry felt there was no reason for him to consider the man a rival for Lannon's affections— yet when the girl had told him that she expected to dine with Gregg that night, Larry had protested.

Lannon and he were both young, impulsive and quick tempered. His protest had been the spark to the flame. There had been a stormy scene. They had quarreled bitterly late this afternoon while Larry had been calling at her home.

With the hour that had passed since then, he had become ashamed of his actions. He had stopped in at the hotel where Gregg was staying, hoping to find Lannon dining with the elderly man, to plead with her to forgive him. But he had been disappointed. He had learned that they had taken a rolling chair and were out on the Boardwalk. Casually he glanced up and down the walk. He realized then that his mission was a very futile one.

11

There was very little chance of his encountering Gregg and Lannon, not on the brightly illuminated Boardwalk that wound and twisted along the shore for over seven miles. Yet even though the possibility of his finding them was so uncertain, he continued to hope in spite of his doubts.

A rolling chair parked close to the outer rail and facing the sea caught Larry's attention. Nearby was a pavilion filled with shadows—but no one seemed to be there. It was growing dark, and Larry could not see the occupants of the rolling chair clearly, for its wicker and glass sides, and heavy top cast a shadow. Yet he knew that there were two people in the vehicle. He wondered if they could possibly be Lannon and Gregg. And as he hesitated Larry found himself becoming more and more certain that it was the two for whom he had been searching.

The chair was but fifty feet away, yet he did not go closer. He felt that by doing so he would make his presence too obvious. It would be better if Lannon did not think he had been following her, searching for her. He wished the meeting between them to appear casual. Afterwards he would apologize.

There was a sudden movement from the chair and a girl stepped quickly out. A slender, golden-haired girl she was, dressed in brown. Lannon Gordon—there could be no doubt of that. But there was something wrong. She hurried swiftly away toward the street intersection that led down from the walk. She seemed to be agitated and paying little heed to her surroundings.

Larry turned to follow her. Then abruptly he halted and glanced back at the rolling chair. He was sure now that Gregg had said or done something which Lannon did not like. She would no doubt tell him what was wrong. He turned and ran quickly down the incline which led to the side street.

As he reached the sidewalk he cursed his moment's indecision. Lannon was gone. There was no one in sight. His eyes searched the length of the block. On the Avenue beyond, the traffic appeared heavy. So many people were passing the corner that he realized the futility of finding her there.

Perhaps Lannon had gone home. He wanted to believe that. He would phone her in a few minutes. Perhaps, possibly, he would run over to the house again later. He would go back first and have a few words with Gregg.

The rolling chair was still parked facing the ocean. As he neared it Larry could see through the window the outline of a man's hat. So Gregg was still there gazing out to sea, not even bothering about Lannon. Larry Benson was mentally fuming. Just one girl among the many, Gregg probably thought. But Gregg would learn that he could not toy with Lannon's feelings without someone coming to her defense.

Larry crossed over towards the chair, then paused as he heard footsteps behind him. A slender, dapper looking man passed slowly by. Hard blue eyes in a dark, swarthy face that ended in a small, pointed beard, stared at Larry.

Benson stood watching as the other turned towards the rolling chair. As he reached it he bent over and leaned into the vehicle as he seemed to speak to the occupant. Strange, thought Larry as he watched, Gregg must be hard of hearing.

Then quickly the other drew back from the chair. He glanced about him. His eyes rested upon Larry.

"I beg your pardon." The man's speech was crisp, abrupt. "Have you been in this vicinity long?"

"Why?" asked Larry shortly. He did not like the abruptness of the question.

"Unusual question, I know." The stranger's manner was quick, alert. "I'll explain—I'm Doctor Fulda of New York. Who are you?"

"Larry Benson." Larry smiled faintly. "Of Atlantic City."

"Good. I'm glad to know your name. I may need it later."

"I don't understand!" Larry looked at the other intently. "What do you mean?"

"My patient, Mr. Watson Gregg—in the rolling chair—he appears to be a bit distressed." Doctor Fulda's hard eyes questioned as he spoke. "Thought you might have seen someone talking to him before I arrived."

"I'm quite sure Mr. Benson saw no one," said a deep voice behind them before Larry could speak.

Both Fulda and Benson turned quickly. They both were a bit startled, for they did not hear anyone approach. A tall, pale-faced man dressed in a dark suit stood there. He wore no hat, and his thick gray hair was like a mane. Beneath heavy brows dark-piercing eyes seemed to smolder. His mouth was thin, sensitive and a little cruel.

"Indeed," said Doctor Fulda ironically. "You seem to know a lot about Mr. Benson. May I ask who you are?"

"My name is Danton—Giovanni Danton."

"Really? And I'm Doctor Fulda—James Fulda. Now you might explain how you know what Mr. Benson may have seen!"

There was a barely perceptible glance from Danton in Larry's direction, a look that appeared to be a warning. But it was not needed. Larry had not the slightest intention of saying that he had seen anyone. It might involve Lannon, and that must not happen.

"Mr. Danton is quite right," said Larry quickly. "I hadn't been here more than a moment before you arrived, Doctor. I've seen no one here during that time."

"I see." There was doubt in Fulda's tone.

Danton smiled. He stared for a moment directly at the little doctor. The latter returned the gaze. Then his eyes faltered.

There seemed to be a tense antipathy between these two men. Was it of hate? Were they foes of long standing, or was it merely that strange animosity that sometimes develops upon sight? Larry could not be sure.

Danton turned suddenly and moved toward the rolling chair. The others watched him. Larry wonderingly. The Doctor with his face placid, expressionless. A moment, and then Danton abruptly leaned over, gazing into the chair.

A few seconds passed. Then he turned quickly toward them. His white hands trembled. The flame was in the deep eyes now, high and intense, as he looked from Larry to Doctor Fulda.

"You'd better get a policeman quick, Benson," he said slowly. "Watson Gregg is dead. He's been murdered—strangled to death by a leather cord!"

2
WHERE IS JOHN HAGEN?

ALREADY A CURIOUS CROWD had began to gather about the rolling chair. Danton was waiting, standing near the chair. He did not permit anyone to come too close, and no one questioned his authority. He was an impressive figure; a wolf may always dominate the sheep.

Doctor Fulda stood near Danton, his dark, swarthy face expressionless, one hand stroking his pointed black beard. His eyes were searching as they peered into the faces of the crowd, as though he were looking for someone.

Larry Benson soon returned with a policeman. He was nervous and a little flustered. Gregg murdered! And Lannon Gordon had been with him last! Memories were taunting him. He could still see Lannon hurrying away from the chair, her face white, frightened—and then her agitation as she ran swiftly off the walk!

Larry and the patrolman pushed their way through the crowd. Officer Hayes stepped forward so that he could gaze at the face of the man in the chair. He thrust the coat collar quickly aside. A peculiar cord of saffron leather had been looped around Gregg's throat and drawn so tight that it was deeply imbedded in his flesh.

"Good God! He's been strangled!" exclaimed Hayes, stating the obvious as he released the cord with nervous fingers.

Larry stood at the inner edge of the crowd watching. He was thinking swiftly. Why had not Doctor Fulda or Giovanni Danton loosened that cord? He glanced at them. There were strange expressions now on the faces of those two men as they gazed at one another.

Larry heard the distant clanging of a bell and knew it was the City Hospital ambulance approaching. He realized it was too late now; anyone could see that. Still they must be sure. The policeman had put in the call for the ambulance as soon as Larry had told him about Gregg. The white-coated figure of the ambulance driver and the surgeon came hurrying across the Boardwalk, the driver carrying a canvas stretcher rolled up under one arm.

A quiet young man was asking questions casually as he moved amid the crowd. He spoke to Danton and Doctor Fulda. Larry realized that he was a reporter. He did not act like the chaps Larry had read about in books and seen on the screen. He had not pulled out any pencil and paper and made notes as they always did. He just asked a question or two and then moved on. Larry was willing to bet that the reporter had not learned a thing.

Two husky, blue-coated figures shouldered their way through the crowd. They were the men from the Accident Bureau. Behind them came two detectives. They pushed their way forward to the chair. They lingered there a moment, and then the elder of the two detectives moved aside and spoke to the reporter.

Larry was standing near them. He could not help listening, did not even try to avoid it, for he hoped that he might learn something. He knew that it was Captain Blake, head of the Detective Bureau, who spoke to the reporter. Larry had seen him often before. He was a man of average size, an old, rugged-faced Irishman with white hair, a man who was said to know his business. He had a mind of his own, Larry had heard.

"Give me all the dope you can, Dave." Captain Blake spoke in a low tone, but Larry heard him plainly. "I want the facts and I want them fast, boy!"

"Watson Gregg, rich theatrical man, found murdered, strangled to death with a leather cord while sitting in a rolling chair on the Boardwalk," the reporter rattled off rapidly. "Officer Hayes has the cord. Gregg was discovered about fifteen minutes ago by his physician, Doctor James Fulda of New York, and two other men—Giovanni Danton and Larry Benson. Benson called Hayes. All three are still here in the crowd. Anything else you want to know, Cap?"

"Of course—a devil of a lot! Was anyone seen with Gregg previous to the time these men discovered that he'd been murdered?"

"There was. A girl, a tall, slender young woman, was seen getting out of the chair a short while before, and she was frightened and seemed to have been crying!"

Larry stood staring dumbfounded at the reporter He had thought that the man had not learned anything vital!

In a flash Benson realized that Lannon Gordon was in danger. He gazed about him anxiously, trying to decide what he could do to help her. His eyes rested upon the tall figure of Giovanni Danton standing by the chair. Larry was sure that Danton would help him— though he did not know why he felt that such was the case. It did not matter—he must ask Danton for aid. He wanted to try and keep Lannon out of this.

Larry moved through the throng toward Danton. Captain Blake was ahead of him. The white-haired Irishman gazed intently into the pale face of the tall man. Larry had come up close enough to listen.

"Your name Danton?" asked Captain Blake sharply, abruptly.

"I am Giovanni Danton." The tall man uttered the words slowly, impressively, like a magician talks when he draws something out of a hat.

"What's your business?"

Danton's deep eyes rested for a moment on the face of Captain Blake, and then a faint smile lingered upon his thin lips.

"I am an actor," he said quietly.

A wave of disappointment swept over Larry as he heard the words. He did not know what he had expected Giovanni Danton to be, but it was not an actor. It was something different—something strange.

"An actor," said Captain Blake. "What sort of an actor?"

Danton's strong white hands moved expressively. For a brief instant his gaze was upon Larry. The latter thought he detected the flutter of a white eyelid and wondered if it could have been a wink. Danton was gazing at Blake again now, his face serious.

"I am but an humble performer in the quaint drama of life," he said in low, rolling tones, moving away suddenly.

Captain Blake stood watching him a moment and then he smiled. Larry was frankly puzzled. He wondered what Danton was talking about. It seemed strange that the Captain had not flared up at such an absurd answer to his question. A performer in the quaint drama of life—what had that meant?

Captain Blake muttered a few words in the ambulance surgeon's car. The limp form of Watson Gregg was placed on a stretcher and covered with a blanket. The police hurriedly made a path through the crowd. In a moment or two the stretcher with its grim burden was being carried swiftly away. The crowd murmured as it passed, and then began slowly to move on.

Larry crossed to Danton and drew him aside. He wanted to learn if it were possible for the tall man to help keep Lannon Gordon's name out of the affair.

"Mr. Danton," Larry said nervously, hesitatingly, "I want you to help me."

"Certainly," said Danton, watching him closely. "But how? Hadn't you better explain?"

Larry thought for a moment before he spoke. After all, would it be wise to mention Lannon's name to Danton? So far as he knew, the other had not the slightest knowledge of the girl's presence in the chair.

"The pretty little blonde girl who got out of the chair—crying," said Danton with a faint smile. "She was a friend of yours?"

"Yes," Larry stared at the other in wonder. "A very dear friend."

"I see." Danton's tone was thoughtful. "And now this very dear friend of yours is in danger—of being implicated in murder!"

"I know—I know," said Larry nervously. "I must do everything in my power to aid her, to try and keep her name out of this mess."

"You may mention her name if you wish, to me," said Danton. "There is very little that I shall tell the police."

"She is Lannon Gordon," said Larry quickly, for he felt that in revealing Lannon's name he was showing his confidence in this man.

"I see." Danton's deep eyes stared into Larry's. "And you are deeply interested in her?"

"Yes." Larry did not resent the question. "And I want to help her. But—that reporter told Captain Blake that a woman was seen getting out of Gregg's rolling chair—"

"So! Did he describe her?"

"No. Merely said a tall, slender woman."

"Then the description is vague—good! There was no one within a block of you when Miss Gordon left the chair. I am sure of that." Again the weird smile came over Danton's face, that never reached his eyes.

"From the distance no one could he quite sure of a face. Don't worry, Benson. Miss Gordon is safe so far!"

The crowd had gone now. Captain Blake and the reporter, Dave Morton, were talking to Doctor Fulda. These three and Danton and Larry were now all that remained. The rolling chair was still standing by the rail.

"I wonder—" said Danton slowly, gazing at the rolling chair. "It might be!"

Larry watched him. Why was he staring at the chair so intently? It was just like countless others, that moved up and down the Boardwalk at intervals. Yet Larry realized that was not quite true. A presence lingered, hovering over this vehicle—like the shadow of Death.

Danton moved to the chair. His white hands were searching, fluttering about within the vehicle. Larry wondered what he was looking for. A clue, of course, but what sort of a clue?

Captain Blake hurried to Danton's side. The latter was holding up an object for all to see. It was a woman's handkerchief, a small, black-bordered square of linen. Larry stared as he saw it. He felt sure it was not Lannon's—hers were always gaily colored. A woman's handkerchief. Whose was it?

"I'll take that if you don't mind, Mr. Danton," said Captain Blake, extending his hand. "Please give it to me."

With an ironical look in his deep eyes Danton presented the handkerchief to the Captain with a low bow.

"A lady's handkerchief, Captain Blake," he said. "A clue, perhaps, but there is something else which might prove more interesting." There was an undercurrent in Danton's tone.

"What's that?" the Captain demanded sharply.

"Have you observed that the man who brought them here, the chair-pusher, is missing?"

"Oh!" Blake smiled. "Yes, I learned that when I first arrived. I sent one of my men to the chair stand to investigate. Here he comes now."

A short, heavy-set man came hurrying toward them—Dan Flannigan, Captain Blake's assistant. He was panting and a good bit out of breath, for it was rather a warm night for a heavy man to move swiftly.

"Well, Dan?" asked the Captain as the other reached him.

"I've been to the chair stand like you said. The fellow who was pushing the chair was a white man named John Hagen. He's missing all right."

"You're sure?"

"Yes, Cap. He should have come back some ago. This Hagen hasn't been working at the chair stand long. He gave the starter a hard-luck story. They were short-handed and took him on. According to what I gathered from the pushers and the starter, Hagen was a hard-faced, sullen bird. Claimed he was from the West, but talked and acted like a New Yorker from the East Side."

"I see. Well, you'd better 'phone a description to the office, Dan."

Flannigan turned away to do as he was told. Captain Blake smiled at Danton. The score was even; Blake had known that the chair-pusher was missing.

"May I see the cord that was around Mr. Gregg's neck?" Danton asked the Captain quietly.

Blake hesitated as he glanced at the other man, and then he slowly drew a leather thong about two feet long from his pocket. He handed it to Danton. For an instant the latter stood gazing at the long, saffron cord. Then his hands trembled slightly, and the flames flickered in his smoldering eyes.

"The Leather Necklace!" he murmured. "*Dio mio!*"

3
"YOU DIDN'T KILL HIM?"

THE WIND WAS MURMURING softly as it floated through the shadows of the night. It peered into windows, rattling at the doors of a rambling stone structure so old that it fairly creaked with the weight of passing years.

Lannon Gordon sat in the living room of the old house, a worried expression upon her beautiful face as she listened to the whispers of the wind. She seemed such a wisp of a girl in the great, shadowy room; the gleam of a tall, solitary candle seemed to reflect only her pale face and golden hair.

There was a pensive, hurt look in her big brown eyes. She could not forget what Larry had said that afternoon. His words had been so bitter. She was sure that he did not love her, and it hurt somehow.

Lannon sat there lonely and frightened—waiting. She was sitting motionless, straining to catch the faintest sound. The old house was creaking and whispering to the song of the wind. Were those footsteps, faint, ghostlike footsteps pattering along the dimly lighted hallway beyond the open door of the room—echoes of steps of other days?—or only the boards creaking softly in the night as they will do when they are old and worn?

Somewhere in the distance a clock struck slowly as though it, too, labored under the weight of years. Lannon counted the strokes. Ten o'clock. Was that all? It seemed to the girl that she had been waiting an eternity.

Lannon turned quickly at the sound of a soft, faint rustle behind her. Terror lingered in her eyes as she peered toward the hall.

A wizened old colored woman stood smiling toothlessly at her from the doorway.

"Oh, it's you, Loona!" There was relief in the girl's tone. "I never realized how creepy this old place could be when the wind was blowing! Hasn't Aunt Ida returned yet?"

The old colored servant shook her white, kinky head. "No, she ain't Missy Lannon," she uttered in a soft cackle. "Creepy yo' say? Lawdy, chil', they's people a-walkin' an' a-whisperin' 'round heah all de time!"

"Ghosts?" Lannon laughed nervously. "There's no such thing, Loona!"

"De ain't?" There was a frown on Loona's ancient face. "Yo' mustn't say dat, chil'—it ain't good to talk data way 'bout spirits. Deed it ain't!"

"Blah— Grow up, honey."

Old Loona shook her head. Her tone changed to a whisper: "If dey ain't no spooks, den what am it dat keeps tellin' me dat ole Mistis is a'goin' to be happy, like she ain't been fo' ten years? What am it dat keeps a-whisperin' an' a-whisperin' dat somethin' done happen tonight? What am it?"

"Oh, please, Loona, don't!" exclaimed Lannon tearfully. "I'm very nervous tonight. You frighten me when you talk that way! I wonder what's keeping Auntie?"

"Don't yo' worry, chil'. She's a-comin' soon! An' she's gonna be happy!" Loona cackled softly. "It's done been a long time since old Mistis been happy—a long time! Many de time I's seen her a-weepin' to herse'f when she don't know dey's nobody 'round. But she's gonna be happy now. I done see it in de tea leaves—dat's it, in de tea leaves!"

The old servant disappeared into the hallway, cackling softly to herself. Lannon stared after her. Loona's words had been so strange. What had she meant? Aunt Ida happy—Aunt Ida, who had traveled hand in hand with a secret sorrow as far back as Lannon could remember. Loona was so old! She had strange fancies. Aunt Ida happy? Lannon sighed. If only that might be so!

The girl turned and stared out of the window. The blind was drawn, but she could see the shadowy forms of the trees which surrounded the old house as they swayed in the wind.

Suddenly a tall, gray-haired woman was standing in the doorway. The shadows of yesterday's loveliness lingered still in the kindly, sweet face, peeping out beyond the marks of sorrow which time had left.

"Lannon, dear," she called in a soft deep voice.

Lannon had leaped to her feet in an instant, and came swiftly forward, delight in her big eyes as she gazed at the other woman.

"Oh, Aunt Ida, I'm so glad you've arrived! I've been worried. I didn't know what on earth was keeping you!"

A strange look passed over Miss Ida Hill's face. For a brief moment there was a gleam in her deep blue eyes. The expression puzzled Lannon. What was the matter with Aunt Ida? She seemed to be laboring under some suppressed emotion. What was wrong? Lannon watched nervously as her Aunt spoke.

"Nothing on earth has been keeping me, Lannon," she said slowly, the bright light still in those blue eyes that must have been so lovely in her youth. "I have found happiness tonight, dearest—happiness that I have hoped and waited for through ten lonely, terrible years!"

Lannon gazed at her Aunt wide-eyed. A change had come over Miss Hill since the last time the girl had seen her, a mysterious transformation that the girl could not understand. Aunt Ida said she was happy, but it seemed such a weird sort of happiness. Lannon wondered what it could mean.

The girl fairly gasped as Miss Hill moved toward her as swiftly as she herself might have done, and kissed her affectionately. It was this which surprised Lannon more than anything. Her Aunt had never been the least bit inclined to become demonstrative. Very seldom did she display the deep affection which she held in her heart for her brother's child.

"It's good to see you tonight of all nights, dear," she said, gazing at Lannon fondly. "But what brings you 'way down here in Margate so late, Lannon? Why, it's almost eleven o'clock."

"I know it is. I heard the clock strike a while ago. I've been here ever since a little after nine waiting for you to return."

"Lannon!" there was an anxious look upon Miss Hill's sweet, faded countenance. "Nothing has happened at home, has there? John—I mean your father—is all right, isn't he?" A bitter smile flashed, then faded from her lips. "Not that he would ever tell me if there was anything wrong. It's a fine state of affairs when a brother and sister live in the same town for nearly ten years and don't even speak to each other!"

"Oh, it is, Aunt Ida! I never could understand why Daddy always refused to have anything to do with you. You would never tell me, you know; and once when I dared to ask him he just swore and walked away."

"Swore, did he?" Miss Hill's tone was scornful. "You never told me that before. That sounds just like John Gordon. It's a wonder he has permitted you to visit me during all these lonely years. Your mother was far kinder to me than my own brother. Oh, if we had never seen that terrible day five years ago when she passed away!"

Lannon's eyes filled with tears. If only that could have been! She had adored her lovely mother—they had been closer than most. They had understood each other so well.

Miss Hill saw the expression on the girl's face and realized what she was thinking. She knew how deeply Lannon had loved her mother.

"You poor, poor baby!" Miss Hill's voice changed, grew lower, and now there was a tender note in it. "You've been so kind to me, darling, kind and good to me all through the long years. Whatever love there might be in the broken heart of an old woman goes out to you. Surely you know that, don't you, dear?"

"Yes, Auntie." Lannon put her arm about the elderly woman affectionately and led her to a divan. "Of course I do. That's why I'm here now. Oh, Aunt Ida, I'm so beastly miserable—"

"Why, Lannon, what do you mean?" Miss Hill looked at the girl. "Tell me about it."

Lannon gazed out of the window. She wanted to tell her Aunt everything, and yet it was so hard to begin. Suppose she did not understand? But she must tell her. She had to tell someone.

"It's—it's about Larry." Lannon paused.

"About Larry? Go on, dear?"

"We—we had a messy old quarrel, and I don't know why—I don't know why. It was a lovely afternoon, and everything was so glorious that it hurt a little bit. You know what I mean, Auntie?"

Miss Hill sighed. She was remembering an old garden, years and years ago—a girl radiant with youth and beauty as she walked beside her lover—there had been moonlight, fragile moonlight kissing the roses

"Yes, dear," she said softly. "I know."

"Honestly?"

"And then what happened, Lannon?"

"And then I told Larry that I was going to have dinner with Watson Gregg—"

"Watson Gregg!" there was a wild light in Miss Hill's eyes now. "Oh, God, Lannon! Tell me you didn't have anything to do with him! Tell me quickly, or I shall go mad!"

"But I did, Auntie, I did!" The girl was frightened now, sobbing wildly.

"Oh, no no! Not you—not my Lannon!"

The blue eyes burned into the white, frightened face of the girl. Miss Hill's strong fingers suddenly clasped Lannon by the throat. The girl gasped as she felt those fingers tightening, tightening.

"Auntie, Auntie!" she cried, her voice choked. "When I think that you had anything to do with that man I could kill you!"

Miss Hill's voice, grim and high-pitched, was ringing in Lannon's ears. Black, giant waves seemed to be dashing over her—then oblivion. Lannon had fainted.

As the girl became limp in her grasp Miss Hill drew her hands away quickly. Lannon fell back against the divan on which they had been sitting. Like someone coming out of a mad dream, the elderly woman passed her hand before her eyes.

She could not realize what had happened. In a dazed fashion she gazed at the senseless girl. On the soft, white throat was a deep, red mark that had been caused by the tight grip of Miss Hill's hands. As she saw it the woman shuddered.

"Oh, Lannon, Lannon!" she murmured tearfully. "What have I done! I must have been mad, insane!" Her frame was shaking with sobs.

It was but a moment before Lannon opened her eyes and looked about her, but to the frightened sorrowful woman who sat beside her it seemed a century. The girl sighed and then sat up weakly.

"Dearest, how can you ever forgive me!" sobbed Miss Hill. "I was mad, Lannon, insane at the mention of that man's name. Did I hurt you very badly, dear?"

Lannon put her hand to her throat. She was still nervous and frightened. That Aunt Ida would ever attempt to hurt her, seemed impossible; and yet she had done so. But she must not let her know how she felt—that would only hurt Aunt Ida's feelings; and she was so excited, so strange tonight.

"It's nothing, Auntie—but—oh, of course it's all right—"

Lannon smiled, and then her eyes filled. In an instant the two women were sobbing in each other's arms, and finding their tears a great comfort.

"Now tell me all that happened," said Miss Hill later, when they had both become calmer. "I won't alarm you again."

"Of course I'm going to tell you everything," Lannon said, smiling now as she patted her Aunt's hand. "You're all the mother I have now, you know. I'd met Mr. Gregg before. I didn't like him, but he had been very nice, and when he invited me to have dinner with him I hated to refuse. I didn't think it would be any harm. We had dinner in the hotel dining room. Afterward he suggested that we go for a little chair ride—"

"A chair ride!" exclaimed Miss Hill, and then she grew calmer. "Never mind—go on, dear."

"We rode up the Boardwalk as far as the Garden Pier. Then he told the chair-pusher to turn around and we started back. All the time he'd been saying—saying things—"

Lannon paused, startled by the look upon her Aunt's face. The elderly woman was gazing out of the window, an expression almost gloating upon her countenance.

"I'm glad," she murmured softly. "Glad!"

"What do you mean, Auntie?"

Miss Hill looked at her and then smiled a strange smile.

"Nothing, dear, nothing. Go on with your story."

"Well—it wasn't 'til we had passed the Million Dollar Pier that—that—what he'd been sayin' sank in. Finally the old freak ordered the chair pusher to park. The chair-pusher walked away. Then Mr. Gregg said— Oh, Auntie, I can't repeat that—" Lannon's tone rose to a frightened pitch.

"I understand," the elderly woman nodded. "I knew Watson Gregg! What happened after that?"

"Then I jumped out of the chair cryin', and headed off the Boardwalk as quickly as I could. When I reached the street I heard someone following me, so I hid in the shadow of a building 'til they had passed. I don't know who it was."

"You saw no one?"

"No. When I came out of my hiding place they were gone. I took the trolley and went home then. After I got all the way home I remembered Daddy was away. He left for New York this morning on some old business—"

"And left you all alone in that big house?"

"But he always does! I'm not afraid. Besides, one of the maids is usually there. But tonight I had to see you. I was afraid that—that beast might telephone or something! I'm going to stay here, too, Auntie. May I?"

"Of course, dear!" Miss Hill turned quickly at a slight sound. The old colored woman stood in the doorway. "Oh, it's you, Loona!" She laughed hysterically. "The tea leaves were right this time! Happiness is coming! The devil is gone!"

"Auntie, what do you mean?" demanded Lannon nervously.

"I mean that Watson Gregg is dead!" There was something like joy in Miss Hill's tone.

"Watson Gregg—dead!" repeated Lannon, dazed.

"De Lord am good!" said Loona, and then cackled softly.

"Yes, he is dead!" Miss Hill's eyes gleamed wildly. "He was found strangled to death in the rolling chair on the Boardwalk shortly after you left him."

"Strangled!" Lannon's hands automatically went to her throat upon which the red mark of her Aunt's strong fingers still was visible. "Auntie, you—you didn't— Oh, God! Aunt Ida, you didn't kill him?"

Miss Hill did not answer. She was gazing at Loona, her eyes gleaming, a smile on her face.

"Whisperin' like dey was tellin' me somethin'," said Loona softly, and then she cackled loudly.

Lannon shuddered and buried her face in her hands.

4
FROM AN UNKNOWN

CAPTAIN JERRY BLAKE sat in his office in the Detective Bureau. At the moment he was a very busy man. The telephone which stood on the desk in front of him rang at frequent intervals. Each time it did so he would lift the receiver from the hook, listen a moment and then give a terse command to one of his men.

Dan Flannigan sat in a chair opposite the Captain's desk. The stout detective was puffing thoughtfully upon a black cigar as he watched Blake.

Again the telephone rang and the Captain lifted the receiver.

"All right, MacFay," he said over the 'phone. "Watch every train that leaves the city over the Pennsylvania tonight. You have that chair-pusher's description, haven't you? Good! If you see him, bring him right in. No, Martin is watching the Reading trains, and the State Police have been warned to be on the lookout for anyone trying to make a getaway over the highways. Right! 'Bye."

"Think that bird Hagen did it?" asked Flannigan as the Captain put the receiver back on the hook.

"No." Blake frowned and shook his head. "But I think he might know who did. This is the damnedest case I've ever worked on, Dan. Watson Gregg was murdered right there on the Boardwalk in plain sight of anyone who might have happened to be passing—and we haven't a bit of evidence that's worth a hoot!"

"It's too bad Hayes didn't have sense enough to use his eyes," remarked Flannigan. "That's the way with some harness bulls, though—they're all dumb!"

29

With an effort the Captain repressed a smile. It had not been more than a year ago that Dan Flannigan had been a patrolman himself. Still, Flannigan was a good man, able to carry out orders in the fullest detail. Blake had found him a valuable aid.

"What you say about Patrolman Hayes is quite right," said Blake thoughtfully. "From what he has told us, he was standing about a block and a half away from the rolling chair all the time. He says that a few people passed him, but he didn't notice them particularly. He remembered seeing that young fellow Larry Benson go by, though. Said he looked anxious and worried and seemed to be searching for someone."

"What do you think about Benson, Cap?" asked Flannigan. "Think he had anything to do with it?"

"I don't know—yet." Captain Blake produced an old black brier pipe and filled and lighted it slowly. "When I questioned Benson an hour or so ago he seemed nervous and a bit excited about something. But that doesn't prove anything. He's young, and I guess his finding Gregg like that was more or less of a shock."

"Sure, it would be," agreed the detective. "It's not the boy but those other two I have my doubts about—Danton and Fulda, I mean."

"I know." Blake nodded. "There's something hard and strange about that little doctor. I haven't quite doped him out yet—but there will be plenty of time to learn more about him. I've warned him not to leave town until this thing is cleared up."

"I hope he likes it here," said Flannigan dryly. "From the looks of things now he may have a long stay."

"I'm not so sure about that. Someone murdered Gregg, and it's up to us to find out who did it. You know, Dan, this Giovanni Dan-ton is a strange bird. I think he knows much more than he is willing to tell. I'm going to give him a long rope and see if he doesn't hang himself."

"Maybe," said Flannigan doubtfully. "But you want to be careful that he doesn't make a quick exit, Cap. He strikes me as a kinda clever guy."

"Don't worry. If he tries to leave the city, the boys have been posted, and they'll bring him in." Blake laughed. "Danton amuses me. He struts around like a ham actor playing a part in a great drama." Then the Captain's expression grew serious. "And yet there is something about the man I don't understand. He's just a bit mysterious. You know, Dan, I haven't the slightest doubt that he could have murdered Gregg."

"Neither have I," said Flannigan. "But I notice you aren't saying that he did do it, Cap."

"No, not yet." Blake shook his head. "I want to learn more about this case first. I don't believe in making an arrest just for the sake of sticking someone in jail. I want to have plenty of evidence against them."

The telephone rang insistently, and Blake picked up the receiver. "Hello . . . Who? . . . oh, Morton, from the *Morning Press* . . . Yes, all right, I'll see him. Send him up."

The Captain had hardly put the receiver-down when there came a knock upon the closed door of the office. Flannigan rose quickly to his feet and drew the door open. Dave Morton, the reporter from the *Morning Press*, stood there, a smile on his good-natured young face.

"Oh, it's you, Dave!" exclaimed Blake as he saw him. "Come in. Shut the door, Dan."

"What's news, Jerry?" asked Morton as he dropped into a chair near the Captain's desk. "Anything further on this Gregg affair?"

"Not a thing that you don't know about, boy."

Jerry Blake and Dave Morton had been on friendly terms for years. The reporter respected the Captain's confidence in him, and by so doing gained a good bit of news for his paper at first hand from time to time. "Have you dug up anything?"

"A little," said Morton. "I had an idea that the gang around the theatres might know something about Gregg—and they did. I pumped a few fellows that I know and learned one or two things."

"What were they?"

"Well, you know one of the shopkeepers along the Boardwalk near where Gregg's chair was parked, said they had seen a woman get out of the chair and she was crying—"

"Yes, a man named Arno who keeps a lace shop. We questioned him, but he couldn't give us a very good description of the woman. Said it was too dark. What about it, Dave?"

"Just that an old flame of Gregg's is staying here in town, a woman named Mercedes La Tona. She's staying at Seafoam Hotel."

"Good!" the Captain quickly picked up a pencil and made a note of the name and address. "I'll send one of my men around to talk to her right away."

"I'm afraid you won't find it much use." Morton smiled. "I've already been to see her. She says she didn't even know Gregg, and won't talk."

"Oh, won't she!" said Captain Blake softly. "We may change her mind about that! Do you think she was the woman in the chair, Dave?"

"You've got me! She's tall and slender—but that doesn't prove a thing. You could find a hundred women who answer to that description, Jerry. I think she may know something, though."

"In that case we're going to find out what it is."

"I'll bet you will, if it can be found," Morton remarked as he rose to his feet. "Well, I've got to get back to the office. Just thought I would drop in and see if there were any further developments."

"There aren't yet," said Blake. "So long, Dave—probably see you tomorrow."

The reporter nodded to the two men and then left the office, closing the door behind him.

"Mercedes La Tona, eh?" said Blake softly, opening a drawer of his desk and drawing out a black-bordered handkerchief. "Now I wonder if this belongs to her?"

"You've got me, Cap. It's a woman's handkerchief, anyway; and it might be hers. Do you want me to go and see her, Cap?"

"Better wait until morning," said Blake. "If Morton has just been there she will be all set for an interview with the police and may be harder to handle. Anyway, I think I'd better talk to her myself."

"That's O.K. with me."

"What time is it?" Captain Blake looked at his watch. "Um, eleven-thirty. I don't think there is much chance of anything else breaking in this case tonight, Dan. I've half a mind to go home and hit the hay. All of you know where to reach me if anything turns up."

"Sure, Cap, and I'm thinking that maybe a little sleep might do you good."

Captain Blake yawned and then stretched as he rose from the desk. He put on his hat and coat, and was just about to leave the office, when the telephone rang again.

He answered it quickly.

"Captain Blake?" demanded a deep voice over the wire.

"Yes. Who's speaking?"

"A friend." There came a soft sound that sounded like a laugh. "If you will drive out over the old Longport Road right away, you may learn something to your advantage."

"What do you mean? Who is this?" demanded Blake.

But the click of a receiver was all that he heard. He called Central and tried to learn the number of the person who had just 'phoned, but he found it was useless.

"Trace the call," he commanded sharply. "This is Captain Blake of the Detective Bureau, speaking."

A minute or so later the operator reported that the call had come from a pay station in Margate. Blake rang the number and found that it was a drug store—but they could not tell him who it was that had telephoned.

"Sounds like a wild goose chase to me," said Blake as he repeated the message to Flannigan. "But I can't afford to take any chances. Come on, Dan. We're going to take a little drive out along the old Longport Road in my car. Hurry!"

5
"A TWO-LEGGED OWL"

IT WAS MIDNIGHT NOW, the ghostly high noon of a grim night filled with strange shadows. A night of silence that somber, brooding stillness which lingers before a storm.

A long, lonely road wandered through the tall pines, like a pale snake twisting through the shadows. The trees loomed black and grotesque against the sky—grim legions of sentinels guarding the road; odd, fantastic shapes swaying slightly in the wind.

Somewhere back in the woods on the left of the dark road an owl hooted mournfully, a strange sound that was weird as the cry of a witch. The sound lingered for only a second. Then all again became grimly silent.

Amid the trees on the opposite side of the road something stirred restlessly in the dense undergrowth. A match snapped and then leaped into flame. For an instant the faint glow revealed the face of the man who sat in a little clearing a short distance from the road.

It was not a pleasant countenance. Even in repose it was slightly sinister. A long, narrow face, cold gray eyes, thin lips that drooped sardonically—the face of a wolf in human form—an impression that was carried further by the long, lean body of the man as with a rapid, snakelike motion he changed his position slightly and lighted a cigarette. He blew out the match and sat there puffing thoughtfully, the cigarette a tiny glowing ember amid the darkness.

The owl hooted again. This time the bird seemed nearer to the right of the road. The cry was repeated twice. The cigarette of the man in the bushes went out suddenly at the repetition of the sound. He sat there tense and motionless.

From the brush on the opposite side of the road, a lean, ungainly figure appeared, dragging a dead tree, which he placed across the road. As he did so two gleaming eyes that grew steadily larger appeared along the highway toward the north. On and on came the approaching car, the headlights shining in the darkness. When it had almost reached the tree the car stopped with a quick grinding of brakes.

The man in the brush saw that there were two people in the vehicle, a man and a woman. As the machine paused, the individual who had placed the tree across the road again stepped out of the shadows. He stood just beyond the gleam of the lights, an evil expression upon his hard face as he watched the people in the car. His eyes rested for an instant upon the rings on the woman's hands, sparkling faintly in the ray of the dash-lamp. He advanced quickly toward the machine, a heavy bit of timber that he had picked up from the roadside now in his hand.

It was not until he stood within the rays of the car's light that its occupants saw him. The woman uttered a startled cry, and the man glared at him belligerently.

The man in the brush had worked his way silently forward until, from where he stood, the conversation was plainly audible. Carefully and silently he drew an automatic from his pocket and stood there in the shadows, waiting.

"What do you want?" the man in the car demanded sharply.

The man with the club grinned as he raised his weapon. "The lady's jewelry!" he stated gruffly. "Hand it over quick!"

"So that's it!" said the man in the car, his right hand groping in the pocket of the door beside him. "A hold-up, eh?"

"Yea—an' if you don't hurry up an' hand over them rings I'll knock you cold!"

"You won't get a damn thing!"

With the words the man in the car suddenly covered the robber with a revolver. A shot rang out. The hold-up man dropped limp and motionless to the roadway. The woman uttered a wild scream.

"God! You've killed him—you've killed him!"

"Why—why that's impossible." The man in the car rose from his seat and stood staring down at the limp form. "I didn't shoot at all!"

The man in the bushes smiled grimly and he placed his warm automatic back in his pocket.

"But you must have!" the woman insisted. "I heard the gun go off and saw him fall!" she glanced about her, pale faced and frightened. "You must have done it! There is no one else here! See—see if he's dead!"

The man leaped from the car and examined the limp form on the road. As he did so there was a faint rustling in the brush as though someone or something were leaving the scene—it grew fainter and then died away. The woman got out of the machine and stood watching anxiously. The man answered her unspoken question with a nod as he stood up.

"Yes, he's dead. Shot through the heart."

"Oh!" the woman's exclamation was a groan. "What shall we do? What can we do?"

"I don't know!" The man shook his head. "It may seem heartless, but the best thing for us to do is get away from here as quickly as possible."

"You mean to leave—leave him there in the road?"

"Yes. The next car that comes along will bring him in. Poor devil, he's beyond aid now. We simply can't afford to be mixed up in this!"

As the man finished speaking he dragged the dead tree to one side. This done, he stood for an instant looking down at the still form. He shook his head slowly as he took the woman by the arm and led her back to the car.

"I did not shoot," he said slowly as they got in. "I wonder—" His eyes roamed over the shadowy trees which lined the road. "Let's get away from here quick."

The motor roared, and the car sped off down the road and soon disappeared.

A few minutes later a low, gray roadster came speeding along. It stopped suddenly as the headlight played upon the still figure in the road.

"Looks like someone had been struck by one of these hit-and-run drivers!" exclaimed Blake to Dan Flannigan as they got out of the Captain's roadster. "These reckless drivers don't seem to have any regard for human life!"

"You said it, Cap!" exclaimed the stout detective, as Blake bent over and examined the man in the road.

"He's dead!" said the Captain. "Shot through the heart!"

With the aid of the headlights on the car Blake went swiftly through the pockets of the dead man. The objects which he discovered were few. Forty cents in change, a grimy handkerchief, and a tattered and torn letter were all.

Captain Blake held the letter up so he could read it, and then uttered an exclamation.

"It's addressed to Mr. John Hagen," he said. "This is the missing chair-pusher—the man who saw Watson Gregg murdered!"

"Looks that way." Flannigan stood staring down at the dead man. "Poor devil—bumped him off because he knew too much, eh?"

"Yes, that must be it." The Captain nodded. "I wonder who did it?"

Both men turned at the sound of footsteps coming along the dark road. A tall figure moved toward them from out of the shadows.

Flannigan swiftly produced a flash-light. For an instant it gleamed upon the pale face of Giovanni Danton.

"Danton!" exclaimed Blake. "What are you doing here?"

"Strolling." There was a sardonical note in the deep voice. "I love to wander in the woodland amid the shadows of the night."

Flannigan dropped the light to the road, and for an instant it fell upon the motionless form of John Hagen. As he saw it Danton uttered a soft exclamation.

"The chair-pusher!" he said. "Is he dead?"

"Yes," Blake answered. "Shot through the heart. Do you know who did it, Danton?"

For an instant that weird smile that never reached his eyes, spread over Danton's face.

"You might try looking for a two-legged owl," he said slowly.

6

THE HOUSE OF SHADOWS

LARRY BENSON had spent a restless night. He had slept but little, for there was much on his mind that worried him. More than once during the long hours he had sat at his window staring out into the darkness; the pale, frightened face of Lannon Gordon lingered vividly in his mind—Lannon as she had looked leaving the rolling chair.

Had Watson Gregg been dead then? No, he could not have been! Larry would close his eyes resolutely as the question pounded at him; and then the ghastly face of Gregg as he had seen it last would appear, the eyes staring, glassy, the countenance purple. It was not a pretty sight to remember.

But more than anything, he worried about Lannon. Where was she? He had telephoned her home last night as soon as Captain Blake had questioned him and let him go, but no one had answered. For hours he had driven up and down the streets of the city in his roadster, hoping that by some strange trick of fate he might catch a glimpse of Lannon. It had been a foolish quest, but his heart would not let him do otherwise.

At last he had returned home utterly worn out, and sought his room. For a long time he had lain on his bed, thinking, tossing. At last, toward morning, he had slept; the deep, dreamless sleep of the weary.

Now it was the morning of a new day. Perhaps he would find Lannon now—he hoped so. He found breakfast a little difficult, for the family were asking questions. They had read the morning paper.

They knew that Larry had been one of the trio who had discovered Watson Gregg, and they demanded explanations.

He told them there was not much to it. He had just been coming along the Boardwalk, the other two men had stopped him, and then they had investigated. It was a brief recital on Larry's part, a bit vague in spots. He said nothing about Lannon, of course.

His father asked him if he had seen in the morning paper that the chair pusher had been found in the woods—shot. To Larry that was startling news. He read the story of the murder carefully. A two-column article on the front page of the *Morning Press*, an interesting article that made one pause and wonder, that made the question more intriguing: Who killed Watson Gregg?

Larry realized that Morton knew his stuff all right; he had all the facts just as they were. Larry smiled to himself—and he had thought the reporter had learned nothing when he had seen him going quietly among the crowd! But what was this about the chair-pusher? Oh yes, here it was:

> John Hagen, who was said to have been pushing the rolling chair in which Watson Gregg was found murdered, was discovered by Captain Blake and Detective Flannigan at midnight last night on the old Longport Road, a bullet through his heart.
>
> Captain Blake stated that it was his opinion that the man had been shot because he knew too much regarding the murder of Gregg.

Larry put the paper down as he heard the telephone ringing. He hurried to answer it, hoping that it might be Lannon.

"Hello?" said a strange voice, that of a woman. "Mr. Larry Benson, please."

"This is Mr. Benson speaking."

"Oh, this is Miss Hill, Mr. Benson."

"Yes, Miss Hill?" Larry was mentally wondering who the deuce was Miss Hill.

A soft laugh came over the wire. "You haven't the faintest idea who I am." Again the woman laughed. "I'm Lannon Gordon's Aunt."

"Oh, yes, Miss Hill—I've heard Lannon speak of you often."

"I'm glad of that. Mr. Benson, I—we'd like you to have dinner with us this evening. Can you do so?"

"Why—why I'd be delighted, Miss Hill. But I'm afraid I don't know just where you live."

"The last house on Locust Road in Margate."

"The last house on Locust Road—I see." Larry wanted to ask if Lannon would be there, but he did not voice the question. "All right. Thank you very much."

"You're quite welcome. We'll expect you at seven-thirty then—goodbye."

"Lannon—" he started to say, but a click on the wire told him that Miss Hill had hung up.

He turned away from the telephone, frowning thoughtfully. He could not quite place Miss Hill. She had a pleasant voice, anyway. He wondered if she were the Aunt Ida that Lannon had mentioned casually once or twice. He felt she must be. If only he could be sure that Lannon was going to be there! Still, Miss Hill had said "we'll" expect you; surely by that she had meant Lannon.

Larry never knew how he lived through the day, the hours seemed so long. He spent them reading books in which he could not become interested, and in writing Lannon letters which he tore up as soon as he had finished them. Finally, he went back to the Boardwalk near the pavilion where Watson Gregg had been found. How different it looked in the daylight! The Boardwalk was thronged with people, with rolling chairs passing the spot, not knowing, not heeding.

It was just ten minutes after seven that evening when Larry's roadster turned north on Locust Road in Margate. It was a dark night, with great banks of storm clouds hiding the stars, and the wind whistling as it rushed by the swiftly moving car.

A mile farther, and Larry had passed the last of the closely clustered houses which had lined the road during the first part of his journey. Now trees and brush began to cast their shadows amid the dancing glow of the roadster's headlights.

Larry realized that the directions which Miss Hill had given him were rather vague. The last house to the north on Locust Road—how far away was that? He began to wonder if he had not already passed the place, when looming ahead and to his right, he caught a glimpse of a well-lighted residence.

This he judged must be Miss Hill's house. He became convinced that such was the case when he found that the road ended a few yards farther on. He turned the car around and then stopped on the road in front of the house, to sit for a moment looking about him.

The house was not very imposing, merely a small and rather dilapidated structure of stone standing in the center of a weedy clearing amid the trees.

Larry felt a foreboding of evil steal over him. The place appeared so forlorn. It was old and badly in need of repair. One corner of the small porch standing in front had sagged and appeared likely to collapse at any moment. The windows with their tightly drawn blinds blinked sardonically at him. Decidedly, if this were the residence of Lannon's Aunt, it was a very uninviting place.

A gravel driveway ran from the road to the front porch, and Larry drove his car along this slowly. He parked the roadster at the side of the driveway and with a feeling of reluctance made his way up onto the dark, ramshackle porch. The upper section of the heavy front door contained a square of red glazed glass, and now a faint light gleamed through this, a light which fell like a splatter of blood upon the floor of the porch.

Larry rang the bell and glanced about him wonderingly. Was Lannon here in this place? It seemed so remote, so lonely and forsaken to him as he stood there amid the darkness of the night. He wondered what sort of a woman Miss Hill might be. Could it be possible that she really desired to live amid such depressing surroundings?

There had been no answer to his ring and he pushed the bell again. As he stood there the red light of the door gleamed weirdly.

From somewhere within the house a faint wind blew the curtains that hung inside the glass to and fro, to and fro. The hallway within appeared to be filled with strange shadows that passed and re-passed in a mad procession.

Finally the door opened slowly and silently. Larry found him-self staring down into the wizened face of an old negro woman, that was as black as the ace of spades.

Beneath the red glare of the light which burned in the hall, the woman stood for a moment looking at him. There was a strange, wild light in her small, black eyes, a toothless, wrinkled grin upon her ancient face. At last she appeared satisfied and moved back so that he might enter, but she did not speak.

"Is this Miss Hill's residence?" asked Larry, as he stepped into the hallway. "I'm Mr. Benson. I believe she is expecting me."

"Yes, suh." The old colored woman uttered a shrill cackle that sent a chill down Larry's spine. "I'll tell Mistis yo' heah!"

The servant closed the front door and then led Larry to a room on the left of the hallway. She indicated that he was to wait there, by a wave of her hand, as she disappeared down the hall.

The room was dimly lighted; its only illumination came from four white candles which stood in pairs in candelabra on either end of the wide mantel. The furnishings were shabby and old, and yet they looked comfortable. Three big chairs and a divan covered with worn leather, a heavy old oak table, and a small writing desk were all the furnishings the small room possessed.

There was an atmosphere about the room, an atmosphere of dim, half forgotten memories—of dead yesterdays. It was as though the old and musty place belonged to another age. Yet Larry felt that something else brooded over the room, dominating it. It was a subtle hint of a strong personality, a personality he now realized hung over the atmosphere of the whole house. A pitiful, valiant effort to make something out of nothing, suggested itself to his mind, a half-ashamed effect of neatness, like that of a woman who had been forced to fix an ancient dress over a dozen times and make it do.

Larry got the impression that this old dwelling had witnessed many scenes during the years which had passed since it had been built. Beneath this roof life had run the gauntlet of emotions, of love and hate and bitter turmoil. He felt that if the house could speak it would tell an interesting story, one which would reveal that the owners of the house had lived in every sense of the word.

Now an uncanny quietness hung over everything, a strange silence that was like the sudden ceasing of the ticking of a clock. The house seemed a place of shadows.

Larry began to pace up and down the room. The grim stillness brooding over the place was so tense that the faint sound of his own footsteps startled him. It had begun to get on his nerves—the uncanny silence. He wondered if Lannon could really be staying in a place like this.

Suddenly he paused abruptly as he heard a faint sound amid the stillness. He stood listening tensely. From somewhere within the house he could hear a woman sobbing as though her heart would break.

He frowned as he listened and then shrugged his shoulders as he continued to pace the floor. It was none of his affair, whatever might be going on within this old house. Then he paused suddenly, a worried expression upon his face. That woman crying—surely it could not have been Lannon. Larry turned quickly, conscious that someone was watching him.

A slim, gray haired woman stood in the doorway, a sad-faced woman who had evidently been very beautiful in her youth, for the charm of her loveliness still lingered. She was dressed in a black evening gown that had been the latest fashion ten years ago. She came toward him with her hand outstretched, a faint smile upon her lips.

"How do you do, Mr. Benson?" she said. "I am Miss Hill."

This sad-faced woman was Lannon's Aunt! Larry felt a wave of pity stealing over him. He sensed that life had not been kind to Lannon's Aunt.

"It was good of you to come, Mr. Benson," she said, simply and graciously, as he took her hand. "I've heard so much about you that I've been very anxious to meet you."

"Really?" asked Larry eagerly. There were times when he was so charmingly young. This was one of them.

"Yes, from Lannon." For an instant a tender look appeared in Miss Hill's blue eyes. "She's a sweet girl, Mr. Benson, a very sweet girl. I don't know what I'd do without her. She's been a great comfort to a lonely woman, a great comfort." Miss Hill sighed as she sank into a chair. "Please be seated, Mr. Benson."

"Thank you!" Larry was watching narrowly as he took a chair near the elderly woman.

He felt that there was something wrong. Miss Hill was visibly agitated, and she appeared to be laboring under a great strain. There was a tenseness about her, her composure was obviously forced. He seemed to he thinking swiftly. That woman he had heard sobbing—had it been Miss Hill or Lannon?

For a moment Miss Hill sat there silently, nervously clasping and unclasping her ringless hands as she held them on her lap. They were like restless, frightened birds beating upon the wires of a cage, white hands that seemed a little worn and tired and weary.

All the time she sat there Miss Hill gazed at Larry. There was a look in her eyes that taunted him, a strange expression that said much and yet told him nothing.

Finally she turned her head. She was not looking at him now. She stared past him into the shadows beyond the candlelight. Her lips trembled, then drew into a straight line. She seemed to sense the question in his mind, to realize that he had observed her agitation.

"Forgive me if I appear a bit excited this evening, Mr. Benson," she said with a faint, odd smile. "My dinner party is really a—well, a celebration, you see!"

A celebration! Larry heard the statement wonderingly. What did she mean—what sort of celebration could she be holding in this lonely old house of shadows? He felt that this was a strange place, a place where skeletons might readily come to the feast. Still, he realized that he had better be tactful.

"Mighty interesting. One naturally becomes a bit elated at such an event," said Larry quickly. He knew that he was being bromidic, but the idea was to keep on talking. "What are you celebrating, Miss Hill, if I may ask?"

For a moment Miss Hill's face shone in the candlelight as she leaned forward. Was it the flickering glow that made it so weird, so fearful for an instant, or was it her expression? The lids dropped over the deep blue eyes as though she wished to hide from Larry what lingered in their depths.

For an instant she ceased to clasp and unclasp her hands, those worn white hands that were even more expressive than her face. Larry gazed at the slender fingers, fascinated. Slowly they reached out a few inches beyond the black gown. They made him think of claws now, the cruel claws of a tigress. Gradually, relentlessly, the fingers closed as though they were squeezing some invisible object, squeezing it to death.

Larry sat there staring. He could not take his eyes away from the grim motion of those white fingers—crushing, crushing. Memories taunted him, they seemed to smother him in their depths. And above all in Larry's mind loomed the recollection of the purple, staring face of Watson Gregg with the leather thong tight about his throat as he sat there in the rolling chair.

7

"WE CELEBRATED DEATH"

Suddenly Miss Hill laughed—a wild, hysterical sound. The hands dropped slowly to her lap and remained there, placid and motionless. The lids lifted from the blue eyes, and now there was a frenzied expression in them, a look of madness. It was gone in an instant, but not before Larry had seen it, and a wave of fear passed over him.

He realized that he must not let her know that her expression momentarily had frightened him. He had to see this thing through. Perhaps Lannon was somewhere in this strange old house and in danger. He had to bluff it out, that was all there was to it. There was no other way of learning the reason for the strange actions of this elderly, faded woman.

"But you haven't told me the nature of the event you are celebrating," he said quietly.

"It is—" Miss Hill fixed her blue eyes upon him intently, and she seemed to be surprised at the calmness in his tone. "Just the sudden happiness of a lonely old woman, Mr. Benson. That is all."

He did not understand. He could not believe that this mad mood of this strange woman denoted happiness—it was not possible. She had merely become evasive, but he felt that she must not suspect that he doubted her statement.

"Mighty good of you to have asked me to join you," said Larry softly. "I'm so glad to learn that you've found—happiness, Miss Hill."

"I wonder if you really think so."

For a long moment the face of faded beauty stared into his, and then Miss Hill smiled. Larry learned then what an unsolved

46

riddle a woman's smile may be. That smile was one of the greatest enigmas that he had ever known.

"If you will pardon me," Miss Hill said as she rose quickly, "I have some instructions I wish to give regarding dinner."

Larry was on his feet instantly, but before he had a chance to speak she had left the room. He frowned at the flickering red shadows of the dimly lighted hall beyond. The frown disappeared, to be replaced by a smile of joyous greeting. His heart was beating fast now, pounding at the sight of the slender figure who appeared in the doorway.

"Lannon, Lannon!" his heart was in the cry. "I—I had hoped you would be here!"

Lannon stood there, her big brown eyes staring at him, a startled look in their depths. Blonde, beautiful Lannon, tall and slender in the candlelight. She came toward him slowly.

"Larry, I—" there was surprise in her tone— "I didn't know—" He found her confusion so sweet. "That is, Auntie didn't tell me—"

"That I was to be here?"

His eyes looked deep into hers, telling her that he loved her, pleading forgiveness.

"No, Larry." Her voice was so quiet, so strange.

"Disappointed?"

"I—please, Larry!" Lannon looked at him nervously.

"There is so much that I must say, Lannon." He held her hand in both of his, and she let it linger, passive, unresisting. "Yesterday—last night—"

"Don't, Larry, please! I don't want to think of last night." He felt her tremble.

"But I must speak of it, Lannon, I must! I love you so. I'm sorry—"

"Sorry you love me?" for an instant there was a hint of the Lannon that he adored in her faint smile.

"No, dear. I'll never be sorry for that! Yesterday I made a mistake, a big mistake. I made my love a little thing—and it isn't that— it isn't! Oh, Lannon, Lannon, I love you so much!"

"Please, Larry! Let's not talk about it now." Lannon glanced about her nervously. "Not here—tonight!"

"Just as you say, dear. Only tell me that you forgive me?"

"I do, boy, I do forgive you."

For an instant Lannon's big eyes gazed deep into his, and there was something lovely, something very precious, in their depths. Larry was drinking deeply of those eyes, knowing that the memory of them would linger with him always, that they would be valiant banners leading him ever onward.

It was a moment to remember, but Lannon had not spoken. Now she turned swiftly toward the doorway. She stood there staring out into the shadowy hallway in which the red light flickered. There was a frightened look on her face; a faint, illusive expression in her eyes.

Larry glanced hastily in the direction of the hall, puzzled by the sudden change in the girl's mood. There was no one in sight, only the shadows swaying slightly in the flickering ray of light. He looked at Lannon.

"What's the matter?"

She did not speak; she continued to gaze out into the hallway.

"Lannon!"

She turned to him slowly, as though she had suddenly become conscious of his presence. There was a strange, worried expression upon her lovely face.

"Larry, why did you come here tonight?" she asked in an undertone, as though she feared her words might be overheard.

"That's easily explained," he answered lightly. "Miss Hill telephoned this morning and asked me here for dinner. It is some sort of a celebration, I believe."

"She asked you to come here for—for the celebration!" she exclaimed. "Oh, why did she do that? Why did she?"

"I don't know." His tone changed. "Lannon, don't you want me here?"

For a moment she stood gazing anxiously toward the hall. Then she turned to him, her eyes looking squarely into his. "I'm so nervous—I don't know what I'm saying. But—oh, there's something I can't explain."

"I know, Lannon." He smiled faintly. "I understand far better than you realize. The situation here at present is—well, rather difficult. There is something wrong. Miss Hill made that quite obvious. Just what it is I don't know, but you can depend on me to stand by you. I love you, Lannon!"

"Larry—" Lannon paused abruptly as Miss Hill appeared in the doorway.

"Dinner is ready, children," said the elderly woman, smiling.

There seemed a look of fear in the swift glance Lannon cast at her Aunt as Miss Hill turned and led the way down the hall. The man and the girl followed without speaking, but Larry took Lannon's hand in his and pressed it for a moment, then gently released it as they entered the dining room.

Here, too, the furnishings were old, and candles the only means of illumination. Six of these stood in the center of the big dining table of heavy oak in a brass candelabrum. To his surprise Larry noticed that places had been laid for four at the table.

Lannon noticed this also, and she glanced at her Aunt wonderingly. Miss Hill seated Larry on her right and her niece on her left, as she sat at the foot of the table. The place at the head remained empty.

The old colored woman entered and served the soup at all four places. As she set a plate at the empty place, the old servant cackled softly. Her little black eyes bore a devilish gleam as she glanced from Larry to Lannon.

"Lannon tells me that you have been abroad, Mr. Benson," said Miss Hill, ignoring the actions of the servant. "Which do you prefer for its beauty, France or Italy?"

Larry observed the look of dread which passed over Lannon's face as her Aunt spoke, and wondered what it could mean. It seemed as though the girl was afraid of what Miss Hill might say. But why? But he knew that he must talk, must try to keep the conversation going.

"I think I like Italy better," he said. "There is something very romantic about it. It is so ancient that it makes you think of all sorts of things. There are spots in Rome where the imagination needs no stimulus to visualize the splendor of ancient days."

"Ah, but there is something about Florence that holds one even more than does the beauty of Rome," said Miss Hill. "When one strolls along the Lungarno, and sees the Ponte Vechio, that quaint old bridge that Dante crossed, one cannot help but think of the contrasts we may sometimes find in life."

"Then you have traveled in Europe?" There was surprise in Larry's tone.

Miss Hill smiled. "I have visited nearly every country in Europe." Her expression changed swiftly; a sad look passed over her face. "But that was long ago." Suddenly she laughed, a sharp, grating sound. "But we must celebrate. Come, Mr. Benson! You must make this a jolly party. Let us all be in high spirits. Have you forgotten that this is a great event?"

"No, I haven't forgotten," Larry answered slowly, his eyes fixed upon Miss Hill's flushed and excited face.

Lannon's hand went to the silk scarf she wore about her neck. She cast a startled look in Larry's direction, but said nothing as she turned her gaze again to her Aunt.

"And you, too, Lannon. You're going to help us celebrate!" Miss Hill looked at her niece, her eyes blazing with suppressed excitement. "You must help us to be merry. Come, this is no time for gloom. Let's be gay!"

"But what is it we're celebrating?" asked Larry, watching the elderly woman intently.

"We are celebrating"—Miss Hill's face gleamed with a strange light as she finished softly—"the death of a man!"

Larry heard Lannon utter a low moan, but he did not take his eyes off Miss Hill's face. As she sat there, the candlelight flickering and casting its dull gleam upon her, the woman's expression was one of madness.

For a moment silence lingered over the room, a strange stillness that was filled with tenseness; a grim, waiting silence that was terrifying and intense in its very lack of sound and motion. It was as if the whole world had suddenly stopped while the man and the elderly woman sat there motionless, staring at each other.

Then, like something swiftly coming into focus, slight sounds that had at first seemed part of the silence came to their ears. Faintly came the dull sputter of the candles and the low moaning of the wind. From somewhere in the old house echoed the shrill cackle of the ancient colored woman.

"The death of a man!" Larry repeated slowly.

Miss Hill apparently had not heard him. She was staring across the table toward Lannon, a startled expression replacing the look of madness upon her face.

Larry turned quickly in the direction of the girl. She lay back in her chair, her face pale, her eyes closed. Lannon had fainted.

From the kitchen there came again the high, shrill cackle of the old negress.

8
"A GOOD LEAD"

DAVE MORTON, police reporter on the *Morning Press*, sat in front of his typewriter, a thoughtful frown upon his face. He paid not the slightest heed to his surroundings, for he was thinking deeply. He was so used to the sounds of the big editorial room that they did not disturb him in the least. He was not even conscious of the other reporters of the late shift, that were scattered about at the various desks. He did not hear the clatter and bang of their typewriters as they turned out copy which, with the coming of morning, would be the news of the day.

Morton's mind was centered on one important fact: It was now nearly midnight upon the day following the discovery of the murder of Watson Gregg, and nothing, so far as he knew, had been done to apprehend the murderer.

Beyond the closed door of the composing room Morton could hear the rumble and click of the linotype machines. He glanced at his watch and realized that he had only half an hour before the deadline on copy for the morning edition. In a very short while the heavy presses would begin to roll, printing those long, endless sheets that, when cut and ready, would be tomorrow's *Morning Press*.

Morton scowled as he savagely thrust a sheet of copy paper into his machine. All day he had been working on the Gregg Case, trying to find some new angle, but he felt that his efforts had been futile. The story which he intended to write now would be little more than a resume of what the public already knew.

He had interviewed Captain Jerry Blake of the Detective Bureau again just an hour ago, and the result had not been at all startling. Apparently Blake knew nothing which Morton had not already learned, or if he did he had decided that it was best to keep his own counsel.

Briefly the reporter summed up the case in his own mind. Watson Gregg had been murdered. He had been found sitting in a rolling chair on the Boardwalk strangled to death with a saffron-hued, leather thong.

Three men had discovered the body almost simultaneously, Fulda, Danton and Benson. Now Morton cold-bloodedly considered each of them in the light of a potential murderer.

He first dwelt upon Larry Benson, though so far as Morton could see the young man was a very unimportant factor in the case. The reporter had looked him up. He had learned that Benson was just out of college and working for his father in the real-estate business. He had merely been passing and Doctor Fulda had stopped him, as he had Danton; and then the three men had investigated and later called the police. Morton was quite sure that Benson did not matter. There was no motive so far as he was concerned. Benson had not even known Watson Gregg.

The reporter felt that the same could not be said regarding Doctor James Fulda and Giovanni Danton.

There was something about the hard-eyed, brusk little physician that Morton did not like. He sensed a cold ruthlessness about the man, which made him wonder. Yet, so far as he had been able to learn, there was not the slightest reason for Doctor Fulda to have killed Gregg. The murdered man had retained Fulda as his personal physician; for the little doctor to have murdered him would have been, in Morton's estimation, to have killed the goose which had laid the golden egg. If Morton knew human nature, that didn't seem reasonable.

As for Giovanni Danton, there was no doubt that the tall, pale-faced man was a very enigmatical individual. There was an air of mystery about him. Morton did not doubt that Danton was quite capable of murder. Still, there was no evidence against him. Upon being questioned by the police, Danton had stated that he had known Gregg only by sight and name; that was all. There was no doubt of the man's cleverness. The reporter had not the slightest idea of dismissing Danton as a vital suspect.

Morton permitted his thoughts to go on to the incidents which had occurred at a later interval upon the night of the murder. At a little after eleven-thirty Captain Blake had received a mysterious telephone message instructing him to come to the Weymouth Woods in Longport. He had done so and had found John Hagen, the chair-pusher who had been pushing Gregg's chair at the time of the murder. Hagen had been shot and killed by a .32 caliber bullet.

The reporter was very much interested in the telephone call which the captain of detectives had received. He wanted to know who had made it, and why. He was sure that there was a very good motive for someone having done so. But what had it been? That was what Dave Morton was very anxious to learn.

He did not know that Blake had encountered Danton near the spot where Hagen's lifeless figure had been found upon the road. Nor had he been informed of Danton's rather cryptic statement regarding two-legged owls. The Captain was willing to work with Morton just as far as he deemed wise, and no further. He felt there were some things better left unpublished until after the murder had been solved.

In his last interview with Blake the reporter lad sensed this. He had been far too shrewd to let the Captain realize that such was the case. He knew that by so doing he would risk the other's antagonism, and thereby lose all possible chance of gaining further information from the head of the Detective Bureau.

Morton had done a good bit of investigation on his own behalf. He felt that he had learned quite as much regarding Watson Gregg as had Captain Blake. A wire to New York had brought back to the reporter a good bit of information regarding the murdered man.

Gregg had been very rich—a retired theatrical producer. He had been in poor health for the past three years. At the suggestion of his physician, Doctor Fulda, he had come to the seashore for an extended visit. Fulda had come with him, as had also his Japanese valet, Tahira Yamada.

The valet, a suave little Oriental who had proven to be exceptionally well educated, and who spoke English perfectly, had been closely questioned by the police. He had proven beyond any doubt that at the time of the murder he had been at the hotel at which Gregg had been staying. Morton felt that the servant's alibi was just a bit too perfect. The reporter was not at all sure that it had not been carefully planned beforehand. He was forced to admit that if such were the case, the Japanese was exceedingly clever.

As far as Morton or the police could learn, Gregg had not been married. He had no relatives, and his friends were few. It was known that a very beautiful blonde girl had dined with him upon the night of the murder, but those who had seen her had not recognized her, and were unable to give her name. It was rumored that Gregg had possessed quite a reputation as a lady's man, but so far as this was concerned the reporter had found it evidently a rumor and nothing more.

Nevertheless, Morton and Blake had learned that a woman known as Mercedes La Tona, a very striking brunette, had been a very intimate friend of the late Watson Gregg. She was said to be an actress, but she had not appeared in any production for three or four years.

Morton had made two attempts to interview Mercedes La Tona and had found himself completely baffled by the complacent cleverness of the woman. He knew that Captain Blake had met with the same difficulties. Mercedes La Tona would make no statement which might involve her in the murder in any way.

She had admitted that she knew Gregg, but had also stated that she had not seen him during the time that they had both been at the shore. She answered all questions with such adroit evasion that Morton and Blake both admitted that she had them licked, for the time being at least.

The Captain of Detectives was not one who gave in easily. He had warned the woman that she must not leave town until the murder was cleared up, and had issued orders to all of his men to be on watch for a possible attempt upon her part to escape. Morton personally felt that the move upon the Captain's part was futile. Mercedes La Tona was not one who would make foolish moves.

"Oh, Dave!"

Morton gave a start as he heard the words. He glanced over his shoulder and saw that Joe Shinn, City Editor of the *Morning Press*, had called to him. The reporter glanced at the blank sheet of copy paper in his machine, and then at the big clock on the wall of the room. He saw that he had only ten minutes left in which to write the morning edition's story on the Gregg case.

"I'll give you my stuff in a moment, Joe," he called quickly. "I was trying to think up a new angle on the case."

"All right," called the City Editor. "Get going—you haven't all night, you know."

Morton did not bother to answer. He turned to his machine and began to write rapidly. Hardly had he finished the first paragraph when the telephone upon the desk in front of him rang. He impatiently picked up the receiver.

"Hello!" he said.

"Hello, Mr. Morton?" came a man's voice over the wire. "I have some news for you. Listen carefully—it's about Watson Gregg. Watch Giovanni Danton. He knows a lot more than he is telling. That's all. Good-bye!"

Before Morton could say a word he heard the click of a receiver and knew that the man on the other end had disconnected. As was his habit, the reporter had automatically taken the other's words down in shorthand. Now he read them over swiftly—and then smiled. He knew that he would recognize that voice if he ever heard it again. He glanced over his shoulder at the City Editor.

"Oh, Joe!" he called.

"What?" demanded Shinn.

"I just got a damn good lead on tonight's story of the murder of Watson Gregg!" and with the words Morton turned again to his typewriter and began to pound away hastily.

9

"A KNIFE IN THE NIGHT"

IT WAS NOT THE PALE FACE of Lannon that Larry remembered clearly afterward. Nor was it Miss Hill, strange elderly woman of mystery, as she sat there for an instant gazing at the unconscious girl, a startled expression erasing the faded beauty of her face. It was the flickering candlelight gleaming down upon the empty place at the head of the table that Larry recalled whenever the picture recurred to his mind. That strange, empty place had been set there as part of the celebration of the death of a man!

The instant Larry realized Lannon had fainted, he was at her side. Miss Hill followed swiftly, but the girl's recovery was rapid. They had hardly reached her before she sat up and opened her eyes

"What happened?" she asked dully. "Funny for me to—to faint—"

"Very strange, my dear," remarked Miss Hill, handing her a glass of water.

"All right now, aren't you, Lannon?" asked Larry tenderly.

"Yes, thanks, Larry." Lannon took a sip of water and then nodded. "I'm sorry, Auntie. Please go on with—um—dinner."

"Certainly." The elderly woman smiled.

Larry frowned as Miss Hill and he moved back to their places. The strange meal went on, a gruesome feast that became more and more unbearable. Every course which appeared was served to the empty place at the head of the table, and every time she put anything down at that spot Loona cackled softly.

The conversation of those at the table was now for the most part devoted to commonplaces, to those stilted marionettes of speech that fill the empty gaps when the mind is otherwise engaged.

Lannon talked but little and appeared to be laboring under the stress of great agitation. Her aunt, too, remained under a spell of nervous excitement, but she talked incessantly and well. Despite the fact that he was ever conscious of the strained attitudes of the two women, Larry forced himself to listen attentively to Miss Hill's constant chatter.

Lannon's Aunt proved to be a brilliant and well-educated woman. She revealed a knowledge of places both in Europe and America which surprised Larry. He had been under the impression that Miss Hill had spent most of her life as a lonely recluse in this old house of mystery.

Even though he made the effort, it was difficult for Larry to act naturally. The obvious nervousness of the girl and her aunt worried him. He knew that Lannon was afraid. She seemed to fear Miss Hill, this strange woman who was under a spell of hysterical joy, almost of madness, over the celebration of "the death of a man."

It was not only the actions of the two women which worried him. Mystery stalked grimly amid the shadows of the old house. From the kitchen he heard a low murmuring that sounded like voices all through the meal. It annoyed him. This was intermingled with the old colored woman's cackling in the distance. The murmuring might have been the old servant talking to herself, but of this he could not be sure. Every time Loona entered the room she gazed at him with a sly light in her black eyes and a grin upon her wrinkled face.

Thoughts taunted him. Over and over his brain pounded at him upon the subject of Watson Gregg. He felt that there was some connection between the murdered man and this elderly woman. But what was it, he wondered. Did Miss Hill know about Lannon having been with Gregg?

He strove valiantly to be loyal and keep the girl out of his jumbled surmises but over and over his disorganized train of thought came back to the starting point: What had happened between Lannon and Gregg before she had left the rolling chair? As for the Aunt, where did she fit into the puzzle? Had she killed Gregg? If so, for what motive?

How had Miss Hill accomplished the deed, provided that she was guilty? To garrote a man required strength, even a sick man such as Gregg had been. Although Miss Hill was tall, she did not impress Larry as one who possessed the muscular ability required. Yet he had heard that a person under the spell of madness sometimes exhibits physical force far beyond normal strength.

It seemed ages to him before the meal was over, but at last the time arrived. With a sigh of relief he rose and followed the two women out of the room.

"I'm sure you young people will excuse me for a short while," said Miss Hill, when they had returned to the front room. "I have some instructions I wish to give Loona."

As the elderly woman silently disappeared into the hall Larry turned anxiously to Lannon.

"What's the matter, Lannon?" he asked softly. "You seem frightened."

"I am, Larry." She drew closer to him and her voice was low. "Scared to death. I don't know what to do!"

"But what's it all about? Can't you tell me?"

"No, I can't tell anyone." Lannon's brave little voice was pathetic. "Not even you! And Larry, I'd always come to you first. You must believe that!"

"Of course I believe you." His tone was tender. "And even if—"

From somewhere within the old house came a wild laugh, followed by a shrill scream which did not seem human. They both stood motionless, listening. In the distance they heard a faint voice murmuring, and they waited tensely.

"Blood, blood! My God, you've killed him!" the words came plainly to the man and girl.

"What was that?" demanded Larry in a hoarse whisper.

"Aunt Ida's parrot." Lannon smiled faintly.

"A parrot!" Larry laughed ruefully. "Good Lord, what a place this is! That was a parrot—you're sure?"

"Of course. He usually is covered up at night and doesn't make a sound. Auntie bought him from a sailor some years ago."

"That bird must have led an adventurous life!" Larry's tame attempt at humor fell flat.

Lannon shuddered. There was a strange look in her lovely brown eyes.

"Death is such an easy topic of conversation in this house," she said softly.

Larry took her hands in both of his; he stood looking deep into her eyes, his back toward the doorway.

"Lannon—this place. There is something wrong. Won't you let me take you home, please, dear?"

"I can't go, Larry." There was a pleading look upon her face. "I must stay here with Aunt Ida. She—she needs me now."

"Needs you?"

"Yes, I—" Her voice broke as she glanced beyond him toward the hallway.

Larry turned quickly, and a startled expression passed over his face as he did so. Giovanni Danton stood there, his pale face weird now, satanic in the rays of the red light of the hall, the deep, burning eyes staring into the room.

Then abruptly Danton smiled.

After an electric moment there came the rustle of skirts as Miss Hill appeared, smiling. Was it the red glow of the hall that made her smile so strangely—so ghastly—or was it Danton?

"Giovanni!" she said breathlessly.

"Ida! I hope that I am not too late." That chill, clear voice of Danton's, his perfect enunciation, seemed to reverberate in Larry's ears.

"Late, Giovanni?" Miss Hill shook her head. "I wonder if it is ever too late?"

Lannon and Larry did not hear what Danton answered. Only the faint rumble of his voice lingered as Miss Hill and the tall man disappeared along the hallway.

Larry's brain was working swiftly. Giovanni Danton here, and on intimate terms with Miss Hill—what could it mean? He turned to the girl.

"Lannon," he said slowly. "Do you know him?"

Lannon did not answer; at first she did not look at him. She stood there, her eyes hidden by her long lashes, a strange expression on her face. Larry thought that it was fright, but he could not be sure.

"Lannon, you do know Giovanni Danton?" Larry's voice was stern.

"Giovanni Danton?" she repeated like one in a daze. "Oh, Larry, you—" She paused abruptly as the old colored servant appeared in the doorway.

"Yo' Aunty want fo' yo' to ask Mr. Benson to 'scuse yo' fo' a few minutes, Miss Lannon," said Loona, grinning.

A look of alarm swept over the girl's face, and then she smiled.

"All right, Loona. Thank you." She turned to Larry. "You'll wait right here, Larry?"

Before he could answer she had followed the old servant swiftly out of the room. Larry frowned. Why had Miss Hill wanted Lannon—was it to meet Giovanni Danton? He dropped into a chair and for a time he sat there thinking, puzzling over the things which had happened.

The minutes ticked slowly by, lingering in the depths of the silence, taunting him. He wanted to know what had happened, what was going on now. Where were Lannon and Danton and Miss Hill?

He could stand inactivity no longer. Intending to penetrate the mystery of the house, he moved to the doorway. The hall was empty, a place of shadows moving slowly beneath the red light.

As quietly as possible he moved down the hall. Opposite the dining room was a closed door leading to a room which he had not seen as yet. As he paused beside this he was surprised to hear a low murmur coming from within. Was this where Lannon had gone at her Aunt's request? Were Danton, Miss Hill, and the girl in there? He had to know.

Cautiously Larry drew the door open slightly and peered beyond. It was a good-sized room which met his gaze, a room faintly illuminated by candles. It was these which first caught his eyes. There were four of them, standing tall and white, one at each corner of a long divan.

As his eyes became accustomed to the dim light Larry gave a gasp of horror. The divan appeared to be a funeral bier. A rug which had been thrown over it, seemingly covered a body.

In the center of the room stood old Loona. She held a candle in one wizened black hand, and her wrinkled face loomed weird, grotesque, as she chanted to the bier in a high, sing-song voice.

"Yo' ain't dah! Yo' ain't nowheres, yo' is daid—daid!" she crooned, wildly waving her hands, the candle casting strange shadows upon the walls of the room. "Yo' ain't gwine nevah brung no trouble to nobody."

Larry felt a wave of horror pass over him. There was something ghastly about the sing-song incantations. She reminded him of some ancient savage witch as he watched her. He shrank back so that the old servant could not see him, and waited, fascinated. As he did so Loona abruptly dropped to her knees.

"Gord Ermity is goo' en kine!" she shouted. "Delibher us—delibber us! Dem dat makes pussons suffah den dat same pusson's gwin git to suffah, too." Madly the old negress beat her hand upon the floor, the candle waving in the other as she did so. "Delibber us, delibber us! A pusson gives trouble to dem dat's innocent fo' ye'rs en ye'rs, but den dat goo' Gord Ermity gwin notice what's a-goin' on some daybress a Lor'! Delibber us, delibber us!"

Old Loona's voice died away to indistinct mumblings. Then with startling clearness came a shrill cry.

"Blood, blood, a knife in the night. Oh, God, you've killed him!"

The servant cackled softly as she heard the words. Larry gazed about him anxiously, and then he smiled a grim smile. He realized it must have been the parrot again. He drew the door of the room silently shut.

He began to move slowly back along the hallway. He was filled with horror at the scene which he had witnessed. A slight sound from the room where he had just heard the old woman chanting her strange prayers, made him pause suddenly.

He crouched as close to the shadowy wall as possible as Loona appeared and walked slowly toward the kitchen, chuckling softly to herself. He waited anxiously until she had disappeared. For an instant there was silence, and then from the distance came the sound of the old servant's unearthly cackle.

Quickly Larry made his way back to the room which Loona had just left. He cautiously opened the door and for a time stood there motionless, staring in. The room loomed weird and fantastic in the dull, flickering candlelight.

Miss Hill had said that she was celebrating the death of a man. Could that man have been lying stark and cold beneath the rug on the funeral bier all during that grewsome dinner party? Larry felt that simply could not be—and yet, why had Lannon fainted?

With reluctant feet Larry slowly entered the room. Once inside the door, his steps faltered. He paused, his eyes upon the divan. Had the rug moved, or were his eyes deceiving him? It was hard to tell in the flickering light of the candles. His heart was heating wildly, and he was shaking all over as he slowly reached out his hand and touched the rug. It felt strange in his fingers. He dropped it hastily.

As his hand fell to his side he again heard the old colored woman cackling in the distance. It seemed as though she were taunting him, laughing at him for his lack of courage. He felt that he must learn what was beneath that rug.

Cautiously he extended his hand again. This time he grasped the rug and pulled it partially aside. He stood there looking down with wondering puzzled eyes. There was nothing beneath it but a pile of sofa cushions!

He had heard no sound, but some sixth sense warned him that he was not alone. He turned to see Miss Hill standing in the doorway, an odd, mysterious smile upon her face. He hastily placed the rug back as he had found it, and then glanced again at the doorway. It was empty. Miss Hill had disappeared. Larry sprang quickly to the opening, but there was no trace of Lannon's Aunt. The hallway was deserted.

Larry hurried back to the room in which Lannon had left him. He felt guilty now, and rather foolish. What right had he to be peering into rooms of a strange house at which he was merely a dinner guest? That Miss Hill was slightly insane, he did not doubt. Still, if she chose to burn candles about a funeral bier of sofa cushions, what business was it of his to question the deed? He was terribly sorry and a bit ashamed, for he felt that in some mysterious way he had caught a depredating glimpse of a woman's soul.

He began impatiently pacing up and down the room. He wished that Lannon was not staying in this house. What could its secret be?

That old cackling negress. And Danton, with his pallid face and burning eyes—what was he doing here? Where was he now? Larry had seen Miss Hill but a moment ago. Had she left Lannon alone with Danton?

His speculations were interrupted by the sound of someone running swiftly along the hall. Lannon rushed swiftly into the room. She was pale and trembling, and her big eyes were wide with terror.

"Larry!" she said quickly. "You'll—have to go. Please!"

"Go? And leave you in this cursed place—exposed to I don't know what? I should say not!"

Lannon looked at him anxiously. "Please, Larry. I ask it!"

Seeing the appeal in her eyes, Larry couldn't resist.

"Well, if you insist. You're sure you don't want me to take you home?"

"Oh, I couldn't leave Auntie. Not now—not now!"

She led him quickly to the front door. As Lannon stood for a moment beneath the ray of the red light, the silk scarf which she wore fell away from her slender throat.

Larry's eyes narrowed as he looked at the girl. On her white skin was the angry red mark of a bruise. He had not seen it before because it had been hidden by the scarf.

"Lannon, how did you get that bruise on your neck?" he demanded.

The girl gave him a startled look but she did not answer.

"How did you get it?" his tone grew suddenly stern.

"Please, Larry. Oh, please don't—"

"But I must know. Lannon!"

She opened the door.

"I—I received it celebrating the death of a man!" she said softly, and then gently pushed him out into the night.

Before he could speak the heavy front door had closed and he heard the latch click. He was alone on the dark and shadowy porch.

10
THE MYSTERIOUS GODFREY FLOSS

MERCEDES LA TONA SIGHED as she gazed at her reflection in the mirror of her dressing table. It was a strange, exotic creature which stared back at her, with hair dark as the shadows of night, and deep blue eyes that were ever a little cynical, a little hard. She was a woman one remembered as a passing smile in the night; alluring, taunting, the least bit alarming, as though one had unexpectedly discovered fathomless depths in shallow water.

Yet it was a strikingly attractive face which was reflected in the mirror, despite the faint wrinkles in her forehead which her frown now revealed. Bright, gleaming jewels sparkled on her long, tapering fingers as she automatically brushed her heavy hair.

Suddenly she paused and leaned toward the mirror, a look of anxiety replacing the frown upon her face. Her eyes were fixed upon the luxuriant mass of raven black hair.

"Nora!" she called to the maid who had been quietly going about the task of arranging her mistress' costume for the day. "Come here, please."

The maid, a placid, middle-aged woman, came to Mercedes' side at once. "Yes, Miss?"

"Oh, Nora!" There was fright in Mercedes' tone. "I've found another gray hair!" She pointed to a strand of her dark locks. "See it? Oh, I'm getting old, Nora, old!"

The maid smiled at her mistress' reflection in the glass. In her years with Mercedes La Tona her maid had thought many things but never that her employer was anything but a strikingly beautiful woman.

"Nonsense, Miss La Tona," she said quietly. "You are still a young woman."

As Mercedes gazed into the mirror she seemed to see herself old and haggard, a faded wreck of her once beautiful self. She shuddered and brushed her hand across her eyes.

"Another gray hair!" she repeated. "Oh, Nora, you don't understand! That means age—age! And for me to become old means oblivion."

"Now, now, Miss La Tona. You're all upset over nothing. You've been acting worried-like ever since—ever since the night before last."

"The night before last. Nora, is that all it has been? It seems centuries, ages." Mercedes paused. "Quick, pull out that horrible gray hair and get the most dazzling gown in my wardrobe before I cry."

Deftly the maid removed the offending hair and handed it to her mistress.

"There it is, Miss. That was the only one." Mercedes gazed at the hair and placed it on the dressing table in front of her.

"How like life it is, Nora; a snap of a tiny thread and life is gone—"

The maid moved quickly to answer the telephone.

"Who is it?" demanded Mercedes anxiously. "That reporter again—or the damn Captain of Detectives?"

"Neither, Miss. It's Tahira. He says he must see you at once. What shall I tell him?"

"Tahira? Tell him to come right up!"

It was but a minute or so later that a suave little Japanese bowed his way into the sitting room of Mercedes La Tona in the Hotel Seafoam.

"Miss La Tona will be here in a moment," said Nora as she ushered him in. "Please wait."

"Thank you." Tahira smiled faintly. "I hope you are well, Miss Kelly?"

Nora sniffed disdainfully as she left the room, but did not answer. Tahira continued to smile as she disappeared, and then his expression changed. Always the maid of Mercedes La Tona had displayed her antipathy toward him. He shrugged his shoulders. It was unfortunate, but it did not matter.

The Japanese bowed as Mercedes entered the room, dressed in her most ravishing costume.

"Good morning, Miss La Tona."

She ignored his greeting, and stood looking at him, an expression of interrogation in her blue eyes.

"Tahira, what's the matter? Why did you come here?"

"A little mission in which you may be interested." The Japanese smiled. "In my capacity as the servant of the late Mr. Gregg I believe that you have always found me—ah, useful?"

"That is a question. There is an undercurrent about what you say that one might find offensive."

"It is unwise to investigate undercurrents too extensively, Miss La Tona. They might be dangerous," said Tahira quietly. "But you misunderstand. There have been times when you have called upon my service—in the most menial capacities naturally, as befitting a servant, such as delivering messages and running a few errands; but I repeat, you have found me useful?"

"Yes, I have:" Mercedes shrugged. "And now?" Mercedes looked at him questioningly.

Again the servant of Watson Gregg smiled. "Now I see no reason why I should cease to be of assistance, when necessary!"

"Just what do you mean by that, Tahira?"

For a moment Mercedes La Tona looked intently at the Japanese as he stood there smiling at her. At last she, too, smiled and moved to a chair.

"You may sit down, Tahira," she said indicating another chair close by.

"Thank you." Tahira bowed and then dropped into the chair which she had indicated. "You are very kind."

"In what way can you be useful to me now, Tahira?"

A faint gleam shone in the servant's dark eyes as he asked: "Have you ever met a gentleman named Godfrey Floss?"

"Godfrey Floss?" Mercedes shook her head. "No. Who is he?"

"Rather an unscrupulous individual, I'm afraid," said Tahira slowly. "You will meet him—in fact, I'm quite sure that he will call upon you today."

"Yes? And why will he do so?"

"When one goes driving with another woman's husband it is not advisable to stop on a lonely road where tramps might be lurking."

"Oh!" Mercedes stared at the servant intently. "I have misjudged you. I never realized before that you were quite so clever, Tahira."

"Modesty is a most becoming virtue."

The faint flicker of a smile passed over the red lips of Mercedes La Tona, to vanish in an instant as she spoke.

"But this Mr. Floss—just where does he fit in?"

"He lives by his wits. That is not always a profitable means of livelihood."

"He is an adventurer, then?"

"No," Tahira shook his head. "His is an uglier title—a black-mailer."

"A blackmailer?"

"Yes. It might prove worth your while to assist him financially."

"Indeed!" Mercedes said scornfully. "And why should I?"

"The reasons are obvious." Tahira waved his hand. "Perhaps you would find it advisable to donate a little gift to the needy, provided Mr. Floss would forget that he saw Martin Woods shoot a man on a lonely road night before last!"

Mercedes grew pale—she gazed swiftly at the floor before she spoke.

"It was self-defense. The man was a robber—he demanded my jewels."

"That may be true. But unfortunately the man who was killed was John Hagen—"

"John Hagen? Who was he?"

"Really, Miss La Tona, it would be wise to read the papers more closely." Tahira smiled. "He was the chair-pusher who was with Watson Gregg at the time he was murdered. The police might find some connection if they were to learn who shot him!"

Mercedes looked at Tahira thoughtfully.

"Tahira, am I to understand that you wish me to bribe this man if he does come to see me?"

"Miss La Tona!" A look of amazement passed over the servant's face. "You wrong me greatly. I merely wish to warn you so that you might be ready to meet Mr. Floss' suggestions."

"Thank you, Tahira. Again I misjudged you!"

"That is better, Miss La Tona. I hope you may always find me useful." He leaned forward in his chair. "If the gentleman becomes—well, shall we say nasty—you might remind him that owls sometimes hoot very insistently!"

"What do you mean?"

"Unless I'm very much mistaken, Mr. Floss will understand." The servant of Watson Gregg rose and bowed. "Good-morning, Miss La Tona."

"Goodbye, Tahira, and thank you."

The Japanese bowed again and left the room. Mercedes smiled as the door closed. "Owls sometimes hoot very insistently." Very well, she would remember.

An hour later Mercedes La Tona sat in her beach chair in front of the hotel. Idly she put down the novel which she had been reading, and sat watching the breakers as they crashed upon the sand. She finally became conscious of a tall, lean man who was watching her intently. He stood near the life guards' stand a short distance away. She leaned back in her chair and gazed at him through half-closed eyelids.

He had a sinister face, she thought; a long, narrow countenance like that of a wolf. She did not like the way those cold gray eyes stared at her. Once she caught a faint smile upon the thin lips that drooped sardonically. She turned her head and gazed in the opposite direction. When she looked again the man was standing close to her, his hat in his hand as he bowed.

"Miss La Tona?" he asked, his voice harsh, grating.

"Yes?"

"Floss is my name, Godfrey Floss."

"Really? I'm afraid I've never had the pleasure of meeting you, Mr. Floss." Mercedes' tone was cold, distant.

"No?" Godfrey Floss dropped into a beach chair close beside her. "That, I should say, was my misfortune."

"A matter of opinion, surely." Mercedes glanced down at her book and pretended to read.

"I hope I don't intrude?" Floss smiled.

"The beach is rather a public place—intrusion is to be expected."

For an instant Floss stared at her and then he frowned angrily.

"Look here, Miss La Tona," he snapped, "you don't need to pull that high hat stuff with me—I know too much!"

"Most men do," she remarked drily.

"I mean too much about you!"

"A number of men have thought even that."

"I saw you with Martin Woods the night before last!"

"Well, what of it? Am I to assume a dramatic pose and exclaim in a horrified tone, 'My God, no'?"

"You actresses all think you are so clever!"

"Oh, no, Mr. Floss, not half as much as some men do!"

"Listen," Floss was scowling deeply now. "I saw you with Martin Woods—"

"What does that make us—brother Elks?"

"Don't be so damn funny! You were with Martin Woods night before last when he killed John Hagen!"

"I see. Insert subtitle: 'Then came the dawn,'" Mercedes smiled. "And what happened then?"

"You don't need to bluff. I saw Woods kill Hagen."

"You did?" Mercedes' eyes narrowed. "Then you probably heard the tramp whom you call John Hagen demand my jewels, saw him raise his club, and then saw Martin Woods kill him in self-defense?"

"No, my recollections are not so vivid. I merely remember Hagen going to the car empty-handed and asking for a ride to town, then suddenly Martin Woods drew a gun and shot the man down in cold blood!"

"Oh, pretty, pretty!" Mercedes gazed at him wide-eyed, in mock distress. "And why did he do that? Was it because fifty years ago John Hagen stole the plans of a secret mine away from Martin Woods? Come now, Mr. Floss, you really must make your story a good one, you know! Was that it?"

"It was because John Hagen knew too much about the murder of Watson Gregg!" A leering smile appeared on the face of Godfrey Floss to punctuate his statement.

"I wonder if he did," she said softly.

"Of course he did!" Instantly Floss frowned as though he realized he had said too much. "He must have," he remarked quickly, trying to cover. "Otherwise Woods would not have shot him."

"But Martin Woods did not kill Watson Gregg. He did not even know that he was dead until he read the paper the next morning."

"The police would be very much interested in learning that he had shot Hagen, nevertheless." Floss smiled again coldly.

"And that you had seen him do it, Mr. Floss."

"Also that you were present, dear lady."

Mercedes yawned frankly. "The point of all this discussion being just what?" she asked indifferently.

"That you might find it advisable to bestow a donation to, well, shall we say a worthy cause, Miss La Tona?"

"A worthy cause?" she looked at him ironically. "Such as what, Mr. Floss?"

"Don't bluff!" Floss leaned toward her and spoke sharply. "You know just what I mean. For ten thousand dollars I could very easily forget that I saw Martin Woods kill John Hagen!"

"For ten thousand dollars even my memory might become a little hazy!" Mercedes smiled. "Just where did you get the idea that I might be rolling in wealth, Mr. Floss?"

"You wrong me. I don't ask that you contribute personally. I merely want you to use your influence with a friend."

"You mean that I suggest to Martin Woods that he pay you ten thousand dollars to keep silent?"

"Quite so!"

"And if I refuse?"

"Both you and Mr. Woods will regret it!"

"Oh! You threaten?"

"Hardly that." Godfrey Floss smiled—he took on a nonchalant air. "A suggestion—merely."

"Mr. Floss, someone warned me that you might make just such a suggestion as you have!"

"And they told you it would be wise to agree to my wishes?"

"On the contrary! They told me to repeat a little message to you." Mercedes' tone was cold and hard.

"And the message was?"

"I was to remind you that owls sometimes hoot very insistently!"

Godfrey Floss's expression changed at the words. His face turned gray. Without another word he leaped from the beach chair and hurried toward the Boardwalk. He did not look back, and in a moment he had disappeared amid the throng.

Mercedes had turned in her chair to watch the departing man, and now she again gazed out to sea.

"I wonder," she said softly to herself, as if unable to decide something in her own mind. "I wonder . . ."

11

THREE MEN

CAPTAIN JERRY BLAKE and his chief aid, Detective Dan Flannigan, stood leaning idly against the outer rail of the Boardwalk. Neither man appeared to have the slightest care in the world, and yet in spite of their appearance of tranquil ease they were both very much alert.

A few hundred yards across from where they stood loomed the ornate structure which was the Seafoam Hotel. Both men were watching the Boardwalk entrance intently.

"Thought so!" said Blake finally, as he caught sight of a small individual who came hurrying out of the hotel and started up the walk. "That's Tahira, the little Japanese servant of Watson Gregg. Now just what was he doing in the Seafoam?"

"You've got me, Cap." Flannigan shook his head. "That ain't the hotel where Gregg had been staying. He had rooms down at the Marine-Neptune."

"I know that," said Blake a bit impatiently. "Use your head, Dan—just who do you think that little Japanese would be calling on here?"

"Well, I can't think of anyone living in this hotel that we have connected with Gregg except the La Tona woman."

"Right—and I'll bet that's just who this fellow Tahira came to see. I'd give a lot to have overheard the conversation between those two."

"I'll bet you would, Cap—and I'm thinking they're just as well satisfied that you weren't listening in on them."

74

"You know, Dan, I'd like to find out who it was that telephoned me night before last and gave me that tip about the Weymouth Woods Road. It was a good one, all right."

"I'll say so!" exclaimed Flannigan. "I wonder what that fellow Danton was doing there, Cap? I ain't figured yet why you haven't put that bird in jail. He acts to me like he's guilty as Hell."

"I know, Dan. But we can't pin it on him yet, can we? I want to give him all the rope that he needs, and let him trip himself up. We haven't any real evidence against him, you know—and sticking him behind the bars now won't do us a bit of good. What we want to learn is just who murdered Watson Gregg, and why."

"Sure, I know that, but it don't look like the easiest thing in the world to do. It took brains to figure out how to murder a man right here on the Boardwalk with people passing all the time—brains and the devil of a lot of nerve."

"Hum!" remarked Blake thoughtfully. "What makes you so sure that it was a man, Dan? A woman might have done it, you know—and there are two of them connected with this case: Mercedes La Tona and that blonde that was with Gregg at dinner on the night he was murdered."

"Funny what became of her." The stout detective looked puzzled. "No one at the hotel remembered ever seeing her before. They gave us a pretty good description of her, though."

"Yes, girl about twenty years old, very pretty. Tall and slender, brown eyes and blonde hair." The captain laughed as he glanced about him at the passing throng. "Look around you now, Dan, and tell me just how many woman you see that might fit that description. I can see at least five of them, and I'm not looking very hard."

"That's right." Flannigan appeared a bit crestfallen. "It is kinda vague at that, come to think about it. But we'll find her, Cap. And I'll bet she knows plenty about the murder."

"Maybe." Blake's tone was doubtful. "I'm not so sure."

He glanced at a uniformed patrolman who was hurrying toward them.

"Here comes Hayes," remarked Flannigan. "And he acts like he has something on his mind."

"If he has, it's about time," commented Blake. "He was standing just a block away from Gregg's chair, and he couldn't remember a thing that was worthwhile before."

"I just remembered something, Captain Blake," said Hayes as he paused and saluted.

"Good!" said Blake drily. "What was it?"

"Well, ever since you talked to me about the case night before last, I've been thinking about it and trying to remember just who I saw near that rolling chair."

"And do you remember now, Hayes?"

"Yes, sir. At least I think so. I told you about the blonde woman getting out and running across the Boardwalk like she was frightened. Well, I remember that the young fellow, Benson his name is, followed her off the walk. While he was gone, three people stopped for a moment at the chair—and seemed to be talking to Mr. Gregg."

"Three people!" exclaimed Blake excitedly. "For the love of Heaven! You saw three people stop there and you're just remembering it now, Hayes!"

"Yes, sir." The patrolman's tone was very meek. "My memory don't seem to be so good."

"I'll say it ain't!" remarked Flannigan.

The patrolman glared at the stout detective resentfully, and Blake observed the look.

"Never mind any side remarks, Dan," he said quickly. "Let Hayes talk." He turned again to the patrolman. "Can you remember what those three people looked like?"

"No, sir. At least I can't describe them very good. One of them was a tall man—I couldn't see his face—but I remember he was leaning over talking to Mr. Gregg, and he was laughing as though they had found something that was awful funny."

"A tall man, eh?" said Blake. "But you didn't see his face. How did you know that he was laughing, then?"

"Oh, I could hear him," said Hayes quickly. "He had a nice jolly laugh, too."

"Hum!" exclaimed the Captain. "Who were the other two?"

"They were both women."

"Women?"

"Yes, Captain. And the first one stopped at the chair just after the tall man went away. She just looked in it and then hurried away. She had hardly gone when the second one came along. She leaned into the chair—and acted like she was talking to Mr. Gregg."

"How were they dressed—have you any idea what they looked like?"

"They were both dressed in black. I can't tell you much more than that, Captain, because they each had a heavy veil down over their faces."

"You are sure that neither of them was the blonde that got out of the chair?"

"Oh, yes. I'm positive about that. She was dressed in brown— and had on a gray fur coat."

"You're improving, Hayes," said Blake. "A gray fur coat eh? And the other two were dressed in black. Is that all?"

"Yes, sir," said Hayes, and he moved away.

"Of all the dumb harness bulls I ever seen in my life!" exclaimed Flannigan as he watched the patrolman move up the Boardwalk. "Maybe if he keeps thinking long enough he will remember who killed Gregg."

"No, Dan," said Blake with a smile. "He won't—but if he keeps thinking long enough we may find out!"

"Lots of news this morning, Jerry?" demanded a voice behind them.

The two men turned quickly, to find Dave Morton standing there smiling at them.

"Oh, hello, Dave!" said Blake. "I wanted to see you."

"Well, here I am, Jerry. What's on your mind?"

"What was the idea of all that truck you had in the paper this morning about the *Press* having received a mysterious telephone call warning them to watch Giovanni Danton."

"No truck about that, Jerry. I received that call at eleven-fifty last night—and so I used it in my story."

"That's a fine trick!" exclaimed Blake angrily. "Tipping Danton off like that! Now he won't do a thing that will give us a chance to get anything on him."

"Gosh, Jerry," said the reporter, "I didn't think you would have any objections to that story. If I had I would have called you up before I used it."

"Yes, maybe you would. I got hauled over the carpet by the Chief on that this morning. He wanted to know why I hadn't arrested Danton."

"And you told him why?"

"Of course I told him!" stated the Captain impatiently.

"I guess you had a good reason, didn't you, Jerry?"

"Certainly." Blake smiled at the reporter. "You needn't think you can lead me on to tell you what that reason was, Dave. There are a few things about this Gregg case I'd rather not see in the papers, you know."

"Oh, sure, Jerry; I understand that perfectly." Morton slapped the Captain on the shoulder. "No hard feelings about my using that 'phone call stuff, I hope?"

"Not at all, Dave—but next time get in touch with me first if you run across anything connected with the murder, will you?"

"You're darn right I will." Morton glanced about him. "This sure is a wonderful day for October, isn't it?"

He turned to the rail and stood gazing down at the beach. A woman in one of the beach chairs in front of the hotel caught his eye.

"Jerry," he exclaimed turning to Blake. "Look! In that second chair there—isn't that Mercedes La Tona?"

"Yes," said the Captain as he looked in the direction the reporter had indicated. "That's her, all right."

"Look at that tall guy over there by the life guards' stand watching her," remarked Flannigan as he stood with the others gazing at the beach. "I'll bet he is trying to get her to give him the glad eye."

"Ever see him before, Dave?" asked Blake, his eyes upon the tall figure of Godfrey Floss.

"No, not that I recall." He, too, was watching the man. "Have you, Jerry?"

"Nope." The Captain shook his head. "We better not all stand here as though we were watching them. Dan, you and Morton turn around. And I'll act as though I am talking to you, and watch those two on the beach at the same time."

The reporter and the stout detective swung around. Flannigan produced a black cigar and lighted it, while Morton leaned idly against the rail.

"He's going over to her now," said Blake, his eyes still upon the two on the beach. "They are talking. Now he has dropped into the chair beside her. They seem to be having quite a chat."

"I don't like that fellow's looks," remarked Morton thoughtfully. "I wonder if he has any connection with the murder."

"Can't tell yet of course," said the Captain, as he continued to watch. "But we're going to find out! The man is leaving now. He looks like he's worried. That La Tona woman must have said something that he didn't like. He's coming this way, toward the steps over there. Dan!"

"Yes, Cap?"

"Shadow that man and see what you can learn about him. But use your head. Don't make any arrest—and don't let him know that you are trailing him."

"Okay, Cap." Flannigan sauntered off down the Boardwalk, Godfrey Floss just a short distance ahead of him.

Blake swung around and looked in the other direction as though he had not the slightest interest in Flannigan's destination.

"I have a hunch," he said slowly. "And it's a good one!"

"What is it?" asked the reporter eagerly.

"I'm sorry, Dave," the Captain smiled, "but it's not for publication!"

12
THE LEATHER NOOSE AGAIN

IT WAS THE NIGHT of the second day following the discovery of the murder of Watson Gregg. Close to the broad expanse of sea that roared eternally as the white-capped waves crashed and rolled upon the hard, white sand of the beachfront, two figures now walked slowly. On their right was the brightly lighted Boardwalk, with its piers and buildings and tall hotels looming like some strange fairyland.

It was a man and a woman who strolled along the beach, a strange couple—Giovanni Danton and Mercedes La Tona—the tall man with the tragic, white face, the dark-haired woman with the deep blue eyes that were ever a little cynical, and cold. Danton and Mercedes La Tona together—the police would have found the fact interesting.

"And I can remember when she was famous. It was before your time, perhaps," Danton spoke softly as they walked along. "Is it any wonder that she should hate so deeply?"

"I know—I know." Mercedes' tone was low, bitter. "A woman forgives much, Giovanni Danton, but she forgets little."

"And you have so much to remember?"

"No, I have so much to forget!"

"Ah, but will you?" That faint, illusive smile crept over Danton's face, to vanish in an instant.

"I can only hope." Mercedes sighed. "What is there about you that makes one hate you and yet tell you so much?"

"I do not know." There was mockery in Danton's tone. "Perhaps it is because I, who am never understood, seem always to understand." His tone changed: "Listen, Miss La Tona, of course you know that the police have learned that a certain actress was on very friendly terms with the late Watson Gregg?"

They had turned away from the sea now and were moving closer to the Boardwalk. For a minute or two they walked in silence. Mercedes appeared to be debating Danton's question before she answered.

"Yes?" she said finally. "And how does that concern me?"

"Surely you are not so dense that you do not get my meaning?"

"Perhaps I prefer not to understand."

"That is rather foolish. If the police question you—and they will, for they have learned that you were a friend of Watson Gregg's—I'd advise you to be careful!"

"Really, you belittle my intellect." Mercedes smiled. "The police—a reporter—they have already questioned me extensively and have found me exceedingly dumb—"

"A very excellent idea, Miss La Tona!" said a voice from the shadows of a pier beneath which they had been passing.

They both turned and looked anxiously through the darkness toward a shadowy form.

"Who is there?" demanded Danton, his long white fingers disappearing within the side pockets of his coat.

The figure in the shadows stepped forward, and a yellow face was revealed in the pale light of the stars.

"Tahira!" exclaimed Mercedes. "You frightened me!"

"Tahira?" said Danton, softly. "I do not think I know the gentleman."

"This is Tahira Yamada," said Mercedes quickly "The servant of Watson Gregg."

"Gregg's servant," remarked Danton slowly. "Interesting—very. You think it an excellent idea that Miss La Tona allow the police to find her exceedingly dumb?"

"Yes, Mr. Danton. Do you not agree?"

"Apparently you are not in deep sympathy, Yamada, with the police!"

"They are occasionally so stupid! The Captain of Detectives has questioned me quite insistently. He seems to think that I might be able to give him a great deal of information should I so desire. In fact, he threatened to place me in jail unless I revealed just what I knew regarding the murder of Mr. Gregg."

"And did you tell him all you knew?" asked Danton.

"I wouldn't say that!" Tahira smiled faintly. "Still—I am not in jail!"

"I see." Danton stood looking down at the Japanese. "I've had a number of interviews with Captain Blake myself. He apparently does not quite trust me!"

"Strange!" Mercedes laughed. "I'm afraid that I agree with the Captain, Mr. Danton!"

"Shall we be on our way?" demanded Danton abruptly. "I'm sure that—"

"Certainly." Tahira bowed. "Have you ever studied the birds, Mr. Danton?"

Danton had started to walk away, but he turned sharply at the words and stood staring at the little servant.

"What do you mean?" His voice was vibrant, sinister.

"Nothing." Tahira smiled. "Only of the night birds the owl is perhaps the most interesting!"

"Oh!" Danton smiled, and then he made a strange gesture with his right hand—a motion which was answered by the hand of the Japanese. "I should like to see you later, Yamada!" Danton's eyes flamed as he spoke.

"It will be a pleasure," Tahira told him, looking directly at the tall man, but he did not smile.

Mercedes observed the glance which passed between the two men. There was something terrible about it. It left her feeling strange and cold, as though an icy wind had suddenly blown over her. The sensation lingered as she and Danton moved on, leaving the servant standing there amid the shadows.

A pale moon was stealing up now from out of the sea—a slender moon that cast long, black shadows in front of the man and the woman as they walked along the beach. They had gone only a short distance when Danton paused and looked back.

Mercedes watched him fearfully. The chill feeling still remained. What had passed between this man and the servant of Watson Gregg? Why did the mention of an owl seem so vitally important? Why was it apparently such a dangerous subject? An owl? The mere name of the bird had caused Godfrey Floss to drop his game of blackmail, for the time at least. It had caused Giovanni Danton and Tahira Yamada to exchange glances that were filled with meaning. An owl—what did it mean? Why should Tahira know so much about it?

"The servant of Watson Gregg," said Danton as he looked back; "strange—I wonder—" He smiled as he left the sentence unfinished. "But we were talking of something else, were we not?"

"Perhaps we were," Mercedes faced him impatiently, "but we are not now, Mr. Danton. I'm tired of all this mystery—these veiled allusions of yours. Who are you, and what's your game? Put your cards on the table—I want to know!"

For a brief instant the man and the woman stood there in the light of the moon gazing at each other. There was an impetuous, defiant expression upon the face of Mercedes La Tona, yet inwardly she was terribly afraid. She realized that it was dangerous to speak as she had done to this tall, exotic individual who stood beside her.

Danton's pallid face was placid now—masklike in its utter lack of expression. The white lids drooped low over the strange eyes, hiding them from her anxious gaze—making her all the more frightened and anxious.

"And if I do not choose to tell you, what then?" His words came slowly and with metallic sharpness, cutting into her consciousness with the keenness of a knife.

"Then I shall form my own conclusions."

"Naturally!"

"And those conclusions are not very flattering to you, Giovanni Danton!"

"No?" The white lids lifted suddenly, and she found those eyes staring deeply into hers, frightening her by the very intensity of their gaze. "That is unfortunate!"

Danton reached out swiftly. His hand grasped her arm. She shuddered at the touch, and shrank away instinctively. As she did so Danton's grip tightened.

"Let me go, damn you!" Mercedes murmured through clinched teeth. "Take your rotten hand off me—you—you murderer!"

"So!" Danton's hand dropped to his side, and she saw that the white fingers were moving restlessly. It seemed to Mercedes that they longed to clasp her throat. "Murderer, eh? You think that?"

Mercedes did not answer. She could not. She stood there trembling with fright and anger, her eyes flashing as she gazed at the pale-faced man in front of her.

Danton was smiling now, a strange, grotesque expression that reminded Mercedes of the Greek masks she had often seen painted upon the curtains in various theatres, characterizing Comedy and Tragedy. It was an uncanny smile.

They both turned at a sound from behind them. They stood staring at a tall figure running swiftly toward them over the sand.

It was a young face, a handsome face that paused and gazed from one to the other.

"Larry Benson!" exclaimed Danton. "What's the matter?"

"Oh, Mr. Danton!" exclaimed Larry. "Ever since early morning I've been searching for you, hoping that I might find you somewhere. I've been all over the city looking for you!"

"Larry! What's the matter, tell me, quickly!"

"You must help me—you must!" Larry paid no heed to Mercedes, did not even seem to notice that she was there. "It's Lannon, Lannon Gordon and her Aunt—"

Danton grasped Larry roughly by the arm: "Quick, tell me what's happened?"

"I was there for dinner last night, as you know—"

"Yes, I know all about that!" Danton interrupted impatiently. "Go on!"

"Later Lannon was called by her Aunt. When she returned she was excited and asked me to leave. Against my better judgment I left, but I was worried about her. I couldn't sleep all night. This morning I drove down to Miss Hill's house, hoping that I might catch a glimpse of Lannon and know that she was all right."

"And did you?"

"No. That's what worries me. All the blinds were down, and the house appeared deserted. I rang and rang the bell, but no one answered. As I started to leave I caught a glimpse of a face peering out from behind the blind at one of the windows."

"A face!" exclaimed Danton. "What sort of face?"

"A yellow face. That of an Oriental of some sort."

"A Japanese?"

"I don't know." Larry frowned. "It might have been."

Danton glanced quickly back toward the pier, and then he looked from Mercedes to Larry and smiled.

"I beg your pardon. Miss La Tona, this is Mr. Benson. Stupid of me not to introduce you before—but I was so anxious to learn the cause of Mr. Benson's agitation—"

"That's quite all right, Mr. Danton." Mercedes smiled and extended her hand to Larry. "I'm very glad to know you Mr. Benson."

"The pleasure is all mine, Miss La Tona."

Danton glanced again at the pier. "Please see Miss La Tona to her hotel, Larry," he said, and then smiled grimly at Mercedes. "I'm sure you'll have no objections if I leave you?"

"Certainly not." There was almost a note of relief in Mercedes' voice.

"I thought not." Danton turned to Larry. "You'll find me in this vicinity later, Larry. I've an interview with a certain gentleman in mind, that must not be delayed. Good evening, Miss La Tona!"

"But, aren't you going to do something? Lannon—"

Giovanni Danton had started rapidly for the shadows of the tall piling beneath the pier. If he heard, he gave no sign.

"Mr. Danton appears to be in a great hurry," remarked Mercedes lightly. "I hope you don't object to my being thrust upon you in such an abrupt fashion?"

"Not at all, Miss La Tona. It's quite an unexpected pleasure!" Larry smiled politely, but his heart was heavy.

He wanted to know what had become of Lannon and Miss Hill. Where were they now? Why had Danton become so excited when he had learned of the Oriental face in the window? Where had he gone now, and who did he expect to find beneath the pier?

"I live at the Seafoam," said Mercedes, after they had walked on for a moment in silence. "We haven't far to go."

Larry's heart leaped as he heard her words. There was the Seafoam towering on the opposite side of the Boardwalk just in front of them. It would take them but a few seconds to get there. He was not at all interested in this woman who walked by his side. He scarcely noticed that she was attractive. His heart was full of Lannon. Besides, he wanted to get back to Danton, to question him and try to learn what had happened at Miss Hill's the night before.

At the entrance to the hotel Larry and Mercedes exchanged a few polite nothings. Then Larry turned and started swiftly back across the walk toward the beach. Now he was again on the sand. He wanted to run, but he did not dare. There were too many people on the Boardwalk. A man running on the beach in the bright moonlight might cause them to wonder, even investigate.

At last Larry reached the shadowy place beneath the pier. It was very dark now that he was out of the moonlight. He paused to let his eyes become accustomed to the gloom. Now he could see better, even though he found the shadows deep around the great pilings of steel and cement which held up the pier.

He grew tense as he thought he saw something move in the shadows to his left. He was not sure about it, but he seemed to have caught just a glimpse of a flitting figure. He realized that he was in a dangerous place. The worst of the city's dregs sometimes gathered beneath the piers. There had been times when people had been robbed, even badly clubbed, when they had resisted. He knew that he must be careful—and yet that figure might be Giovanni Danton. He decided to take a chance.

"Danton!" he called softly.

"Yes!" The figure took definite shape and moved toward him. "That you, Benson?"

"Right."

In an instant Danton had reached his side.

"Danton, what's wrong? Where are Lannon and Miss Hill?"

"I don't know. But this much I can tell you. They are safe—no harm has come to either of them."

"But that face I saw in the window? What about that?"

"I may be able to explain that later." Danton moved toward the other side of the pier. "Come on, let's get out of here!"

Larry followed and then stepped around the opposite side of one of the pilings from that which Danton took. As he did so his feet struck something soft. Startled, he leaped back instinctively. He looked down and saw a shadowy form stretched out before him.

He must have cried out, for Danton turned and came quickly to his side.

"What's the matter?"

"Look!" said Larry. "There's something on the ground there! It looks like a—a body!"

Danton produced a small pocket flashlight. In its ray the figure of a man was revealed, a man who lay with his face buried in the sand. Danton handed Larry the light, and then stooped to turn the man over. It was the face of Tahira Yamada that stared up at them. As Danton looked, he uttered an oath. The slim white fingers reached quickly for the throat of the Japanese. In a moment Danton stood up, a long brown leather cord in one hand.

"The leather necklace again," he said softly.

"Is he dead?" asked Larry, staring down at Tahira.

Danton leaned over the motionless form again. He pressed his ear close to the servant's chest. He could hear the man's heart beating faintly.

"No!" Danton exclaimed as he got to his feet. "I think he has a chance—but we got here just in time!"

"I wonder who did it?" said Larry.

"Probably the result of discussing too freely the subject of owls," remarked the tall man.

Larry did not speak. He was watching the restless white hands of Giovanni Danton as they played with the leather thong.

13
"THE SUBJECT OF MOTIVES"

LANNON GORDON had found her visit to her Aunt a trying ordeal. With each passing hour things had become more and more difficult. Now it was the third night that the girl had spent in the strange old house, and she found herself held in the grip of a blind, unreasonable fear.

To Lannon it was now a night of strange sounds and whispering shadows. Sounds beat upon her ears, noises that made her quiver with fright. She shuddered as she gazed out through the half-open door of her bedroom. The sound of footsteps came to her from the hallway, the soft *pad, pad* of someone passing in the darkness. She wondered why her aunt had put out the light in the hall. It was so dark out there—so terrifying, somehow.

Lannon sat huddled up in one corner of the big bed, her lovely eyes wide, her soft lips trembling, her heart fluttering wildly. Deep within her was something telling her that she must be brave, and she did not feel she could. She wanted to scream hysterically, to gather the bedclothes in a heap and dive beneath them, and yet she just sat there staring into the darkness beyond the half-open door.

Memories of the past twenty-four hours were running through her brain: a night that had been a thing of terror and day that had been worse. A long, weary day of silence it was, of drawn blinds and hushed voices, mysterious actions which she did not understand.

She had not wanted Larry to leave. Yet her Aunt had sent for her and had requested her to dismiss him at once. Even now

Lannon did not know why, but she had felt it unwise to go against her Aunt's wishes.

The girl wondered what had become of Giovanni Danton. Where was that pale-faced man with his strange eyes? She had never seen him before last night. It was strange that she had not been able to tell Larry that, yet she had been so nervous, so excited, that she had hardly known what she was doing. She had thought that when Miss Hill had sent for her it was to meet Danton, but such had not been the case; the elderly woman had been alone. And she had told her to send Larry away.

Again Lannon heard steps in the hall, and then a soft cackle came out of the darkness. A wave of relief swept over Lannon. Then it was Loona who was passing.

"Loona!" Lannon called softly. "Is that you?"

The soft cackle came again, but there was no answer to her call. The footsteps passed and then died away. It seemed strange that the old servant had not answered, it had been Loona, of course. Who else could it be? Lannon decided that Loona had not heard. Perhaps she was a bit deaf. Still, she was a little afraid of the old servant.

Memories of the day which had just passed lingered in Lannon's brain. Aunt Ida had come to her early this morning, hysterical with excitement and almost begging her to stay in her room until she called her. How well Lannon remembered the long interval which had followed! At last the girl had found she could stand it no longer and had opened her door. She had had a brief glimpse of a strange yellow-faced man passing through the hallway—the face of a Japanese or a Chinaman, she had thought.

The afternoon had been even more difficult than the morning. She had wanted to write to Larry, to telephone him and assure him that she was all right. She knew that he would be worried, and he loved her. Finally she had written a little note, and then tried to get out of the house to mail it, or at least to telephone him. Her aunt had appeared every time she approached the door, pleading with her not to leave, apparently afraid that she would not return. At last Lannon had given up in despair. She had realized it was no use, she could not escape—not without openly offending her aunt, and she did not want to do that.

Now she was very much worried about Larry. He had known that she was frightened and anxious the night before. How well he understood—the afternoon they had quarreled about her having dinner with Gregg was the only time he had failed her. If only she had listened to him then! But he had been so sweet about even that, though. He had pleaded with her to forgive him—and it was so easy to forgive Larry.

For a long time Lannon sat there on the edge of the bed staring out into the dark hallway. Finally she again heard footsteps in the hall, and a moment later Miss Hill stood in the doorway. She smiled and then entered the room and dropped down on the bed beside the girl.

"Lannon, dear."

"Yes, Auntie?"

"I have been cruel—I did not think."

"Cruel, Auntie?" Lannon gazed at Miss Hill anxiously. "Why?"

The elderly woman shook her head. It seemed to the nervous, overwrought girl that the strange expression, of insanity almost, which she had observed in her Aunt's eyes had increased in intensity, but of this she could not be sure.

"Explanations are always difficult, Lannon," Miss Hill said slowly. "Usually they only make things worse."

"But, Auntie, I—I haven't asked you to explain anything!"

"I know that, dear. That is why I feel that my silence, the weird actions you could not have failed to observe here—" Miss Hill smiled faintly. "I don't wonder you have been a little worried."

"Only because of you, dear!"

"You're sweet, Lannon." Miss Hill patted her niece's hand. "I don't wonder that Larry Benson loves you so much!"

Lannon did not look at her Aunt. Her heart leaped at the sound of Larry's name, and a thrill passed over her at her Aunt's words. She realized that Larry loved her, but how did Miss Hill know?

"What makes you think that, Auntie?" she asked innocently.

"Oh, child, child!" Miss Hill smiled. "One would have to be blind, not to see it. It's in his eyes every time he looks at you." Suddenly she became thoughtful. "How old is Larry?"

"Twenty-four. Why, Auntie?"

"Nothing, dear. I was just wondering, that's all." Miss Hill sighed. "Love is such a strange thing, Lannon. Either we are consumed by its flames or we find ourselves raking its ashes."

"I'm afraid I don't quite follow."

"No, perhaps not. It does not matter."

For a moment Miss Hill was silent. Visions, faint yesterdays, pale hues of half-forgotten dreams, lingered in her heart.

"Auntie."

"Yes, dear?"

"Can't you tell me what's worryin' you?"

"Yes, Lannon, I will tell you. It is hard to keep the heart sealed forever. It is the old, old story—"

Miss Hill turned suddenly and gazed at the doorway. Lannon followed the direction of her glance. Old Loona stood there, a glum, anxious expression upon her withered countenance.

"Loona, what's the matter?" Miss Hill stood up, startled by the old servant's expression.

"Trouble." Loona shook her head. "De's a man downstairs dat says he must see you."

"Who is he?"

"Dat Doctor Fulda."

An expression which Lannon did not understand, passed over her Aunt's face—a look that was cold and hard.

"Doctor Fulda here!"

"Yes 'm."

"But how did he get in? Why did you let him in, Loona?"

"I didn't go fo' to do hit, 'deed I didn't!" Loona's voice was tearful. "I just open de do' an' fo' could say 'boo' he just walk right in! Dey ain't nobody home I says—'tell Miss Hill I'm heah' he says—an' dat's all!"

"All! Good heavens, Loona, don't you realize what it may mean to have Doctor Fulda here?" Miss Hill turned to Lannon hysterically. "Oh, Lannon, you must help me! This man Fulda—he is Watson Gregg's physician. He— Oh, what am I saying?"

"Please, Auntie," said Lannon hurriedly, trying not to show the alarm which she felt in her heart. "What's it all about?"

"I can't explain now. But I don't dare see this man alone. You must come down with me. Will you, Lannon?"

"'Course I will, Auntie." Lannon moved swiftly over to the mirror and gave her hair a few hurried pats. "Lead on."

Doctor Fulda rose and bowed as the two women entered the room. His hard eyes were fixed intently upon Lannon as he stepped toward them.

"Please pardon the intrusion," he said, "but it was vitally important that I see you, Miss Hill."

"It's quite all right, Doctor Fulda." Miss Hill answered him far more calmly than Lannon had thought she could speak. "Only your visit was rather unexpected. This is my niece, Miss Lannon Gordon."

The dark, swarthy-faced doctor bowed low over Lannon's hand as she acknowledged the introduction.

"This is indeed an unexpected pleasure!" he said softly.

"You said you wished to see me about something vitally important, Doctor?" asked Miss Hill coldly as she sank into a chair and motioned Lannon to one by her side.

"Yes." Fulda released Lannon's hand reluctantly and turned to her Aunt. "As the physician of the late Mr. Gregg I am naturally very much interested in the solution of the murder."

"Of course," said Miss Hill calmly, as Lannon took the chair beside her. "But in that case I should think that the police would be the ones for you to look up."

"Quite so." Doctor Fulda stood there looking down at Miss Hill. "In murder cases the first thing to look for is a possible motive. Don't you agree, Miss Hill?"

"I suppose that is so." Miss Hill smiled faintly. "Really, Doctor Fulda, I haven't studied the subject of murders very extensively."

Lannon's fingers beat nervously upon the arm of her chair. She felt that there was something terribly dangerous to her Aunt in the presence of this small, swarthy man with his pointed beard and his hard eyes.

"Well, I have studied the subject," said Fulda. "And I know that such is the case."

"Still I must say I don't see why you have something of vital importance to see me about."

Miss Hill sat calmly gazing at the doctor, but Lannon noticed that her hands trembled slightly, and she was controlling herself with an effort.

Doctor Fulda smiled.

"It was the subject of motives which brought me," he said. "Who would have more reason to hate Watson Gregg now than Dolly Marden?"

"Dolly Marden!" exclaimed Miss Hill, leaning forward in her chair, glaring at Doctor Fulda. "You mention that name now?"

"Yes," the Doctor answered calmly. "Dolly Marden, the woman whom Watson Gregg made a star on Broadway and then grew tired of and deserted for a new love!"

"No! You can't say that!" Miss Hill was standing now as she faced the Doctor. "Dolly Marden was different from the rest—from the others."

"Yes? In what way?"

"She was the wife of Watson Gregg!"

"His wife?" Fulda's tone was incredulous. "Is that true?"

"Yes, as true as I am standing here!"

"I see—I believe you." Doctor Fulda frowned. "Now I understand lots of things that have always been very vague and mysterious. The wife of Watson Gregg— How that woman must have suffered!"

Something in the way the Doctor looked at her as he spoke made Lannon turn to her Aunt, a question upon her lips.

"Auntie, who is Dolly Marden?"

Miss Hill looked at her for an instant before she spoke.

"Oh, Lannon, Lannon, why do you ask that?" she said finally, in tears. "Dolly Marden was my stage name, dear!"

Lannon did not speak. She sat staring at her Aunt, dumb with amazement.

"And Dolly Marden was the wife of Watson Gregg," said Doctor Fulda. . . . "We were discussing motives!" . . .

14

BLUFF

IMPRESSIONS LINGER IN THE MIND. Larry Benson never forgot the long moment that he stood beneath the pier, his eyes watching the strange white hands of Giovanni Danton as the latter played with the leather cord. There was an illusive expression upon the pallid countenance of the tall man as he stared down at the motionless form of the Japanese upon the cold, gray sand.

Questions passed swiftly through his brain. Who was this Japanese? It was the same face that he had seen staring from the window of Miss Hill's house that morning. He was sure of that. Now there was a faint smile upon Danton's face as he stood there looking down. There was something sinister, evil, in the expression. Had Danton drawn tight the leather thong?

Larry wanted to know what Danton had meant when he had asked him who had strangled the Japanese. "Probably the result of discussing too freely the subjects of owls!" Danton had said. But why speak of owls—and with whom?

The cord which Danton had drawn from the throat of the man on the sand—he had called it "the leather necklace—"

The Japanese moaned and then changed his position slightly. Danton glanced at Larry, a strange expression in his weird eyes.

"Our friend appears to be recovering rapidly." Larry felt that deep voice of Danton's was always a bit sinister. "He is fortunate that we discovered him in time."

"Who is he?" asked Larry. "Do you know him?"

94

"Yes. He is Tahira Yamada, the servant of the late Watson Gregg." Giovanni Danton's expression was very thoughtful. "Was this the man whom you saw looking out of the window of Miss Hill's residence?"

"Yes, it is the very same face. Oh, Danton, what do you suppose happened to Lannon and Miss Hill? Where are they now?"

"Don't worry, my boy." Danton's tone was quiet, soothing. "You will probably find them both just where you left them!"

"But if they were there, why didn't they let me see them?"

"Why should they?" Danton smiled ironically. "I judge they might wish seclusion after the—ah—celebration."

"What were you doing there last night?" Larry demanded.

For an instant the flame leaped high in Danton's eyes. The long, slender fingers tightened upon the leather thong that he still held in his hands. He stared down at it, and then smiled faintly.

"You're rather a fool at times, Benson," he remarked slowly. "It is fortunate that I like you, otherwise your daring to question my actions might not be advisable!" There was a dangerous note in the deep voice.

Larry felt cold, he shook as though an icy breeze had swept over him. He realized that he had made a mistake. Danton had been right when he had called him a fool. It had been dangerous, foolhardy, to have questioned this man. How did he know that Giovanni Danton was a friend—that he could be a friend of anyone?

A wave of relief swept over Larry as he realized that the Japanese was sitting up now. The man's actions relieved the tension. Danton no longer looked at Larry, he was staring at the servant.

Tahira got slowly and weakly to his feet. His eyes were fixed upon the face of Giovanni Danton, his countenance placid and devoid of any sign of emotion.

"Feeling better now, Yamada?" Danton spoke softly, politely, the leather thong still in his hands.

"Much better, thank you, Mr. Danton." Tahira was equally quiet and polite, his gaze now upon the leather cord in the tall man's slender fingers. "I am very fortunate in receiving such prompt assistance. Thank you again, Mr. Danton."

"You are quite welcome, although I do not deserve your gratitude. It was Mr. Benson here who discovered you in the shadows."

"I am indeed indebted deeply to you, Mr. Benson." Tahira bowed low in Larry's direction. "You have placed me under an obligation I fear I may not be able to repay."

"Oh, that's all right," said Larry quickly. "Mighty glad we found you in time!"

"Have you any suspicion as to who tried to strangle you?" asked Danton.

"One may always have suspicions, Mr. Danton." Tahira looked again at the cord in the ever-moving hands. "Motives are sometimes more difficult to fathom!"

"There are many subjects upon which one may speak too freely at times, Yamada!"

"For instance?"

"That of owls!"

For a long moment Giovanni Danton and Tahira stared deep into each other's eyes, a tense moment during which Larry Benson waited for he knew not what. Then suddenly the two men smiled, and the action seemed almost a pact of friendship between them.

"Your words are pearls of wisdom," said Tahira, still smiling, and then his expression changed, grew serious. "You have reason to suspect that that which you have mentioned might be so?"

"An owl sees with splendid vision in the dark!"

"True," remarked Tahira. "And they are far more capable of discerning many things when traveling in pairs—"

A slight sound came from the opposite side of the pier. The three men turned abruptly in that direction. A shadowy figure approached them slowly, stepping in a zigzag course around the pilings.

Danton again brought his small pocket flashlight into play. Its ray gleamed upon the hard, wolflike countenance of Godfrey Floss. He stood there, his lips parted in a snarl, his eyes blinking in the unexpected light.

"Good evening." Danton's voice rang out cold and dangerous from behind the light.

"Who's there?" demanded Floss.

"Friends, I assure you!" There was a sarcastic note in Danton's voice.

"Maybe you are," growled Floss. "But I'd be more certain if you'd take that damn light out of my eyes."

"I beg your pardon." The light went out. "I hope that's better, Mr. Floss?"

Godfrey Floss stepped forward and stared into the pallid face of Giovanni Danton.

"You appear to know me," he said slowly. "But who the devil are you?"

"The question is really quite debatable," the tall man smiled. "But my name is Giovanni Danton."

"Giovanni Danton!" exclaimed Floss.

"The very same—and quite, oh, very much at your service!"

Larry glanced at Tahira. The little Japanese was smiling faintly as the blackmailer and Danton confronted each other. Larry was wondering who this evil-looking man could be. Why had Floss been so startled at learning Danton's name?

"Danton, eh?" repeated Floss. "And these other two?"

"Again, pardon. I have been rude." There was still that sarcastic undercurrent in Danton's tone. "This is Mr. Larry Benson and Tahira Yamada."

Larry and Tahira bowed as Godfrey Floss glanced from one to the other and then turned again to Danton.

"You and Benson were the ones who discovered the murder of Watson Gregg, were you not?" he asked.

"Either your powers of deduction are remarkable or you read the papers," said Danton drily. "Why do you ask?"

"Nothing vital," answered Floss. "I was just wondering."

"Yes, wondering just what we were doing here, were you not, Mr. Floss?"

"I was!" Floss frowned as he answered, and his hand disappeared within the side pocket of his coat. "I'd like to know."

"Since you insist, I shall tell you." Danton turned to the Japanese. "We were practicing our vocal lesson, weren't we, Yamada?"

For an instant Danton and the servant gazed at each other, and then suddenly the latter smiled.

"Quite so, Mr. Danton," he said softly. "We were."

Danton smiled and then moved closer to Godfrey Floss. The blackmailer instinctively stepped back.

"Oh, don't let me alarm you, Mr. Floss," said Danton. "I merely wish to make a suggestion. It is that you remember the message that was conveyed to you by a certain charming lady this morning—"

"You mean Miss La Tona?" Floss spoke before he thought.

"Yes." Danton's eyes gleamed. "I believe she informed you that owls sometimes hoot very insistently?"

"She did!" Floss snarled as he began to back slowly away. "But what's that to you?"

"Observing bird—an owl," said Danton quietly, his hand also disappearing within the side pocket of his coat. "But as I was saying, Yamada and I have been practicing our vocal lesson. Listen!"

From Danton's lips there suddenly came the realistic hoot of an owl. Once only he voiced the cry, and then turned to Tahira. From the lips of the latter came a repetition of the sound.

"Very observing," repeated Danton, and then abruptly his tone changed. "I wouldn't advise that, Floss! My automatic works quite as well as yours!"

Godfrey Floss glared at the pointing bulge in Danton's right-hand coat pocket, and then dropped back into his own pocket the automatic which he had half-drawn. Slowly he turned and moved away. He did not look back—he did not speak.

Giovanni Danton sighed softly as he drew his long white hand from his pocket.

"I'm afraid that our friend, Mr. Floss jumps too readily to conclusions," he remarked slowly. "I really must buy myself an automatic—it might prove useful!"

15
HEADWAY

CAPTAIN JERRY BLAKE was scowling as he slowly read over a report which he had received from the New York Police Department upon the subject of Watson Gregg. The bright light of his green-shaded desk lamp gleamed down upon the papers in front of him as the head of the Detective Bureau turned page after page of the report. A clock beside him pointed to the hour of midnight, but at present Blake was unheedful of time.

Finally he thrust the papers swiftly aside with a grunt of disgust. He ran his stubby fingers through his thick white hair, and then gazed reflectively out of the window. For a few moments he sat there thinking deeply. He finally turned with a start as he heard a soft rap upon the closed door of his office.

"Come in!" he commanded gruffly.

The door opened, and Dave Morton stepped into the room. Blake glared at the reporter for an instant without speaking. The younger man merely grinned and then dropped into a chair.

"Evening, Jerry!" he said, and then laughed as his eyes observed the clock. "Or maybe I should say good morning!"

"What do you want?" demanded Blake abruptly.

"Why, news, of course," answered Morton, a faint twinkle in his eyes. "The public is clamoring for it—begging, pleading. They want to know who murdered Watson Gregg."

"Yea?" Blake's scowl grew deeper. "Well, so do I!"

"Echo answered ditto!" remarked Morton. "Why the grouch, Jerry?"

"Who wouldn't be sore at the world with a case like this?" asked the Captain. "We haven't gotten any further than we were two nights ago. I want action!"

"So does the City Editor of the *Press*." Morton grew serious. "What a bawling out I got tonight! Shinn told me that the dumbest reporter on the staff could have learned as much about this case as I have so far!"

"Oh, he did!" exclaimed Blake, beginning to brighten up. "And what did you say?"

"What could I say? I told him I'd go and see you as soon as I could. Listen, Jerry—we've been good friends for some time, haven't we?"

"We sure have, Dave—and I hope we always will be." Blake frowned. "But we won't keep on being if you make any more breaks like you did by using that 'phone call you received about Danton."

"Forget about that, will you? I told you it was a mistake." The reporter drew a package of cigarettes from his pocket, and lighted one. He sat gazing at Blake thoughtfully as he took two or three puffs. "That's not the point, Jerry. We're friends all right. Now what I want to do here and now is have a little confidential chat about this Gregg affair."

"Sure, and if we do I'll read all about it in the paper tomorrow," snorted the Captain. "That's a grand idea!"

"You've got me all wrong, Jerry." Morton shook his head. "What we say here tonight won't be for publication. I want to try and help you—I know you well enough to realize that if something breaks in this case you're going to give me first crack at it from a news angle."

"All right. I'll grant you that much." Blake nodded, his eyes fixed intently upon the other man. He knew Morton and trusted him, but he also realized that gathering news was a dominating idea with the reporter—at any cost. "What's the rest of it?"

"I think it might be a good idea for us to argue this thing out—that's all, Jerry. You are bound to have some personal opinions as to the guilty party—and I know that I have. So let's talk the case over from every possible angle that we can think of now. What do you say?"

Blake did not answer at once. He reached into his desk drawer and produced his old black brier pipe. He was thinking swiftly as he filled and lighted it. Morton was right—there would be no harm in talking over the case. The Captain realized that the reporter had already given him some good tips. Mercedes La Tona had been a discovery of Morton's, and Blake felt that she was an important link in the murder.

"All right, Dave," he said slowly. "I'm willing. Now just what did you have in mind?"

"How about the subject of motives?" asked the reporter thoughtfully. "Whoever murdered Gregg didn't do so without some good reason. That crime wasn't one that was committed upon the spur of the moment, Jerry. The person that did it planned it beforehand."

"What makes you think that?"

"Well, in the first place, how about that saffron cord? It is not the sort of thing that anybody would be likely to carry around with them unless they had some logical reason for doing so. And in this instance the reason was murder!"

"There may be something in what you say," remarked Blake. "You know that cord has been puzzling me. It's rather an odd-looking thing. The leather necklace, Danton called it."

"I know he did, and I've been wondering why ever since. But at present that cord is a link in the puzzle that doesn't quite fit. Let's try the question of motives again and see where that leads us, Jerry. As far as has been learned there are a number of suspects."

"Granted. The first three of these are Danton, Fulda and Benson."

"I don't think you can count the boy," said Morton. "There is no motive as far as he is concerned—and I believe he was telling the truth when he said that he did not even know Gregg."

"All right. We'll leave Benson out of it for the time being at least. We still have Danton and Fulda."

"That's true. And don't forget there is one more, Jerry. That's Gregg's Japanese servant, Tahira."

"How can you count him in? His alibi is perfect."

"That's just the trouble—it's much too perfect to suit me. He told me that he was in Gregg's apartment in the Marine-Neptune at the time of the murder, didn't he?"

Blake nodded. "And I had one of my men go to the hotel and investigate. They reported at the hotel office that Tahira had asked for his room key at five-thirty—and left word at the desk that if Mr. Gregg wanted him he would be in his room."

"Seems to me he went to a lot of trouble to tell the clerk his business. Does it seem logical to you that if Gregg wanted his personal servant he would call down to the hotel desk for him? He wouldn't—he would 'phone Tahira's room direct."

"Hum," Captain Blake stared thoughtfully into space for a moment before speaking. "Come to think about it, I believe you are right. You say Tahira's alibi is too perfect—what makes you so sure of that?"

"I went to the hotel myself this afternoon, and I used the old idea of the halfwit who found the horse by thinking where he would go if he were a horse. I started figuring just what I would do if I were Tahira and I wanted to get out of the hotel without being seen."

"What did you decide?" asked Blake eagerly.

"That I would use the freight elevator," Morton smiled. "It was only an idea, mind you—but in following it up I ran into a bit of luck. The night operator doesn't go on the freight elevator until seven. I found the day man was still on duty this evening and questioned him. He remembered that at six p.m. on the night of the murder he had taken Tahira down to the trunk room!"

"How did he know the time?" asked Blake calmly.

"Tahira told him that he wanted to see the head porter about a trunk which Mr. Gregg was expecting on the six-thirty train from New York. The elevator operator realized it was still early, and looked at his watch to make sure. He then told the servant the time. Tahira merely smiled and said that Gregg liked his orders to be carried out in plenty of time."

"I see." The captain nodded thoughtfully, and then smiled. "Did the freight operator bring Tahira back up after he had talked to the head porter?"

"No—he didn't see him again that evening. I hung around and questioned the night man. He said he had taken Tahira up to the eleventh floor at two o'clock the next morning!"

"Good!" exclaimed Blake. "Now we are getting somewhere, Dave. Did the night man notice anything strange about the Japanese? Was he nervous or excited?"

"Not in the least, as far as the elevator man could recall. He did say that he observed one thing which struck him as rather strange. It was that Tahira's clothes were all dusty and dirty, his shoes muddy."

"I don't see how that fits in very well, unless Tahira had been hiding under the Boardwalk."

"Neither do I," said Morton, "but at least we know that his alibi was just a bit too perfect. Tahira was out of the hotel at the time that Watson Gregg was murdered! That gives us a reason to suspect him."

"Sounds like a good angle to me," remarked Blake. "Now let's get back to the question of motives. Why should Tahira wish to kill Gregg?"

"There you've got me." The reporter frowned. "I feel the same way about him that I do about Doctor Fulda. For either of them to have murdered Gregg would be to more or less kill the goose that laid the golden egg."

"What do you mean by that?" began Blake, and then he nodded. "Oh, I see. Gregg was supporting both of them. It was his funds that paid them—and when he died they were both out of luck."

"Right. That's just the way that I figure it. But that doesn't eliminate Danton."

"I know it doesn't. Have you thought of one thing, Dave? It has been in my mind ever since night before last when the murder was discovered." The captain paused and looked at the other man intently. "All that I'm telling you tonight is confidential, isn't it? No newspaper stuff?"

"I gave you my word, Jerry." Morton looked the least bit offended. "All of this is just between ourselves."

"Fair enough." The Captain appeared to relax as he leaned back in his chair. He drew at his pipe, found that it had gone out, and relighted it. "In spite of your argument against Fulda not having any motive, there is something which I don't understand."

"What's that, Jerry?"

"This—as we know from their stories, Benson was passing the chair, then Fulda appeared, glared at the young fellow, and then walked over to where Gregg was sitting. All right. He leaned into the chair—and then came back to Benson. Fulda knew that Gregg was dead—or at least dying at that moment. Why didn't he release that leather cord from around his patient's throat?"

"Great snakes!" exclaimed Morton excitedly, sitting erect in his chair and staring at the Captain. "I never thought of that! And don't forget that the same question might be asked about Danton, or Benson for that matter. None of the three touched the cord. Hayes removed it from Gregg's throat."

"I know it," Blake said. "And it's been worrying me ever since. Since this is a very confidential chat, I'm going to tell you a few things more."

"Please do. I think we are beginning to get somewhere now. That angle about the leather thong is a darn good one. What's the rest of the dope, Jerry?"

"Well, this afternoon—or rather this noon, when you found Flannigan and myself standing on the Boardwalk—we had just been talking to Patrolman Hayes."

"I knew that. I saw you." The reporter laughed. "And I sure wish that I had been listening in. What did Hayes have to say, Jerry?"

"Hayes recalled a few things he had seen and forgotten on the night of the murder. First he saw Benson, as you know—"

"Yes, and there is one other thing that puzzles me. Why didn't he see John Hagen? Someone had to push the chair to the rail, you know."

"Of course. I asked Hayes about that when I first questioned him. He said that the chair must have been parked there for some time before he noticed it. He is one of the dumbest policemen I have ever run across!"

"One of the dumbest!" Morton laughed. "Jerry, that man is so dumb he doesn't even know he is living. But what else did he re-member?"

"As I said, first, he saw Benson, and then the blonde girl getting out of the chair and hurrying off the Boardwalk crying—"

"How I'd like to find that blonde!" exclaimed the reporter. "I beg your pardon, Jerry. Please go on."

"Then Benson left the walk. While he was gone, three people stopped at the rolling chair." Blake hesitated as if he half-expected the reporter to interrupt him again, but the latter made no comment. Morton sat listening intently as the Captain continued: "One was a tall man who appeared to be having a very amusing conversation with Gregg. Although Hayes was not close enough to hear their words, he did hear the man laugh heartily. He went away, and later two women stopped at the chair."

"Two women!" exclaimed Morton. "Can Hayes identify them?"

"Hayes!" the Captain snorted. "He couldn't identify his own mother if he saw her ten feet away, I don't believe. No, all he knew about them was that they were both wearing heavy veils."

"Gee, that's a tough break. A tall man and two women, eh? Jerry, do you think the man could have been Giovanni Danton?"

"Of course it might have been!" said the Captain. "But what we've got to do is to prove it. Now it seems to me—"

He broke off abruptly as there came a knock upon the closed door of the office. At a word from Blake the door opened and Detective Flannigan entered. There was a sheepish expression upon his round face as he nodded and then sank wearily into a chair.

"Well, Dan?" demanded the Captain. "What's on your mind?"

"Plenty!" The detective looked at Blake anxiously, as though doubting how the latter would take his next words. "That guy I was trailing got away from me. He gave me the slip clean as a whistle. He musta been wise that I was shadowing him. Of all the eels I ever run across, that bird's the worst. I'm sorry, Cap!"

Blake did not speak, he merely sat there staring intently at the stout detective. Flannigan grew more and more restless under the Captain's gaze. He tried to look around the room. He glanced at Morton, but the reporter had lighted a second cigarette and was gazing at it thoughtfully. The detective looked again at Blake.

"For the love of Heaven, Cap!" he exclaimed nervously. "Will you say something! Give me a good bawling out if you want to—but don't just look at me like that!"

"You lost him, eh?" said the Captain slowly. "Seems to me you were making some pretty personal remarks about dumb harness bulls this noon, Dan!"

"I know." Flannigan nodded soberly. "And Hayes ain't a bit dumber than I been to lose that guy—but I couldn't help it, Cap. Honest I couldn't. He went into a movie, and I followed him—but he must have beat it out an exit—that's all."

"That's enough," growled the Captain. "I'll overlook it this time, Dan, but don't ever let it happen again."

"It won't," said Flannigan, a note of relief in his tone. "If I run across that guy again I'll bring him in so quick he won't know what happened!"

"Yes, that's just what you would do. Now listen, Dan, I told you to follow that man, to shadow him and try to find out all about him—but not to bring him in! That still goes—understand!"

"Yes, sir," answered Flannigan, his eyes upon the floor.

Blake and Morton smiled at each other as they heard the meekness in the other's tone.

16
MERCEDES

As she stepped through the revolving door of the Hotel Seaform and out onto the Board-walk, Mercedes La Tona glanced casually about her. To her right and to her left stretched the Boardwalk, the smooth boards gleaming in the bright sunlight of the October morning. Already a long procession of rolling chairs was moving up and down, and there were quite a number of people moving about drinking in the invigorating sea air.

Mercedes mentally breathed a sigh of relief as she saw that there was no one about whom she recognized. She had been afraid that Captain Blake of the Detective Bureau, or that young newspaper reporter Morton, might be waiting in the vicinity in the hope that she might appear.

She drew her expensive fur coat closer about her and started strolling slowly down the walk. Ever since she had left Danton on the beach the previous night she had been worried. The tall man's actions had been so strange. His conversation about owls with Tahira—and his sudden decision to find someone when he had heard young Benson's story—it had all left a feeling of fear in the heart of Mercedes that still lingered.

She wondered where the little Japanese servant of Watson Gregg was at the present time. She hoped that no harm had come to him if he had remained there in the grim darkness beneath the pier. She smiled to herself as she walked along. Tahira had been quite right in what he had said the previous morning. She had found

107

him useful, and now—the woman's eyes clouded—now she felt that Tahira's services were at an end.

Yet as she let her mind dwell upon the subject she realized that was not quite so. Tahira was still useful to her—had said that he intended to continue being so. That warning which he had given her about Godfrey Floss had aided her materially in her first encounter with the evil-faced blackmailer. She had been prepared for the man's threats and insinuations, and by so doing had managed to frighten him away, for the time at least.

Mercedes did not feel that she had seen the last of Floss by any means. If there was anything which she felt that she knew, it was the character of men. Floss was the type who would not abandon a project easily, particularly if he felt that there was money in it; and he had named ten thousand dollars as the price of his silence. It was very doubtful, Mercedes thought, that Floss would long remain intimidated by the mere mention of the subject of owls.

The woman felt that she would like to know much more about that same subject herself. That the name of the bird could have proven such a dangerous subject, was rather surprising, to say the least. Yet it had frightened away Floss—struck terror to his heart— and it had proved to be filled with meaning when discussed by Danton and Tahira. Mercedes dwelt upon the subject for a moment or so and then dismissed it from her mind. Perhaps she would question Tahira about it later. He would tell her the meaning of it all.

It was Danton that she found uppermost in her thoughts. The man was a mystery. He had casually walked into the hotel the previous evening, discovered her sitting in the lobby, and introduced himself. The man had impressed her with an uncanny sense of power. She had not resented his speaking to her in the casual fashion that he had done—and not even realized that she might have done so until now. He had interested her intensely. So much that when he had suggested that they take a walk along the beach she had readily consented.

Now as she thought it over she realized that Giovanni Danton had learned so much about her that she had thought she would never reveal to anyone. There was something weird in the way the man inspired one to confide in him, and yet he told nothing regarding himself. Yet he had seemed to tell so much.

Mercedes La Tona suddenly realized now that someone was walking a short distance behind her. At first she thought nothing of it. There were quite a number of people on the walk—and not the slightest reason why someone should not be following her without intention.

She increased her pace lightly, and it seemed to her that the person in back of her did the same. Mercedes was far too clever to turn and look back, even casually. Something in a shop window apparently caught her eye and she moved in that direction. As she stood gazing in at the articles on display, the Boardwalk at her back was reflected dimly in the glass of the window.

Mercedes bit her lip as she saw a tall, lean figure standing by the outer rail of the walk, seemingly quite oblivious to her presence. It was Godfrey Floss. For a brief instant panic swept over Mercedes. She glanced quickly up and down the walk—and then turned and started hurriedly back in the direction of her hotel. She had gone only a short distance when she heard Floss' voice close to her, soft and insistent.

"I'm sorry, Miss La Tona," he said, "but I really must have a word with you at once!"

"Yes?" she wheeled and faced him, her eyes flashing, her face set and hard. "And why have you anything further to say, Mr. Floss?"

"It would be advisable." He smiled coldly. "I'm afraid you won't find me so readily bluffed today." He was looking at her intently. "At least, not by the mention of the subject of owl."

Mercedes merely stood there looking at him, but she felt a sinking steal over her. His abrupt dismissal of the subject which she had found a potent weapon, frightened her—she had depended upon it subconsciously. It had been the first thing which she had thought of when she had realized who it was that had been following her. And, now she found the verbal threat contained in the mention of the night bird useless. She realized that the situation was dangerous—she would have to think and act fast.

"You know I really found your fear of owls rather amusing," she said, smiling at Floss in quite a charming fashion. "You did not strike me as the type that would be easily frightened by a mere warning."

"I'm not," Floss told her shortly. It was obvious that he was puzzled by her abrupt change of front. He could not understand the sudden cordial manner which she displayed toward him. It worried him and left him uncertain. "Nothing frightens me."

Mercedes refrained from smiling with an effort. There was something amusing in his statement—there was an air of bravado in his words. She knew that he was puzzled, and she did not intend to lose the advantage which she had gained.

"You say you want to talk to me," she remarked casually, with rather an eager lilt to her voice. "After all, why not? When you first appeared you startled me. You will pardon my rudeness?"

"Certainly." He had evidently decided that if she wished to put their discussion on a friendly basis he was quite willing to follow her lead. It might be to his advantage to do so. One could never tell with a woman of the type of Mercedes La Tona, he knew. "And I hope you will grant me the same favor, and forgive mine."

"A pleasure, Mr. Floss." Mercedes glanced about her. "But, really, don't you think that under the circumstances you've selected rather a public place for any discussion which we might have?"

"You're right." He was quite obviously becoming even more worried now—her willingness to seek a more secluded place to talk things over was something which he had not dreamed that she would suggest. "Where shall we go? Perhaps you have some place in mind?"

"I suggest that we might take a chair ride down toward Ventnor." She smiled again. "Doubtless it would be wise if we give ourselves an opportunity to understand each other thoroughly."

"A chair ride?" he said in surprise. "You would really like that after—after what has happened?"

"Oh," she laughed musically, "I see you think that the fact that Mr. Watson Gregg was found murdered in a rolling chair might intimidate me in regard to the vehicles. Far from it—that doesn't make the slightest bit of difference to me. If anyone refused to ride in motor cars merely because a certain percentage of the population had been killed by them—wouldn't that make things difficult?" She moved toward a near-by stand. "No, come, Mr. Floss—let's get our chair and be on our way."

"All right," he said as he followed her. "Just as you say."

Something in his tone made her pause abruptly and look at him quizzically. He stood frowning down at her, but he did not speak.

"I wonder if you might not have some personal dislike for rolling chairs yourself, Mr. Floss?" she demanded, watching him closely as she spoke. "And perhaps you hope that the chair-pusher will not be as observant as John Hagen this time."

"Damn you!" he muttered softly. The mask had slipped now, and he was no longer the polite gentleman he had been for a time. "What's your game, anyway? I haven't anything to say to you further save to tell you that Martin Woods had better have that ten thousand ready for me within two days or there is going to be trouble!"

"I'll be delighted to inform him of the facts." She knew that she could outbluff Godfrey Floss. "But I'm afraid he won't be very much interested, Mr. Floss!"

"He will be—if he is wise!" snarled Floss.

"Possibly. Sorry you changed your mind about the chair ride," said Mercedes as she turned away. "It might have proven interesting."

Floss did not answer. He merely stood there glaring at her as she moved on up the Boardwalk in the direction of her hotel.

That the blackmailer did not follow her, surprised Mercedes greatly. She had half-expected that he would do so. It was with a feeling of relief that she realized that she was again rid of the man, temporarily at least. He was not a pleasant companion, and she had found it rather difficult to pretend to be nice to him. Yet she realized that by her unexpected change of front she had won a victory. Her statement regarding Floss' dislike for rolling chairs had been a blind stab in the dark, but her words had apparently struck home. That they had done so, gave her food for thought.

It was not until she had reached the Hotel Seaform again that Mercedes really understood how much her brief interview with

Floss had unnerved her. She was tense and excited, though she displayed no outward sign of emotion as she walked slowly along the wide corridor which led to the lobby. It was with difficulty that she suppressed a startled cry as someone behind her spoke her name softly.

She wheeled abruptly to find herself staring into the smiling countenance of Tahira. The little Japanese bowed politely.

"Pardon, me, Miss La Tona," he said quietly. "I had no wish to alarm you. If you have a moment to spare I should like to say a few words."

"Certainly, Tahira." Mercedes glanced about her nervously. "But isn't this dangerous? For all we know the police may be watching. If they see us talking together they may think it strange."

"No doubt," said Tahira drily, his gaze sweeping swiftly about the corridor. "But I am sure that Captain Blake has no one watching us at the moment." He bowed politely. "Still, if you would prefer a more secluded spot—"

"I would," said Mercedes. "I'll meet you in the writing room in the east wing of the hotel in ten minutes. I'll go there at once—you follow later."

"Very well," Tahira nodded and turned away as Mercedes moved on along the corridor.

Ten minutes later the actress sat in a corner of the writing room. Her chair was screened from casual observation by a number of potted plants. She had not been there long when Tahira moved quietly into the room.

The servant hesitated as he observed a man who sat with his face buried in a newspaper. He felt that someone might be watching him, but he quickly dismissed the idea. He was quite sure that the other was merely a guest. It was very unlikely that he had the slightest interest in either Miss La Tona or the servant of Watson Gregg.

"What happened last night?" demanded Mercedes, as Tahira reached the spot where she was sitting. "That conversation you had with Giovanni Danton worried me. When he left me abruptly there on the beach I was afraid. I thought something terrible might happen."

"Your fears were justified," said Tahira quietly. "Mr. Danton and Mr. Benson found me with a leather thong drawn very tight about my throat—very tight!" the servant put his hand to his neck above his collar, and as he did so Mercedes observed an angry red mark. "It was very fortunate that the two gentlemen arrived when they did!"

"Tahira!" exclaimed Mercedes excitedly. "You mean that last night someone tried to strangle you as they strangled Watson Gregg?"

"Yes. The effort was rather successful!"

"Was it Danton?" Mercedes looked at the servant as though she already knew the answer as she voiced the question. "Was it, Tahira?"

"I don't know." Tahira shook his head. "It was very dark beneath the pier. Before I realized what had happened, someone leaped at me from out of the shadows. He was larger, stronger than I am. We struggled, and then he looped the leather cord about my throat and drew it tight. I became unconscious. But why should it have been Danton?"

"I don't know," answered Mercedes nervously. "That man—there is something sinister, almost uncanny, about him. I don't believe that he would stop at anything to get what he wanted—not even murder!"

"Possibly. But what motive would he have in killing me?"

"How can I explain that? Last night, there on the beach, before that young boy came running up to us, I accused Danton of the murder of Watson Gregg!"

"That was dangerous—or I have misjudged Mr. Danton," said the servant quietly. "What did he say?"

"Nothing that was vital." Mercedes shuddered. "He just looked at me—and there was something in his expression which made me terribly afraid. Tahira—we must be careful. That man—he knows too much!"

"Knows too much? You puzzle me, Miss La Tona. What is for him to know which might concern us?"

"A number of things." Mercedes leaned forward in her chair, her eyes fixed intently upon the expressionless face of the Japanese.

"Listen, Tahira, you told me that you still wished to be of service as far as I was concerned."

"And I spoke truly, Miss La Tona."

"Then we must be frank. You know that I was on the Boardwalk on the evening that—that Watson was found dead! You saw me not three blocks away from where the rolling chair was standing."

"That is quite true. It is a little detail that I intend to forget permanently. And for you to forget that you saw me in that vicinity might also be very wise. My movements that night are covered. The police believe that I did not leave the hotel—"

"I'm afraid that you misjudge the police," said a voice from behind the potted plants, and Captain Blake stepped quickly into view.

Mercedes uttered a startled gasp—and then sat there staring at the head of the Detective Bureau, white faced and alarmed. Tahira leaped to his feet and bowed.

"This is an unexpected pleasure, Captain Blake," he said quickly. "But I am afraid that you did not continue your eavesdropping to the proper extent."

"What do you mean?" demanded Blake gruffly, glaring at the servant. "I heard enough to confirm a few suspicions that I have had for sometime!"

"Perhaps you may think so—but you are wrong," said Tahira, and there was an earnest note in his tone which carried conviction to the Captain in spite of himself. "I was saying when you interrupted me that my movements for that night were covered—"

"Oh, were they?" exclaimed Blake. "Well, I happen to know that you left the hotel that night by the freight elevator! And you did not return until two a.m.!"

"My respect for the police increases!" said Tahira. "If you had not felt that my alibi was a bit too perfect, I should have been greatly disappointed."

"Huh?" Blake looked at the Japanese sternly. "What are you driving at, anyway?"

"I think that now it might be very wise if I endeavor to explain a few little details," said the servant slowly, and he glanced at

Mercedes. "Captain Blake, I would like very much to have a confidential talk with you at your office."

"That won't be difficult. I've made up my mind that you are going there, anyway. It is part of the police station you know. I'm going to hold you as a material witness, Tahira Yamada!"

"As you wish." Tahira bowed. "But I think I can convince you that my arrest will be a mistake." He waved his hand expressively. "Of that we shall speak later!"

Blake turned with an expression of relief as Dan Flannigan came lumbering into the writing room.

"Thought this was where you said to find you, Cap," remarked the stout detective. "And I was right."

"Take this man to the station and hold him there until I arrive," commanded Blake briskly. "I'll be along later. I want to have a little talk with Miss La Tona."

Tahira glanced at Mercedes as Flannigan started to lead him away. She sat gazing at him with an anxious, worried expression in her eyes.

"The promise of service will be a lasting one," said the little servant as he left the room with the detective.

The Captain's manner changed abruptly as he dropped into a chair close to where Mercedes sat. He now seemed in the most amiable of moods. The actress did not like the detective's satisfied expression. There was a placid serenity about him that reminded her of a cat that was just about to eat the canary.

"Tahira's desire to be of service is very touching," Blake began softly. "A most unusual servant—exceptionally well educated, and one judges rather clever."

"He went through college in this country," said Mercedes casually, determined to follow Blake's lead in facing the situation calmly. "I believe that he served Mr. Gregg both as a valet and a sort of secretary."

"Oh, he did. That's very interesting." Abruptly Blake leaned forward in his chair, and his face grew stern. "Miss La Tona, you were the woman who was seen getting out of the rolling chair on the night of the murder!"

"It's not true!" exclaimed Mercedes excitedly. "I was not that woman, Captain Blake." Her slender fingers played with a ring on one hand. "I'm tired of these accusations! Tired of being followed—and spied upon. I did not kill Watson Gregg. I—can't stand it any longer—I could not have killed him, I tell you!"

"Why not?" asked Blake softly, his eyes fixed intently upon the woman's face.

"If I tell all I know, will you promise to stop hounding me and let me alone?"

Blake considered a moment. Then:

"Yes, Miss La Tona. If you can convince me that you were not the woman who got out of that chair!"

Mercedes was thinking swiftly. Her only thought now was for herself. It did not matter whom she might implicate, so long as she could hold Captain Blake to his promise. What she had told him was true. He had gotten on her nerves by his constant questioning, and she felt sure that she had been shadowed since her first interview with him.

"I was not the woman in the chair, Captain Blake," she said slowly. "And I could not have killed Watson Gregg. I'll tell you why—and it is not easy to do. I could not kill him because I loved him—loved him better than life itself!"

Blake looked at her in amazement. That she might have been in love with Gregg was a thought that had never entered his mind. His opinion of her was of a woman hard and cold. He had felt that she would be ruthless toward those who went against her wishes. Yet now she said that she had loved Gregg, that she had loved him more than life itself. There was a ring of sincerity in her tone which startled him—he did not know whether to believe her or not.

"If you were not the woman in the chair," he said slowly, "do you know who she was?"

"Yes," said Mercedes quietly, "I do. She was a young girl—a blonde. That is the woman you must look for, Captain Blake."

"I know that she was young and blonde," remarked Blake with a smile. "But do you know her? Remember you promised to tell me all that you know if I would stop hounding you!"

"I don't know her. I have never seen her," said Mercedes tensely. "But this much I can tell you: Her name was Lannon Gordon!"

17
THE DESERTED CABIN

THE BRIGHT MORNING SUNLIGHT crept through the lace curtains at the windows in the bedroom of the old house of Miss Ida Hill. It was reflected upon Lannon Gordon as she stood gazing at herself in the mirror. The girl had changed. Her eyes were brave, resolute. She suddenly made a funny little face at her reflection as she talked to herself.

"Ya dawgone freak—dim-wit! Ever since you left that—that rolling chair you've been actin' like a dumb—bunny! Only last week you were raving at Kismet 'cause nothing ever happened! Oh, no, nothing ever happens! You've had enough excitement since then to keep you in hysterics for life!"

She leaned closer to the mirror, the sunlight from the windows gleaming upon the lovely blonde, bobbed head.

"What if Larry is worried? He doesn't know what's happened to you. He loves you!" Lannon smiled at herself in the glass. "Don't hate that idea, do you? He should be worried when you flop over in a faint over something someone else says! Gotta tell the old soul that you're alive and doing noble!"

With a wave of her hand to her other self Lannon turned and rushed out of the room. She went swiftly down the stairs, taking pains not to make any unnecessary noise for she did not wish to disturb her Aunt.

She was thinking of the elderly woman as she descended. Poor Aunt Ida! Doctor Fulda had lingered but a few minutes after he had revealed the fact that Miss Hill was Dolly Marden and the wife

118

of Watson Gregg. Lannon had wished to question her Aunt. She wanted to learn the whole story from her lips, but the Doctor's visit had left Miss Hill terribly nervous and upset. She had gone at once to her room and had remained there ever since.

Lannon had reached the front door now. In an instant she was outside the house and speeding swiftly down the road toward the trolley line half a mile away. A pay station was in the corner drug store there. From this she could telephone Larry.

"Wonder what Aunt Ida will think when she finds I'm gone?" she said to herself as she walked briskly down the tree-shaded road. "That'll go over big! Reckon she'll think I'm in on a massacre!"

Lannon chuckled gleefully as she went along. She was forgetting the horrors that she had gone through. She only knew that she had taken herself in hand—she was young and it was good to be alive.

She reached the drug store at last. To her disappointment she found someone was using the 'phone booth. It seemed to her that it took people a long time for their phone calls. As she waited, she grew impatient and nervous. Suppose Larry wasn't home? She smiled as she realized that the fat man who had been phoning had left the booth at last.

"Neptune Six Four Seven Two Two," she called as she dropped in her nickel. "Hello, is Mr. Larry Benson there?"

"Just a moment. I'll see." It was a woman's voice that had answered.

"Hello?" came Larry's voice in a few seconds. "Hello, Larry—it's Lannon!"

"Lannon!" there was delight in his tone. She had always liked the sound of his voice over the 'phone. "You're all right?"

"Sure 'nough."

"Atta lady! Lord, but it's good to hear your voice!"

"Kinda crave the noise you're making—"

"Lannon," seriously, "you're feeling all right, dear?"

"Yes, Larry."

"Where are you now? I must see you!"

"I'm down at Ford's drug store in Margate."

"Wait for me there—I'll be right down!"

"Good-bye, dear."

Lannon came out of the 'phone booth smiling. The drug clerk preened himself, smoothing his hair. Funny how the women all fell for him! Lannon passed him without even knowing he was there. He frowned. She needn't be so high hat—she wasn't so pretty anyway. The drug clerk went on about his work angrily—his whole day spoiled.

Lannon stood waiting outside the drug store. Every few seconds she would glance up the avenue toward Ventnor, two miles away. She wished that Larry would hurry. There was so much that she wanted to tell him. Cars passed swiftly by, but she was watching for Larry's roadster.

At last she saw it moving fast, and she knew that he had hurried. A quick grinding of brakes and the car halted at the curb. Larry leaped out and ran toward Lannon. His eyes were on her face hungrily, feasting upon her beauty as though he could never get enough of her loveliness.

"Lannon!" Her hand was in his now as they stood there in the bright morning sunlight smiling at each other.

The drug clerk glanced through the window at them, commenting mentally. So that was who she was waiting for! Huh, of all the goofy looking birds! With a gesture of disdain the drug clerk turned away from the window.

"Right decent sort of a day—isn't it?" said Lannon inanely, timidly.

"It is now that I've found you!"

"Be your age!" Lannon smiled at him.

"If I acted as old as I feel I'd be a hundred and ten!" Larry grinned as he opened the car door.

"What nice white whiskers you have, grandpa! Why so ancient all in a rush, playmate?"

"It's quite a long story." Larry's tone became serious.

"Tell me!" Lannon leaped into the car and curled down on the seat. "I'm dyin' to know what's happened since I saw you last. It was night before last, wasn't it?"

"Woof!" remarked Larry. "Be still and let me tell you what's happened!"

As they started off down the avenue he related briefly what had occurred since he had left her. She smiled at him softly, her eyes a bit misty, as he told her how he had worried about her and had returned to the vicinity of the old house on the following morning. Dear Larry, she thought—he did care, and—well, she didn't quite hate him!

"And after Danton had frightened this man Floss away, we stood there talking. Finally Danton told me to run along home. He assured me that you and Miss Hill were both all right. I went of course, but as I turned away Danton and the Japanese looked at each other rather strangely."

"Sure sounds mysterious," said Lannon. "Have you any brain-throbs on what it's all about, Larry?"

"No." Larry shook his head. "Only I'm sure that the subject of owls has something to do with the murder of Watson Gregg."

Lannon sat silently gazing at the road ahead as the car sped along. At last she spoke quietly, not looking at Larry.

"This Mercedes La Tona, the woman whom you met with Mr. Danton—was she very pretty?" she asked casually.

"I guess so. I didn't notice particularly. She seemed quite attractive."

"Oh," said Lannon shortly; then: "Do tell me about her, Larry," she said very sweetly.

"Nothing to tell," Larry replied casually as he guided the car through traffic, "Danton just calmly turned her over to me and asked me if I wouldn't see that she got home safely."

"But what did she look like?"

"She was a brunette. Had rather pretty eyes and a most mysterious sort of smile. She said she was an actress."

"Oh, an actress!"

Lannon was mentally fuming. No, he had not noticed her particularly pretty eyes and a mysterious smile. Lannon was not jealous—she never got that way—she was just mad!

They were at the lower end of the island now, running slowly through the sandy streets of Longport, the brave little township that had been so often the plaything of the sea. Completely surrounded by water on three sides, it had ever borne the brunt of innumerable severe storms.

The car came to a stop at the very end of the island. In front of them stretched an expanse of rolling beach, while beyond they could see the waters of the bay which lay between Ocean City and Longport.

"Let's walk along the beach," said Larry, smiling at Lannon.

"All right!"

What was the use of being angry at Larry? Besides what did it matter if the mysterious lady did have pretty eyes? Lannon leaped out of the machine and started on a run for the beach.

"Beat you to the water's edge!" she called back over her shoulder.

A flash of slender, lovely limbs showed below the edge of a blue skirt. Lannon sped swiftly over the sand, with Larry in close pursuit. A laughing, carefree pair they were, drinking deep of the wine of youth.

They had forgotten the weird whispering of the grim nights, the murmured words of death. They were young and happy, and that was all that mattered now.

"Whoopee!" came Lannon's gay shout as she reached the water's edge a full yard ahead of Larry. She turned, smiling. "Where've you been, old boy? I've been waiting here a coupla centuries!"

This was Lannon, his Lannon once again.

"Why, you conceited little devil. Think you can run, don't you?" he taunted her.

Lannon disdained to answer. How bright the sunlight was on the sea! Ocean City looked like a fairyland in the distance. It was such a noble day, she thought. The happiness that lingered in her heart was peeping out through her lovely eyes.

"Lannon, won't you tell me what happened at your Aunt's house?" he asked her suddenly.

Her eyes clouded at the question, driving the smile from her face. She had forgotten the trying ordeal which she had gone through, and now his question brought it all back to her. She had been so happy and carefree!

"Won't you tell me, Lannon?" he pressed.

He was awakening grim memories, driving the fear back into her heart. A wave of guilt swept over her. She had no right to leave Aunt Ida as she had done. Aunt Ida was waiting for her, alone, back there in that lonely old house. What would she say when she returned—what would she do?

"Please, Lannon?"

As she stood there Lannon wondered why Larry was so insistent. She did not want to tell him what had happened. After all, it was so foolish. There had been so much of it that had been caused by her own imagination. She could not tell him that. She did not want him to think that she was a simpleminded idiot, afraid of shadows. She could never forgive herself for having fainted at that weird dinner party.

"Lannon?"

"I can't tell you, Larry," she said impatiently, wondering why he kept on asking.

"But you must, Lannon! For your own good I need to know!"

She stared at him for an instant, and then turned her eyes away. She did not like the tone he used. It was just a bit too commanding. She was angry now. Orders from Mr. Benson—the thought was not a pleasing one.

"Really?" she said finally, her deep soft voice cold. "Well, I'd prefer not to say anything about it!"

He realized that he was wrong. The subject was far from an agreeable one. Larry felt that he was an idiot not to have waited. She would have told him just what had happened when she was in the mood. She always told him about the things which mattered. They were such good pals.

"I'm sorry, Lannon," he said softly.

"That's all right, Larry," remarked Lannon, still a little constrained.

She realized that he was really sorry, but why did he always want to spoil things? The other afternoon when they had quarreled about her dinner engagement with Gregg—and now this lovely day! Of course she would forgive him, but she would not be so quick about it this time.

They had reached the spot where the beach circled to the left as it followed the sea. There was no one in sight anywhere about them. They were alone on the white sand. Close to where they now stood was an old, tumble down shack built of logs. Its door sagged and its windows were battered and broken from the buffeting of winter seas that had dashed upon it.

Lannon dropped down on the lower step of the old cabin with a smile at Larry.

"All right, I'll forgive you this time," said Lannon, still smiling. "But don't let it happen again!"

"I'm so glad!"

As he voiced the words Larry felt that the statement was so feeble, so inadequate. He wanted to take her in his arms, to kiss her sweet lips, but he did not dare. Lannon had never said that she cared—that she loved him. He knew that she had her creed, even though she was young; modern Lannon Gordon only gave her kiss as part of the gift of her heart.

"Damn!" exclaimed Lannon, suddenly, looking about her anxiously. "I've lost my vanity case. Reckon I dropped it somewhere along the beach."

"I'll go look for it," said Larry promptly. "Coming with me, Fair Lady?"

"No, I'll wait here." She cast him a soft glance from the big eyes. "But hurry back!"

With a smile and a wave of his hand Larry moved swiftly off along the beach in the direction from which they had come. Lannon watched him, her lovely eyes filled with something precious; something which he had never been sure of, lingered in their depths.

She had suddenly realized that she loved him—loved quite as much as she knew that he loved her. Her heart was calling to him as he reached the curve in the beach. Perhaps he sensed her call, for he turned and waved his hand again as he disappeared. Lannon sighed softly, contentedly—for she found it such a lovely day.

"What beauty one may find amid solitude!" a harsh, grating voice spoke suddenly from the door of the cabin behind her.

Lannon rose swiftly to her feet, swung around as she did so. She was startled and alarmed as she stood staring at the open doorway.

A face peered out at her, a long narrow countenance like that of a wolf. Cold gray eyes swept her slender figure boldly, an expression in their depths which left her cold and a little ashamed. An instant later a tall, lean man stepped out of the cabin and moved toward her.

Lannon looked about her wildly. There was something about this man that was utterly terrifying. She did not know quite what to do. Larry was out of sight. He had not the slightest idea that there had been anyone else upon the beach besides themselves.

"Surely you are not afraid of me, dear child whom I only know by the lovely name of Lannon?" Godfrey Floss' voice was low, suave; it was when the man was most dangerous that his speech became flowery.

Lannon did not speak. She began to back away, wide-eyed with fright. Questions were passing through her brain with lightning speed. Who was this man—why had he been hiding in the old cabin? Where was Larry—she needed him now!

"Who—who are you?" she demanded tensely.

"A friend!" said Floss quickly.

She started to speak again, but with a quick step Floss was beside her. His hands shot out. She felt his fingers tighten about her arms as he caught hold of her, and she shuddered. Slowly he began to draw her closer to him. She struggled wildly, kicking at him with her tiny feet, but he was strong and agile, her efforts were futile. She could not get away.

Now she could feel his hot breath upon her face as he drew her closer and closer. She was filled with stark horror. Madly she threw back her head and screamed at the top of her lungs.

With a swift motion Floss released his grip on her arms. Before she realized what had happened, he had lifted her from the beach and started toward the cabin, with her clasped tightly in his strong arms.

18
"SPEAKING OF MOTIVES—"

CAPTAIN BLAKE BORE a very satisfied expression as he walked swiftly out of the Seafoam Hotel. The conversation which he had over-heard between Mercedes La Tona and the servant of the murdered man had been very interesting. He was sure that now it would not be many hours before he had solved the riddle of the Gregg case.

Upon receiving the information from Mercedes that the girl in the chair had been a blonde by the name of Lannon Gordon, Blake had kept the promise which he had made to the actress. He had not questioned her further at any length. He had by no means aban-doned the idea of Mercedes being a possible suspect. That she had loved Gregg only made the Captain all the more convinced that she might have been the one who had committed the murder. It might have been that the retired producer no longer cared for Mercedes, and Blake was a firm believer in the old saying that "Hell hath no fury like a woman scorned."

The head of the Detective Bureau smiled as he moved along the Boardwalk. He was now on his way to his office, where he felt that his interview with Tahira might prove exceedingly interesting.

"Well, Jerry, you certainly are in a good humor this morning," said a voice behind him, and Dave Morton moved up beside him. "You must have some news?"

"Oh, hello, Dave!" Blake replied good-naturedly. "Yes, I guess I have a little bit of news at that. I just placed Tahira under arrest."

"Tahira!" exclaimed Morton, in surprise. "Why pick on him, Jerry?"

"I have plenty of reason," said the Captain calmly. "I might tell you more about it—if you are willing to turn in a story containing just the facts. Tahira arrested, and to be held for questioning and that sort of thing—and nothing else now, Dave!"

"Suits me," the reporter told him. "I gave you my word on that before, Jerry. What's the latest?"

Swiftly Blake related the conversation which he had overheard between Mercedes and Tahira. Morton listened eagerly as the two men walked along.

"And she said that the girl in the chair was named Lannon Gordon!" exclaimed the reporter as the Captain finished. "Now we are really getting somewhere, Jerry. You are going to have your men try and find this girl, of course?"

"Certainly!" Blake nodded. "And I have every reason to suspect that she will be able to tell a great deal about the murder!"

"You said it! Both the La Tona woman and the Japanese admitted that they were on the Boardwalk at the time the murder was committed, eh?"

"They did—to each other, but not to me." Blake smiled grimly. "Tahira is a very smooth article. The way he acted, you would almost think that he was elated over the fact that I had arrested him. I'm going to my office now to question him. You can come along if you wish, Dave."

"Thanks, Jerry, that's mighty decent of you. I appreciate it. And I won't use anything which you don't want me to turn in—yet. But when this is cleared up, what a first-page story it's going to make!"

The two men had turned off the Boardwalk now and were walking along one of the side streets which led to Atlantic Avenue, upon which the police station was located. A short while later they had reached the building and gone directly to Blake's office.

"Sit down, Dave," said the Captain, waving his hand toward a chair. He removed his hat and overcoat and then went to his desk. "I'll have Flannigan bring Tahira up here right now."

Morton nodded and then dropped into a chair and lighted a cigarette as Blake picked up the telephone and issued a few terse commands.

"They will be up here in a few minutes," the Captain remarked as he placed the receiver back on the hook. "Have you learned anything new, Dave?"

"Not a thing," answered the reporter. "I was just going into the Seafoam to try and have another interview with Miss La Tona when I saw you coming out, and followed you. I'm sure glad that I did."

Blake merely nodded and then spoke as there came a knock on the closed door of the office. At his command Flannigan entered the room with Tahira beside him. The little servant glanced at Morton and then at the Captain as though he were surprised at the reporter's presence.

"Well, Yamada," said Blake, "you said that you might have a few things to tell me privately." He indicated a chair near the desk. "Sit down."

"Thank you, Captain Blake." Tahira looked again at Morton. "You wish to have me speak freely before this gentleman? I know who he is. Perhaps it would not be wise to have a gentleman of the press hear our little talk?"

Morton looked at the Japanese in surprise. As far as he knew Tahira had never seen him before, and yet he had known at once that he was a newspaper man.

"How did you know I was a reporter?" asked Morton. "Did you ever see me before?"

"No, not that I remember," answered Tahira. "As to your being a reporter—that is very simple." He waved his hand in a deprecating gesture. "I but observe. For instance, I judged that you are a reporter from glimpsing a bit of gray paper which the men in your profession so often use, sticking out of your pocket. You also carry a number of pencils, some of them are sharpened, some are not. Obviously you find it necessary to write hurriedly. It was quite simple."

"Humph!" exclaimed Blake, studying the Japanese intently. "You think you are a good bit of a detective, don't you?"

"On the contrary," answered Tahira. "And at the present time I am quite conscious of the fact that I am a prisoner under arrest."

"Can you tell me just what you did on the evening that Watson Gregg was murdered?" demanded the Captain abruptly. "Where did you go after you left the hotel by the freight elevator?"

"I first strolled down the Boardwalk, where I encountered Miss La Tona walking in the opposite direction. Then I took a trolley car to Ventnor. I was obeying Mr. Gregg's instructions."

"Gregg's instructions! What were they?"

"That I continue placing Mr. Gregg's residence in order."

"Residence?" Blake looked at Tahira, a puzzled expression upon his face, while Morton and Flannigan sat listening with interest. "What do you mean?"

"I mean a very attractive cottage which Mr. Gregg had recently leased in Ventnor."

"A cottage in Ventnor, eh?" exclaimed the Captain slowly. "Why didn't you tell me about it before?"'

"I thought you probably knew about it already," said the servant blandly.

"Hum! For how long did he lease it?"

"He told me that he had paid the rent for six months in advance, as I believe is the custom in Ventnor."

"Do you know why he took it?"

"I believe he was tired of hotel life—and Doctor Fulda had insisted that he remain at the seashore on account of his health."

"I see," said Blake. "And you were at this cottage after you left the hotel on the night of the murder?"

"Yes. As I said before, I was obeying Mr. Gregg's instructions."

"Why did he want you to go there on that night?"

"He requested me to put the cottage in presentable shape as he expected to visit it during the evening. He further instructed me that my presence after nine o'clock was not desirable."

"Why not?"

"I have no wish to defame my employer's character, but I was under the impression that he had—" Tahira hesitated and then smiled—"an engagement with a lady!"

"Who was this lady?" demanded Blake.

"Mr. Gregg neglected to inform me," said Tahira tranquilly.

The Captain glared at the little servant as he heard the words. The Japanese did not appear at all alarmed by Blake's glance. He merely sat there motionless, watching the other man.

"And you left the cottage at nine?" asked Blake finally. "Had the, ah, lady arrived by then?"

"No, sir. I saw no one while I was at the cottage." Tahira shook his head. "I wish that I had."

"Why do you say that?"

"Because later that night Mr. Gregg's cottage was entered and robbed. This occurred during my absence."

"Robbed! What do you mean?" exclaimed Blake. "There wasn't anything to take, was there?"

"On the contrary. Fifty thousand dollars in cash was taken from a safe where Mr. Gregg had placed it early that afternoon!"

"Speaking of motives," remarked Morton abruptly, "that's a wow!"

19

"FIGHT, LARRY, FIGHT!"

LARRY BENSON WHISTLED SOFTLY as he walked along the beach. He had searched every foot of the way that Lannon and he had walked. He had finally discovered that she had left her vanity case in the roadster. Now it reposed safely in his pocket, and he was hurrying back to the girl.

A shrill, terrified scream came from around the curve in the beach ahead of him. It had sounded like Lannon. Larry went tearing over the sand now, running as fast as he could.

A moment later he had turned the curve. Before him stretched the wide expanse of beach, the old cabin in the middle distance. He shouted angrily and moved even faster as he caught sight of Godfrey Floss entering the cabin with Lannon in his arms.

Larry was in a frenzy of rage as he ran. He was determined to show the man that he could not treat Lannon like that. He would show him just as soon as he reached him. He was angry enough to kill!

Larry reached the cabin just as the old, sagging door swung shut. He leaped up the steps and threw his weight against it. It quivered and shook under the impact of his body, but it remained closed. From within he heard Floss laugh harshly. Again he threw himself with all his might against the door. There was a sound of cracking wood. He realized that he had broken something that time. The upper portion of the door now leaned backward, like a prize fighter a little groggy from a blow.

The next time would tell. *Slam!* Larry's strong young shoulder again pounded the door. A splintering crash—and it fell within the cabin.

Larry stood in the open doorway glaring inside. Floss had put Lannon down at the first sound of the onslaught upon the door. Now he stood calmly waiting for Larry's next move.

Lannon stood near the back wall of the cabin, watching and waiting. Her eyes moved from the face of one to the other. This lean, wolflike creature—he was so strong! Could Larry prove his match? They were both tall men, but Floss was older, and the girl felt, more experienced.

"Well?" Floss's lip curled into a snarl.

Larry did not bother to speak. He moved slowly forward. His eyes were fixed upon the sinister face in front of him, his lips were drawn in a thin, straight line.

Lannon gazed at him fascinated. This was a different Larry than she had ever known. Here was no foolish, carefree boy. Here was a man—

A short laugh that was almost the bark of a wolf, and Godfrey Floss's hand shot out. It landed upon the side of Larry's face. He winced at the sting of the blow, and growled angrily. There was something which rankled in the other man's having slapped him with his open hand. It had been a contemptuous gesture. Larry leaped at Floss, both fists flying. The latter's guard was up now. He was ready, quite ready.

Godfrey Floss had lived a life in which he had often found it essential to take care of his own welfare. He had encountered the onslaughts of pugnaciously inclined individuals before.

Slam! His right fist shot past Larry's guard and landed on the boy's mouth. Larry sputtered, and a faint drop of red appeared on his lip. But in a split second his left fist tore past Floss's defense and thudded on his right eye.

Lannon stood in the corner of the room, watching eagerly. "Sock him, Larry, wallop him! I'm rooting for you, boy!" ran through her mind. She had forgotten to be frightened now. After all, one can get a mighty big kick out of having two men fighting over you! Particularly when one is only twenty.

Thud, thud! Both of Floss' fists landed in rapid succession on Larry's chest, knocking the wind out of him, leaving him breathing heavily.

"That's it, Larry! Now you're getting him! I'm depending on you, boy!" Lannon was silently rooting as she watched. Her heart was telling her that he was fighting for her, that he loved her.

A hard blow from Larry landed on Floss's chin; the man's head snapped back. He recovered instantly, and a heavy uppercut sent Larry reeling against the wall of the cabin, a blow that left him dazed and half blind. *Slam!* Another followed closely before he could recover. His fists were beating out blindly, feebly, now.

Lannon suddenly grew nervous and hysterical as she watched. Terror was creeping into her heart. Larry was losing, he was being beaten. The thought was pounding home to her. Larry was losing—fighting a game fight, but losing. He loved her—perhaps the sound of her voice might help. But what could she say, what might encourage him most? She knew that she must think quickly, must act at once or it would be too late. She knew what to say—surely that would make him do his best.

Larry was fighting blindly now. Floss was pounding, pounding at him. His whole body was one terrible ache from the blows. He was so tired—what did anything matter?

"Oh, Larry, dear, win—win for me!" he heard Lannon's voice coming to him from a great distance!

Win for her sake—sure, of course, he must. He knew that all right. . . . Floss's right fist landed on his cut lip. Lord, but that hurt. *Bam!* Landed that time, anyway. If only he wasn't so groggy, if he just had a little more pep!

"Larry! Fight, boy, fight!" Lannon's voice came clearer now, the words ringing in his ears. "Oh, I—I love you!"

What was that she had said? Not that she loved him? Yes, that had been it! "Fight!" He felt he could lick the whole damn world after hearing that. Larry flew at Floss like a madman, pounding, beating, as he tore through the other's guard.

He landed a right to the jaw! That's it—you stagger around a little, it's your turn now. *Thud!* Here's another to keep that first one company. "Lick me, will you? not while I've a bit of breath left in my body. She loves me—she loves me!" Larry was mentally saying it over and over as he kept time with flying fists.

Godfrey Floss was panting, worried now as he tried to stop the constant rain of blows. This fellow was mad. He had taken enough punishment to stop any ordinary man, and here he was coming back twice as strong.

Lannon stood gazing proudly at Larry, a glorious light in her eyes. He was winning—winning! Had it been her words? She did love him—she was so sure of that now.

A dull, sickening thud sounded as Larry landed on Godfrey Floss's chin with all his strength. The man's head jerked back, he shuddered and then fell limply to the floor. For an instant Larry stood over him, and then he turned to Lannon.

His lip was swollen and bleeding, one eye was beginning to grow suspiciously dark, but Lannon never loved him more than at that moment.

"Say it again, dearest!" he said with a crooked smile.

Somehow Lannon found herself in his arms, and she was kissing the poor, bruised cheek.

"Say it, Lannon!" his voice sounded in her ear.

"I love you, Larry!"

Godfrey Floss slowly opened his eyes as he lay on the floor. He looked about him, and then rose slowly to his feet. His hand moved toward his back pocket as he did so.

"Lannon, dearest, my own Lannon!"

The boy and the girl did not see Floss. They were unheedful of their surroundings now. Their heads were far in the clouds. It was the most precious moment they had ever known.

Floss slowly drew a blue-steel automatic from his pocket and very carefully began to level it at Larry, as the latter stood with his back toward him, Lannon held tight in his arms.

"I really would not advise that, Mr. Floss!" said a deep voice from the doorway of the cabin.

All three turned in that direction. Giovanni Danton stood there, his strange eyes fixed upon Godfrey Floss, an automatic held carelessly in one slender hand.

20

GREGG'S COTTAGE

FOR A MOMENT THE THREE MEN in the office of the Captain of Detectives stared at the Japanese as they heard his startling statement that fifty thousand dollars had been stolen from Gregg's cottage. Finally the little servant spoke.

"According to all established customs, would not an examination of Mr. Gregg's residence prove wise?" he asked softly.

"Yes, it most certainly would," said Blake sharply. "I intended to do that just as soon as you told me about the place." He looked intently at Tahira. "And you are coming with me!"

"Perhaps that will be easier," said Tahira. "If you recall, you have as yet failed to ascertain the exact location of the cottage!"

The Captain gazed at the servant for a moment. Then, realizing that the man spoke truly, he muttered an oath under his breath. "Where is the house?" he demanded.

"It is located on the south side of Suffolk Avenue, No. 169A. It is the cottage nearest the beach."

Both Blake and the reporter jotted down the address. At a word from the Captain, Flannigan hurried from the room to have a car in readiness for the trip to Ventnor. Blake did not wish to take his own roadster. It was too small. And besides, he preferred one of the police automobiles so that he could give his undivided attention to the Japanese.

Little was said as they started on their four-mile journey, although Tahira, who sat in the rear of the machine between Blake and Morton, made several attempts at conversation. Finally the reporter decided to do a bit of questioning.

"How did you know that Gregg had fifty thousand dollars in the cottage on the night of the murder?" asked Morton, looking at the servant.

Tahira's eyes were fixed upon the broad back of Flannigan as the latter sat in front of the machine beside the driver.

"It was brought to him by messenger from New York at four o'clock that afternoon," answered the Japanese. "Mr. Gregg signed for the money—we were both at the cottage then. The messenger, to make doubly sure, as it was a large sum, insisted that Mr. Gregg have someone else sign the receipt. I did so at Mr. Gregg's request. Naturally I saw the amount which had been received."

"I see," remarked Morton. "Why did Mr. Gregg send for such a large sum of money. Do you know?"

"That I cannot answer." Tahira shook his head. "I suspect it had something to do with the meeting which he planned at the cottage last night."

"And you claim that meeting didn't occur," said Blake quietly. "Are you sure of that, Tahira?"

"Quite sure, Captain Blake. As I said before, I remained at the cottage until nine, and no one appeared."

"Where were you between nine that night and the time you returned to the hotel at two a.m. the next morning?" demanded the Captain.

"I'm sorry, Captain," said the servant slowly, "but I would rather explain that later."

Blake started to say something further, and apparently changed his mind. He lapsed into silence, but he was listening closely as Morton asked another question.

"You said that the money was stolen from a safe in the cottage, didn't you?" he demanded.

"Yes, that was quite true. I realize that you probably consider it quite unusual for a safe to be found in a furnished cottage. It was not there when Mr. Gregg rented the place. He had it put in later himself." The servant suddenly sat forward. "This is Mr. Gregg's residence, gentlemen."

The car had stopped beside an attractive white stucco dwelling that stood within a short distance of the Boardwalk. The four men got out, leaving the driver sitting in the machine. Tahira led the way up the front steps to the porch. When he reached the front door he produced a key from his pocket and unlocked the door. He pushed it wide open, and bowed as he permitted the three men to precede him into the house.

The first floor consisted of a living room, dining room, and kitchen. Leading from the kitchen was a small butler's pantry connecting with the dining room. It was all attractively furnished, but there was a stuffy air about the place which indicated that it had not been lived in for some time.

Blake, Morton and Flannigan moved about slowly, examining everything carefully. The reporter noticed the remains of a number of half-burnt cigarettes in the stone fireplace in one corner of the living room. He took a package of cigarettes from his pocket, placed one in his mouth and lighted it, and then turned to Tahira. The Japanese stood near by watching Blake and Flannigan, who were examining a small steel safe which stood near the stairs.

"Have a cigarette?" the reporter asked the servant casually.

"Thank you, but I don't smoke." Tahira shook his head.

"Maybe you're right." Morton walked over and threw the cigarette he had been smoking into the fireplace. "Smoking is probably what affected Mr. Gregg's health."

"No, I don't think so," said Tahira, still watching the detectives as they examined the safe. "He smoked very seldom, and never a cigarette."

"Oh, he didn't?" Morton glanced again at the many cigarette stubs in the fireplace. "Then I guess he can't blame poor health on that."

The Captain ceased examining the safe, and turned to the servant.

"Was this locked when Mr. Gregg left here on the afternoon of the murder?" he asked.

"Yes," answered Tahira. "I am quite sure of that."

"Do you know the combination?"

"No, I do not."

There came the sound of a bell in the distance.

"That is probably the grocery boy," Tahira volunteered. "He usually comes at this time. Pardon me a moment while I unlock the back door."

Blake nodded as Tahira turned and went in the direction of the kitchen. When he was convinced that the man was out of earshot, the Captain spoke in a low tone.

"That bird knows a lot more than he is telling. I'm glad I placed him under arrest." He turned to Flannigan. "You better go after him, Dan. He might try to make a break—though I doubt it."

The stout detective nodded as he hurriedly left the room.

"Someone spent quite a time here—either on the night of the murder or since then," said Morton. "And they made themselves very much at home." He indicated the half-burnt cigarettes in the fireplace. "Whoever it was, had time enough to smoke all those before leaving."

"It might have been Tahira," remarked Blake.

"No it wasn't. I just offered him a cigarette, and he said that he didn't smoke."

"How about Gregg? He might have left him."

"I don't think so. Tahira says that Gregg rarely smoked, and never cigarettes."

They both turned as Flannigan came bursting into the room. He was panting and evidently had been running.

"I've been all over the house!" he exclaimed. "I even went down in the cellar, but it's no use. He put one over on us. That damn little Heathen has beat it!"

"Are you sure?" demanded Blake.

"Of course I'm sure. Ain't I looked everywhere? I even run out and asked Brown, sitting in the car, if he had seen the Jap. He ain't seen nobody. Who the devil rang that bell?"

The reporter was gazing at a slight rise in one corner of the rug.

"Tahira rang the bell himself," he said, moving to the spot. "Listen!"

Morton placed his foot over the spot in the rug, and from the kitchen came the faint sound of a bell.

21
GREGG'S LEATHER NECKLACE

THE BRIGHT AFTERNOON SUNLIGHT gleamed upon the face of Miss Ida Hill, seeking the beauty, the radiant youth, of the girl who had been known on the stage as Dolly Marden.

Miss Hill sat alone in the living-room of her old house, the room in which Lannon and Larry had stood but two nights ago, the room in which Larry had learned to hope from the things which a woman's eyes may say.

In her hands the elderly woman held a square box. It was a pretty, fragile sort of thing tied with ribbons that were worn and shabby with age.

How like love it was, she thought—pretty, fragile, and yet lasting even though it was a little tired and weary with the years it had known. She smiled faintly. A pretty fancy, but was it really true? Love had not meant that to her. It had brought only bitterness and sorrow and humiliation.

Life is made of lights and shadows, she felt. Just now the box basked in the radiance of sunlight. It was a thing of memories, of faint treasures of bygone days. Miss Hill sighed as she gazed at the ribbons, her blue eyes hazy with the veil of remembrance. With fingers that trembled slightly she untied the ribbons. It had been so long since she had last looked within this old box! Would the fragile, foolish things that had been sacred to the heart of a girl still be there? Memories were stirring in her heart, dim-felt pain that was somehow sweet as she raked the ashes of yesterday.

The box was open now. She sat gazing at its contents. An old play-bill, "Dolly Marden in 'The Girl from Rome'"—the recollections were growing clearer. Old scenes, old faces, that she thought she had forgotten, crept into her mind: Johnny, the little call boy, who had always smiled knowingly when he had brought her the many, many flowers from her admirers—Johnny knocking on her dressing-room door: "Fifteen minutes, Miss Marden"—Johnny— she had seen his name in the cast of a new play just a week or so ago. The old call of the footlights stole over her, the roar of the clapping hands as Dolly Marden stepped from the wings and bowed again. It all came back to her so vividly!

Miss Hill sighed. How proud she had been then. Pride—it was a damnable thing. It had wrecked her life—made her face so many bitter, unspeakable things. The wife of Watson Gregg—how well he had crushed that pride!

Swiftly her mind traveled back over the years. Bright memories—a lovely old garden bathed in the white light of a slender moon. A tall young man, white faced as he walked slowly toward the stone gateway. A beautiful girl sobbing as she watched him go. Too proud to call him back, and yet wanting him so. Pride, pride— how cruel you may be!

Nothing had mattered afterward. The man whom she adored had gone out of her life forever. Later she had met Watson Gregg, when she had come to New York and started her career on the stage. One sometimes learns to love those who help them to their heart's desires. It was through Gregg's efforts that she had become the brilliantly successful Dolly Marden.

She had married Gregg then. She had given him all that she had to give, the love of her very heart and soul. He had been good to her at first. They had spent six months abroad, and when they had returned he had used his influence, for he had been rich and powerful even then. He had made her a star on Broadway. The critics had been lavish in their praise, and for a time Watson Gregg had been proud of his lovely wife.

Three years went by. How happy and successful they had been! Then had come that ghastly fourth year. She shuddered at the memory of it. Watson Gregg's love had grown cold. He had become cruel in the little ways which hurt women most—the little things that had wounded her pride, gradually had grown bigger, the hurts deeper and deeper. Never could she forget the taste of bitterness which she had found within her heart when she had seen the name of another woman blazing in electric lights, and had known that her husband had placed it there.

The shock of the realization had been too much; it had caught her unawares, and she had broken under the strain. She had learned to love Gregg deeply in spite of his faults. Always she had hoped that he might change, always she had clung to the faint dreams that even a woman whose heart is breaking may dare to keep until the very end.

Miss Hill sobbed softly as she remembered the gray, desolate days which had followed. She had become desperately ill and had remained so for weeks. Someone else had taken her part in the show in which she had been the star, but she was too ill to even know or care then.

All during those long weeks she had asked each day for her husband, but he never came to her, never made the slightest effort to see her—the woman who was his wife. Broadway did not know that—they had never known—for Gregg had suggested that they keep their marriage a secret. He had said it would be better for her career.

As she had lingered there in the hospital, ill and heartbroken, Gregg had sent her money sometimes, but he never came near her. The bitterness of it, the cruel hurt, still lingered in her heart. At first she had been too proud to take what he had sent. Later she had had to do so in order to live.

When she had recovered from her illness she had gone to see her husband. Never would she be able to forget the humiliation of that interview. It had taken courage for her even to speak to him, for she had been proud, terribly proud. She had finally faced her husband and demanded her rights as his wife. Gregg had only laughed at her. He had told her that the marriage had not been legal—that the minister had been a fraud, an actor whom Gregg had hired. It had not been until long afterward that she had learned that he had lied. The marriage had been legal, the minister genuine.

Blindly, hopeless with shame and sorrow, she had left Watson Gregg then. He had convinced her that he told the truth—she was not his wife. It had been the last straw that she had clung to so desperately. At first she had thought of suicide, but she had been proud and would not admit defeat, even then.

From somewhere within the silent house there came to Miss Hill's ears the weird cackling of the old negress. Lannon's Aunt smiled faintly.

During all the weeks that she had been ill, Miss Hill had possessed but one friend. That had been the colored woman, then middle aged, who had been her maid. Dear, dear old Loona! Through everything she had stood by. She had tried to help all she could in her poor, ignorant way.

Time had gone on. At last Miss Hill had been unable to stand it any longer. Her weeks of illness had faded her beauty, affected her voice for a time. Her disillusions had made her haggard. Managers were no longer interested in the shadow of what had once been the lovely Dolly Marden. It was too much for her proud spirit—the weary rounds of the theatrical offices—broken promises, stalls— and waiting day after day with never an offer of a part. Again she had broken under the strain.

Weeks later they had come to the seashore, Dolly Marden and her maid. She had hoped that the salt air would help her regain her health and beauty. For a while they had lived in boarding houses; Gregg still sent her money at times.

Finally there had come a day when they could no longer afford even that. Although her husband had not ceased sending her money, the sum had grown smaller and smaller each time.

Miss Hill had learned of the house in which she now lived. It was old and far away, and even said to be haunted, but that had not mattered. She had sold the jewels which her husband had given her, and which she had clung to in spite of her poverty, and had bought this place very cheaply.

She smiled grimly at the box in her hand. Such bitter memories!

She wanted to try to forget them now. Surely there were others that were kinder.

She put the play-bill aside, and drew something else from the box. What was this? A withered, crumpled thing—a rose from the old garden. Sweeter memories came now. The other man, the man who had loved her always—she had plucked it for him that night on which they had quarreled. How well she remembered standing there, watching the rose slowly slip from his fingers as he turned away.

With a swift motion Miss Hill placed the withered rose to her lips. The old love was stirring in her heart, restless from its long sleep. Yet it had been such uncertain slumber. So often she had heard it whispering, berating her in the still watches of the lonely years, for hearts cannot understand why they must suffer.

So lost was Miss Hill in the rainbow hues of reverie that she did not hear the faint ringing of the doorbell, nor see Loona as the old colored woman passed along the hall.

A moment later a tall figure appeared in the doorway. Giovanni Danton smiled as he stood there, a smile that was different. A wistful, sad smile that lingered in the deep eyes as he noticed the box which Miss Hill still held.

She looked up as he entered, and then she too smiled; her expression changed to one of trust and confidence.

"You've kept it all these years?" he asked, his deep voice soft and strange, his eyes still upon the fragile box.

"Yes, Giovanni." Miss Hill looked at him bravely, the beauty of the girl of long ago lingering now in her tired face. "There are some things that one simply cannot part with. Forgetting is not always easy."

"I once thought one could do everything, even learn to forget— forget when everything in life taunted me, when everything whispered 'Remember'." Danton dropped into a chair beside her. "No one will ever know how hard I tried to forget. I went wandering over the world trying, always struggling to put the old memories away from me. Then would come a star-filled night that held the bitter fragrance of recollection. A night that tore at my heart, that made me call out in anguish a name I thought I would never dare to speak again!"

"It meant so much to you?" The girl of yesterday spoke in Miss Hill's soft voice. "So much you could never forget?"

"Yes, Ida, so much. I've never forgotten for a moment. I wonder if you could know what that has meant—the sudden sharp pain that would come to the heart when least expected?"

"If I could know! Oh, Giovanni, how can you say that! Do you think it has ever been easy for me to forget—I who have so much to remember?"

"Yet you knew happiness, Ida!"

"Happiness!" The untold bitterness of her laugh appalled him. "You suffered so much?"

"Suffered, Giovanni. The wife of Watson Gregg—suffered! I have been through years of hell. Suffered—what can you know of the torture that a woman may find, who is married to a man she loves and who does not love her? To have your pride beaten down and torn into shreds by a man who is little more than a beast?

"A woman can forgive much, Giovanni, even unfaithfulness if a man is kind. Women learn to face big things—even death. It is part of our lives, part of the lives of all women, Giovanni. Your lovely Italian mother faced it when she brought you into the world.

"Oh, yes, we can face big things. It is the little ones that tear at our hearts. Trifles perhaps to you, but so much to a woman. The little, foolish things that a man no longer remembers to do. A kind and loving word that is no longer spoken. A word perhaps that has been so much a part of a woman's life. When it is forgotten, it leaves such an empty space. Oh, why, why can't husbands realize that a woman marries her lover?"

"But a woman does not always marry her lover, Ida," said Danton very quietly. "At least not her first love!"

"Please, Giovanni! Don't say that as you do now, with bitterness in your tone." She looked at him pleadingly. "Was I altogether to blame? I was very young—I did love you, Giovanni, but a girl cannot always be sure of her heart. Perhaps if I had been older—" She paused uncertainly.

"Have I ever said that you were to blame, Ida? That quarrel in the garden—it was my fault. I was such a foolish, headstrong boy.

To say now that I am sorry—it's so futile, so inane. But why tear open old wounds? I came on a mission."

"A mission?" Miss Hill looked at him in surprise. "What do you mean?"

"Lannon sent me here."

"Lannon sent you?"

"Yes."

"Where is she now?" There was an anxious note in Miss Hill's voice. "I thought she would be back by now. I was sure she had gone merely to tell Larry Benson that she was all right. Where is she, Giovanni?"

"Don't worry, Ida, she is quite safe. Probably home now, or out with Larry Benson. That boy has courage, far more than I at first suspected."

Briefly Danton related what had happened in the old cabin on the beach at Longport. He gave a vivid description of the fight between Floss and Larry, for he had witnessed the greater part of it through a window.

"Then I took the automatic away from Floss and ordered him to leave the vicinity," he said in conclusion. "He obeyed at once. I walked back to the car with Lannon and Larry. She asked me to call to tell you she was not coming back until tomorrow or the next day."

"The poor child!" Miss Hill sighed. "I can't very well blame her. It has been very lonely and terrifying for her here, I'm afraid."

"Yes. Your celebrating—" Danton paused, the sentence half finished as he smiled grimly.

"I know—I know," said Miss Hill quickly. "It was a strange thing to do, but I had a purpose, Giovanni. I knew that Lannon cared for the boy greatly. I wanted to see how he would behave under mysterious, even terrifying, conditions. That was the reason I invited him to my mad dinner party—my celebration of death! That was one reason why I permitted poor old Loona to give free rein to her emotions. The funeral bier, the empty place at the end of the table, were her ideas, and I humored her, let her carry them through."

"Then Loona has taken this thing that has happened very seriously?"

"In her ignorant way she feels the death of—" Miss Hill halted, and then went on, her voice stumbling over the name swiftly—"of Watson Gregg is the most wonderful bit of happiness that could ever come into my life." She smiled sadly. "I don't feel that way, Giovanni. For a time when I first learned of it, I thought that I did. But I was wrong—I know that now. He was very cruel, very brutal to me, but he left memories. I think he did love me once in his vain, selfish way. One forgives the dead so much because they are gone. How ironical life may be! To think that the cruelest thing he ever did to me was returned to him a hundredfold—"

"I don't quite understand!" Danton looked at her questioningly. "What do you mean, Ida?"

"But you do, Giovanni, you understand so well! Don't you remember when you first returned to this country after an absence of so many years? How in some way you found this poor shadow that had once been the girl you loved? Found her in a hospital deserted by the world?

"You offered to help me then, Giovanni, but I couldn't let you. I clung vainly to the hope that the man whom I had married was at least kind. There was a very valuable pearl necklace which he had given me, that was still in his possession. I wrote to him and asked him to send me that, if he would not aid me in any other way—if he would not come to see me. You were there with me, Giovanni, when I received the package which was his answer—don't you remember?"

"Remember? I'll never forget! The brutality of it—the damnable cadishness of the action!" Danton's eyes flamed. "Oh, if I could have found him I would have killed him then!"

"Yet it was merely a long, saffron-colored, leather cord, and a card saying, 'Here is a necklace for you. I have other use for the pearls.'" Miss Hill shook her head. "And he was murdered by a leather thong, Giovanni!"

"Yes," said Danton softly, an odd expression upon his white face as he gazed at her; "he was, Ida!"

"The leather necklace that he sent me—I've always kept it." Miss Hill rummaged amid the contents of the box on her lap. "It is here somewhere, I'm sure."

Danton watched her silently as she searched. Over and over she went through the contents of the box, and then she turned to him with a startled cry.

"It's gone, Giovanni! The saffron cord isn't in the box!"

"Didn't you know it was missing, Ida?" he asked quietly.

"No." She shook her head, puzzled by a note in his deep voice.

"You are sure?" he was gazing at her intently now, his strange eyes fixed upon her face.

"Yes, Giovanni. Why do you ask?"

"Because it was your leather necklace that was found around the throat of Watson Gregg—I know, for I examined it!"

"My necklace?" She looked at him with horror in her eyes. "The saffron cord that Gregg sent me?"

"Yes, Ida, your necklace!"

"Oh, and you thought— The police have questioned you so much, Giovanni, what have you told them?"

"Nothing." Danton smiled drily. "They appear to be growing a little tired of silence. Captain Blake has made it very plain that I had better speak soon or I shall be arrested for murder!"

"And you have remained silent because you thought that I—" Miss Hill hesitated and then went on bravely—"that I killed Watson Gregg? Oh, why, why, didn't you speak, Giovanni?"

Danton leaned forward in his chair, and his strange eyes gazed deep into the blue ones of Miss Hill. There was an expression in his gaze that she thought had gone forever—but it was in his eyes now, and she felt instinctively that it would ever be there.

"I did not speak because I love you, Ida," he said, his voice deep and tender as he spoke the words.

22
THE SAFFRON CORD AGAIN

IT WAS NOW OVER AN HOUR AND A HALF since Flannigan had announced that Tahira had disappeared. The three men had searched the house from top to bottom quickly, but they had not found the slightest trace of the Japanese servant. They had continued their search throughout the neighborhood, and had been unable to find anyone who had even seen the man.

During the hunt they had run across Officer Cremmens, a motor-cycle patrolman of the Ventnor police, and had enlisted his aid. He had covered all of upper Ventnor on his machine, but had been unable to catch sight of Tahira.

What made the man's sudden disappearance all the more mysterious was the fact that there was an open lot in the rear of Gregg's cottage. For Tahira to make his get-away in this direction, it was necessary for him to cross the open space which was clearly visible from the Boardwalk. He could not have left by coming around either side of the house and out to the street, for if he had done so Brown, the driver of the police car, would have seen him. Brown had not seen anyone, he was quite sure of that.

There were a number of people on the Boardwalk, and although the detectives questioned them, none recalled seeing a man answering to Tahira's description.

"That's the dumbest trick I've ever done," said Blake angrily, as he walked back to the cottage with the reporter. "I place a man under arrest because he is a suspicious character in a murder case. We come down here and a bell rings. He says it is probably the grocery boy and goes to answer the door—and like a damn fool I let him go alone!"

"No use crying over spilt milk, Jerry," said Morton. "He made a clever get-away, that's all. I doubt that he will be able to leave the city, though."

"No, I don't believe he will—I agree with you there. He knows that we have all the railroad stations watched—the highways, too, for that matter. He's a smooth little devil—he will probably remain in town and try and hide some place until this case blows over."

They had reached the front porch of the cottage now, and Morton sat down on the steps and lighted a cigarette. Blake glanced about him, and then sat beside the reporter. Flannigan moved over to the police car, where he stood talking to Brown.

"That fifty thousand that Tahira says Gregg received, gives us a nice little motive for the murder," remarked Morton thoughtfully, his eyes fixed upon the smoke from his cigarette. "We've learned a lot in the last few hours, Jerry."

"Yes, I know." Blake nodded. "In the first place, we know definitely that both Mercedes La Tona and Tahira were on the Boardwalk at the time that the murder took place. The day he was killed, Watson Gregg is said to have received fifty thousand in cash. That is missing—if there really was such a sum."

"There must have been. What would be the point in Tahira telling you a thing like that if it was not true? He had nothing to gain by it, and everything to lose. He must have realized that he was only implicating himself. You had already placed him under arrest. To tell that Gregg had been robbed of the money, only placed more suspicion upon him."

"I realize that." The Captain frowned. "I wish Flannigan had not let that tall man we saw talking to the La Tona woman get away from him. I certainly would like to have a little talk with him!"

"So would I!" said Morton dryly. "I'd like to talk to the blonde that was in the chair—Lannon Gordon, Miss La Tona said her name was, didn't she?"

"Yes. Rather an unusual name. I don't believe it will be very difficult to find her if she is still in the city. I think she knows a good bit about the case, but I have a funny hunch that she did not murder Gregg."

"What makes you so sure of that?" asked the reporter. "She was in the chair with him. To my mind she had the best opportunity. When she left the chair she was frightened and crying. Something must have happened. Wonder if she was the woman that Gregg planned to bring down here to the cottage?"

"I don't know. With all the talk of this one and that as a possible suspect, we haven't mentioned Giovanni Danton or Doctor Fulda."

"What has become of those two? I haven't seen the physician since the evening that Gregg was discovered in the rolling chair. He is still in town, isn't he?"

"Yes, staying at the Seafoam. I have one of my men shadowing him constantly. He has been keeping very quiet."

"How about Danton? Is he being shadowed, too?"

"No, not as yet. I didn't want to try it with him. I was afraid that I would put someone on the job who would blunder as Flannigan did with that tall man. Danton has brains—if he was sure he was being watched he would be very careful to do nothing which might be in the least suspicious. As I said before, I feel that if I give Danton enough rope he will hang himself."

"He might, at that," said Morton. "But it strikes me that you are taking a long chance in letting him roam around without keeping tabs on him, Jerry."

"Maybe I am, but that's the way I intend to let things work out with him. I'll give him about one more day, and then I am going to throw him into jail. He won't talk—and I don't like that. He has acted ever since this thing started as though he were shielding someone."

"When you overheard the conversation between Miss La Tona and the Jap at the hotel this morning, did they mention Danton's name?"

"I'm not sure of it," said Blake. "I sat there pretending to read the paper for a few minutes after Tahira came into the writing room. When I sneaked up behind the potted plants I was just in time to hear Miss La Tona say, 'Tahira, we must be careful—that man, he knows too much!'"

"And you think she meant Danton?"

"I don't know. I wish I had heard a little more of the conversation. He might have been the one whom she meant. Or perhaps it was that tall man that Flannigan let get away."

"Sure, or Doctor Fulda!" The reporter laughed. "It might even have been you or myself. I think she is a little afraid of you, Jerry. She hasn't found detectives quite as dumb as she expected they would be."

"No?" Blake grinned. "Nor reporters either, eh?" He rose to his feet. "Let's go through the cottage just once more, and then I must be getting back to my office."

"Suits me," said Morton as he followed the Captain into the house. "We went over the place in an awful hurry last time. Still, I don't think Tahira would be foolish enough to remain here."

"Neither do I," said Blake.

They went quickly through the first floor of the house and then descended to the cellar. They found nothing which they considered of interest in either place.

"Looks like we've drawn a blank so far," remarked Morton as they ascended the stairs leading to the second floor of the cottage. "I sure would like to know just how that little Jap got away so quickly."

"I have a few ideas on the subject," said Blake. "I'll tell you about them later."

They had reached the second story now. There were five rooms on this floor. Two of these had a small bath connecting. The doors of all rooms opened into the hall. The stairs were at the far end. Blake walked into the room which was nearest, and stood there looking about carefully. The room was tastefully furnished. A single bed stood in one corner, and next to it a bedside table upon which stood an ornate reading lamp. In the corner opposite the bed was a small writing desk. A tall dresser had been placed against the wall between two windows which faced out toward the Boardwalk.

As the Captain and the reporter looked about them, they saw

that the room had evidently not been occupied for some time. However, it was carefully cleaned and dusted and it was obvious that it, as well as the rest of the cottage, had been prepared for the new tenant to move in.

Morton went to a closed door in one corner of the room and drew it open. It proved to be a clothes closet. There were a number of coat hangers dangling from a rod which ran from one end of the closet to the other, but no garments hung on them.

"Nothing here," said the reporter. "And I'll bet the rest of the place is the same way, Jerry."

"Probably. But I won't be satisfied until we have gone through every room. We may not find anything, but I want to have a very good picture of this place in my mind. It might prove useful. You never can tell."

Morton merely nodded as he followed the Captain into the hall and they moved on to the next room. This also proved to be a bedroom. It was quite as tastefully furnished as had been the first that they had entered, and in a similar fashion. The reporter drew open the door of a closet as Blake pulled out one of the upper drawers of the dresser and looked inside.

"Find anything?" asked Morton as he observed the Captain's actions, and then, as Blake shook his head. "Neither did I."

"Let's try the next one," said the Captain, moving toward the door.

The reporter followed. The two men stopped when they reached the next room. This was also a bedroom, but it was larger than had been the other two—and there were twin beds at one wall. But it was not the size of the room which had caught the attention of Blake and Morton. It was an overturned chair. The rest of the house had been in such perfect order that the misplaced bit of furniture surprised them.

"What do you think of that?" cried Morton, indicating the chair. "I don't know just how to figure it myself, Jerry."

"It might not mean anything," said Blake slowly, his eyes studying the floor about the chair intently. "The rug has been turned up as though someone caught their foot in it and did not bother to fix it."

The reporter had moved toward a closed door in one corner of the room. He drew the door open and then leaped back with a gasp of horror as a limp form fell out of the closet and landed face downward on the floor.

"Good God!" exclaimed Blake, as he hurried to where the reporter stood. "Who is it?"

"I don't know." Morton stared down at the body at his feet. "I didn't see his face."

"We'll know in a minute!" Blake said tensely as he leaned down and turned the body over. Then he cried in momentary horror: "Why, it's Doctor Fulda!"

For a moment the two men stood staring down at the body of the little physician. His hard eyes were fairly sticking out of his head, and a saffron hued leather thong had been drawn tight about his throat.

The Captain of Detectives leaned over and examined the still figure.

"He's dead, all right," he said slowly. "The saffron cord again!"

"Yes, but how did he get here?" demanded the reporter. "Where did he come from? Who killed him?"

"If I knew the answers to those questions I wouldn't be still working on the Gregg Case," Blake told him. "He might have entered the house by the back while we were sitting out front—and there might have been someone with him." The Captain looked about him quickly. "You stay here, Dave. I'm going out to the Boardwalk and ask a few questions. I saw a man sitting out there on a bench through the window of that first room we looked in." Blake turned toward the door. "Don't touch anything until I get back."

"Don't worry," said Morton, with a glance at the body. "I sure won't!"

As the Captain hurriedly left the room the reporter moved closer to all that remained of the physician of Watson Gregg, and stood there gazing down intently. Questions and conjectures were passing swiftly through Morton's mind. He realized that it might have been possible for Fulda to have entered the house during the interval in which they had been searching the neighborhood for Tahira—but he thought that very unlikely.

The people whom Captain Blake had questioned upon the Boardwalk had stated that they had observed no one in the vicinity of the house. To enter the house from the rear, the Doctor would have been forced to cross the open space, and would have been readily seen.

Morton was inclined to believe that Blake had been right when he had said that he thought Fulda must have come into the cottage while the Captain and the reporter were sitting out on the front steps discussing the case. If that were so—what Morton wanted to know was: Who had come with him?

The reporter turned as he heard someone running up the stairs. In an instant Flannigan came bursting into the room. He stopped abruptly as he caught sight of the limp form upon the floor.

"The Captain told me you just found him," said Flannigan, with a nod toward the body. "Another one killed with that damn leather cord, eh?"

"Right! I'm afraid Captain Blake will have to show results pretty quick—unless he wants half the town wiped out. God! Where is this going to end? Where is Blake now?"

"Talking to some feller out on the Boardwalk," answered Flannigan. "He said he would be back up here in a few minutes."

"Did you see anyone around the place when you were standing outside?" asked the reporter.

"Nope." The stout detective shook his head. "No one near the cottage. There's been a few people passing on the Boardwalk, and one man sitting on a bench for some time. He's the feller that the Captain is talking to now."

"Here he comes," said Morton as he heard someone enter the house and start up the stairs. "That you, Jerry?" he called.

"Yes," answered Blake as he entered the room. "We were right—Fulda drove up in his car. He parked it in the next street—it is all wide-open beach between this street and that along here, as you know. Then he walked over to the house and entered through the back door. That chap sitting on the bench saw him."

"So far so good!" exclaimed Morton. "But who killed Fulda?"

"I don't know," said Blake, "but Johnson, the man on the bench, said that a few minutes after Fulda entered the house a woman came out the back way."

"A woman!" exclaimed the reporter in amazement. "What did she look like?"

"She was slender and rather small—and from the distance Johnson judged that she was a blonde!"

23
"TOMORROW AT TEN-THIRTY"

LANNON GORDON sat in the living room of her home, a happy, radiant expression upon her lovely face. Larry had just left her a little while ago—her Larry, who had fought and won for her. How good it was to know that the boy to whom she had given her heart had proven himself a man when he had found the girl he adored was in danger!

It had been with such a strange feeling of relief that both Lannon and Larry had turned as they stood there in the old cabin to find Giovanni Danton covering Floss with an automatic. Even now the girl shuddered as she realized what might have happened if Danton had not appeared. She did not doubt that Floss would have shot Larry. He might even have killed him. Lannon did not like to think of that. Now she only wanted to think of Larry. She loved him, there was not the slightest doubt of that in her mind and heart now. It had been her heart that had made her cry out and tell him so, there in the cabin.

Afterwards they had both been so shy about it. It had been Danton who had talked the most as they walked back to Larry's roadster. The tall, white-faced man had made them both feel that he was their friend. It had been his suggestion that he tell Miss Hill that Lannon was safe, and would not return to the weird old house of her Aunt for a day or so. Danton had realized that the trying ordeal which the girl had gone through had unnerved her to a certain extent. He knew that the best tonic in the world for her now was to be alone for a time with the man whom she loved.

For an hour or so after Danton had left them Larry and Lannon had driven aimlessly around. Their destination did not matter. It seemed to them that there was so much they had to say to each other, so many words that their hearts must voice; yet they had said so little. Lannon smiled now as she realized that Larry had not even asked her to marry him. They were both young, and they had found such contentment in just being with each other. Nothing else had mattered.

Larry had been tactful. He had asked nothing further regarding what had happened during the time that Lannon had remained at the old house of her Aunt. Because he had been so sweet and understanding and had not questioned her, Lannon had told him all about it. She had found it easy to tell him of her fears, of her nervous terror of those things which she realized had been for the most part the product of her own fevered imagination. Larry had not found those fears foolish, as she had been afraid that he might have done. He had been interested and tender and sympathetic. Lannon laughed happily as she thought about it now. Dear Larry— she did love him so much!

The girl looked up with a start as she heard the doorbell ring. It was now five in the afternoon. She wondered who it was that had rung the bell. For an instant she thought it might be Larry returning for some reason. She quickly dismissed the idea; he had said that he would return at eight that evening. If not he, who then?

Lannon looked at the maid anxiously as she entered the room.

"A gentleman to see you, Miss Lannon."

"Oh, who is it, Hilda? Do you know?"

"No, Miss." The maid shook her head. "An elderly gentleman, and very polite and nice he seemed, too."

"All right, I'll see him," said Lannon. "Show him in, please."

The maid nodded as she disappeared. A moment later an elderly, white-haired man entered. He smiled in a friendly fashion as he saw the beautiful blonde-haired girl who rose to greet him.

"Miss Gordon?" he asked as he came forward. "Miss Lannon Gordon?"

"Yes, but I'm afraid that I don't quite know—" Lannon hesitated.

"Of course you don't know who I am." He laughed. "I'm Captain Blake."

"Oh!" Lannon grew tense, but she controlled herself with an effort.

Then this was Captain Blake, the head of the Detective Bureau, and he had come to see her! Perhaps he had learned that she was the girl who had been in the rolling chair upon the night that Watson Gregg had been found murdered. Larry had told her so much about Captain Blake!

"Yes, Captain Blake, of the Detective Bureau. But please don't let my being here alarm you. I assure you that my mission is of a most friendly nature."

"Thank you, Captain Blake," said Lannon as she dropped into a chair and indicated another near by. "Won't you sit down?"

"With pleasure. Miss Gordon, it's necessary that I ask you a few questions."

"Naturally," said Lannon with a smile, but there was fear in her heart, for she felt that what she might say would implicate her Aunt, and she did not want to do that. "Just what would you like to know, Captain Blake?"

"Perhaps it would make things easier for you if I explain that I am already quite certain that you were the girl who was seen getting out of Watson Gregg's rolling chair, crying—" Blake hesitated, and his smile took the sting from his words as he continued—"on the night that he was found—dead."

Lannon heard the announcement with almost a feeling of' relief. She had realized it was inevitable that the police would learn the identity of the girl in the chair. She had known, too, that she would have to explain her actions that night. Captain Blake's attitude was a friendly one. She had feared that when the time came for her to be questioned by the police, she would encounter a blustering type of individual who would make the interview a trying ordeal.

"That is true," she said slowly. "I was in the chair with Watson Gregg—and I did leave it crying. Oh, Captain Blake. I must make you understand! He—he was not dead then. I left him because of the things he said to me. I can't explain—but—but he was awfully insulting."

"You need not explain that, Miss Gordon," said Blake softly. "I have been able to gather rather a good impression of the late Mr. Gregg's character since I have been working on this case." He frowned. "I regret that such a lovely girl as you should be mixed up in this matter at all."

"That's mighty sweet of you, Captain," said Lannon, gratitude shining in her lovely eyes as she gazed at the detective. "I'm so sorry that I agreed to have dinner with him that night. It was just—just the impulse of a foolish kid, that's all. And now I'm going to be sorry for it all my life!" Her soft lips trembled as she finished.

"Now, Miss Gordon, please!" exclaimed Blake soothingly. "You really must not feel that way about it. In order that we may clear up this case and find the person who is guilty, it is necessary to question everyone. I wish I could feel that I could make you an exception, but I just can't. I'm sorry."

"It's right noble of you to feel that way," said Lannon. "But I've told you about all that I know now."

"Not quite all, I'm afraid. Where did you go after you left the rolling chair, Miss Gordon?"

Lannon hesitated for an instant before she answered. She was very reluctant to tell the detective that she had gone to her Aunt's house. Yet she did not wish to lie to him. She felt that he had been so kind and so friendly that it would be far wiser to tell the truth.

"I went to my Aunt's house," she said slowly. "I've been staying there ever since. Daddy is away in New York on business, and I was afraid to stay here that night."

"Why?" asked the Captain quietly. "Do you mind telling me?"

"Of course not. It was just—just that I was afraid Mr. Gregg might phone me or come to call on me here. After what he said—there in the chair—I never wanted to see him again as long as I lived!"

"I understand. And from what you have told me, and what I know about the man—you were quite right."

"You—you're mighty nice!" exclaimed Lannon. "You're not at all the way I thought a detective would be, Captain Blake. Reckon I've had some rather quaint brain throbs on the subject."

Captain Blake laughed sincerely. He had a daughter of his own about the same age as this girl, a daughter that he adored; and Lannon Gordon was so much like her. He heard her words with an understanding heart.

"I'm afraid that you have an entirely wrong impression of a Captain of Detectives," he said. "Like all police officials, we have our duties to perform. Some of them are a bit difficult and unpleasant, of course—but after all we are human, at that."

"I know." Lannon nodded seriously. "You've made me realize that, Captain." She smiled at him frankly. "I've been awfully afraid of what would happen when the police found out that I was the girl in the chair. And well, just talking to you, now, hasn't been so—so ghastly!"

"Of course not. Why should it be?"

"I don't know now. But when you get thinking of things which you don't know anything about, they grow mighty big and frightening in your mind."

"And when you do learn about them they are not so terrible, are they?" asked Blake with a smile.

"No," Lannon shook her head. "They are not!"

"After you left the chair you went to your Aunt's house," said the Captain thoughtfully. "Where does she live, Miss Gordon?"

Lannon had fully decided that she would answer any questions which the Captain might ask, though she still had a number of mental reservations so far as her Aunt was concerned. She did not know where Miss Hill had been on the night of the murder. The thought that her Aunt might have killed Gregg still lingered in the girl's mind. The way the elderly woman had acted upon that night— her insane rage when she had learned that Lannon had been with the murdered man—her mad celebration—they all had left a vivid impression in Lannon's mind. Yet she felt that she must tell Captain Blake the truth. The girl was fundamentally honest, exceptionally so in some ways. She would not lie about anything if she could help it.

"She lives in Margate," Lannon answered; "the last house out at the end of Locust Road."

"I see—and her name?"

"Miss Ida Hill." There was one thing which Lannon had determined that the police would never learn from her. That was the fact that her aunt had been the wife of Watson Gregg. "You're not going to question her, are you, Captain Blake?"

"I don't know. Probably not," said Blake. "I judge it would be very unlikely that she knows anything about the murder, don't you?"

"I can't see how she could," said Lannon quickly. "She lives such a lonely, sheltered life. For days at a time she hardly ever leaves that old house of hers."

"Sort of a recluse, eh?" remarked Blake, with a nod. "I see. Miss Gordon, did anything unusual happen during the time that you were visiting your Aunt?"

"Unusual?" demanded Lannon, striving desperately to keep the alarm out of her tone. "What do you mean?"

"Nothing in particular," said Blake slowly. "To be frank about it, I can't even explain what prompted me to ask the question."

"I can't either. Funny you should ask me that, isn't it? But nothing happened that you would be interested in."

"Did you have any visitors while you were staying there?" asked Blake casually.

"Yes, Auntie invited Mr. Benson to have dinner with us the second night that I was there. I reckon you know *him*, Captain Blake. He's the finest, dearest boy that ever lived!"

"Larry Benson!" exclaimed Blake. "Of course I know him—I have talked to him quite often since the night of the murder. I agree with you perfectly, Miss Gordon. He is a mighty fine boy. I judge you are rather fond of him."

"I am," Lannon nodded, her eyes shining. "I just adore him!"

Captain Blake smiled. It seemed very obvious that the girl was in love with Larry Benson. Blake made a mental note of the fact. It cleared up a few things which had been puzzling him.

"When did you leave your Aunt's house, Miss Gordon?"

"This morning," answered Lannon promptly, and then she frowned. "Larry and I have had a very trying experience since then."

"You have?" Blake looked surprised. "Won't you tell me about it?"

Lannon hesitated. She wondered if she had already said too much. Yet she felt it might be wise to tell Captain Blake all about the man named Godfrey Floss. He was a dangerous character. He might harm Larry even yet. Perhaps it would be wise to relate what had happened. In doing so she might be insuring Larry's safety— that was the first consideration in her mind.

"Yes, Captain," she said. Then hurriedly she related how she and Larry had gone for a walk on the beach on Longport. She told of how Floss had picked her up and carried her into the cabin. How Larry had broken the door down and then had fought with the other man. Told that Larry had won, but she did not mention that it had been her words of love which had inspired him to greater efforts. Finally she related the entire story, finishing with the very opportune appearance of Giovanni Danton.

"Then you know Danton?" asked Blake as she finished.

"No," Lannon shook her head. "I only know his name. But I sure was glad to see him standing there in that cabin door this morning."

"I don't doubt it." Blake smiled, and then grew serious. "Can you describe this Godfrey Floss?"

"I'll try to. He is a tall man, and he has a wicked-looking face. Like a wolf you'd say, I guess."

"Hum," said Blake, remembering the man he had seen on the beach talking to Mercedes La Tona. "Dark hair, and lips that are drooping?"

"Yes, that sounds like him." Lannon nodded. "He's a bad man, Captain Blake—and I'm afraid of what may happen if he finds Larry again. Couldn't you arrest him?"

"Certainly," said Blake quickly. "And I intend to do so. My men are out searching for him now. I don't doubt that one of them will bring him in very soon. I wonder why he'd want to kidnap *you?* . . . never mind that now. He'll be under arrest in a few hours, I'd say."

"I'm glad of that." Lannon shuddered. "He frightened me so!"

"You needn't worry any more about him." Blake looked at his watch. "I'm sorry. I've been keeping you here talking for quite some time. But there are still one or two more questions I would like to ask you."

"Be glad to answer them if I can."

"Do you by any chance know just about where you were at one-thirty to-day?"

"Of course." Lannon looked at the Captain in surprise. "I was out riding with Larry Benson."

"You didn't happen to drive anywhere near Suffolk Avenue here in Ventnor, did you?"

"No, Captain. We rode around Margate and Longport mostly—and then Larry brought me on home. But we didn't go near Suffolk Avenue. That's twenty blocks away from this house, you know."

"Yes, I know. It doesn't matter. The only reason I asked was that I saw a girl who might have been you in that vicinity."

"It must be someone who looks like me," said Lannon, a puzzled expression upon her lovely face. "I haven't been near there lately. I haven't even walked down the Ventnor Boardwalk since last week."

"I believe you!" Blake rose to his feet and Lannon did likewise. "That's about all, Miss Gordon, and thank you very much."

"Not at all, Captain Blake," said Lannon as she followed him to the door. "It is a relief to have finally been questioned by the police. I dreaded it so!"

"I'm glad you feel that way about it," said Blake, and then he looked at her his face serious: "Now there is just one more thing which I must ask of you."

"Certainly, Captain," said Lannon. "What is it?"

"That you be at my office at ten-thirty to-morrow morning. It is vital that you do so!"

Lannon did not speak as Captain Blake bowed and left the room. She stood there staring in the direction in which he had gone—a look of terror creeping into her lovely eyes.

24

"YOU HATED WATSON GREGG"

As Dave Morton hurried into the city hall the next morning in answer from an urgent telephone message from Captain Blake, he glanced around him in surprise. The Atlantic City Police Department was located in the big red brick building, and now the Law appeared to be exceptionally active. Uniformed officers and plainclothes men were hurrying about, and each one of them was evidently carrying out important instructions.

When the reporter reached Blake's office he found the place a scene of turmoil. The Captain sat at his desk, constantly barking orders into the telephone in front of him—or to those of his men who entered and left the room in a steady stream.

"Hello, Dave!" said Blake as he saw the reporter. "Sit down. I'll be with you in a minute."

The reporter nodded as he dropped into a chair and sat watching and listening. Five minutes later Blake dismissed the last of his men and turned to Morton.

"Wheeh! This has been a morning!" he remarked. "But I think I will get action on this Gregg case now."

"What's the idea?" demanded Morton. "Why all the sudden excitement? I don't get it, Jerry."

"You will before the morning is over," said Blake with a grim smile. "I've ordered everyone connected in any way with the murder brought in right away. I had bench warrants sworn out for the whole bunch—they will be here all right—and soon, too!"

"But, Jerry, they won't talk!" exclaimed the reporter. "You and I have both questioned most of them and drawn blanks."

"I'm not so sure about them not talking," Blake laughed, and then looked at the reporter intently. "I haven't been working at this case blindly for the past few days, Dave. I've learned a great many things that I have thought it wise not to tell any one."

"Been holding out on me, eh? Well, I don't know that I blame you. As long as I am in alone on the finish—that suits me."

"I told you that you would be, didn't I?" demanded the Captain. "None of the reporters received a phone call telling them to come around here this morning. When this thing breaks, you get it, Dave. And from the way it looks to me it is going to be a whale of a story."

"Now you're talking!" exclaimed Morton. "Come on, Jerry. Tell me who killed Watson Gregg?"

"That's something you will have to figure out for yourself," said the Captain slowly. "But when I get through questioning those connected with the case, you are going to have a lot to think about—or I'm all wet."

"Who did you send for?"

"Every one. Mercedes La Tona, Giovanni Danton, Larry Benson, Lannon Gordon and her Aunt, Miss Ida Hill."

"Lannon Gordon! You've found the girl then?"

"I have. I had a long talk with her yesterday afternoon. She is in love with Benson—and he with her."

"What has her Aunt got to do with it?" asked Morton eagerly.

"Plenty!" said Blake laconically. "She is going to be one of my best witnesses, I think."

"How about the Jap, and that tall man that gave Flannigan the slip?"

"Oh, Tahira and Godfrey Floss, you mean? Don't worry about them. You'll find this morning very interesting. I strongly suspect that this little session we are going to have will last longer than the morning, though. Probably take the whole day to get through with this thing."

"That's all right with me. My deadline is not until midnight you know—the *Press* is a morning paper."

"Maybe that's just as well. One thing I must get straight here and now—that is, you let me do all the talking. This is official business. Both the Chief and the Director of Public Safety happen to be out of town today. Maybe that's just as well—gives me a free hand. And it won't do me any harm if I can produce the murderer of Watson Gregg and Doctor Fulda when they get back tomorrow."

"I hope you can. But you have to show me, Jerry."

"I expect to show you and a few other people. I'll bet there are some who are connected with this case that think I'm just about the dumbest mortal that ever lived." The Captain frowned, and then brought his fist down upon the desk with a bang. "But they are all wrong! I've been in the Police Department for ten years—and I think I have learned to use my brain. I've done the devil of a lot of thinking, and I've come to the point now where I want to ask a lot of questions—questions which I expect will have some rather surprising answers."

"Motives and all that sort of thing?" asked Morton. "That what you mean?"

"Yes, and then some. Listen, Dave, if I wanted to I could give you a logical reason why every one of these witnesses that I am having brought in now might have murdered Gregg. I know the man's history back for at least ten years. He was rotten all the way through—I haven't the slightest doubt about that now. Each and every one of these people that are connected with this case had some reason to hate him—and they did hate him!"

"How about Larry Benson?" the reporter asked. "He didn't even know the man."

"Maybe he didn't—but he had one of the best reasons in the world for disliking him. That was jealousy. Gregg had been devoting a good bit of his attention to Lannon Gordon, and Benson is in love with the girl. We don't know what happened yet—but we may find out that Benson had reason to want to kill him." The Captain frowned. "And from what little the girl has told me, I don't know that I blame him."

"What did she tell you?"

"There's no use going into that now. She will be here this morning. I'm sure of that. You'll learn just where she fits in when I question her." He glanced at his watch. "Most of the men that I sent after these various witnesses left some time ago. The ones that I was just talking to have other orders."

Both Morton and Blake looked at the door eagerly as Flannigan entered the room.

"All set, Cap," said Flannigan with a nod. "The whole bunch are waiting for you up in the council chamber."

"Good!" exclaimed Blake as he rose to his feet. "We'll go right up. Come on, Dave."

A few minutes later the reporter followed the Captain into the council chamber. In one corner of the room sat Giovanni Danton, and close to him Ida Hill, whose sad and careworn face evidently had once been lovely. She was very nervous, and she continually clasped and unclasped her hands. Danton appeared quite calm. He smiled and bowed without rising as he saw Blake.

A short distance from Danton and Miss Hill sat Larry Benson and a beautiful blonde-haired girl. Morton realized that this must be Lannon Gordon, and he looked at her with interest. The girl was pale and she, too, was very nervous as she glanced from time to time in the direction of her Aunt.

On the opposite side of the room sat Mercedes La Tona. She was very beautifully dressed and seemed quite calm and undisturbed. To his surprise the reporter found that Officer Hayes was also in the room.

As he caught sight of a wizened old negress who sat apart from the others, Morton frowned.

Blake moved to a flat-top desk which had been placed near the center of the room, and sat down in the chair behind it. He motioned Morton to another close by. In front of the desk and facing it was a third chair, evidently placed there for the various witnesses to sit in as they were questioned. Flannigan and another detective now stood at the door, which was the only exit from the room.

The Captain placed upon the desk a stack of papers which he had brought with him. He glanced about the room as though debating whom he would call on first. His gaze rested upon Mercedes.

"Miss La Tona!" he called. "Will you take this chair, please?"

"Certainly." Mercedes rose and moved over to the chair which Blake had indicated. She sat facing him calmly.

"Miss La Tona," said Blake looking at her intently, "there are a few questions which I must ask you here and now. I advise you to answer them truthfully and fully!"

"I intend to do so, Captain Blake," Mercedes' eyes narrowed slightly. "I am in the habit of telling the truth!"

"I did not intimate that I doubted it," said Blake calmly. "Where were you at six-forty on the evening of October sixteenth, Miss La Tona?"

"On the Boardwalk."

"What part of the Boardwalk?"

"I was walking up the Boardwalk in the direction of the Inlet. I judge that I was about four blocks away from the Seafoam Hotel."

"Did you encounter anyone whom you knew in those four blocks?"

"I don't remember."

"Oh, yes, you do, Miss La Tona! Wasn't that when you passed Tahira Yamada, the Japanese servant of Watson Gregg?"

"No!" Mercedes smiled. "I met him about two blocks farther away."

"I see." Blake frowned as he realized that the woman had gained a point. "Did you speak to him?"

"I did not. I merely bowed as I passed."

"Then Yamada continued down the Boardwalk?"

"I don't know. I did not bother to watch the direction in which he went. When he passed me he was going down the Boardwalk."

"How far up the Boardwalk did you go, Miss La Tona?"

"To the other side of the Million Dollar Pier—then I turned around and came back."

"At seven-fifteen didn't you stop for a moment beside the chair in which Watson Gregg was sitting?"

Mercedes hesitated a moment before she spoke, and then she nodded.

"Yes, I did."

"What did you say to Mr. Gregg?"

Mercedes cast a quick glance about the room. "Is it necessary that I repeat that now?"

"It is, Miss La Tona."

"Very well. I told him that I deeply regretted that I would be unable to keep my engagement with him for that evening."

"When I first questioned you about this case you told me that you did not know Watson Gregg. Why was that, Miss La Tona?"

"The answer is quite obvious." Mercedes smiled faintly. "I did not wish to be involved in this case if I could help it. I thought it best to deny my acquaintance with Mr. Gregg."

"That was a mistake."

"I realize it now."

"Before you reached the chair, did you see anyone else about?"

"Yes, a tall man was walking down the Boardwalk. I did not recognize him. His back was toward me."

"Mr. Gregg was alive when you spoke to him?"

"He was. He assured me that my being unable to keep my engagement was quite all right."

"Will you be kind enough to tell me where you had intended meeting Mr. Gregg that night?"

"Is that necessary?"

"Yes, Miss La Tona."

"I was to be at his cottage in Ventnor at nine-thirty."

"And you did not go there?"

"I did not." Mercedes smiled. "I just told you that I broke the engagement."

"Quite so. Why did you break it, Miss La Tona?"

"I had other plans for the evening."

"I see."

To Mercedes' surprise, Blake did not appear at all interested in what she had done during the remainder of the evening. "How long have you been in Atlantic City, Miss La Tona?" he asked finally.

"About three weeks. I have been in rather poor health, and I thought a rest at the seashore advisable. I've been staying at the

Seafoam Hotel ever since I have been here." Mercedes smiled engagingly at the Captain. "But you probably know all that."

"Quite so." Blake fumbled with the papers upon the desk in front of him. "So you have been here three weeks. Do you know very many people here, Miss La Tona?"

"No. I have been rather inactive socially. As I told you, I came down here for a rest."

"Previous to that you lived in New York, did you not?"

"Yes, for a number of years."

"You knew Mr. Gregg in New York?"

"I did."

"When did he arrive in Atlantic City?"

"A few days after I did." Mercedes looked directly at the Captain. "But surely you know that as well as I do, Captain Blake."

"Granted." Blake looked quickly about the room. All of the others present had been listening intently to his cross-questioning of Mercedes La Tona. "Just how well did you know Godfrey Floss, Miss La Tona?"

Mercedes appeared slightly startled as she heard the name of the blackmailer. For the first time during the interview she was obviously nervous. She hesitated, and glanced around the room, before she answered Blake's question.

"Answer my question please, Miss La Tona. How well did you know Godfrey Floss?"

"I saw him for the first time in my life a day or so after the discovery of the murder."

"About eleven-thirty a.m. on the morning of October eighteenth, wasn't it, Miss La Tona?"

"Yes." Mercedes looked at Blake in startled surprise. "How did you know?"

"That does not matter. You met him on the beach in front of the Seafoam Hotel. You talked with him for ten or fifteen minutes, then he left you hurriedly. Isn't that true?"

"It is, Captain Blake

"Will you kindly tell me the subject of your conversation, Miss La Tona?"

"Is that necessary, Captain Blake? Our talk was purely personal."

"You just told me that you saw Mr. Floss for the first time in your life that morning. That your conversation should be of a personal nature, seems rather surprising."

"I'll grant you the point, Captain Blake. Nevertheless, it was personal, and I would prefer not to discuss it here and now."

"I'm sorry, Miss La Tona, but I must insist that you give me some inkling as to the subject under discussion at the time."

Mercedes looked at Giovanni Danton. He was sitting gazing at her, an interested expression upon his strange white face. He smiled faintly as he heard her next statement.

"We were discussing the subject of owls," she said slowly.

"Hum!" Blake had difficulty in suppressing a smile. "I would not consider owls a topic of very personal nature!"

"Mr. Floss appeared to find it so. I am afraid that he found the subject not only personal but decidedly annoying."

"Why should he have felt that way?"

"I don't know." Mercedes shook her head. "I have wondered about it myself."

"I happen to know Mr. Floss' record," said Blake slowly. "He is rather a dangerous individual. From all reports, he lives by his wits, and by prying upon the mistakes of others." The Captain's tone grew suddenly stern. "Miss La Tona, why did Godfrey Floss try to blackmail you?"

Mercedes gasped, and her face grew pale as she heard the words. She looked about her wildly, and then touched her handkerchief to her lips. For a long moment she sat staring at Blake.

"I refuse to answer that question, Captain Blake," she said finally, her voice so low that the others present had difficulty in hearing it. "I won't answer!"

"Then Godfrey Floss did attempt to blackmail you? You admit that?"

"Yes." Mercedes did not look at the Captain as she answered. "But how did you know that?"

"I didn't know it," said Blake dryly. "It was merely a supposition upon my part, based upon Mr. Floss' reputation."

"Oh!" Mercedes bit her lips, as she realized that the Captain of Detectives had been too clever for her.

"Don't you think it would he advisable for you to explain why Mr. Floss felt it possible to attempt blackmail, Miss La Tona?" said Blake. "If you don't explain, I am afraid it may be necessary to arrest you for the murder of Watson Gregg!"

"You think that—that I killed Mr. Gregg—and Mr. Floss attempted to blackmail me for that reason?" demanded Mercedes excitedly. "That's not true, Captain Blake! It's a lie, I tell you. When I last saw Mr. Gregg he was alive. I am positive of that!"

"But I am not, Miss La Tona!" abruptly Blake brought his fist down upon the desk top. "To my mind that is the only logical reason for this man's attempt to blackmail you—and you have admitted that he has made such an attempt! In order to clear yourself of very grave suspicion it is necessary that you tell me just what happened on the night of October sixteenth."

"I did tell you all that!" exclaimed Mercedes nervously.

"Oh, no you didn't! You only told me what happened up to the time that you stopped at the rolling chair in which Watson Gregg was later found murdered! Murdered, Miss La Tona—and it is up to you to convince me that you did not commit that crime!"

"All right—all right," said Mercedes hysterically. Her first thought was for herself now—as it was always when she faced danger. "I'll tell you—everything!"

"Very good!" Blake relaxed and leaned back in his chair. "What happened after you left the rolling chair that night?"

"As I said before, I had an engagement with a friend of mine. I met him a block or so away from the hotel. He suggested that I go for a drive with him in his car, and I did so."

"What was this friend's name, Miss La Tona?"

"I prefer not to mention that. I don't believe it is at all necessary."

"Very well. We shall consider that later. Did anything unusual happen during the drive?"

"Yes. While we were driving along a lonely road in the vicinity of Longport, we saw something ahead which forced my friend to stop his car abruptly."

"What was it that made him do that?"

"A dead tree had been dragged across the road in such a way that it made it impossible for us to pass. We had hardly stopped before a rough-looking man appeared from the dark trees at the side of the road. He had a club in his hand, and he roughly demanded my jewelry."

"What happened then?"

"The gentleman whom I was with, reached into the side pocket of the car and produced a revolver, with the intention of frightening the other man away. As he did so I heard the sound of a shot. I screamed, for I thought that my friend had shot the robber—"

"Why do you say that you *thought* he had shot the other man?"

"Because my friend swore that he had not fired his revolver. Later he showed me that the revolver was fully loaded—not one bullet had been fired!"

"The man who was killed before your eyes was John Hagen, the chair-pusher who had been missing when Watson Gregg was found murdered, was it not?"

"Yes. But I did not know that until a day or so later."

"Why not, Miss La Tona? The fact was mentioned in the paper the next morning."

"So I understand. As it happened, I did not read the paper. I do so very seldom."

"What happened after this shot was fired?"

"My friend got out of the car and examined Hagen. He found that he was dead. Then the gentleman whom I was with, removed the tree from the road and we drove away."

"Leaving John Hagen lying there on the road, dead? Wasn't that rather a heartless thing to do, Miss La Tona?"

"I—perhaps it was," Mercedes stammered nervously. "I realize that now. At the time I was dazed—when my friend thought it best for us to get away from the scene as quickly as possible, I did not think to protest. I—I wish I had done so now!"

"The reason for your hasty departure was that you did not wish to be implicated in the killing, I judge," said Blake calmly. "That and the fact that the gentleman you were with was a married man! Isn't that true?"

For an instant Mercedes stared at the Captain in blank amazement. Finally she nodded.

"That is quite true," she said slowly. "But I can't see how you guessed that, Captain Blake."

"I didn't guess," said the Captain with a faint smile. "From the very first moment we learned that you were involved in the murder of Watson Gregg you have been watched very closely, Miss La Tona."

"But yesterday morning when I talked to you in the hotel you promised that you would not hound me any longer!" protested Mercedes.

"That is quite true," said Blake. "I did not think it would be necessary after to-day. I hope that I am right." He looked at the actress intently. "As I have just told you, Miss La Tona, you have been watched very closely, to a greater extent than you suspect. Every telephone call which you have made during the past day or so has been recorded in shorthand by one of my men. It is not so very difficult to listen in over a hotel switchboard, you know."

"So you have had your men spying on me all the time!" Mercedes' face grew hard and cold. "I hope they found my telephone conversations interesting!" Her tone was bitter.

"Perhaps not as much so as I did the reports which I received upon the subject, Miss La Tona." Blake smiled. "Particularly your conversation with Mr. Martin Woods. That, coupled with what you have just told me, has been most interesting. I see now that Mr. Floss had a very excellent reason, to his way of thinking, for the idea of blackmail!"

"Very well!" Mercedes sighed with relief. "Then you are convinced now that I did not murder Watson Gregg?"

"I'd hardly say that as yet." Blake frowned and shook his head. "No, Miss La Tona, I am not convinced. You had every reason to hate Mr. Gregg, even though you did admit to me, when I talked with you before at the hotel, that you loved him!"

Miss Hill tittered a startled exclamation as she heard the words of the Captain. She half rose from her chair, but sank back again as Danton placed a restraining hand upon her arm. The woman who had been the wife of Watson Gregg sat there motionless, glaring at Mercedes.

"Hate him!" exclaimed Mercedes excitedly, not even noticing Miss Hill. "Why should I have felt that way? Tell me that, Captain Blake—tell me! Surely you are such a clever detective that you have learned everything about me. Everything—even my reason for hating Watson Gregg as you say that I did?"

"You really want me to tell you that?" demanded Blake. "You are sure that you would not rather have me spare you?"

"Spare me!" Mercedes laughed wildly. "How amusing that sounds, coming from you! You've hounded me and spied upon me every moment since Watson Gregg was found dead! You have accused me of the murder—"

"Oh, no I haven't, Miss La Tona! I merely said that you would force me to accuse you if you did not tell me what happened that night."

"What does it matter? You have brought me here before all these people and asked me all sorts of personal questions. And now, when you say that I might have killed Watson—the man I loved—because I hated him, you talk of sparing me! Tell me why you think I hated him, Captain Blake—go on, tell me. Go on!"

"All right, I will tell you!" Blake's face grew stern. "I tried to make things easier for you, Miss La Tona—but you wouldn't let me! Now I am going to tell you the truth. You hated Watson Gregg because you knew that he was tired of you! For two years you were his common-law wife, but he grew tired of you as he has of a number of women during his lifetime. Someone else had taken his fancy—"

"It's a lie—I won't have you say such things!"

"Oh yes, you will, Miss La Tona," said Blake impatiently. "I know that you were to meet Watson Gregg at the cottage which he had rented in Ventnor. You were to meet him on the night that he was found murdered. Probably you know as well as I do that on that day he had fifty thousand dollars in cash sent down to him from his bank in New York—"

"Fifty thousand dollars!" exclaimed Mercedes.

"Yes; and he intended to offer you that money to leave him alone for the rest of his life!"

"That's not true!"

"It is true, Miss La Tona, and I can prove it!" Blake glared at the woman. "You had every motive to kill Watson Gregg, and I am not so sure you did not do it!"

Mercedes did not answer. She buried her head in her hands, and her sobs came loudly through the grim silence of the Council Chamber.

25

"PLAIN BROWN LEATHER"

FOR A FEW MOMENTS no one spoke. Finally Mercedes ceased her sobbing and looked at Blake. She brushed the tears from her eyes as she did so. "Are you through questioning me now?" she asked nervously.

"Yes, Miss La Tona," the Captain answered. "That will be all at present. However, I must ask you to remain here until I have talked to the others involved in this affair. I'm sorry, but it is necessary."

Mercedes merely nodded as she rose unsteadily from her chair in front of Blake's desk. She did not look at the others present as she moved slowly across the room and took another chair. She had taken a place that was remote from the rest, and yet her position was such that she could clearly hear all that the Captain might ask his next witness.

Dave Morton sat studying the actress without her realizing that he was doing so. The reporter was mentally going over the cross-questioning which he had just heard. He was not at all convinced that Mercedes La Tona's motives had been strong enough for her to have killed Gregg, though he was willing to admit that Blake's case against her had been a good one.

Both Lannon and Miss Hill were extremely nervous now. The extensive questioning which they had just heard the actress go through, had made them fear that it might be their turn next. They did not know what the Captain might suspect or surmise, and they were both sure that the interview would be difficult.

Giovanni Danton appeared quite calm and serene. He had listened to the questioning of Mercedes La Tona with great interest—and once or twice Morton had noticed that the white-faced man had smiled to himself as though he had found the interview amusing.

Larry Benson had known that Lannon was worried. His first thought was of the girl, and now he tried to comfort her all that he could. From time to time they had talked together in low tones—and Lannon seemed to find his presence reassuring.

Patrolman Hayes and Flannigan and the other detectives who stood at the door had listened stolidly to all which had occurred. The investigation was merely a matter of duty to them. They did not seem to have the slightest personal interest in the questioning of the various witnesses in the Gregg case.

Miss Hill's old colored servant, Loona, had listened eagerly. At times she had nodded her head wisely as though she thought that she knew all about it. It was with surprise that Larry realized the old negress had not uttered her uncanny cackle once during the interview.

Captain Blake gazed about the room as though deciding whom he wished to question next. He stared at Miss Hill for an instant, and then he looked at Danton. The latter half rose from his chair as he caught the Captain's gaze upon him.

Blake smiled faintly and turned his eyes toward Lannon and Larry.

"Mr. Benson," he called, "come here, please."

Larry smiled at Lannon as he rose and moved toward Blake's desk.

"Sit down, Mr. Benson." The Captain motioned to the chair which Mercedes La Tona had just left a few moments ago.

Larry dropped into the chair and sat there gazing at Blake, an earnest expression upon his good-looking young face that still bore the marks of his battle with Godfrey Floss. He waited for the Captain to speak.

"You were on the Boardwalk at six-forty on the night of October sixteenth, were you not, Mr. Benson?"

"Yes, sir, I was, as I believe you know, Captain Blake."

"Why were you on the Boardwalk at that time?"

"I was looking for Miss Gordon."

"You knew that she had gone for a chair ride with Mr. Gregg?"

"I did. I had stopped at the hotel in which Mr. Gregg was staying in the hope of finding Miss Gordon there. I knew that she had planned dining with Mr. Gregg that evening."

"And you learned at the hotel that they had left in a rolling chair?"

"Yes, sir."

"Why were you so anxious to find Miss Gordon at the time? You knew that she had an engagement with Mr. Gregg."

"I would rather not answer that question, Captain Blake."

"Very well. Where was Mr. Gregg's rolling chair when you first saw it that evening?"

"Parked near the outer rail of the Boardwalk in the same position that you found it later."

"Did you go close to the chair when you first discovered it?"

"No, sir. I sat on a bench a short distance away."

"You knew who was in the chair at the time?"

"I did not. I learned that later."

"Miss Gordon was in the chair at the time?'

Larry hesitated for an instant before he answered. Finally he nodded.

"Yes, sir—she was."

"Is it true that she got out of the chair crying and apparently very much excited about something?"

"Yes, it is, Captain Blake—and she told you the reason for her agitation." Larry's eyes flashed. "If I had known the cause of her distress I would have made trouble for Watson Gregg!"

"Rather a reckless statement, Mr. Benson," said Blake, and then he smiled. "Though I don't know that I would blame you. What happened after Miss Gordon got out of the chair?"

"She hurried off the Boardwalk. I started to speak to Gregg, and then decided that I would follow her and try to learn what was wrong first."

"Did you follow her?"

"Yes, sir, but when I reached the street I found that she had vanished. I went all the way from the Boardwalk to Pacific Avenue and back looking for her. I have learned since that she heard someone following her and hid."

"How long do you think it took you to go from the Boardwalk to Pacific Avenue and back?"

"I don't know. Less than five minutes, I judge. As you know, that is rather a long block."

"Then it was possible for someone else to have stopped at the rolling chair during your absence?"

"Quite possible." Larry nodded. "In fact, I am sure that someone must have stopped at the rolling chair during that time."

"Why?"

"Because Mr. Gregg was alive when Miss Gordon left the chair, and he was dead when I returned to the Boardwalk."

"That seems probable." Blake nodded thoughtfully as he leaned back in his chair. "Why didn't you tell me about Miss Gordon's having been in the chair when I questioned you before?"

"Because I hoped that she would not be implicated in the murder," answered Larry slowly. "I was sure that she was not guilty, and I hoped that you would find the real criminal before it would be necessary to question her."

"Are you so positive that you were not just a bit doubtful as to the part which she played in this affair?" asked Blake. "I've watched you closely, Mr. Benson—and you have been greatly worried ever since the night that you and Mr. Danton and Doctor Fulda found Mr. Gregg in the chair. Deep in your heart you have feared that Miss Gordon—" the Captain smiled faintly—"the girl you love, was involved in this affair to a greater extent than you knew about. Isn't that true?"

"I guess so." Larry uttered the words slowly and then nodded. "Yes, you are right, Captain Blake. I did know something was wrong—but I do love Miss Gordon, and I have all the faith in the world in her. The fact that she left the rolling chair frightened and crying, has worried me. But it doesn't now, for she has explained the reason for her state of agitation! Watson Gregg was alive when Lannon—when Miss Gordon left the chair."

"How did you happen to visit Miss Hill's residence upon the following evening?"

"I received a telephone message from Miss Hill inviting me there for dinner that night. I accepted, of course."

"Had you ever met Miss Hill before?"

"No, but I knew that she was Miss Gordon's Aunt."

"And you knew that Miss Gordon was staying there?"

"No." Larry smiled and glanced at Lannon who was listening nervously. "But I hoped so!"

"Did anything unusual occur during the evening that you spent at Miss Hill's home?"

Miss Hill and Lannon looked at each other anxiously—and for the first time old Loona uttered a shrill cackle.

"Not in the least," answered Larry quietly. "It was a very enjoyable evening."

Blake frowned as though he doubted Benson's statement, but his next question seemed to indicate that he had dismissed the subject from his mind.

"How long have you known Giovanni Danton, Mr. Benson?"

"The first time I ever saw him was on the night of the murder."

"And since then?"

"What do you mean?"

"You only saw him on the Boardwalk that night?"

"No, I have seen him a number of times since then." Larry looked at Blake. "Miss Gordon has told you that Mr. Danton arrived at a very opportune moment when I fought Godfrey Floss in the cabin down in Longport."

"That's true. But before that? Haven't you seen Mr. Danton at any other time?"

"Yes, sir. I saw him on the beach on the second night after the murder."

"What was he doing on the beach?"

"He was walking with Miss La Tona."

"Oh, was he?" An expression of interest passed over Blake's countenance. "What happened when you met them?"

"Mr. Danton introduced me to Miss La Tona, and asked me to take her to her hotel."

"Why was that?"

"I don't know. Mr. Danton said that he had an interview with a certain gentleman in mind, that must take place at once. He told me to look for him later."

"And did you do so?"

"Yes. I found him under the Steel Pier."

"Had the interview which he mentioned taken place?"

"I don't know. Mr. Danton did not say." Larry hesitated, and it was quite evident that he was debating whether he should say anything further.

Captain Blake sensed the fact, and in doing so asked a leading question.

"Did you and Mr. Danton find anything unusual under the pier?"

"Yes, we did," answered Larry slowly. "We found Mr. Gregg's Japanese servant, Tahira—and he had been nearly strangled to death with a leather thong—just as Mr. Gregg was murdered!"

There were muttered exclamations from the others in the room as they heard Benson's words. This was something new and startling. Then the Japanese had nearly met his death in the same way as had his employer!

Morton looked at Benson with added interest. The reporter had felt that up to the present time the questioning of the boy had not been very exciting. Now he realized that Benson had a new angle on the case—and it was one worth a good bit of thought and consideration, Morton was quite sure.

"So Tahira was found under the pier with a leather thong about his neck," said Blake. "Was it the same sort of saffron cord that was found about Mr. Gregg's throat?"

"Not quite the same," answered Larry. "Saffron is rather a yellow color, isn't it?"

"Yes," Blake nodded.

"I thought so. This cord was made of plain brown leather it seemed to me, though I did not examine it after Mr. Danton removed it from Tahira's neck."

"Then Mr. Danton was the one who found the Japanese?"

"No, sir, I did. I stumbled over him as Mr. Danton and I were walking out from under the pier."

"Mr. Danton was under the pier before you arrived?"

"He was."

"Then it would have been possible for him to have attempted to garrote Tahira?"

"It might have been," said Larry slowly, the thought of Danton's white hands as he played with the leather thong returning to his mind; "but I don't believe he did it."

"What did Mr. Danton say when you discovered Tahira?"

"I didn't quite understand him. I asked him who he thought had tried to kill the Jap, and he said that it was probably the result of the too freely discussed subject of owls!"

"Owls again!" exclaimed Blake excitedly. "I've heard so much about those damn birds since this case started that I'm likely to start hooting at any moment. What the devil have owls to do with it, anyway?"

"I don't know. I just repeated what Mr. Danton said. A short while after that Tahira recovered, and then he and Mr. Danton started to talk about owls!"

"And still more owls!" snorted the Captain. "Of all the fool subjects for grown men to talk about, that's just about the worst. Forget about the owls, Mr. Benson. What else happened?"

"As we were standing there, this Godfrey Floss appeared. He questioned Mr. Danton and wanted to know what we were all doing under the pier."

"What did Mr. Danton tell him?"

"He said that he and Tahira had been practicing their vocal lesson."

"Doing what?" demanded Blake with a frown.

"Practicing their vocal lesson," Larry smiled.

"Then what happened?"

"Mr. Danton hooted like an owl and Tahira echoed the sound."

"Oh, they did, eh?" exclaimed Captain Blake. It was evident that he was beginning to see a light upon the troublesome subject of owls. "I see." The Captain glanced at Danto, who sat listening, an expression of interest upon his face. "What did Floss do then?"

"He started to draw a gun, but Mr. Danton warned him not to do so as he had him covered from his pocket."

"And then what?"

"Then Mr. Floss went away. Mr. Danton said he was afraid that Floss jumped too readily to conclusions."

"What did he mean by that?"

"I don't know—only Mr. Danton said that he really must buy himself an automatic, that it might prove useful."

"Huh! So Danton bluffed Floss—is that it?"

"Yes," Larry nodded. "I am quite sure of it. But Mr. Danton had an automatic when he appeared at the cabin yesterday. I guess he must have bought one since that night on the beach."

Larry looked at Danton. The latter smiled and nodded as though confirming the other's statement.

"Mr. Benson," said Blake abruptly, "wasn't Mr. Danton at Miss Hill's residence on the night you were there for dinner?"

"Why—yes, he was," said Larry slowly.

"I thought so. Did he have dinner there that night?"

"No, sir. He arrived later in the evening." Larry grew suddenly nervous. He did not want to tell what had happened during that weird dinner party at Miss Hill's old house, yet he feared that Blake might make him do so. "Please, Captain Blake, I have already told you all that I know about this case. Won't you let me stop answering questions now?"

"Not yet, Mr. Benson," said Blake. "I'm afraid that you don't quite realize the seriousness of this affair so far as you personally are concerned."

"So far as I'm concerned?" Larry was startled; he looked at the Captain of Detectives anxiously. "What do you mean?"

Blake did not speak for a few seconds. He sat looking down at the papers on the desk in front of him. The Captain was an old and clever hand at the game of cross-questioning. He realized that there was nothing which created a greater aspect of suspense than silence at times when an answer to a question was vital to the person most concerned.

Larry watched him, and in doing so he grew more nervous. The fear that something which he had said might have implicated Lannon more deeply, lingered in his mind. Not only that, but he now realized that he might have drawn the noose of guilt closer about Miss Hill. He hoped that such was not the case, but he could not be sure that Blake had not found something which might point to Lannon's Aunt as the one who had committed the murder in what had been said.

As for the Captain's intimation that Benson himself might be more deeply involved than he realized, Larry considered that only vaguely. The remark had made no real impression upon his mind.

"I'm afraid I don't understand, Captain Blake," he said, after waiting what seemed an interminable time for the detective to speak. "Won't you please explain?"

"All right, I will. You admitted that you saw Miss Gordon get out of the rolling chair in which Watson Gregg was later found murdered. You also insist that Mr. Gregg was not dead at the time. You have stated that you would have made trouble for Gregg if you had known what he had said to Miss Gordon—"

"That's true!" interrupted Larry. "And I would have done so—if I had known. You said yourself that you would not have blamed me!"

"Perhaps I did say that." Blake frowned grimly. "But I did not say that the fact would excuse you, if it were to be proven that you were the one who murdered Watson Gregg!"

"But—but that's impossible!" exclaimed Larry. "I didn't do it, Captain Blake. I didn't even know that he was dead until Mr. Danton and Doctor Fulda told me so!"

"That's what you say!" said Blake sharply. "But you must not forget one thing, Mr. Benson! That is, that you have admitted you were alone on the Boardwalk for a few moments after Miss Gordon left the chair. You knew that Gregg had done something which had frightened and offended the girl you love. I only have your own statement in regard to your having left the Boardwalk, Mr. Benson. When Doctor Fulda passed a few minutes later, you were still on the Boardwalk—and you were standing near the rolling chair then." The Captain brought his fist down upon the desk in that gesture which all of those in the room had already learned to dread. "You might have killed Watson Gregg, you might have done it, Larry Benson! Mind you, I don't say that you did—but I do say that you might have done so—and you did have a motive!"

Larry frowned, and his face turned pale. He merely sat there gazing at the Captain. He realized it would be useless for him to try to say anything further.

26
TIME AND MOTIVE

AT A WORD OF DISMISSAL from Captain Blake, Larry rose and moved
over to the chair in which he had been sitting beside Lannon.
Blake's final words had come as a shock, but his fight with Floss
had changed Larry. It had made him a man in situations in which
he had acted the part of a youth before. He realized that the Captain had intimated that he might be guilty of the murder. It was
something which he had not even considered before, and now, after the first reaction of the Captain's words, Larry had again grown
confident and sure of himself.

His attitude showed in the way that he smiled at the girl he
loved. He leaned over and spoke to her softly.

"Don't you worry, honey," he said in an undertone. "Everything
is going to be all right."

"Oh, Larry," whispered Lannon, her eyes upon his face
adoringly, "you were just—just noble, that's all. I know that I'm
going to be scared to death when he questions me! You are sure
everything is going to be all right?"

"Of course, dear." Larry was still smiling. "And you must be
brave, Lannon!"

She nodded—and they drew apart as they realized that Captain
Blake was gazing at them thoughtfully. Lannon waited fearfully
for Blake's next words. She was positive that he intended to question her now, and she was afraid that when he did so she would
make things difficult for her Aunt.

Lannon still wore a scarf about her slender throat, and faint red marks that had been caused during that mad moment when her Aunt had choked her, still remained. Explanations would be hard to make—she knew that the Captain's eyes were keen.

To the surprise of all Blake did not call upon any of those present at the moment. He turned in the direction of the door and beckoned to Flannigan. The stout detective came at once to the Captain's side. Blake muttered a few words in an undertone. Flannigan merely nodded to show that he understood, and then left the room.

Blake turned again to those who had not as yet been questioned. He glanced from one to the other, and then back again. He seemed to be having difficulty in making up his mind as to the next witness which he would call before him.

Morton glanced at his watch. It was now after eleven-thirty. Blake had taken over an hour to question Mercedes La Tona and Larry Benson. The reporter felt that the time had been well spent—there were a number of things which had been vague in his mind, and had now assumed much clearer proportions. Morton realized that Blake not only desired to learn the identity of the murderer—if he did not already know just who that person was—but also every possible detail of the case. In this the reporter was in accordance with the Captain. His training had been to get all the facts—and it was on this method that Blake now seemed to be working.

"Mr. Danton!" called Blake finally. "Come here, please!"

Danton rose slowly to his feet and moved toward the chair in front of the Captain's desk. He sat there without the slightest suggestion from Blake that he do so. His deep, intense eyes were fixed upon the head of the Detective Bureau—and as Blake started to speak he smiled faintly, that strange smile of his that never reached his eyes.

"Please, Captain Blake," he said in his deep, rolling tones, "let's not begin with these rather childish questions regarding my whereabouts upon the night of October sixteenth."

"Just as you wish, Mr. Danton." Blake's eyes twinkled, though his face was serious. "The actor in the quaint drama of life now has the stage!"

"Thank you," said Danton with a nod. "But if you don't mind I would rather wait until Detective Flannigan returns from the little mission upon which you just sent him. If I am not mistaken—and I am so seldom, Captain—my recital will be much more interesting then!"

"Then you think you know why I just sent Flannigan out of the room?" demanded Blake, looking at Danton intently. "I wonder if you really do?"

"Frankly, I don't," said Danton. He waved one white hand, and the motion was exceedingly expressive. "But I have hopes." He glanced at the door. "Ah, I see my hopes have been doubly granted!"

Flannigan had reentered the room, and beside him walked Tahira Yamada. Behind them came another detective, and with him was Godfrey Floss.

Morton's jaw sagged as he saw the two prisoners. For the first time in his career the reporter was startled out of his usual rather cynical calm. That the police would be able to bring in those two men in such short order, was what the reporter had least expected. Impulsively he rose and moved to Blake.

"Where did you find them, Jerry?" he demanded excitedly.

"Never mind that now, Dave." Blake frowned and shook his head. "Maybe you have not realized it, but since this thing started, the police, my department in particular, have been on their toes."

"What's the idea in placing me under arrest?" snarled Floss as he came closer to the Captain's desk.

"Idea!" exclaimed Danton. "It's a positive inspiration upon the part of Captain Blake!"

Blake merely grunted, but he seemed pleased at Danton's statement. The Captain motioned the two detectives to take Tahira and Floss to a group of chairs which were near by. Flannigan and the other man obeyed. The four sat there watching and listening as Blake turned to Danton.

"Now, Mr. Danton, please proceed."

"Certainly." Again Danton smiled his weird smile. "First, in order that you will not find it necessary to ask the question, I was on the Boardwalk at the time of the murder."

"And your reason for being there?"

"As I believe I informed you once before, I love to stroll amid the tranquil stillness of the nocturnal hours."

"Did you murder Watson Gregg?" barked Blake abruptly.

"No!" Danton's answer was just as abruptly given.

"I don't believe you," said Blake firmly.

"Good—I like a man who forms an opinion and sticks to it." Danton shook his head. "But I am afraid that you are not working in your usual way, Captain. You have voiced a number of leading questions that have built up a charming array of motives with the two other witnesses you have just talked to. Don't you think you had better do the same thing with me? I like motives; the police are so good at digging up a lot of circumstantial evidence."

"Never mind about motives," remarked Blake, "or lectures upon your opinions of the police, for that matter. You've thought that I and my men were a bunch of half-wits ever since the case started."

"Oh, Captain Blake, you wrong me! When you did not arrest me on the night of the murder, my respect for you went up at least a hundred per cent. I was so obviously in wrong. I was on the Boardwalk at the time that Watson Gregg was murdered. I'll grant you that being on the Boardwalk in Atlantic City is just about the same as saying that a man was on Broadway at a certain time. There is so much of both to cover—and my merely being on the Boardwalk that night really doesn't prove such an awful lot."

"I'm not so sure about that!" said Blake.

"Of course not, but still you get my point. However, I have admitted that I was in the vicinity of the murder. Considering the fact that Benson, Doctor Fulda and I were the only ones who found Mr. Gregg, for me to deny that I was there would be the height of folly!" Danton looked at the Captain, and as he did so his expression grew serious. "When was Doctor Fulda murdered, by the way?"

Blake glared at Danton. The tall pale-faced man had trumped one of Blake's best cards when he asked the question. None of those present as yet knew that Doctor Fulda was dead. The Captain had even prevailed upon Morton to keep the news from his newspaper. The reporter had been very reluctant to do so, for he had realized that it was not ethical, and besides, if those above him learned that he had suppressed such an important bit of information, he would probably lose his job. It had only been upon the promise of Blake that the Gregg case would be solved today, that Morton had finally consented to withhold the news.

"How do you know that Doctor Fulda has been murdered?" demanded Blake.

"I don't know it." Danton smiled again. "Really, Captain, do you think I would admit such a thing? Fortunately, my usual facility to be in the vicinity when things happen, failed me this time. It is just as well. I appear quite involved in this affair as it is now. To arrive at the scene of a murder just after it had happened three times in succession might be bad luck."

"What do you mean by 'three times'?"

"You know very well what I mean, but I shall tell you if you insist. I found Watson Gregg—with the others, of course. I just happened to be strolling through the woods when you came across John Hagen—and I wasn't there when you found Doctor Fulda."

"I haven't admitted that we found him at all. I haven't even said that he was dead."

"Of course not. But he isn't here, Captain—and everyone that is in any way connected with the case is present. Even the policeman who was standing two blocks away. If you could have produced the physician of the late Mr. Gregg you would have done so. I am quite sure of that!"

"How do you know that I won't produce him before this investigation is over?" demanded Blake.

"I certainly hope you do," said Danton. "It will revive my faith in miracles!"

"You seem quite certain that Doctor Fulda is dead, for one who claims to know nothing about it."

"I seem to have blundered again." Danton sighed. "I'm afraid I became carried away by my interest in the little game of guessing. You know, Captain Blake, I don't believe I have ever met a detective who is quite as clever at that same game as you are. You hit the bull's-eye nine times out of ten. It is a pleasure to watch you work."

"Thank you, Mr. Danton." The Captain's tone was mocking. "You are very flattering to my vanity. . . . How well did you know Watson Gregg?" demanded Blake, changing his tone abruptly.

"I've known of him for at least fifteen years," said Danton calmly; "yet I never spoke to the man."

"You had a very good reason for wishing him dead, did you not?"

"Certainly, one of the best. I may as well admit that now, Captain—if I don't you will think of one before this interview is over."

"I don't need to think of one," remarked Blake calmly. "I know your motive already. It is because Watson Gregg wronged the woman who had always meant everything in life to you, Giovanni Danton!"

"That's true," said Danton slowly. "And my hearing you make that statement only increases my respect for you, Captain Blake. I did have a motive for killing Gregg. There has been so much bitterness in my heart against him that I was glad when I found him— dead. You may have sensed that hatred by something which I could not make myself do at the time—something which would have been my first impulse if it had been anyone else but Watson Gregg in that rolling chair."

"And what was that something, Mr. Danton?"

"It was to attempt to loosen the saffron cord—that leather thong that was drawn tight about the neck. You noticed that I did not do so, of course?"

"I did—and I have wondered about it since then."

"I thought so. But there is one other thing in connection with the subject of the saffron cord which may not have occurred to you, Captain Blake."

"You mean the fact that Doctor Fulda also made no effort to loosen the thong when you three men found Gregg?"

"Yes, that's it," said Danton, and he appeared just a bit surprised. "I disliked Doctor Fulda intensely from the first moment I saw him. He struck me as rather a treacherous individual, and those hard eyes of his were—well, there was something dangerous in their depths."

"Then you think that Doctor Fulda might have killed Mr. Gregg?"

"No, not if he is dead now, and you have led me to believe that is the truth about the Doctor, Captain Blake."

"I have not said anything of the sort!" exclaimed Blake.

"It hasn't been necessary for you to say so. As I told you before, if it were possible for you to produce the physician you would do so by now. You haven't revived my faith in miracles as yet!"

"Never mind about that now!" said the Captain impatiently. "Why do you think that Doctor Fulda did not remove the saffron cord from Mr. Gregg's neck?"

"Because the Doctor hated his patient—I am sure of that. From what I know about the case, Larry Benson was standing on the walk a short distance from the rolling chair. He heard someone approaching, turned and found that it was Fulda. The Doctor went at once to the chair, looked in and saw Gregg with the leather thong drawn tight about his throat. Then it was that Doctor Fulda should have removed the saffron cord. Perhaps if he had done so Watson Gregg would still have been alive." Danton's eyes flamed, and his fingers tightened unconsciously. "I am glad that Doctor Fulda hated his patient!"

Blake did not speak. He was going swiftly through the papers upon the desk in front of him. Danton sat waiting patiently for the Captain's next move.

During the lull in the questioning of Danton the reporter glanced about the room. It was in the two latest arrivals that Morton was most interested. Godfrey Floss sat between Flannigan and the detective who had brought the blackmailer into the room. The Japanese sat on the opposite side of the stout detective. Both Floss and Tahira were quite calm and serene to all outward appearances. They were watching Danton and Captain Blake. They had listened intently to all that had been said.

Once or twice Tahira had glanced in the direction of Mercedes La Tona. Morton was sure that the servant of Watson Gregg wondered if the actress had been questioned as yet. There was no way of Tahira having learned such was the case.

Godfrey Floss had not looked once toward the woman he had attempted to blackmail. He seemed to be avoiding her gaze as though he feared the woman.

"Now, Mr. Danton," said Blake finally, "I want to ask you a number of very important questions. And I don't want the answers to be long-winded evasions!"

"Naturally not, Captain," said Danton, with his strange smile appearing upon his face for an instant. "Evasions clutter up the wheels of justice and all that sort of thing. Proceed with your questions—I shall try to answer them to the best of my ability."

"Very well. You admit that you were on the Boardwalk and in the vicinity of the scene of the crime on the night of October sixteenth, do you not?"

"I do."

"Just where were you then, Mr. Danton?"

"I was sitting in the little pavilion located about half a block from where the rolling chair stood. I saw the chair-pusher, John Hagen, park the chair in the spot where it stood all during the remainder of the evening."

"Oh, you did! Then you know where John Hagen went after he left the chair?"

"Yes. He walked away slowly, and finally went down the steps which lead off the Boardwalk and onto the beach. A few seconds later Mr. Benson appeared. He was walking swiftly, and frowning as though worried about something. He sat down on a bench."

"How long did he remain there?"

"Not very long—probably two or three minutes at the most. Then I saw Miss Gordon suddenly step out of the chair. She was frightened and crying, as you already know."

"Did Mr. Benson follow Miss Gordon as he had already stated?"

"He did, after hesitating for a moment and gazing toward the chair as though debating whether to speak to Gregg first."

"But he did not approach the chair at the time, Mr. Danton?"

"No, he did not. He left the Boardwalk hurriedly."

"What did you do then?"

"I remained sitting in the pavilion."

"Did anyone else approach the chair during the time that Mr. Benson was off the Boardwalk?"

"Yes, three people, as you know. So far I am afraid that your questions appear to be mostly reiteration, Captain Blake."

"Not necessarily," said Blake drily. "You failed to tell me that you were sitting in the pavilion before." He changed his tone. "Can you tell me who the three people were that stopped at the chair?"

"The first was a tall man. He appeared to be on very friendly terms, for I heard them laugh heartily—at least the tall man laughed."

"Who was this tall man?"

"It was Godfrey Floss!"

The blackmailer snarled as he heard Danton's words. The latter glanced at him and smiled, then turned again to Blake.

"You are positive?"

"Quite positive. I saw his face clearly." Danton looked at the Captain. "You'll grant it is a countenance which one would remember!"

Blake nodded.

"Do you know where Mr. Floss went after he left the rolling chair?"

"He disappeared in a dark doorway of a shop which was already closed for the evening a little farther down the Boardwalk."

"Why do you think he did that?"

"I'm not at all positive about it, but I think he had decided to watch Mr. Gregg's chair for some reason."

"I see. And did you recognize the second person who stopped at the chair?"

"Not at the time. I merely knew it was a woman. I have since learned it was Miss La Tona, of course."

"Had you met Miss La Tona at any time previous to the murder, Mr. Danton?"

"I had not. It was not until a day or so later that I first spoke to her."

"Why did you do that?"

"I was anxious to try and learn her connection with the case."

"Did you do so?"

"Yes, to a certain extent. But really, Captain, I am growing a bit weary of all these questions. They take up so much time. Suppose I tell my story in my own way—and supply all further details later."

"Go ahead!" Blake leaned back in his chair, and sat watching the pale-faced man closely.

"I did not know that Miss La Tona was the second person who stopped at the chair, because she was wearing a veil and I could not see her face clearly. At the time I would not have recognized her anyway, for I had never seen her before.

"Miss La Tona said a few words to Mr. Gregg. At least she looked into the chair, and I judged that she was talking to him. Now I am not so positive about that."

"Why not?"

"Because during the time that both Mr. Floss and Miss La Tona paused at the rolling chair they might have placed the saffron cord about his throat and drawn it tight!"

"Oh!" the sudden exclamation came from Mercedes La Tona who had been listening tensely to every word which had been said. "He lies! I did not do it—I did not!"

"Silence, please, Miss La Tona!" commanded Blake sharply. "I am interviewing Mr. Danton now! Proceed, Mr. Danton. Where did Miss La Tona go after she left the chair?"

"She continued down the Boardwalk in the direction of the Seafoam Hotel."

"And the third person who stopped at the chair?" Danton hesitated before he answered.

"It was a woman," said Danton slowly. "I do not know who she was!"

"Why not? You saw her, didn't you, Mr. Danton?"

"Yes, but she, too, was wearing a veil."

"What happened after she left the chair?"

"She continued down the Boardwalk. When she reached the doorway of the shop in which Mr. Floss had disappeared, he stepped out and spoke to her." Danton looked again at Floss, who was glaring at him angrily. "His sudden appearance evidently startled her, for she leaped back as though she was frightened. He said something to her—and then she handed him something and hurried on up the Boardwalk."

"What was it that she handed him? Do you know?"

"No, I do not," said Danton. "But I had a vague impression that it might have been money."

"Money!" exclaimed Blake. "You mean you think this woman tried to bribe Mr. Floss for some reason?"

"That might have been what happened."

"Where did Mr. Floss go then?"

"He went down the steps to the beach, the same steps that John Hagen had descended a short while previous."

"Did he remain on the beach?"

"I judge so," answered Danton. "I did not see him again, nor did I see Hagen—that was why I told you that the chair-pusher was missing. A moment later Larry Benson came back on the Board-walk, and at the same time Doctor Fulda appeared." There was a very thoughtful expression upon the pale face of the man who was being questioned. "It would be very interesting to know just where Doctor Fulda was previous to that time."

"The rest of the story from that point we know," said Blake; "at least up until the time that you left me after I questioned you there on the Boardwalk. What did you do after that, Mr. Danton?"

"Really, Captain, do you mean to say that one of your men has not been shadowing me ever since then?" Danton appeared to be sincerely surprised. "I supposed of course that would be the first thing you would order done."

"As it happened, it wasn't. I was working on a little different theory so far as you were concerned, Mr. Danton."

"You intrigue me. What was that theory, if I may ask?"

"That if you give a man enough rope he will hang himself," said the Captain. "And I have given you so much since this case started, Mr. Danton. Have you stopped to consider that you are about the same height as Mr. Floss? We only have your own statement to prove that you were sitting in the pavilion during all that time."

"Oh, pretty—beautiful!" exclaimed Danton. "Up to your old tricks again, eh, Captain? The question of motives, evidence and what-not. I told you how the police loved to produce a lot of cir-cumstantial evidence—and I judge you have gathered plenty of it where I am concerned."

"That is true, and there are a number of things which you have failed to explain as yet, Mr. Danton!"

"For instance?"

"What were you doing out in the Margate Woods upon the night of the murder? And what is all this foolishness about owls?"

"I knew you would get to that in time, Captain." Danton shook his head in mock sadness. "It's no use—you think of everything!"

"And if you knew what I was thinking at the present time, Mr. Danton—" began Blake.

"But I do. You think that I am guilty of the murder of Watson Gregg. Really, Captain Blake! You have thought everyone you've questioned was guilty—and that isn't possible!"

"It is your guilt that I am concerned about at the present time, Mr. Danton," said Blake. "Never mind about the others. If you want to clear yourself you had better answer my question. What were you doing in the woods on the night of the murder?"

"Captain Blake," said Danton slowly, "I realize just as well as you do that I am deeply implicated in this affair. In order to have any hope of clearing myself, I must try and explain all of my actions since the time that Watson Gregg was found murdered."

"You certainly must, Mr. Danton," said Blake.

"I flatter myself to be a good enough judge of human nature to feel that you have already picked some certain individual as the real murderer. You have some real reason of your own for all this browbeating. I don't doubt that when the time comes you will be able to prove the person's guilt very conclusively!"

"That may or may not be so, Mr. Danton," remarked the Captain. "However, I must insist that you dispense with generalities and get to the answer of the question which I asked you a few seconds ago. What were you doing in the Margate Woods that night?"

"After you had finished questioning me at the rolling chair that evening, I returned to the scene of the crime. Be sure and note that fact, Captain. I believe that criminals are supposed to display a tendency to return to the spot where their evil deeds took place! Anyway, I went back to the Boardwalk and to the spot where the rolling chair had stood."

"Was there anyone about at the time?"

"Merely the usual passers-by. No one so far as I know that was in any way connected with the murder. I wandered about aimlessly for a few minutes and found nothing at all of interest. Finally, as I was just about to depart, the face of a man who was passing caught my gaze—"

"Who was that man?"

"It was Godfrey Floss, Captain." Danton made an expressive gesture. "And I must again ask you to consider the supposition that a criminal—a murderer in particular—finds it difficult to resist the impulse to return to the scene of his crime."

"Look here, Captain Blake!" protested Floss as he heard Danton's words. "Are you going to let this man accuse me of murder without permitting me to say a word on my own behalf?"

"Silence, please, Mr. Floss," said Blake with an impatient wave of his hand. "I'll hear your side of the story later. Mr. Danton is being questioned now."

"I know that Mr. Floss is not unwilling to do anything, even to committing murder, if he feels that it would be to his own advantage to do so!" stated Danton slowly and coldly.

Floss again started to speak, but Flannigan placed his hand warningly upon the man's arm, and the blackmailer lapsed into sullen and angry silence.

"What do you mean by that statement, Mr. Danton?"

"Just this: On the night of the murder I followed Mr. Floss to the Margate Woods without him realizing that I was doing so. I hid in the brush beside the road." Danton's eyes gleamed. "Merely upon impulse I hooted once in what I believe was a fairly good imitation of an owl. To my surprise, the call was echoed by another hoot which sounded exceedingly human!"

Tahira was listening interestedly now, a faint, amused smile on his face. Danton glanced at him and he, too, smiled.

"So that's what all this business about owls has meant?" said Blake. "Go on, Mr. Danton—and then what?"

"Then John Hagen appeared from out of the brush a short distance away from where I was hiding. Previous to that, Mr. Floss had ignited a match in order to light a cigarette as he was crouched amid the undergrowth on the opposite side of the road. He put the cigarette out very quickly when he heard the hooting of the owls. I suspect that he must have sensed there was something just a bit unnatural in the sounds."

"Go on please, Mr. Danton," said Blake as the other paused.

"Then Hagen dragged out an old, dead tree and placed it across the road. Miss La Tona told you the rest of the story of what happened after that."

"She did, but she insists that the man whom she was with did not fire his revolver. Is that true, Mr. Danton?"

"I have reason to believe so, Captain. When Hagen approached the car he did have a club in his hand. I strongly suspect that his main object had been to force someone to drive him out of this part of the country as quickly as possible—for all I know the man may have had a police record, and realized that things would prove difficult for him if he was mixed up in the murder."

"We have investigated. John Hagen did have a record—he was a bad egg. But you say that the man in the car did not shoot him. Then just who did kill Hagen?"

"It was Godfrey Floss," said Danton. He swung around in his chair so that he faced the blackmailer, pointing a long, white finger in the direction of the other man. "That man there is the one who killed John Hagen!"

"How do you know?" demanded the Captain.

"Because just before Hagen fell I heard the bark of an automatic and saw a flash of flame coming from the spot where Floss was hiding!"

"You damn liar!" shouted Floss, starting to leap from his seat— only to be drawn roughly back again. "You're smooth—smooth as hell—but you are only shielding yourself. I know that you murdered Watson Gregg, and you are trying to throw the blame on me. Don't let him get away with it, Captain Blake! Make him prove that he did not kill Hagen himself because the chair-pusher knew too much about the murder!"

"Keep quiet!" growled Flannigan, shaking Floss roughly. "The Captain said you could do your talking later!"

"Have I convinced you that I am telling you the truth?" asked Danton calmly.

"No!" roared Blake, bringing his fist down upon the desk. "You've told just the sort of clever and well-concocted story I thought you would tell! To my mind you come very close to being guilty, Mr. Danton. You had plenty of time to murder Watson Gregg. When Tahira Yamada was found under the Steel Pier with a leather thong about his neck you were the only one in the vicinity. You knew entirely too much about Doctor Fulda's having been murdered!" The Captain suddenly changed his tone. "That will be all for the present—I will talk to you again later!"

"Once more you produce your motives, Captain Blake," said Danton as he rose and bowed. "I hope our later interview will be as interesting as this one has been!"

Blake did not answer. He was staring sternly at the white-faced man as the latter moved back to his place beside Miss Hill. It was quite evident that the Captain was not through with Giovanni Danton.

27
GREGG'S WILL

As DANTON MOVED AWAY, Morton again glanced at his watch. It was now twelve-thirty. The latest of the Captain's interviews had taken a full hour. The reporter felt that the time had been more than well spent. As he had listened to the cross-questioning of the three witnesses, Morton had realized that more and more the mysterious elements which were connected with the murder were coming to light. He had a far better idea of just what part each one of the three people to whom Blake had talked had played in the Gregg affair.

Morton had agreed with Danton's statement. It was hardly possible for everyone connected with the case to be guilty. Yet he knew the array of motives which the Captain had produced against each and every one, was worthy of careful consideration.

Giovanni Danton had been clever: there was no doubt about that in Morton's mind. Nevertheless, the reporter felt that Danton's reckless disregard for the way in which he implicated himself, had been dangerous. The very plausibility of his story placed him all the more under suspicion in the reporter's mind.

Blake was again looking about the room. As he did so, those who had not already been questioned waited nervously. They had heard enough of the Captain's tactics during his interviews to feel very much as though they awaited a verdict from an executioner.

Lannon leaned over and whispered to Larry. Her low, musical voice was soft and appealing as she said:

"Reckon I'm next, Larry. And I'm simply scared to death. I don't know what he is going to ask me—oh, honey, I'm so afraid!"

"Now, Lannon! There's no reason why he should ask you anything that would worry you, Babe!"

"I'm not so sure about that." Lannon shook her lovely blonde head. "He's been finding every one guilty—and maybe I will be, too, when he gets through talking to me."

Blake was watching the boy and the girl as they whispered together. He smiled faintly—and they would have been amazed at what was going through his mind. He was merely thinking that Lannon was so much like his own lovely daughter that he adored. He felt glad that his child had not been mixed up in a sordid affair like this murder case.

The Captain had liked the way that Larry Benson had taken his hints that the boy might have committed the murder. He realized that Larry had faced things like a man—and he had defended the girl that he loved so far as he could during the interview which he had had with Blake.

"Miss Ida Hill, please," said Blake finally.

Lannon's Aunt looked about her nervously. She was already frightened. The thought of having the tragedy of her life revealed before all these people, was one which she found hard to face.

Blake must have sensed her mood as she walked slowly to the chair in front of his desk. He rose and stood waiting for her to seat herself. When she had done so, he returned to his position behind the desk.

"I'm sorry that I find it necessary to question you at all, Miss Hill," he said gently, his eyes upon the sad-faced woman who sat opposite him. "Perhaps it will make things easier for you if I explain that I already know quite a bit about your past."

"Really?" Miss Hill asked the question timidly, and she was again clasping and unclasping her restless hands in her lap. "I don't quite understand, Captain Blake."

"When one investigates a man's past history as I have done regarding Watson Gregg," said Blake quietly, "it is not remarkable that he should learn the part which a certain woman has played in his life. The information which I have gathered regarding you, Miss Hill, has made my feeling towards you one of the deepest, both in sympathy and admiration."

"That is very kind of you," said Lannon's Aunt, and it was quite obvious that she was growing less agitated after the Captain's soothing words. "Thank you, Captain Blake."

"You must not get the idea that because a man happens to be a police official, he is not also a human being," said Blake. "I understand your case very well, Miss Hill. In doing so I realize that there are certain things which you would prefer not to have brought into our present interview. So far as it is possible for me, I shall dismiss them at this time."

"You are very kind. But I am ready now for your questions, Captain."

"You were the wife of Watson Gregg?"

"I was."

Mercedes La Tona uttered a smothered exclamation as she heard the question and the reply. She placed her handkerchief swiftly to her lips, then drew it abruptly away again as she stared at Miss Hill.

"Did you see Mr. Gregg upon the night that he died, Miss Hill?"

"No." Miss Hill shook her head. "I was not on the Boardwalk that night. I leave my house so seldom. You see, I am rather a lonely old recluse, Captain Blake."

"At the time you married Mr. Gregg, you did so very much against the wishes of your family, did you not?"

"Yes." Miss Hill's face clouded. "My brother, Lannon Gordon's father, has never forgiven me for having done so."

Blake was silent, thoughtful, for a full minute. "Miss Hill, I can't quite explain it—but I have a feeling that you are keeping something from me—something which I judge that it would be best that you tell me."

"I had intended to tell you everything, Captain," said Miss Hill. "Only I have found it rather difficult to begin. You say that you have learned my past. Then surely you already know of the way Watson Gregg treated me—the way that he left me, the woman that he married—ill, and with only the most meager funds. You know, too, how I finally came to Atlantic City with my maid—that old faithful colored woman over there—" She turned and looked at Loona—"You know that I finally bought the old house in which I now live. You do know all that, don't you, Captain?"

"Yes, Miss Hill, I do."

"Then it will not be necessary for me to go into details. The day before Mr. Gregg was murdered, I met his servant, Tahira—that Japanese sitting over there. From him I learned that Mr. Gregg had rented a house in Ventnor. Tahira and I had always been quite friendly. He had been with Mr. Gregg in the old days.

"Tahira told me many things which had happened during the ten years since—since I had been Mr. Gregg's wife. The new love which had taken my place had died." Miss Hill turned and smiled coldly at Mercedes La Tona—the other woman turned her head away. "But there have been many others since then!" A sting in the way she voiced the word, carried to every one in the room.

"I was desperate and in need of money. When Tahira informed me that Mr. Gregg had planned a meeting with a woman at his cottage the next evening, I pretended I was that woman.

"Upon the night of October sixteenth I went to Mr. Gregg's cottage. I was certain that he would not see me. I knew that if I rang the doorbell and gave him an opportunity to learn who I was, he would probably have Tahira get rid of me in some way. At the time I did not even think of the possibility of Mr. Gregg's not being there.

"When I reached the cottage I stole around to the back door and fortunately found it open. I slipped into the kitchen. After I had waited and listened for a few moments, I realized that the place was deserted. I was bitterly disappointed, but I determined to remain there in the hope that Mr. Gregg would eventually arrive.

"I wandered through the cottage in an effort to pass away the time. In the living room I discovered a small safe. With no particular thought in mind I tried the handle of the dial. The safe opened easily at my touch. When I looked inside I found that the only thing which the safe contained was a large package of bills—money in large denominations—"

Miss Hill paused and looked about her nervously. Captain Blake smiled at her reassuringly.

"Please continue," he said softly.

"At sight of the money, all of the old hatred which Mr. Gregg had placed in my heart because of his inhuman treatment, returned to me. I determined that at least I would have something which might comfort me in my old age for my years of suffering. I wrapped the money up in an old bit of wrapping paper that I found, and left the cottage. I no longer had any desire to see Mr. Gregg. I just wanted to get away—" Abruptly Miss Hill's voice faltered and broke. "So—so you see I have been a thief, Captain Blake. But at the time I did feel that my action was justified!"

"I still feel that it was, Miss Hill," remarked the Captain. "There are some crimes, such as the one that you committed, that even the Law should be willing to condone." He smiled. "Fortunately, you have every legal right to Mr. Gregg's possessions. I have found in going through his things at the hotel, that he did one thing which showed there was at least one strain of decency in his character."

"What was that?" asked Miss Hill listlessly, and Mercedes La Tona leaned forward in her chair.

"He made a will leaving all of his property to you, Miss Hill— the woman who was his wife!"

"Oh!" there was bitterness in Miss Hill's exclamation. "And I have wronged him! I have been glad—glad!" Larry and Lannon watched her nervously as they realized that the old flame of madness was in her eyes. "I had been glad that he was dead! Oh, Watson, Watson, I have been cruel, heartless! But no more so than you were to me." She gazed about her with a faraway expression in her faded blue eyes. "I'm sure that wherever you may be now, you will know and forgive—your wife!"

Miss Hill dropped hack in her chair and sat there motionless. Blake produced his handkerchief and blew his nose with unnecessary vigor. Lannon's eyes were filled with tears as she turned to Larry. He reached out and took her slender hand and held it in his for an instant.

"The old fool!" murmured Mercedes La Tona vindictively, half to herself. "Did he think those twenty thousand dollars worth of bonds he gave me would last forever? To think of Watson Gregg—the old rotter—getting soft and leaving everything to his wife!" She laughed harshly. "The fool!"

"Silence, Miss La Tona!" roared Blake.

With a frown the actress passed into a sulky silence. Morton smiled faintly as he gazed at her. Every time she had been mentioned in the papers since the case had started she had been called "the actress." The reporter felt that in doing so they had been rather hard on the rest of the profession.

"Is there anything else, Captain Blake?" asked Miss Hill finally, when she had again gained control of herself.

"Just one more question, Miss Hill," said Blake quietly. "When did you know that Watson Gregg was dead?"

"At about nine-thirty of the night he was murdered," answered Miss Hill. "I met Tahira shortly after I left the cottage—and he told me that Mr. Gregg had been murdered, strangled to death by a leather thong."

28
"THERE'S YOUR MURDERER!"

AS HE HEARD MISS HILL'S STATEMENT, Blake glanced at the Japanese servant. Tahira smiled placidly as he caught the detective's look. He seemed quite satisfied with all that went on.

Blake turned his eyes in the direction of Godfrey Floss. The tall, lean, wolflike man now wore a sullen expression, as though he knew that he would be questioned next and he feared the ordeal.

"Mr. Floss," Blake snapped abruptly, "come here!" The Captain indicated by his tone that he had no liking for the blackmailer.

Floss rose from his chair as he heard Blake's words. Flannigan did likewise, but seated himself again at a word from the Captain.

"That's all right, Dan. Stay where you are," ordered Blake, and then as Floss dropped into the chair in front of him: "From what the witnesses this morning have said about you, Mr. Floss, I haven't a very good opinion of your character."

"You haven't a thing on me and you know it," Floss said, his voice vibrant. "I doubt if an investigation like this is even legal!"

"That's just where you are wrong, Mr. Floss. As Captain of Detectives I have every right to question those connected with this case, either singularly or collectively. As for my having nothing on you—to use your own words—first you were brought in by one of my men as a suspect in the murder of Watson Gregg; second, on hearing the testimony of Miss La Tona, I place you under arrest on a charge of attempted blackmail; and third, I charge you with murder in the first degree!"

"You can't do that!" exclaimed Floss. "I did not kill Watson Gregg!"

"We will go into that point later," said Blake sharply. "I base my charge against you upon the known fact that you deliberately shot and killed one John Hagen!"

"That's a lie!" shouted Floss. "You are accusing me of that to shield Martin Woods! He was the one who shot Hagen!"

"My charge against you stands," said the Captain grimly. "Do you realize the penalty for murder in the first degree in the state of New Jersey, Mr. Floss?"

"Oh, go ahead and ask your questions," snarled Floss, with a change of front. "I'll answer them—and I'm going to make it mighty hot for somebody when I do." He turned and glared at Danton. "You had your chance to put me on the rack—and now it's my turn, damn you!"

"You will confine your remarks to me, please, Mr. Floss!" said Blake.

"All right!" The blackmailer swung around.

"In the first place, you admit that you knew Watson Gregg?"

"Yes. I've known him for at least five years. We had always been very good friends." Floss's lips curled in a sneer. "This is one time when your favorite topic of motives doesn't work, Captain Blake."

"That is for me to decide. Did you stop at Mr. Gregg's rolling chair on the evening of October sixteenth?"

"Yes, I did. What of it? He was alive when I left him."

"What did you say to Mr. Gregg?"

"I stopped to tell him a new joke that I had just heard."

"What was that joke, Mr. Floss?"

"I would rather not repeat it now. There are ladies present." Floss turned and glared at Mercedes La Tona. "At least some of them are!"

"You will please make your statements a little less personal, Mr. Floss," growled Blake angrily.

"You asked me a question and I answered it. What more do you want?"

"You insist that Mr. Gregg was alive when you left the rolling chair?"

"Yes, he was! How many times do I have to tell you that?"

"Quite a number to convince me of the fact. Why did you hide in that doorway farther down the Boardwalk?"

"I had a hunch that something might happen to Gregg."

"What made you feel that way?"

"I don't know. I just told you it was a hunch."

"You live by your wits, don't you, Mr. Floss?"

"You might call it that."

"Did you know Mercedes La Tona previous to the night of the murder?"

"Only by sight. I had seen her quite often with Martin Woods."

"Yet you knew them both well enough to recognize them when their car was stopped by Hagen, did you not?"

"Yes, I knew them when they stopped, all right."

"Then you admit that you were in the woods on that night?"

Floss scowled as he realized that Blake had led him into a trap.

"No, I don't," he said shortly.

"It is unnecessary to attempt to deny the statement, Mr. Floss. We know that you were in the Margate Woods that night. You have practically admitted it yourself."

"All right, I'll admit it," said Floss. "What of it?"

"Then you did kill John Hagen?"

"No! I've told you that Martin Woods did it."

"I'd advise you to tell the truth, Mr. Floss. Why did you become so alarmed at the mention of owls?"

"I refuse to answer."

"Then I will tell you. You were afraid of the subject because you thought that the person who had hooted like an owl there in the woods had seen you kill John Hagen!"

"I tell you I didn't kill Hagen!"

"What made you go all the way out to the woods, Mr. Floss?"

"Aw, what's the use?" exclaimed Floss impatiently. "I followed the chair-pusher. I found him hiding under the Boardwalk when I went down the steps. I told him that Watson Gregg had been murdered—"

"You did!" broke in Blake. "I thought you said that he was alive when you left the rolling chair?"

"He was," said Floss quickly. "I did not learn that he had been murdered until later."

"Just how did you learn that Watson Gregg had been murdered? You left the Boardwalk before the crime was discovered."

"I know I did." Floss slowly nodded his head. "Danton told you of the woman that I stopped just after she left the chair. My sudden appearance startled her. She leaped back in fright, whispered: 'You saw me!'"

"And what did you say?"

"I said: 'Yes—I saw you.' Then she handed me a bill—it was a hundred dollars—and whispered: 'Don't tell anyone—there will be more later'."

"You accepted the money?"

"I did," said Floss. "I was broke—desperate."

"You are always rather desperate when money is concerned, are you not, Mr. Floss?"

"What do you mean?"

"You must be if you would kill John Hagen in order to blackmail someone else!"

"Again I tell you that I did not kill Hagen!"

"What did Hagen do when you told him that Mr. Gregg had been murdered?"

"He was scared to death—so much so that he got confidential. He told me that he was going to beat it. He said that he was going to hang around down at the lower end of the island and try to get a ride out of town. He didn't want to get mixed up with the police. I felt the same way about it. I told him that I would meet him on the old Longport Road at eleven-thirty, and we would both make a get-away."

"Did you do so?"

"No. When I got down there, he wasn't in sight. I didn't want to be seen by any passing motorist, so I hid in the brush and waited."

"Then when Hagen finally did appear and dragged the tree across the road you were still waiting?"

"Yes."

"In that case you did kill Hagen!"

"No!" Floss' denial was weaker than any of those which he had given previously. It was easy to see that he was beginning to break under the cross-questioning of the Captain of Detectives.

"You did not recognize the woman whom you startled after she had left Gregg's rolling chair?"

"I did not," said Floss slowly. "She was wearing a very heavy veil, and it was dark when she stopped and I spoke to her."

"The Boardwalk is usually very brightly lighted by seven p.m. at this time of year," remarked the Captain. "You are sure that you can recall nothing by which you might identify her?"

"I can't at the moment." Floss looked thoughtful. "Perhaps I may think of something later."

"I advise you to think hard!" said Blake grimly. "What were you doing under the Steel Pier upon the third night after the murder?"

"I had been taking a walk along the beach. I heard voices and I grew curious."

"And you found Mr. Danton, Mr. Benson and the Japanese there?"

"Yes, I did. But Mr. Danton did not frighten me away by hooting like an owl," said Floss defiantly. "I intended to leave anyway."

"From what Mr. Danton has told me, you attempted to draw a revolver and he bluffed you out of it."

"There's no use in my saying that he was lying," growled Floss. "You wouldn't believe me, anyway."

"We know that you had an automatic. One of my men took it away from you when he caught you coming up from Longport last night. Has it dawned upon you, Mr. Floss, that it might be of the same make and caliber as the one that killed John Hagen? An autopsy has already been performed, of course!"

"What of it?" demanded Floss. "Even if my gun should use the same caliber bullet, it doesn't prove that I killed him."

"Then you still deny it?"

"Of course I do. You think you are mighty clever, Blake—"

"Captain Blake, please!"

"You think you are damn clever! But you aren't going to make me admit that I killed John Hagen. I didn't do it, I tell you!"

"Have you ever seen an electric chair, Mr. Floss?"

"Oh, stop—stop, will you?" Floss fairly screamed. "Let me alone. Stop pounding at me. I can't stand it!"

Blake reached into his pocket and produced an object which he set upon the desk in front of him. It was a long, saffron-hued cord made of strong leather.

"Did you ever see that before?" he demanded abruptly.

"No." Floss shuddered, as he sat staring at the cord, fascinated.

"That is the saffron cord," said Blake as he picked up the thong, and formed it into a noose by running the end of it through a knot which he had quickly made. "The leather necklace it has been called." He began playing with the cord. "And Watson Gregg was murdered with this thong!"

"Put it away," murmured Floss. "I—I never saw it before."

"Rather an unusual weapon," said the Captain thoughtfully. He glanced casually about the room. "I want you to have some idea of how this works, Mr. Floss." He reached across the desk and handed the saffron cord to the blackmailer. "Take it," he commanded.

Floss grasped the cord gingerly.

Again Blake looked about the room. His gaze fell upon Tahira, who happened to be nearest to the desk.

"Try it on the Japanese," said Blake, and then he smiled. "Just throw it over his head gently, I mean."

Tahira looked mildly astonished as he heard the Captain's words. Floss hesitated a moment, and then rose and moved toward the Jap. When he reached the servant, the wolf-faced man dropped the saffron cord over Tahira's head. He was watching the Jap intently as he did so. Suddenly Floss jerked the cord tight. Tahira gasped, and Blake leaped quickly to his feet.

"Floss!" shouted the Captain. "Let go of that thong!"

The blackmailer, startled, dropped the saffron cord as he heard Blake's words. Tahira reached quickly to his throat and tore the thong away with both hands.

"He—he nearly got me again!" panted the Jap, glaring at Floss. "That is the man that tried to kill me with the leather thong beneath the Steel Pier the other night. I recognize that scar on his left hand!"

"He's right!" exclaimed Floss. "I did try to strangle him. He threatened to kill me if I did not stop annoying Miss La Tona. But it was *his* leather thong that I choked him with! He tried to use it on me first—but I was too strong for him!" The blackmailer suddenly reached out and grasped one of the hands of the Japanese. "Look! That odd Oriental ring that he is wearing—I saw it on the hand of the 'woman' that killed Watson Gregg! There's your murderer, Captain Blake!"

"Prove it!" said Tahira slowly.

29
"I AM GUILTY"

BLAKE'S EXPRESSION WAS VERY GRIM as he stared at the Jap for an instant. Finally he smiled coldly and waved his hand toward the chair in front of the desk.

"Sit there, Yamada," he commanded gruffly as he picked up the saffron cord and moved back to his seat behind the desk. "I am not going to ask questions this time," he said as he settled himself. "I am going to tell you a few things." Swiftly he glanced about the room, and then nodded as though having reached a decision, "And I am sure that those present will corroborate my statements. Tahira Yamada, you murdered Watson Gregg!"

"I suggested before: Prove it," said the little servant quietly.

"I will," said Blake shortly. "From the very first I have felt that it was the second woman who stopped at the rolling chair who killed Mr. Gregg. There has only been one thing which has puzzled me. That was the fact that a woman would hardly be likely to possess the necessary strength."

"May I say a word, Captain?" asked Giovanni Danton from where he sat beside Miss Hill.

"What is it?"

"I believe that it will do no harm for me to state that the saffron cord which you have there, was once the property of Miss Hill. It was sent her at one time by Watson Gregg as an ironical gesture when she had asked him for a very valuable pearl necklace which belonged to her."

215

"It was because you knew to whom this saffron cord belonged that you have refused to answer questions, Mr. Danton?" Blake smiled. "And that was why you called it the 'leather necklace'?"

"Yes, Captain." Danton nodded. "That was it. Late yesterday afternoon Miss Hill discovered that the saffron cord was missing. She mentioned the fact to me. Afterwards, she recalled when she had last seen it."

"When was that?"

"A day or so before Mr. Gregg was murdered," said Danton slowly. "As Miss Hill has already told you, she had met Tahira. Since that first meeting he had called at her house once or twice. She realized afterward that he must have been the one who had taken the leather thong."

"*That* would be rather difficult to prove," remarked Tahira softly.

"You're wrong there!" said Blake quickly, looking at the Japanese. "Oh, Dan!" he called.

"Yes, Cap?" Flannigan rose to his feet. "Bring in Hinkle now."

The stout detective departed. In a few moments he returned with a little gray-haired man.

"Sorry to keep you waiting so long, Mr. Hinkle," said the Captain.

"That's all right," said Hinkle, in a mild voice.

"You are a harness-maker, aren't you?"

"Yes, sir. I do nearly all sorts of work with leather."

"On October fourteenth, didn't this man come to your shop and want some work done?" Blake pointed to Tahira.

"Yes, he did." Hinkle nodded. "But there wasn't much work to it. He just wanted me to match a kinda orange-colored leather cord that he had with him."

"A saffron cord?"

"I guess you'd call it that," said the harness-maker. "Anyway, I matched it for him all right. Good strong leather it was, too."

"That's all, thank you, Mr. Hinkle," said Blake with a smile. "You may go now."

"Huh?" Hinkle looked surprised as he moved toward the door. "I thought you were gonna ask me a lot of questions," he mumbled under his breath.

"There were two saffron cords, you know," remarked Blake, as the harness-maker disappeared beyond the door. "We found the other one about the throat of Doctor Fulda yesterday at noon when we discovered his body in the closet of a room in Mr. Gregg's cottage in Ventnor."

"And Tahira was the blonde woman that was seen leaving the cottage!" exclaimed Morton. "He had been hiding there all the time. While we were searching the neighborhood for him, he was somewhere in the house!"

"Yes, probably hidden in one of the clothes closets in a bedroom. I'm afraid that we went through the place too quickly that first time, Dave."

Tahira smiled faintly, as though he found the Captain's statement amusing, but he said nothing.

"When one of my men found you last night," said. Blake, turning to the servant, "you had just checked a suit case in the parcel room of the Pennsylvania railroad station. We have secured that suit case—and it had two complete outfits of women's clothing in it—also a blonde wig."

"I suspected Tahira," put in Danton. "That was why I have been so interested in his actions since this case started. That night when I met him walking on the beach—as you know, I was with Miss La Tona at the time. When we stopped, then he mentioned the subject of owls. He did so in order to learn if I had been the one who had answered his call, or rather repeated it after he had answered mine. It amused me when he seemed to feel that the way in which I waved my hand was some secret signal."

"Is that true, Tahira?" demanded Blake suddenly.

The servant shook his head. "You said you would not ask questions this time, Captain Blake."

"Very well. It was true!" The Captain turned to Danton. "Why do you think Tahira went out to the woods that night?"

"He may have been lurking somewhere under the Boardwalk and heard Floss talking to Hagen. He probably felt that Mr. Floss knew too much, and followed him later in the hope of getting a chance to get rid of him."

"That's just what I think," said Blake. "Here's the way I sum up what happened: Tahira, dressed as a woman, stopped at the rolling chair and murdered Watson Gregg. He went on down the Boardwalk. Floss stepped out of the doorway and startled him. He handed Floss the money and then went on. Floss went down off the Boardwalk. Tahira probably did the same thing—"

"He did, Captain!" exclaimed Patrolman Hayes, speaking for the first time. "I remember that the second woman went down on the beach after she had passed by where I was standing."

"If you could remember things a little quicker it would be a great help, Hayes!"

The patrolman merely nodded, and again lapsed into silence. Flannigan glared at him, then shook his head sadly.

"All right, Tahira went down on the beach," continued Blake. "He overheard the conversation between Floss and Hagen—as Mr. Danton has said. Then he probably hurried down to Mr. Gregg's cottage. I am sure that was what he did—and he went there to get the fifty thousand dollars which was his motive for murder!"

"May I make a suggestion?" asked Danton.

"Certainly, Mr. Danton."

"I believe that when Tahira reached the cottage Miss Hill had left, and he found the money gone. But I also believe that he found Doctor Fulda waiting for him. I think that the little physician suspected the Jap. When Tahira arrived, still dressed in his woman's costume, no doubt Fulda was sure of his guilt."

"In that case," said Blake slowly as he considered what Danton had said, "why didn't Doctor Fulda tell me who committed the murder?"

"Because he, too, wanted that fifty thousand dollars! I know that he came to call on Miss Hill. I believe that he did so in an effort to try and learn if she had the money."

"It is all true," said Tahira quietly, "all these statements and questions that I have heard have been very tiresome. I am guilty, Captain Blake. I might as well admit it. I have waited my chance for years. I hated Watson Gregg for two reasons. First because he always treated me like a dog. I am an educated man. I did not like to see the suffering that those whom he had treated so cruelly were forced to go through. Miss Hill—Miss La Tona—and there were others—I think that deep in their hearts they may feel that I have been of service!"

"Service!" exclaimed Blake. "You have a strange way of looking at things, Tahira!"

"Perhaps," said the Jap. "I knew that Mr. Gregg was ill. Miss Hill had been taken care of in his will. When he was gone there would be nothing for me. You were right, Captain; it was the fifty thousand dollars that made me commit murder. Doctor Fulda did see me that night at the cottage. He must have waited there some time—for he smoked many cigarettes. He suspected—he hated Gregg—and he wanted the money. I am not sorry. The mind of the East is not the same as that of the West. I have killed two men; I would have done the same with Mr. Floss, but he was too strong for me."

The Jap's hand had been in his pocket as he talked. Now he brushed it across his lips as though he found them dry.

"I hoped to escape detection," he went on slowly. "I 'phoned you that night and told you to come to the Longport Road, for I knew you would find Mr. Floss and the chair-pusher there. I did not know Hagen would be—dead! The next night I telephoned the newspaper. They put Mr. Morton on the wire, and I warned him to look out for Mr. Danton." Tahira smiled. "In doing so I hoped to shield myself. . . . That's also why I left the woman's handkerchief in the rolling chair."

"Captain," Danton put in, his eyes on Tahira, "Watson Gregg's murderer will never face the electric chair!"

"Your words are pearls of wisdom, Mr. Danton," said Tahira, his voice growing weaker. "The hand I put to my lips a moment ago held a very effective poison." The little servant shuddered. "I still think—that Miss Hill and Miss La Tona . . . will grant . . . I have been of service . . . East is East—and—" With a convulsive shudder Tahira Yamada's body grew limp and he fell to the floor.

Miss Hill uttered a low moan. Lannon screamed, and then buried her head on Larry's shoulder.

30
AN AWFUL THOUGHT

LARRY BENSON SIGHED as he finished reading the article on the Gregg Murder Case which had appeared in the *Morning Press*. How strange to think that it was all over now!

Tahira the murderer—and dead!—Godfrey Floss was in jail awaiting his trial.

It startled Larry to realize that it had only been three days since the fight in the cabin—the fight that had brought him so much, for it had made him sure of Lannon's love. Ever since then he had felt older, somehow; so much more a man. He had fought for the woman he loved, and he had won.

To-night he was again to have dinner with Lannon and Miss Hill. Although he would not admit it even to himself, he was still a little afraid. The vivid recollection of that last mad dinner party still remained. He understood far better now. He realized how much the death of the man who had been her husband, had meant to Miss Hill. Poor woman, it was no wonder that she had been under a spell of madness, of strange hysteria over Watson Gregg's death. That was only natural.

The long day passed slowly, but at last Larry again found himself standing beneath the red light of the doorway of Miss Hill's old house. A pale moon hung high in the sky. Its light changed the old place, made it seem peaceful and serene in its very antiquity.

Larry rang the bell. A moment—and Lannon herself came to the door, her eyes soft as she smiled at him. Does it matter that they found the shadows kind? That for a moment he held her close in his arms, and knew that her lips were soft and lovely? Heart was whispering to heart, saying over and over the things which love has always said. Would new words make an old song sweeter?

Lannon and Larry entered the house. Miss Hill and Giovanni Danton stood in the hallway smiling at them. There was something about Lannon and Larry radiant with the fires of youth that brought back memories to this man with his strange eyes, and to this lovely, sad-faced woman. The faint call of yesterday lingered in their hearts.

"Danton!" exclaimed Larry, smiling at the tall, white-haired man. "I'm so glad to see you here!"

There was no doubt in the boy's mind now—no lurking sense of danger. Giovanni Danton was a friend, and one that was so worthwhile; a man who would always be a mystery, and yet would always understand.

"And I am glad to be here!" Danton replied, glancing significantly at Miss Hill.

She knew that his eyes were saying things which his lips did not utter—things which he had said to her in a garden long ago. But she did not dare to look at him. Not yet—not now. She was not brave enough to face even the thought of happiness so soon.

"Lannon has been telling me interesting things about you two," said Miss Hill, smiling as she took Larry's hand. "Is it true, Larry?"

"Don't you answer any questions, Larry," said Lannon quickly. "I haven't told a thing!" and Lannon actually blushed.

"Why, Lannon!" exclaimed her Aunt. "You did. You told me that you and Larry were going to be married!"

"We are!" Lannon grinned impishly at Larry. "When he asks me!" She held up her hand in protest as he started to speak. "No, not now—be your age! A nice time to propose—as unromantic as—" She paused uncertainly.

"How am I going to know when?" asked Larry.

"I don't think you will find that difficult," said Danton, and for the first time since Larry had known him the pale-faced man's smile reached his eyes. He looked at Miss Hill. "Come with me a moment, Ida," said Danton quietly; "I have something I, too, must say."

Ida did not speak as he led her down the hall. Not yet had Miss Hill dared to look deep into the eyes of Giovanni Danton—those deep, burning eyes that perhaps were only banked fires before the altar of an old love.

Lannon and Larry stood watching them as they disappeared down the hallway.

"Speaking of romantic moments—" Lannon paused, smiling.

"Lannon, dearest, I love you so! Will you marry me?"

"It's an awful thought," her arms went about him; "but I guess I will!"

THE CELL
MURDER
MYSTERY

1

THE LURKING MENACE

TED AMES MOVED STEALTHILY through the grounds of the vast, gloomy estate of Fosdick Martin. He knew his mission was dangerous, for he had come to steal Martin's famous collection of unset diamonds.

Over Ames hung the ever-present shadow of that strange, sinister individual known as The Lizard. It had been The Lizard who had sent him, a shadowy figure in the grim darkness of the stormy night. He had to get the jewels no matter what the risk might be. The Lizard would not permit failure. That was not his way.

Ames clung to the shadows of the trees as much as possible, running hastily across the open spaces that intervened. The journey from the hedge which surrounded the grounds to the huge house seemed long. He breathed a sigh of relief when he finally found himself close to the porch.

Beneath a tall oak, fifteen feet away from where Ames stood, a figure dressed in black remained motionless, watching. A black mask completely hid its face, and only the hard eyes that stared through the holes in the cloth were visible—so well did the figure blend with the deep shadows about the trunk of the tree.

The man beneath the tree had observed Ames' furtive progress through the grounds, and had apparently found his actions amusing, for he had chuckled softly once or twice as he saw the other scamper from tree to tree like a frightened rabbit.

For a moment Ames stood gazing at the light gleaming through a pair of French windows that opened out onto the porch. He did not realize that the light was reflected faintly upon his face, and that for the moment he was clearly visible to a slender woman who stood in the shadows of the porch. She stared at him, then covered her face with her arm and stepped back to avoid detection.

Ames did not see her—had not the slightest inkling that she was there. He considered mounting the porch and trying to see what was in the lighted room beyond the French windows, but finally decided against it. Silently he turned and disappeared around the left side of the old mansion.

The woman on the porch began to edge along the wall until she had reached a spot where she could peer in through the French windows. Here she paused and stood watching and listening intently.

The masked man beneath the tall oak had not moved. He remained there patiently, his eyes fixed upon the light streaming through the French windows.

Five minutes later there was the sound of a window being slowly and cautiously jimmied in the dining-room of the house. For a brief instant Ames' figure was outlined against the night as he climbed noiselessly through the opening.

When he was safely inside he stood very still, listening. In one hand he now held an automatic, while the other gripped a flashlight he had not as yet brought into use.

He thought he detected voices somewhere in the distance, but he could not be sure. He placed the automatic in the side pocket of his coat. He was satisfied that he was alone in the room and turned to the window and silently drew down the thick green shade.

He switched on the flashlight, certain that there was little possibility of its beam being observed from outside the windows. Slowly the bright beam began to circle the room and paused at a closed door. Apparently this was the object of Ames' search for he went to it at once.

He switched off the flashlight as he drew the door open slowly, inch by inch. He was taking no chances of encountering the unexpected on the other side. Finally he found himself peering into a long, dimly lighted hallway. He started to draw the door closed again as he heard someone approaching, and then changed his mind. He wanted to know who was out there in the hall. He stood close against the dining-room wall and peeped through the crack in the door.

A small black-haired man appeared within Ames' range of vision. His eyes were dark, and there was a sharpness about his pointed face that gave him a rat-like appearance. He did not even glance toward the dining-room as he hurried down the hall.

"Fulson," murmured Ames softly. "Fosdick Martin's secretary. I wonder if he knows where the old man keeps the diamonds?"

Ames slowly widened the crack in the door. As he stuck his head around the edge he heard the murmur of voices. Even from the distance he was sure it was two men quarreling bitterly, though he could not quite distinguish their words. The sounds appeared to come from the other end of the hall.

Ames had put the flashlight away, but his fingers clung to the automatic in his coat pocket. He realized he was taking a long chance by venturing about the Martin residence so early in the evening, yet he was only obeying instructions.

Ames stepped out into the hall, then crouched close to the wall as he spied a figure in the distance. It was Perry Fulson, the strange, furtive little man who was Martin's secretary. Fulson had his back to the dining-room. He was leaning against a closed door, his ear pressed tightly against the panel as he listened to the conversation in the room beyond.

Ames realized that Fulson was listening to the quarreling voices that now came indistinctly to the man against the wall. They ceased abruptly. Fulson glanced about him without seeing Ames, who was well-concealed by the shadows. Hastily, the secretary went to a switch on the wall and pushed the button. At once the hall was plunged into darkness.

Ames began to move forward. He went for some distance through the darkness, feeling his way along the wall. He did not dare to use his flashlight now. The risk was too great, for he felt that Fulson still lurked somewhere ahead of him. But why had the secretary turned out the lights?

A thought struck Ames and he paused abruptly. Had it been because Fulson had seen him after all? Was he standing there at the switch waiting for Ames to come nearer so he could turn on the lights again and confront him?

He waited tensely as he heard a slight sound. He tried to peer through the darkness but it was impossible to distinguish anything. The hall was black and his eyes had not as yet become accustomed to the gloom.

Suddenly there came a startled exclamation. Ames could not make out the words, but he knew it was a masculine voice that spoke. This was followed by a rustling and shuffling sound. Then he clearly heard a hoarse whisper.

"I've got you, damn you!" came the whispered tones. "I told you I would! I've been waiting for this!"

Ames found a sinister note in the whispered words. There was vindictiveness in every syllable, a cruel venom that was ruthless in its very speech.

"I—oh—" the words came in another voice, a wail of terror that died away in a feeble groan.

Ames heard the soft thud of a heavy object evidently falling upon a thick rug. A door closed distinctly, with a click of a latch. Then the house grew grimly silent. As he stood there in the darkness, Ames found that a shuddering stillness seemed to hang over every-thing. For what seemed an eternity he remained motionless, strain-ing his ears for some slight sound. But he heard nothing further.

At last he felt he could stand it no longer. He knew that he must investigate. There had been something ominous in the whispered words and the groan which had followed. The soft thud had sounded like that of a falling body. Ames was sure that what he had heard was murder.

He moved along the hall slowly, guiding himself by the wall at his side. He held the flashlight in his left hand, but as yet he had not risked turning it on. From time to time the fingers of his right hand touched the automatic in his pocket. He experienced a sense of comfort in the feel of the cold steel against his hand. He knew that danger, perhaps death, lurked somewhere about him, and that he might stumble upon it at any instant. But he was ready for what-ever he might encounter.

He was prepared for anything—anything except what he now heard. It came abruptly from out of the darkness ahead. For suddenly there came to him the soft, whispered words of a woman. He was so startled that for an instant he forgot the flashlight in his hand. He just stood staring dazedly into the darkness.

"Go! Oh, please go at once!" came the woman's voice. It was more of a soft, musical undertone than a whisper, and Ames realized she was speaking to him. "Don't let them find you here." Her tone was pleading. "Hurry—they've phoned for the police!"

Ames thought of the flashlight. He switched it on, determined to see the woman who spoke. The light gleamed upon a slender white arm, as a dim figure disappeared around the edge of a door opposite the one at which the secretary had been listening. As the arm vanished Ames caught a glimpse of an odd-looking snake bracelet made of hammered gold. Then the door closed and he heard a key turn in the lock.

Ames swung his flashlight about the hall. There was no one in sight now. The door beside which Fulson had stood was closed. Ames realized that the woman was right. It would never do for him to be found there. She had said that someone had sent for the police. He felt he had better go quickly. He turned and ran back along the hall. A moment later he had raised the shade and climbed out the dining-room window. A swift run through the rain which was now pouring down brought him to the hedge at the side of the house.

When he reached the shadow of the wall of evergreen, he paused and looked back. The house was dark and silent as it sat brooding in the rain. But he saw that a bright light still gleamed through the French windows on the lower floor. He wondered what was now going on within that room.

Ted Ames frowned as he stood there, a tall rain-soaked figure in the shadows. He realized he was safe. As yet he saw no one in pursuit, nor any indication of the arrival of the police. He had left no clue, nothing to indicate he had been in the house. But who was this woman who had whispered to him? How had she known he was there in the dark hall? And what would The Lizard say when he learned that the man he had sent had failed to get Fosdick Martin's collection of diamonds?

2

IT'S MURDER!

AN AIR OF EXPECTANCY brooded over the private office of the Chief of
the North City Police Department, a lingering hush not unlike the
moment before the curtain rises upon a tense drama, a silence in
which the sounds of the night played a muted symphony. Rain beat
with liquid fingers upon the windows that were gleaming black
squares reflecting the grim darkness of the stormy night. The noises
of the city were vague echoes lost in the moan of the wind.

A green shaded drop-light hanging from the ceiling cast a bright
glow upon the face of the heavy-set grey haired man who sat silently at the flat-top desk. A frown wrinkled his broad forehead
and made his thick, dark eyebrows seem like shields that half hid
the observant blue eyes beneath them. There was more than a hint of
aggressive firmness in the chin that was faintly shadowed by a blue-
black beard that was always closely shaven. An evil-smelling briar pipe
was in one corner of the strong, sensitive mouth, a pipe from which
faint wisps of blue smoke rose at intervals. His strong, stubby fingers
drummed noiselessly upon the green blotting-pad in front of him as
he gazed at the rain beating upon the opposite window.

Chief John Kenny finally ceased his contemplation of the storm.
He appeared to find no answer to his thoughts in the wailing of
the wind or the pounding of the rain. His eyes wandered over the
articles on the desk in front of him. The official-looking papers
stacked neatly in a wire basket held no interest for him, nor did
the telephone that stood beside them. The little brass clock that
ticked softly on its stand between two brass ink-wells provided

something for his gaze to linger upon for an instant. Then it traveled to the small ivory elephant that stood with upraised trunk as though trumpeting at the vast desert of green blotting paper which it contemplated with stately derision.

At a slight sound, Kenny turned his head. He glanced at the shadowy figure sprawling indolently in the comfortable leather chair just beyond the rays of the green, shaded light. Detective Sergeant O'Shay merely grunted when he found the chief staring at him. He did not feel that words were necessary. The silence between the two men was one of complete understanding. Though Kenny was O'Shay's superior in the Police Department, they were old friends, and had been friends for years. They had often sat as they did now, each lost in his own thoughts and yet finding an unvoiced pleasure in their mutual companionship.

The years they had spent as members of the North City Police Department had made them seem phlegmatic. To outward appearances they were both unemotional individuals, for it was part of their duty to face life and death cold-bloodedly, yet it is doubtful that anyone could really consider John Kenny or Tim O'Shay heartless or unfeeling.

As they sat silently listening to the sounds of the storm each realized that the other was under a feeling of suspense. They were like blood-hounds straining at their leash. Both men knew that their attitude of passivity was merely a mask beneath which they concealed their impatience.

The sudden, insistent jingling of the telephone-bell broke the spell with startling abruptness. It was the signal for which the two men had been waiting, and they showed it plainly.

O'Shay leaned forward in his chair. His round, red face with its fringe of sandy hair outlining his bald head now gleamed clearly in the light, as he watched and listened.

The frown had disappeared from Kenny's countenance as he reached out and lifted the telephone receiver. He was very much alert, and voiced a crisp, "Hello." The conversation on the part of the chief was terse and much to the point. O'Shay realized that as he listened.

Finally Kenny jammed the receiver back on the hook. He swung around so that he faced O'Shay, and though he gave little indication of it from his expression, the detective sergeant realized that the chief was excited.

"It's murder!" said Kenny quietly.

"Murder." O'Shay repeated the word slowly, as though he found it the answer to a question in his own mind. "I was afraid it would be," he nodded. "Afraid—hell, I was sure of it!" A thought struck him. "Was that Coroner Blake on the phone?"

"Yes—calling from the hospital. Said he arrived there shortly after they brought Fosdick Martin in. Blake says he's sending his report to me by Dave Heath of the *Morning News*."

An expression of surprise swept over the round face of the detective sergeant when he heard the chief's words.

"Why doesn't the coroner come himself?" he asked. "Blake usually wants to work with you when a murder-case breaks, and this sure is one."

Kenny hesitated for a moment before he spoke. He seemed to have a doubt in his mind about something.

"That's true," he said finally. "But Blake couldn't see me tonight. He's catching the ten-fifty for Washington. Said he had to be there the first thing in the morning on official business."

"Oh, yeah!" A slow grin spread over O'Shay's face. "Seems to me that murder is what you'd call official business for a coroner!"

"Right!" Kenny laughed, and then suddenly grew serious. "I wish he hadn't gone though. Of course there was no use in my arguing with him about it. Blake knows his business. Told me to get Doctor Wilson if we needed him."

"The Deputy Coroner, eh?" O'Shay shook his head. "And what a tough bird he is to get along with. That guy must have an ingrown grouch." He looked intently at the chief. "Anything about this trip of Blake's strike you as queer?"

"What do you mean?"

"Nothing. Only I've heard rumors that Blake and Fosdick Martin never got along very well together."

"At it again, eh, Tim?" Kenny laughed. "I've never worked with you on a case yet that you didn't jump right in, suspecting everybody, no matter who they were. And you're starting now with Coroner Blake!"

"Well, we gotta start somewhere," exclaimed O'Shay. "And Blake's gone."

"I guess he has." The chief glanced at the clock on the desk. "Ten forty-five now. Blake didn't have much time."

"I'll bet he made it all right. It's not far from the hospital to the station. So Fosdick Martin died?" The detective sergeant leaned back in his chair. "I was afraid he would when we found him out at his house half an hour ago. Both of those knife wounds were deep and nasty."

"They certainly were!" A thought struck the chief, and he frowned. "Tim, the papers will eat this up when they get hold of it."

"When they get hold of it!" interrupted O'Shay, derisively. "With Dave Heath already up at the hospital! Huh, I'll bet he's phoned the News long before this."

"You're right. I can see the headline now. FOSDICK MARTIN MURDERED. BANKER STABBED TO DEATH."

"Sure," said O'Shay. "And don't forget they'll say—POLICE ARE BAFFLED," he grunted. "They love that one."

"I know." Kenny scowled. "It's too bad this had to come right on top of that series of jewel robberies that have been going on in North City. There'll be plenty of excitement in town tomorrow."

"Plenty is right," agreed O'Shay. "Say, Chief, this makes things look tough for Grant Ellery. He was the last one to see Martin alive, according to what Perry Fulson says. You weren't so dumb in holding those two birds as material witnesses."

"Perhaps not." Kenny thoughtfully played with the elephant paper-weight on the desk. "I'm not at all satisfied with Fulson's story. The fact that he was Martin's private secretary doesn't mean a thing to me."

"I've got a hunch that he's lying. You know, he might have stabbed Martin himself. Fulson's a rat, if I've ever seen one."

"Another suspect, Tim?" Kenny laughed. "That makes two you've found in the last five minutes."

"No, three." O'Shay grinned as he sat in the semi-darkness beyond the light. "Don't forget Grant Ellery."

"I'm not forgetting anybody now," stated Kenny grimly.

O'Shay rose from his chair and walked over to the nearest window. For a few seconds he stood staring out into the bleak and stormy night.

"Still raining hard," he remarked, his back to the chief. "Sure is rotten weather."

Kenny did not even hear him. He was lost in thought, as he slowly filled and lighted his pipe. For a few seconds he sat smoking.

"Tim," he said finally, as he reached a decision. "Bring Grant Ellery here. I want to talk to him again."

"Aw, what's the use?" The detective sergeant swung around so he could look at Kenny. "Ellery won't talk—you know that. Didn't you try it before and he refused to say anything until he had seen his lawyer in the morning. It's just a waste of time, Chief."

Kenny glared at him. There were times when O'Shay seemed to forget who was Chief of Police. Such instances were rare, and usually instigated by well-meaning blunders on the part of the detective sergeant. Kenny seldom noticed such lapses, but now he was in an impatient mood.

"Never mind what you think about it!" The chief's tone was sharp. "I want to talk to Ellery! He doesn't know that Martin is dead. Bring him in, Tim!"

"All right, all right," said O'Shay soothingly. "I'll get him."

He grinned at Kenny as he started toward the door. The chief scowled, and then he laughed.

"I must have a grouch," he said quietly.

"Sure," said O'Shay without looking back. "I don't mind, but it's gonna be tough on Ellery—I'll bet."

Kenny was still smiling faintly as the door closed upon the stocky form of the detective sergeant. A good man, O'Shay, even if he was a bit free and easy in his ways. Still, the chief felt that O'Shay should have a mind of his own. The North City Police Department was small and Detective Sergeant O'Shay was really the head of the Detective Bureau, though he and his men took their final orders from the chief.

The telephone on Kenny's desk rang sharply, and the chief picked up the receiver at once.

"Hello," he said into the phone. "Oh, the *Morning News*, eh? Sure, Clark, I'll tell Heath to call up as soon as he arrives. He's on his way down from the hospital now. You're welcome—'bye."

Kenny placed the receiver on the hook and leaned back in his chair, his mind going carefully over the events of the night. The steady patter of the rain and the wailing of the wind came dimly to his ears, but he paid little heed. He had more important things to think about at the moment.

At nine-thirty Desk Sergeant Cunningham had received an excited telephone message from Perry Fulson, secretary of Fosdick Martin, one of the wealthiest of North City's citizens. Fulson had requested the police to come at once, intimating that there had been a murder committed.

Kenny, O'Shay, and two detectives had started immediately for the house in a police automobile. When they arrived there they found that Fosdick Martin had been stabbed. He was lying face downward on the floor of his study, bleeding badly from two knife wounds, one in his right arm, the other in his back just above the heart. There was no trace of the weapon.

Both Perry Fulson and Grant Ellery had been at the house when the police arrived. Fulson had met them at the front door and led the way to Martin's study, which was in the left wing of the lower floor. Here they had found Grant Ellery awaiting them calmly.

Upon being questioned by the chief, Fulson had hysterically accused Ellery of murdering Martin. Ellery had refused to make any statement, merely saying that he intended to see his attorney first. As far as the police could learn there had been no one else in the house that evening after eight o'clock except the three men. Martin's two servants, a man and a woman, had been given an evening off, and they had left the house a little before eight.

At the same time that Perry Fulson telephoned the police, he had put in a call to the North City hospital for an ambulance. This had arrived shortly after the police reached the house and Fosdick Martin, who was still alive, had been rushed to the hospital at once.

Chief Kenny had arrested both Ellery and Fulson as material witnesses. The two men were now lodged in the city jail. This was located in the rear of the big building which housed the North City Police Department. Two detectives had been left on duty at the Martin residence.

At the house, Kenny learned from Fulson that Martin had wanted a private interview with Ellery. For that reason he had permitted the servants to take the night off as soon as they finished serving dinner for the three men.

Grant Ellery had been Martin's partner in a number of business deals. Ellery had just returned to town that night after an absence of some months. Kenny had heard vague rumors of a serious breach between the two men, but he was inclined to take all such hearsay about Fosdick Martin as something more or less to be expected—a man who was rich and powerful might well be expected to have enemies.

Martin had had an aggressive, ruthless way about him that made him cordially hated. It had often been said that he never increased his wealth without causing someone suffering, so Chief Kenny realized there were a number of people who probably would not regret the murder of Fosdick Martin.

Kenny glanced at the clock. It seemed as though O'Shay had been gone a long time. To his surprise, the chief found it had been less than ten minutes since the detective sergeant left the room. It was now eleven o'clock.

A moment later the door opened and O'Shay entered. With him was a tall, broad-shouldered man who bore a sullen expression upon his dark, handsome face. In business or the social world Grant Ellery was seldom considered a very docile individual.

"I resent all this, Chief Kenny," he said, and his tone was angry and blustering. "I see no reason for being treated like a common criminal. It's outrageous! Locked up in that cell with that gibbering idiot down the row howling and screaming all the time. Fortunately his cell is some distance from mine, but it's bad enough as it is."

"Sit down, please, Mr. Ellery." Kenny waved his hand toward a chair close to the desk, a chair which brought its occupant fully within the light which hung from above. "I want to have a talk with you."

Ellery dropped into the chair with a growl, and sat glaring at the chief. The latter paid not the slightest heed to the other's belligerent attitude as he calmly knocked the ashes from his pipe and put it aside.

O'Shay had carefully closed the door of the office, and now he returned to his chair at the left of the chief.

"I told you I would say nothing until I had seen my attorney," said Ellery. "Nothing! And Mr. Naimark will not be in the city until tomorrow morning."

"Very well then," said Kenny slowly. "Suppose I talk and you listen. I think you'll wish you had not been quite so reluctant to speak."

The chief's tone was very calm, but Grant Ellery seemed to sense a hidden menace in the words. His eyes were fixed upon Kenny's face as he spoke.

"What do you mean?" he asked anxiously.

"That we have been considering facts, Mr. Ellery, just plain facts. You were at Fosdick Martin's house tonight. You quarreled with Martin, according to Perry Fulson's statement."

"And do you think you can frighten me into talking by telling me all that?" Ellery laughed. "You have nothing on me." He shook his head. "What if I was at Martin's house when he was stabbed?"

"Fosdick Martin was murdered!" The chief uttered the words slowly and coldly.

Grant Ellery seemed to wilt as he heard Kenny's statement. He ran his linger inside the collar of his soft silk shirt as though he had suddenly found it too tight for him. A blank expression swept over his face, and he gazed at the chief in amazement.

"You—you mean he is dead?" he asked in a low voice. "Dead?"

"Yes, murdered." Kenny leaned forward, his eyes fixed upon the face of the other man. "You were with him there in his study—you know where those knife wounds came from. And now he is dead—"

"How do you know he's dead?" Ellery asked the question as though grasping at a straw. "Tell me."

"Coroner Blake phoned me from the hospital a little while ago—and he told me that Fosdick Martin had died. Died from those wounds he received while you were with him there in the study—while you were alone with him Mr. Ellery." The chief deliberately became melodramatic. "Can't you see him lying there on the floor, his hand outstretched—the hand that has been offered to you in friendship."

"Oh, stop it, stop it," exclaimed Ellery: I tell you I won't talk—I won't!"

"I'm not asking you to talk." Kenny's tone was grim. "I am only telling you that you're in a very precarious position. You were the last person to see Fosdick Martin alive. You haven't denied that—"

"Denied it! How can I, when I know that anything I say will be used against me?"

"What makes you so sure," the chief smiled ironically. "Why, the statement itself might be considered an admission of guilt!"

"Guilt!" exclaimed Ellery excitedly. "You mean you think that—that *I* killed Fosdick Martin!"

"I'm not saying what I think. I'm merely stating facts, Mr. Ellery." Kenny spoke quietly and calmly. "You were alone with Martin. Somebody killed him. Your silence makes me wonder."

"I didn't do it." Ellery forced a laugh. "Fosdick and I were friends, the best of friends."

"And yet you refuse to speak—you alone must know who killed him. Killed the man with whom you were the best of friends—and you are silent!"

"Don't! I don't know what to say—can't you see I'm all confused?" Ellery nervously ran his fingers through his thick black hair. "I tell you I didn't do it. Why, Martin and I were partners—you said that yourself."

"I did, and I know you were partners."

"Then if you do, surely you can see that I would have no motive for murdering him." Ellery's tone was eager. "Don't you see that, Chief?"

"I'm not so sure I do. Perry Fulson says he heard you threaten Mr. Martin tonight."

"Fulson is a liar! A rotten little sneak, that's what he is! Ask him where he was when—" Ellery broke off abruptly, a startled expression on his face as he realized he had said too much.

"—when Martin was murdered?" asked Kenny softly. "Was that it?"

Ellery shuddered. He did not speak. He sat staring down at the floor, his face white and drawn. For an instant the only sound in the room was the patter of the rain on the windows, the faint voice of the wind, and the ticking of the clock on the desk.

"You must have heard the rain beating against the windowpane, just as it is now, when you stood there looking down at Martin," said Kenny softly, but his voice was like a dagger cutting the silence.

"Oh! I can't stand it—this pounding at me like this. Everything you have said has made me feel guilty. I'm nervous—upset—I don't know what to say. I'm afraid that if I tell you the truth you won't believe me—oh!" Ellery groaned and buried his head in his hands.

Kenny glanced at O'Shay. The detective sergeant nodded his head slowly. Both men felt that they would learn something new. The interview had proven too much for the shattered nerves of Grant Ellery. He had reached the point where he would talk.

"Come, Ellery," said Kenny soothingly. "The truth is all we ask of you—that is what I have been trying to get you to tell me all the time. I don't want to believe you guilty, but only you can convince me of your innocence—"

"What do you mean?" Ellery raised his head.

"Tell me what happened out at Fosdick Martin's house tonight."

"All right." Ellery got himself under control with an effort. "I'll talk—but will you give me just half an hour to think things over. I'm so nervous now. Just half an hour, please, Chief—and I will have a lot to say."

"Certainly, Mr. Ellery." Kenny glanced at the clock. "It's eleven-fifteen now. O'Shay will take you back to your cell, and I will come there and talk to you about a quarter to twelve."

"Thank you, Chief Kenny." Ellery got to his feet as O'Shay walked over to him. "I'll be waiting for you in my cell."

Kenny merely nodded as the detective sergeant took Ellery by the arm and started out of the office.

"Oh, Tim," called Kenny as the two men reached the door. "Bring Fulson back with you when you come."

Ellery glanced at the chief as he heard the words. He smiled, and there was something about his smile that left Kenny sitting there with a puzzled frown as the door closed. What did Grant Ellery know?

3

THE LIZARD LISTENS

THE LIGHT FROM THE FLOOR LAMP close beside his easy-chair gleamed down upon the grey-haired man who sat reading. His attitude was one of languid repose, and the glance he cast from time to time at the expensive little clock that stood on the smoking-table at his right hand was quite casual. One could not have detected by Glynn Landor's actions that he was expecting a visitor.

Finally, he carefully marked his place and put the book on the table beside him. He yawned, but there was an alert expression in his dark eyes as he gazed about the room. The place was very tastefully furnished and yet there was an air of informality about it that reminded one of a suite in a luxury hotel. Glynn Landor never left any real trace of himself behind. That was not his way.

He rose slowly to his feet, a tall, carefully dressed figure, a smoking-jacket replacing the coat of his evening clothes. There was a gliding, snake-like motion to his walk as he went to the window. It had been that strange and rather sinister gait that brought him the name by which he was known throughout the Underworld, The Lizard.

There was nothing unusual about the man except his strange gait. In fact, he was rather good-looking in a bold way, and in the eyes of the world the suave and urbane Glynn Landor had no connection with that ruthless criminal known only to the Underworld as The Lizard.

For a few moments Landor stood at the window staring out at the rain-swept street four stories below the floor upon which his bachelor apartment was located. Finally he turned as he heard a doorbell ring once, then twice, then once again.

Landor smiled as he glided out of the room. He returned in a few seconds and a tall, good-looking young man was with him. The latter appeared nervous as he took the chair that Landor offered him.

"Nasty night, isn't it," said Landor casually, as he dropped back in his easy-chair.

For a moment he studied the younger man, then he reached for a carved cigarette-box on the table. He passed it to his companion, the latter took a cigarette mechanically, lit it and then ran the fingers of his left hand impatiently through his thick blond hair.

"Well, why don't you say something?" he demanded harshly.

"Why should I?" Landor appeared surprised. "I rather expected you to talk. What happened, Ames?"

"Plenty!" Ted Ames stated grimly. "I was a fool to have ever let you rope me into all this."

"Really?" Landor blew a cloud of smoke toward the ceiling as he leaned back in his chair. "It seems to me it's a little late for regrets."

"I'm not so sure about that." Ames' tone was impatient.

"I would be if I were you." Landor's tone was still casual, but the younger man detected a menacing note in it. "Suppose we consider the situation a bit more carefully. Six weeks ago I met you in a speakeasy. You were in a very dejected mood. In fact, as you stated, you didn't give a damn what happened—"

"I was a fool!" interrupted Ames.

"Granted," said Landor calmly. "But that's neither here nor there. Since then we have joined forces. The police have been rather bothered by what they seem to consider—," he smiled, "shall we say 'baffling jewel robberies'."

"Yes, and you committed those robberies!"

"Of course." Landor's tone was soothing. "I'm not denying it, dear boy. Only you seem to forget that you provided very valuable assistance."

"Yes, acting as lookout while you looted rich men's homes."

"And thereby eliminating any possibility of the police appearing unexpectedly." Landor turned his head so he could look at the other man. "As I have just said, you were a great help, Ames."

Ted Ames did not speak, but sat staring sullenly at the floor. Landor frowned as he watched him. He did not like the other man's mood. From the time he first encountered Ames in the speakeasy, and decided that he might prove useful, the younger man had proved docile clay in The Lizard's hands. But now there was a defiant attitude about the other that did not please Landor.

"What happened tonight?" he asked.

"Not what you expect." Ames raised his eyes and looked at him. "I didn't get the diamonds."

"That *is* a disappointment. The first job I let you handle alone, and you fail." Landor shook his head. "You can hardly expect me to be pleased."

"No?" Ames glared at him. "Well, suppose I tell you that I don't give a hoot how you feel about it—what would you say then?"

Glynn Landor hesitated before he spoke. He appeared to be carefully debating the question. His dark eyes were staring steadily at the younger man.

Ames suddenly found himself uncomfortable under that close scrutiny. He moved restlessly in his chair, and finally dropped his eyes to the floor.

"I should say that your not giving a hoot, as you put it," Landor remarked finally, "is rather unfortunate for you."

"What do you mean?"

"I have had a lot of hard things said about me, but no one has ever dared consider me a fool." Landor was sitting erect in his chair, his eyes fixed on the other man's face. "You're in this much deeper than you realize, Ames—and if you start getting nasty you may force me to show you just how I've got you hooked." The Lizard smiled. "It will be more or less like a worm squirming on the end of a pin, I'm afraid."

Ames appeared not to heed the other's words. He was still staring at the floor. His face was pale and he seemed to be laboring under a great strain. Finally he sighed.

"I guess you're right," he said halfheartedly. "And I'm sorry I slipped up on getting the diamonds."

"That's better, much better." Landor nodded. "I knew you would see I was right when you had thought things over a little." He smiled, "Now tell me just what went wrong at the house."

"Well, as you know, you told me to be there early. It was just about nine when I reached the grounds. I managed to get up to the house without being seen—"

"You're sure of that?" interrupted Landor. He watched the other man closely as he spoke.

"Quite sure." There was an expression of surprise upon Ames' face. "Why do you ask?"

"It's not important." A faint fleeting smile swept over Landor's countenance. "Go on!"

"I jimmied a window in the dining-room and climbed in. Then I opened a door leading out into the hall and peered out. Perry Fulson passed me, without a glance in my direction. A few seconds later I heard the sound of voices. I couldn't make out the words but I am sure it was two men speaking and they were quarreling."

"Quarreling, eh?" remarked Landor softly, as Ames paused. "That's fine. And then what?"

"I looked down the hall and saw Fulson listening at a closed door."

"Delightful!" Glynn Landor laughed. "I can picture him doing it—he always was a furtive soul."

"He sure is," agreed Ames. "A moment later Fulson switched out the lights in the hall. Then I heard a man mutter something—and then the whispered words—" He paused.

"Go on!" Landor exclaimed with excitement in his voice. "That's no time to stop."

"A man's voice whispered, 'I've got you, damn you. I told you that I would. I've been waiting'—that was all. Then I heard another voice, and a groan, and a soft thud as though a body had fallen."

"What did you do then?"

Ames hesitated before he answered. For some reason which he could not explain, he found himself reluctant to mention the woman who had uttered the whispered warning that had sent him from the house. He finally decided to leave her out of his story altogether.

"I ran back along the hall to the dining-room, and sneaked out the window. I was sure that a murder had been committed and I did not want to be found in the house."

"You were very wise." Landor leaned back in his chair again. He lit another cigarette and blew a smoke-ring in the air. "And that was all that happened?"

"That's all I know about," replied Ames wearily.

Landor started to speak, and then changed his mind as the telephone on the stand beside him rang softly. He picked up the receiver.

"Hello," he said. "Yes, speaking—oh!" His eyes narrowed as he listened to the voice on the other end of the wire. "Hum, quick work on their part. Of course I understand perfectly. Yes, all right, good-bye."

Landor's expression was very thoughtful as he put the receiver back on the hook and looked at Ames. Then suddenly he smiled, a strange, mysterious smile that the other man did not understand.

"As I said before, you were very wise to leave the house when you did," he remarked. "Fosdick Martin has been murdered. The police have already placed Martin's partner, Grant Ellery, and Perry Fulson in jail. They're being held as material witnesses."

"Fosdick Martin murdered!" Ames rose to his feet excitedly. "I knew it—it happened while I was there!" He scowled at Landor, who sat calmly watching him. "I'm through, I tell you—I won't be mixed up in this."

"So you're starting that again." The Lizard's tone was cold. "I warned you it was dangerous." With a cat-like leap he was on his feet and standing close to Ames. "Now you listen, you *are* in this—and you're going to stay! I've had enough nonsense from you. If you make any false moves I'll swear that you murdered Fosdick Martin!"

"That *I* did it!"

"Yes. You were at the house tonight. You could have done it." Landor laughed harshly. "That was why I sent you there—I knew what was going to happen."

"But you said the diamonds—"

"Oh, yes, the diamonds." Landor's hand went to the pocket of his smoking jacket, and produced a chamois bag. "Well, here they are."

"You got them!" Ames gazed at him wildly. "Then you—you are the man who killed Fosdick Martin!"

"No, you're wrong," Landor said softly. "That was the real murderer who just phoned."

"Who was it?" asked Ames and as he spoke he realized that the words were futile and inane.

"That is a little question we had better leave to the police." The Lizard laughed. "And now that we understand each other, I hope you will pardon me." He glanced at the clock. "It's ten o'clock— and I have an appointment at ten-thirty." He bowed. "I must change my clothes so I can leave at once. I think you can find your way out alone."

Ted Ames nodded as he moved toward the door. He was dazed. As he stepped out into the hallway of the apartment house, he murmured softly to himself, "I wonder if I *can* find my way out alone?"

4

GRANT ELLERY DOES NOT TELL

CHIEF KENNY GLANCED at the clock on his desk. Ever since O'Shay and Ellery had left the room, he had been thinking deeply. He was surprised to find that so much had passed through his mind in the past few minutes.

The knowing smile upon Grant Ellery's face still puzzled Kenny. He found himself regretting the half hour's respite he had given the man. It would give Ellery a chance to become more certain of himself. In half an hour he would be able to tell a convincing story which, no doubt, would completely exonerate him of any participation in the murder. Kenny felt that Ellery's story would have to be absolutely water-tight before he would even consider dismissing him from the list of the principal suspects in the case. The chief was sure that his next talk with the man would prove interesting.

Kenny was still thinking when O'Shay returned with Perry Fulson a moment later. As Kenny gazed at Fosdick Martin's secretary, his demeanor changed. He became a ruthless, hard-faced Chief of Police. He disliked the small, black-haired man who stood nervously in front of him, his thin, pointed face white and drawn.

"Sit down, Fulson," Kenny commanded, pointing to the chair which Grant Ellery had recently vacated. "You're going to talk!"

The secretary sank into the chair. He was already badly frightened by the chief's tone. He looked about him anxiously, his dark rat-like eyes blinking as the light gleamed down on his face. The night had proven a thing of terror to him. His every act and gesture was

247

instigated by fear—and of all things, his fear of the police was the most potent.

"Yes sir," he said, and his voice trembled. "But I've told you all I know."

"You have not!" stated Kenny. His tone was harsh, for above all he hated a craven, and this cringing creature was obviously a coward. "I expect more from you than the excited babble you gave me at Martin's house. Tell me everything, Fulson!"

"But—but where shall I begin?" stammered the secretary, his voice shaky as he watched Kenny with the same expression in his eyes a mouse might have when it knew a cat was hunting it. "Won't you tell me?"

Kenny knew the value of suspense. He thought for a moment before he spoke, his eyes fixed intently upon Fulson.

"What time did Mr. Ellery arrive at the house?" he asked finally.

Fulson sighed with relief. He found the question far simpler than he had expected.

"At seven o'clock this evening," he answered promptly. "He came on the train that arrives from the West at six-fifty and came right out to the house in a taxi."

"Hum, do you know why Mr. Ellery had made a trip West?"

"Yes, sir. To investigate some oil fields in which he was interested." Fulson was growing calmer. So far the interview had proved far easier than he had thought. "He had been gone about six months."

"Was Mr. Martin also interested in those oil fields?"

"No, sir, I don't believe he was. Most of Mr. Martin's financial interests are here in town, as you probably know." Fulson ventured to smile at the chief as he uttered what he considered a flattering statement. "The police are so clever about such things."

Kenny glared at him. "You knew Mr. Ellery?" he barked. "That is, you have met him before tonight?"

Fulson looked surprised. He found the question a strange one and he could not understand why the chief had asked it.

"Of course," he said slowly. "Grant Ellery was Mr. Martin's partner."

"Why do you say *was?*" asked Kenny abruptly, watching the secretary intently.

Fulson slumped back in his chair, a startled expression upon his face. His fingers closed and opened nervously, and he glanced about the room wildly as though seeking some means of escape.

O'Shay was not even watching the secretary. The detective sergeant was making little marks on a pad on his knees. It was his habit to jot down such interviews as this in shorthand whenever possible.

"Why did you say it?" repeated the chief.

"I—I thought Mr. Martin was so badly wounded that—" Fulson's voice faltered and then went on. "That I was afraid he was dead." His tone grew excited. "And Ellery did it—I know he did!"

"You *know* he did?" questioned Kenny. "How is that?"

"Because Ellery was alone in the study with Mr. Martin. I heard them quarrel. Their voices grew loud and Ellery said, 'Damn you, I'll kill you for this!'" Fulson nodded his head. "I know it was Ellery who stabbed Mr. Martin."

"But did you see it done?" asked the chief.

The secretary shuddered. The words appeared to have brought a vision before his eyes. A strange expression swept over his face. It was gone in an instant, and yet Kenny had observed it. It puzzled him. Fulson did not look at the chief as he answered slowly.

"No, I did not see it done."

"Where were you when you overheard Ellery make the threat?"

"Listening at the door of the study." Fulson spoke before he thought.

Kenny smiled grimly. "I thought you were. Why?"

"I expected a quarrel, and I was afraid for Mr. Martin's sake. I felt that Mr. Ellery would be very angry when he learned what had happened."

"What do you mean by that?"

Fulson frowned and then shook his head. He was becoming more and more agitated all the time. He seemed to feel that every question that Chief Kenny asked was leading him into a trap. The thought grew in his mind until he was in a state of constant terror.

He was afraid to speak, and yet he realized that if he did not answer he would only make things all the more difficult for himself.

"Answer my question!" The chief's tone was sharp.

"I—I'd rather not!"

"You *will* answer!" Kenny brought his fist down upon the desk
with a thud, and he scowled at Fulson. "What do you mean?"

Fulson half rose from his chair, then sat down again abruptly.
He was weak, so frightened that his legs would not support him.
His eyes were fixed upon Kenny's heavy list as it rested upon the
desk. It seemed to fascinate him.

"Tell me!" growled the chief.

"Ellery had learned that Mr. Martin tricked him out of a lot of
money, and he threatened to kill Mr. Martin if he would not sign a
paper giving the money back—"

"You're lying!" interrupted Kenny abruptly.

"No, I'm not." Fulson spoke eagerly now, for he realized that it
was to his advantage to implicate Ellery. "I was listening outside
the closed door of the study. I heard it all. Ellery gave Mr. Martin
five minutes to decide whether he would sign the paper or die. Mr.
Martin laughed. He told Ellery that he was bluffing, and he wasn't
afraid—"

"Go on!" said Kenny tersely, as Fulson paused.

"'Remember, five minutes, that's all,' was what I heard Grant
Ellery say. Then I could no longer hear their voices. As I stood there
in the hall, the light in the study went out—"

"How did you know that?" broke in the chief. "You just said the
door was closed!"

"Yes, but the light was shining through a crack at the bottom. I
know it went out, for I switched off the hall lights to be sure. I
listened and heard nothing for a moment—" The secretary wrung
his hands nervously. "And then—then I heard a groan and a thud.
It sounded like a body falling—and it was—it was!"

"What did you do then?"

"Nothing." Fulson looked surprised at Kenny's question. "I just
stood there. I was too frightened to move."

"I believe you! Go on, then what?"

"A few seconds later, Mr. Ellery opened the door and I noticed that the lights in the study were burning again. Ellery told me that Mr. Martin had been stabbed, and ordered me to phone the police and the hospital at once."

"Ellery ordered you to phone the police?" Kenny was puzzled, and still he realized that if Grant Ellery were the one who had stabbed Fosdick Martin, the request for the police was a clever move upon his part. "You're sure of that?"

"Quite sure. Mr. Ellery told me to phone here." Fulson found it a relief to dwell upon what he considered unimportant details. "He said something about having walked through the French windows and out into the garden at the side of the house."

"Oh he did, eh?" Kenny glanced toward the nearest window. The rain was still pouring down steadily, as it had been ever since morning. "Mr. Ellery must have had a delightful time strolling in the garden tonight."

O'Shay clucked as he heard the chief's words. The detective sergeant glanced at Fulson, and then jotted down a bit of short-hand upon the pad which had been in constant use since Kenny first started to question the secretary.

"That's what I thought," said Fulson as he caught the meaning of the chief's remark. "His clothes were not the least bit wet, and it was raining hard."

"He's right," remarked O'Shay. "I noticed that myself when we were at the house, Chief."

"So did I," said Kenny dryly. "Go on Fulson, what else did he say?"

"He said that when he reached the garden he turned and looked back. As he did so, the light in the study went out—"

"That's just what you said happened," interrupted Kenny. "Is it true?"

"Yes, the light did go out—but I think Ellery was still in the room. He said something about someone brushing past him in the dark as he ran back." The secretary tried to smile knowingly, but it merely proved an inane grin. "He lies—there wasn't anybody else." A thought struck him. "And Ellery stole the diamonds!"

"What diamonds?" exclaimed Kenny tersely.

"Why, Mr. Martin's collection of unset diamonds. They were worth at least fifty thousand dollars—"

"You idiot!" shouted Kenny, half rising from his chair in his excitement. "Do you mean to say that fifty thousand dollars worth of unset diamonds are missing and you've said nothing about it until now?"

"I—I forgot," stammered Fulson. "They were in a wall-safe behind a picture in Mr. Martin's study. I looked there just after I phoned the police and the safe was empty." He became more and more excited as Kenny glared at him silently. "Ellery took them—I'm sure of it—he took them and killed Mr. Martin. He killed him!" The last words were a tearful wail.

"That will do, Fulson," said Kenny as he saw that the secretary was becoming hysterical. "Take him back, Tim. I'm through."

Fulson was trembling as O'Shay rose slowly from his chair and came toward him. The secretary looked at the chief pleadingly, and there was a sob in his voice as he spoke.

"Please don't lock me in that terrible jail again, Chief. I didn't do anything. Please, please let me go. I can't bear it much longer—this place is driving me mad!"

"I'm sorry, Fulson," said Kenny, quietly but firmly. "But I must continue to hold you as a material witness. That will be all, Sergeant."

The chief frowned as O'Shay and Fulson left the room. The diamonds were an entirely new angle, and he did not know whether to believe the secretary or not.

Finally Kenny picked up the phone and called the Martin residence. One of the detectives who had been left on guard there answered.

"Hello . . . who's this? Oh, Voring, Kenny speaking. Where are you? In Martin's study? Good. Look around and see if you can find a wall-safe behind a picture I'll hold the wire." The chief sat patiently waiting for a few seconds, the receiver at his ear. "Oh, there is one then? Empty and unlocked, eh? I see. Thanks, that's all, Voring."

The chief glanced up as O'Shay entered the room. The latter smiled as he sank slowly into a chair.

"I don't blame Fulson for not wanting to go back in the cell tonight," he remarked. "That dope fiend in number five has been making quite a racket."

"You mean Danny Lester?" asked Kenny. O'Shay nodded. "What's wrong with him?"

"Aw, you know how them guys get. He's howling and mumbling in his cell. Yeager is the turn-key on duty now, and he's tried to shut Danny up, but it don't do much good." O'Shay laughed. "Kinda tough on the other three guys that's locked up. Ellery and Fulson ain't getting much kick out of it."

"You mean the other four, don't you?"

"No, I'm not countin' Tom Hogan, that drunk in number one. He's been sleeping it off for the past five hours."

"What about that confidence man?"

"Oh, Harry Brown. I guess he's used to jails."

"You picked him up this afternoon, didn't you, Tim?"

"Sure, at the Allen Hotel. He passed a lot of bad checks over there on banks that never heard of him. The manager got wise. I caught Brown just as he was leaving." The detective sergeant grinned. "And now he'll be with us for a while."

"What did you think of Fulson's story?" asked the chief.

"Same thing as before. He's lying, that's all. You know, Chief, I kinda think he might have done it."

"I don't." Kenny shook his head. "That would be too obvious. This is not a case that is going to be so easy to solve. I've a hunch about that."

"When you get one of them hunches you're usually right," said O'Shay. "What time is it?"

"Eleven-thirty. I must have talked to Fulson for about fifteen minutes."

"You did, and Ill bet it was the longest fifteen minutes he ever spent."

The chief started to speak, then lapsed into silence as there came a knock on the closed door of the office.

"Come in!" commanded Kenny.

The door swung open and a tall, sandy-haired man walked into the room. He wore a water-soaked soft hat and a yellow slicker covered his lean body. A half-smoked cigarette dangled from the corner of his mouth.

"Oh, hello, Heath," said the chief. "Thought it was about time for you to show up."

"Then you've been expecting me?" Dave Heath unbuttoned his slicker as he spoke. "I hung around the hospital for awhile after Blake left." He took a long white envelope from his inside pocket. "He said to give you this. It's his report."

"Thanks." Kenny smiled at the reporter as he took the envelope. "Did Martin die?"

"You've got me." Heath dropped into a chair. "They were giving him another blood transfusion when I left. Not much hope of it doing any good though."

"Coroner Blake felt the same way about it when he phoned me. Let's see if he's changed his mind." Kenny tore open the envelope and read the coroner's report. "Just the same. His report is murder by person or persons unknown."

"Huh, just like him to make a report before Martin died," remarked O'Shay. "He might have been sure of it before he left town." The detective sergeant looked at the chief. "Told you there was something fishy about Blake didn't I?"

"Still at it, Tim?" Kenny smiled. "Go ahead, but you're running up a blind alley."

"Maybe, but that don't stop me runnin'," O'Shay grinned.

"Oh, Heath." A thought had struck the chief. "The City Editor of the *News* phoned a little while ago. Said for you to call him when you got here."

"Thanks." The reporter rose and moved over to the desk. "Mind if I put a call through on your phone, Chief?"

"Go right ahead."

Heath nodded as he picked up the telephone. "North 8934. City Desk, please. Hello, Clark? Heath talking. Yes, in Chief Kenny's office. I just came down from the hospital. Blake's report is murder by person or persons unknown. Little hasty on the coroner's part. Martin wasn't dead when I left the hospital. No, Blake went to Washington on the ten-fifty—on official business—" Heath stopped speaking abruptly and swung around as the door of the office burst open suddenly. "Hold the wire a minute!"

A uniformed policeman stood in the doorway. He was breathing deeply as though he had been running, and he was very much excited.

"Yeager!" exclaimed Kenny rising from his chair and moving around the desk. "What's the matter?"

"The man in cell seven," exclaimed the turn-key. "Grant Ellery— I found him lying on the floor. He's been murdered! Stabbed to death!"

For an instant the three men stood staring at the excited figure in the doorway. Then the reporter seemed to realize that he was still holding the telephone in his hands.

"Clark!" he said hastily over the wire. "Hold what I've given you on that Martin affair. One of the witnesses has been found murdered in his cell. No, don't know anything yet. I'll call you back!"

As the reporter hung up he saw that Kenny and O'Shay had already started to leave the room. As they disappeared through the doorway, the telephone rang sharply, insistently. Without thinking, Heath answered it.

"Oh, Chief!" he shouted. "Here's a call for you."

Kenny heard him from out in the hall and hastily re-entered the room. He picked up the receiver, uttered a few words and then hung up.

"Hospital calling," he announced tersely. "That last blood transfusion successful. Martin will probably live." He glanced at the clock. It was just eleven-fifty. "But Grant Ellery won't tell me anything now!"

5
EXOTIC LADY

A STRANGE, EXOTIC AIR OF MYSTERY hung over the luxurious apartment of Lily Lawton. It was a place of dim lights and perfumed shadows. That night the living room was a black oasis bathed here and there by pools of subdued light that streamed from the floor lamps placed about in seemingly heedless arrangement. There was an Oriental atmosphere about it all, a sense of subtle unreality that blended all too well with the character of the woman who dwelt there.

Lily Lawton was as strange as her apartment. Dark hair framed the deep brooding eyes in a pale face that was like the frigid beauty of ice. The crimson lips beneath the slender nose were a little petulant and hard. In her way, the woman was very lovely, but it was the flint-like beauty of one who has seen much of the world, and knows the value of enhancing her charms by every possible artifice.

Lily Lawton did not possess the fresh, fragrant beauty of glorious youth, but the fascination of a very suave and sophisticated woman who had lived deeply and recklessly. Seeing her in a crowd you would realize that here was a woman who might be considered dangerous. A woman with such lure might prove as fascinating and as stupefying as some Oriental drug.

As she moved about the room she was a scarlet flame, a tall woman in an evening dress whose bright hue made the whiteness of her face seem all the more startling. Yet the gown that clung close to her tall, slender figure was exceedingly becoming.

Though she moved about slowly, almost majestically with the train of her dress trailing over the soft rug, she appeared to be nervous. She picked up a cigarette, lit it and then sank languidly down on a chaise-longue. There was just the trace of a frown upon her smooth white brow as the telephone hidden in the quaint stand made in the form of a leering Indian god rang softly.

"Hello," she said, her voice low and mellow as she picked up the receiver. "A Mr. Stevens to see me?" She hesitated for the fraction of a second. "Mr. Homer Stevens," she repeated. "Very well, ask him to come up, please. Thank You."

Her expression was very thoughtful as she replaced the receiver. She could not recall anyone among her acquaintances whose name was Homer Stevens. Yet some subtle intuition had told her that she had better see the man. She glanced at the costly diamond-studded wrist watch on her arm. It was just midnight.

A few moments later Lily opened the door of the apartment. A stout, well-dressed man stood gazing at her, a beaming smile upon his round face. He gave the impression of a fat, middle-aged cherub.

"Miss Lawton?" he demanded in a deep and booming voice, and then as she nodded without speaking, "I'm sorry to intrude like this, and at such a late hour, but I have some information which I'm sure you will consider vital."

"Really?" Lily's tone was cold. "I rather doubt my interest!"

"That remains to be seen." For a second Homer Stevens no longer smiled as he looked directly into the woman's eyes. "But I think you would rather learn what I have to say, from me, than from the police!"

Lily flinched at his words, but she gained control of herself instantly.

"Won't you come in, Mr. Stevens," she said quietly.

"Thank you, I'll be delighted." Stevens bowed and then stepped through the door, as she moved aside to let him pass. "It's very kind of you, Miss Lawton."

Lily closed the door and led the way into her living-room. She motioned Stevens to a chair beneath a tall floor lamp, where he seated himself calmly, apparently not at all disturbed by the fact that the light gleamed directly upon his face.

Lily slowly sank down on the chaise-longue. She produced a quaint case and offered Stevens a cigarette.

"Thank you." He shook his head. "I never smoke them."

Lily placed a cigarette between her lips, lit it, and then looked at Stevens, her eyes inscrutable.

"And now just what is it, Mr. Stevens?" she asked quietly. "Blackmail?"

"Miss Lawton!" he laughed, a jolly hearty laugh, that seemed sincere. "How you have misjudged me!"

"Then what is the reason for this visit?"

"Merely a desire to help you." Stevens' expression grew serious.

"And what makes you feel that I am in need of assistance?"

"I'm sure you are," stated Stevens calmly. "And that's why I'm here."

"It all sounds rather mysterious." Lily looked at him, and then smiled. "But you hardly appear the dark and sinister villain, Mr. Stevens."

"Of course not," he smiled. "And I'm not—I'm merely a private investigator."

She grew tense as she heard his words. She leaned forward, staring at him, the cigarette in her hand forgotten.

"Then you are from the police?"

"No," he shook his head. "I'm afraid they have never even heard of me. As I said I am a private investigator—my work is strictly of a confidential nature."

"I see," said Lily slowly. She was very much on guard. It was obvious that she did not believe him, and yet she wanted to learn more. "But why have you come to see me?"

"Because of what happened to-night." Stevens' tone was matter of fact. He appeared to expect her to understand without any further explanation. "I rather felt that you might need my services."

Lily hesitated before she spoke. In spite of the suaveness of his tone, she sensed an undercurrent of danger. She realized that this man was evidently very clever. It was best to proceed carefully.

Somewhere back in Lily's brain, she seemed to hear a voice warning her, telling her to remember that anything which she might say would be used against her.

"But I don't understand?" Lily looked at Stevens, and her expression was that of a child who has been given a riddle too difficult for it to solve. "What has tonight to do with it?"

"Quite a lot." Amusement mingled with admiration was on the round, fat face as he watched her. Homer Stevens realized that Lily Lawton was an extremely astute woman; she played her game well. "You see, Miss Lawton, I have often found it useful to dig up all the information about people that I can. In a town of this size, it usually isn't very difficult to do so."

"Naturally not. And I suppose I am among those you have all nicely tabulated, like various specimens of butterfly or something of that sort? Is that it, Mr. Stevens?"

"To an extent, yes. But one cannot gather much more than the known facts." He smiled. "And all of us usually have little details about our lives that we prefer not to have known by the world. But I do know a few things about you, Miss Lawton. For instance, you are the leading lady with the Troupers' Stock Company here in North City."

"Remarkable!" Lily laughed delightedly. "A discovery worthy of a paragon of detectives—or should I say Private Investigators. To think of it—you have discovered what everyone who has been to the Globe Theatre knows. I'm afraid you will have to give me a more brilliant example of your work than that, if you wish to impress me, Mr. Stevens."

"And still we work at cross purposes." Stevens shook his head in mock sorrow. "It's all so futile." His tone changed and his face grew serious.

"Listen, Miss Lawton, I want to help you. I really mean that. It is my motive for coming here tonight."

"Again we return to the noble motives which instigate your visit, Mr. Stevens."

He studied her for a moment before he spoke. He appeared to be debating a question in his mind. She waited with growing impatience for his next word—sensing that now it would reveal the real reason for his unexpected visit—and half fearing what he might say.

"I think I can make myself clear as to how much I really know about you, if you will permit me to ask you one question," he said finally.

"What is that?"

"Just why do you hate Grant Ellery so bitterly?"

"Grant Ellery?" She spoke before she thought, startled surprise in her tone. "What have I to do with him?"

"That's just what I've been wondering," said Stevens quietly. "You know of course, that he is in jail now—held as a material witness in the Fosdick Martin case?"

"Why, yes, so I heard."

"Your hearing is excellent," stated Stevens with a smile. "As yet no one is supposed to know anything about it but the police. Of course, there will be a story in the Morning *News*—but this isn't New York, Miss Lawton—tomorrow's paper does not appear in North City the night before. How did you learn Grant Ellery was in jail?"

"Why don't you tell me how I learned that, Mr. Stevens?" she parried. "Surely a clever detective like you would know!"

"Of course," he said quietly. "And I do know. You were at Fosdick Martin's house tonight—you know what happened there—but you don't know who stabbed Martin!"

Lily glared at him like a cat about to spring. Her slender white hands fluttered nervously, the cigarette in her fingers unheeded.

"I wasn't there!" she exclaimed hysterically. "I don't know anything about it. Oh, what are you trying to do to me? Why did you come here—why—why?"

"Please, Miss Lawton." Stevens shook his head, a serious expression on his round face. "It will do you no good to deny your having been at Fosdick Martin's house tonight. As a matter of fact, I was just about to suggest that you go and tell your story to the chief of police."

"The chief of police! Why should I?"

"Because that will be just what Chief Kenny will not expect. For you to go to his office and tell him just as much as you wish about what has happened, will make things easier for you in the long run." Stevens smiled. "I think you can be depended upon to handle the situation gracefully, Miss Lawton."

"Thank you," she nodded coldly, as she considered his advice. She did not as yet understand the motive that had brought him here, but still she realized that Homer Stevens, as a detective, could take her to the police himself and she would be forced to go. Perhaps it would be best to agree to what he asked of her.

"I'll go," she said finally. "I shall call on Chief Kenny the first thing in the morning."

"No, I don't advise that." The stout man shook his head. "Go at once." He glanced at his watch. "It's twelve-fifteen now. You should reach the police station by one. I'm sure that Chief Kenny will still be there then."

"Very well," said Lily slowly. "I'll go just as soon as I change into a more suitable costume for weather like this."

"Good." Homer Stevens rose to his feet. "You won't be sorry, Miss Lawton." He laughed. "I have enjoyed my visit immensely." He bowed. "And you may depend upon me to be of service."

"That is very kind." Lily rose and moved with him toward the door of the apartment. "But I still do not understand the reason for your interest."

"Life is full of enigmas, Miss Lawton, mostly because we make it so." Stevens had paused near the door—his gaze fell upon a thin silver cigarette case tossed carelessly on a table—a man's case on which the initials G. L. were engraved. "Goodnight, Miss Lawton, I hope you will follow my advice."

"I shall, I assure you." She held out her hand. "Goodnight, Mr. Stevens—and thank you."

Stevens took her hand for an instant, muttered a few polite words and then departed.

Lily closed and locked the door. For a few moments she leaned against it, thinking deeply.

Finally she shrugged her shoulders, as she went to change into something more suitable for a call upon the chief of police.

Stevens smiled as the door closed behind him.

"G. L." he said softly, as he walked down the hall toward the apartment elevator. "Glynn Landor, eh." There was a satisfied expression upon his round face. "I rather thought she might know The Lizard!"

6
THE DEATH CELL

THE CORRIDOR WHICH RAN DOWN THE CENTER of the jail was grimly silent. There was something forbidding about the rows of heavy steel barred doors on either side. The lights which hung from the ceiling gleamed brightly, and yet there was a ghastly whiteness about their glow.

The four men stood in front of cell number seven gazing through the bars of the closed door. The chief, O'Shay, Yeager, and the police reporter had all encountered death before. It was part of their job. Yet the face of each was set and stern as they stared at the grotesque figure that sprawled face downward within the cell.

There was something about Grant Ellery as he lay there that told each man that Fosdick Martin's partner was dead. Chief Kenny had been right. The man in cell seven would not tell him anything now.

For a moment only, the four men stood motionless, a moment during which each was lost in his own thoughts of death, and then the chief stepped forward. He tried the door of the cell but it did not open. Kenny glanced at Yeager. The latter stepped forward, producing his keys as he did so.

"I locked it when I went to get you, Chief," said Yeager as he placed the key in the lock. "The murder must have happened while I was chasing the dope in cell five."

Kenny glanced at the turn-key, but he said nothing. Now he would waste no time in questioning Yeager. That would come later, after he had inspected the scene of the murder.

263

It was Heath who found the turn-key's statement interesting, and he turned to O'Shay.

"What does he mean by 'the dope'?" he asked the detective sergeant softly.

"Feller we got locked up in the last cell down there." O'Shay waved his hand down the corridor to his right. "Name's Danny Lester."

"And he nearly got away," murmured Heath. "Hum, sounds interesting."

The chief paid little heed to what the others were saying, though he heard every word. That Danny Lester had nearly made his escape was interesting, but Kenny would learn more about that later. As Yeager opened the cell-door the chief stepped inside. The turn-key moved back and stood beside the others as they watched.

Kenny paused just inside the doorway, his gaze roving about the interior of the cell. It was a bleak, barren spot that met his eyes. High in the ceiling a single bulb cast its glow down over the cold grey walls, the iron cot upon which Ellery had carelessly tossed his coat, and upon the motionless figure on the hard, stone floor.

Ellery's arms were stretched above his head, as though he had made one last desperate effort to catch himself as he fell. The back of his soft white silk shirt was stained with blood. There was no doubt that he had been brutally stabbed.

Kenny knelt down and examined the limp form slowly and painstakingly. Finally the chief rose to his feet. He glanced at the others, a frown upon his face.

"He's dead all right," he said. "Stabbed through the back so that the weapon reached his heart."

Both O'Shay and Heath nodded. There had been little doubt in their minds that Grant Ellery was dead.

"Just the same way that they tried to get Martin," remarked Heath thoughtfully. "Looks like the same person had it in for them both, doesn't it, Chief?

Kenny seemed to be debating the question for an instant before he answered, and then he nodded.

"Yes. I'm positive it was the same person."

The chief turned his back on the others and began to wander about the cell. Ellery's coat lying on the bunk caught his eye. He picked it up and examined it carefully. As he finished, he glanced at the spot where the coat had been. His face lighted with interest as he observed an object gleaming faintly in the light. It was a thin, keen-bladed knife, obviously blood-stained.

Kenny gazed at the dagger-like blade for a long time. There was something strange about it as it rested upon the blanket folded over the bunk. It was the weapon with which Grant Ellery had been murdered, of course, but its presence in the cell puzzled the police official. He felt that the murderer was clever, far too clever to have left the knife where it might easily be found unless there was some reason for the act.

Finally the chief uttered a low grunt and shook his head. The motive for the knife having been left there would have to be looked into later. Now there was work to be done. He took a clean white handkerchief from his pocket and dropped it carefully over the weapon before he picked it up. He lifted it gingerly, holding it in only one place. He did not wish to risk blurring any possible fingerprints of the murderer's hand.

"Find somethin', Chief?" asked O'Shay, who had been interestedly watching, though he could not see what Kenny had picked up, as the latter's back shielded him from the others. "Is it a clue?"

"The knife the murderer used," answered Kenny quietly, as he turned and moved out of the cell, the weapon covered with the handkerchief as he held it in his hand. "It's a clue, all right."

"What's it look like?" demanded the reporter eagerly, edging closer to the chief. "Let us see it, will you?"

"I'll show you later," the chief smiled and shook his head. "I don't want to touch it any more than I can help now. Fingerprints, you know."

O'Shay started to speak and then lapsed into silence as there came an uncanny howl from the far cell on the opposite side of the corridor. All four men turned in the direction of the sound, but could see nothing.

"It's that drunk," said Yeager. "He must have woke up an' found bein' in a cell is not to his likin'. It's the first he knows about it, for it's dead to the world he's been for I don't know how long."

"Go see if you can't quiet him, Yeager," ordered the chief impatiently, as there came another howl from the cell at the far end of the row. "Make him stop that noise!"

Hurriedly the turn-key started to obey. As he reached the cell where Tom Hogan had been lodged, the door suddenly flew open. Yeager leaped forward and slammed it shut again and locked it before Hogan realized what had happened.

From within the cell Hogan, a big rough looking man clad in a blue shirt and overalls blinked as he caught sight of the blue-uniformed figure of the turn-key. He shambled forward and caught hold of the bars of the door with his grimy hands, and glared at Yeager.

"Let me out of here!" he roared. "I ain't gonna be locked up!"

"Shut up!" growled Yeager. "Or I'll come in there with me club an' shut you up!"

Hogan glared at him. It slowly dawned upon the man in the cell that the turn-key had meant just what he said. Hogan groaned but moved back to his bunk and dropped upon it heavily.

Yeager walked across the corridor and tried the door of Danny Lester's cell. The next cell was empty, so the turn-key did not bother with it at all. The third cell on that side of the corridor was also vacant and Yeager passed it by. The fourth was that in which lay the motionless form of Grant Ellery.

The turn-key again crossed the corridor. He paused in front of the cell directly opposite that in which Ellery had been placed. This was where the confidence man, Harry Brown, was being held. The latter was lying on his bunk with his back to the door. Yeager tried the heavy, steel-barred door. It was unlocked, and he locked it swiftly. He moved on to the next cell, that of Perry Fulson. The secretary sat on his bunk, his head buried in his hands, and he did not look up when Yeager tried the cell-door and found it also unlocked. As he locked it, the turn-key glanced anxiously at the chief.

"What's the matter?" asked Kenny, hurrying to Yeager's side.

"The cells," answered Yeager in a whisper. "I've just found three of them unlocked." "Unlocked?"

"Yes, Chief."

"Which ones?"

"Hogan's, Brown's and Fulson's."

"I see." Kenny's expression indicated that he was puzzled. "All right, Yeager." He turned away.

"Something new, Chief?" asked Heath as Kenny returned to where the reporter and O'Shay stood near the door of Ellery's cell.

"It might be important," answered the chief. "We've just learned that three of the other prisoners' cells were unlocked at the time of the murder."

"Which ones?" demanded Heath. "Hogan, Fulson and Brown."

"Then any one of them might have done it!" exclaimed O'Shay. "Don't you think so, Chief?"

Kenny did not answer until he had thought the question over carefully.

"Yes," he said slowly. "Any one of them might have killed Ellery, but I wonder if any of them did." He apparently dismissed the matter from his mind for the time being, as he glanced at the detective sergeant. "Oh Tim, you'd better phone Doctor Wilson, he's deputy coroner you know. Have him come here at once and give us a report on Ellery."

"O.K.," said O'Shay and he left to carry out the chief's instructions.

"Yeager," called Kenny. "Tell the Desk Sergeant to put another man on guard here for a while. I want to talk to you. Hurry back, I'll wait right here."

The turn-key saluted and hurried off in the same direction O'Shay had gone.

"What do you make of this case, Chief?" asked Heath, as the reporter found himself alone in the corridor with Kenny. "It's a whale of a *News* story."

"I guess it is," the chief smiled. "But it is just a bit more than a news-story to me, Heath."

"I know that, Chief." The reporter nodded soberly. "Still a murder like this is a good break for me. It's news with a capital 'N'. Front page stuff—and if you can give me any further dope, that makes it all the better. How about it?"

"I'll be frank with you, Heath, I can't tell you very much now. I don't quite know what I'm up against yet. So far it's all vague in my mind—as vague as hell." Kenny shook his head and his face was serious. "I'll have to think awhile before I give out any statements. Let it go at that for the time being, will you? You know just about everything that's happened so far, as it is. So let it slide."

"Sure, Chief." The reporter grinned. "No statements it is!"

"Well," Kenny laughed. "We *are* working on the case you know."

"I get you. Chief Kenny states that the police are working on a clue which is expected to lead to the arrest of the murderer in a very short time. Don't worry, I'll have the usual tag-line to my story." Heath glanced at his watch. "It's late—got to gallop along and write this up pronto. Clark will be ravin'. I'll give you a ring just before we close in case there's a last minute flash. So long!"

Kenny smiled and waved his hand as the reporter dashed away. He watched Dave Heath as the latter disappeared along the corridor. A good newspaper man, and one who knew his business. He had not missed very much of what he had heard and seen tonight. The chief knew that he would read the *Morning News* with interest.

Yeager appeared with a blue-coated figure by his side. Kenny nodded as the other policeman saluted, then the chief motioned to Yeager to follow him back to his office.

"Now tell me just what happened," Kenny said as he sat at his desk again. "Start from the very beginning and give me all the details." He smiled at the elderly officer who stood before him. "You can forget the regulations for the time being and sit down, Yeager."

"Thank you, sir." The turn-key sighed as he dropped into a chair. He had spent a busy evening and he was weary. "Well, to begin with I was walkin' down the corridor between th' cells. I was just opposite the two at this end—"

"Between Ellery's and Fulson's cells, eh?"

"No, sir." Yeager shook his head. "Between Ellery's and Brown's. Fulson is in the next one down on the right."

"Good!" Kenny smiled. "I just wanted to test your memory. Go on."

"Well, as I was walkin' along somethin' made me turn and look back down the corridor. Just then I seen this Danny Lester sneakin' out of his cell. I run after him of course, but before I could even get near him he had run down the back corridor and out onto Eastern Avenue."

"Was the Eastern Avenue door open?"

"Yes, it was that, Chief. Wide open and swung back against the wall."

"How did that happen?" Kenny looked sternly at Yeager. "I ordered that door kept locked at all times!"

"I know that, sir. And it was, not more than half an hour before I seen Danny Lester runnin' away, for I tried it then."

"Hm, was it bolted or just locked?"

"Just locked. The bolt is broken. I reported it to Sergeant Sprong yesterday."

"Then anyone could have unlocked it if he had had the right key?"

"Yes, sir. I guess they could, at that."

"I see. Go on."

"I chased Danny to th' corner of Eastern and Waltham Avenues before I caught him. The little devil nearly got away from me, what with the storm an' all." The turn-key glanced at the windows of the chief's office. "I guess you could have seen me if you'd been looking out."

"Unfortunately I wasn't." Kenny's tone was dry. "How long did it take you to catch Lester and bring him back?"

"I couldn't say for sure. He was half crazy when he knew I had him, an' he fought me all the way. I guess about ten minutes— maybe longer. I ain't positive."

"Do you think someone could have murdered Ellery while you were chasing Lester and bringing him back?"

"I don't know, sir." Yeager appeared perplexed. "I wasn't gone long."

"A man could do a lot in a short space of time if he worked fast, and the murderer did just that. Was there anyone in the corridor when you got back?"

"Not a soul did I see. I locked Danny up in his cell an' started to come an' tell you he'd tried to make a break. As I passed Ellery's cell, I seen him lyin' on the floor just like you found him. I went in and looked close, then come arunnin' to you."

"You entered the cell then?"

"Yes, sir."

"Was the cell door unlocked?"

"No, sir." Yeager frowned. "That's the funny part of it—it was locked tight just like it was when we came back later."

"Hm-mm, all right, that'll be all. You go back on duty now and call me as soon as the Deputy Coroner arrives—"

Kenny stopped speaking as the telephone rang. He motioned to Yeager to remain where he was and then reached out and lifted the receiver.

"Hello . . . oh, all right, Sergeant, send him right in." The chief hung up. "That's Doctor Wilson now. You can go, Yeager." Kenny glared at the policeman. "Finding those cells unlocked looks like a bit of carelessness on your part."

"But it wasn't, sir." The turn-key was on his feet as he uttered the protest. "I tried them all just a little while before I seen Danny tryin' to sneak away, an' every one of them was locked."

"Very well." Kenny dismissed Yeager with a wave of the hand.

As the door closed behind the turn-key, the chief sat staring fixedly at his desk. Finally he smiled to himself. He glanced at the telephone as though the instrument had suddenly become a very vital factor in his mind.

"I should have thought of that." He murmured softly. "Yes, it was against orders." A thought suddenly struck him. "Of course, I sure am dumb!"

Hastily Kenny reached into a drawer of his desk and fumbled around. He frowned as he drew out a bunch of keys.

"Strange," he said softly. "I was sure these would be missing, but they're not. Hum, maybe I was wrong." He shook his head. "Maybe!"

He glanced up as there came a knock on the door. At a word from the chief the door opened and Doctor Wilson appeared. He was a short, stocky man who wore horn-rimmed eyeglasses, and at present he was not in the most cordial of moods.

"What's the idea of my being called out on a night like this?" he demanded abruptly. "Your man O'Shay phoned me that it was very vital, or I wouldn't be here. What's wrong? He refused to tell me over the telephone."

"Tim is getting some sense in his old age," said Kenny. "You're deputy coroner, aren't you, Doctor?"

"Certainly, you know that. At least you should know it."

"I do," said Kenny tersely. "And I know that you are supposed to take over Coroner Blake's duties when he is away, and he's gone to Washington."

"All right. Here I am, what's it all about?"

"We just found a man murdered in his cell a little while ago."

"Murdered! Who was it?"

"Grant Ellery, did you know him?"

"Grant Ellery! Good God! Of course I knew him. He was Fosdick Martin's partner. Grant Ellery dead!" Doctor Wilson dropped weakly into a chair. "Murdered! Why we were old friends—went to school together years ago. How did it happen?"

"That's just what I would like to know." Kenny smiled sardonically. "You see I did send for you regarding something vital, Doctor."

"Yes, I realize that now." Doctor Wilson nodded. "I'm sorry, Chief. I'm afraid you've found me in rather a bad humor this evening."

"This night hasn't been one to make me dash around shouting 'goody, goody'," stated Kenny. "That's all right, Doctor."

The physician assumed his professional manner. He got to his feet. "I suggest that you let me see the, ah, body."

"Right." Kenny rose from his desk. "Come with me."

The chief hastened out of the office with Doctor Wilson beside him. The two men walked along the hallway which led from the door of Kenny's office to the center of the building. As they moved along, the police official briefly related the events of the night. The physician listened eagerly, asking a question now and then.

A few seconds' walk and the two men had turned sharply to the left. They passed through an open doorway and found themselves in the part of the station house which contained the jail. Here the corridor between the cells led to the rear of the building where it connected with the corridor which ran at right angles and terminated at one end at the door leading out to Eastern Avenue, and at the other at a door which opened on to Oakland Avenue.

Yeager appeared as Kenny and Doctor Wilson reached the corridor between the cells.

"You'll find him in there," said the chief indicating cell seven. "Officer Yeager here will be at your service, Doctor." He smiled. "And now if you'll pardon me for a few minutes. I have just thought of something which I should like to ask the Desk Sergeant."

7
QUESTIONS

NORMA BURTON SIGHED PENSIVELY as she sat curled up on the window-seat staring out into the darkness of the stormy night. Behind her the big studio seemed a vast and awe-inspiring place, compared to the lovely, slender figure in the dark green lounging-pajamas. The girl's pretty little blond head lay a touseled mass against the dark wall of the far end of the padded window-seat.

For a long time Norma had sat there lost in her own thoughts. Vague fancies they were—rose-hued, indefinite dreams that tumbled about in her mind. The visions of one who is very sweet and very young.

But that night she found that she did not enjoy her dreams as much as she had at other times. A talented and gifted young artist, she was a child of many moods. There were times when life seemed futile and death was a knight in gleaming armor that she liked to play with only because she found it a daring gesture. Still tonight she did not want to think of either life or death—there were reasons that made her wish to drive such topics from her mind. Yet she had learned, in what seemed so long ago, that one cannot always rule one's thoughts. The mind has a will of its own when it desires to assert itself.

Norma found herself wishing that Billie had not had an engagement that evening. Billie was such a nice practical soul, and yet such a charming girl. Norma had liked dark-haired, grave-eyed Billie from the moment the two girls had met three years before.

The big studio apartment they now shared was in a way the realization of a dream for both of them.

To Norma, it meant that she had become successful in her work—and it was true, for she was one of the highest paid fashion-artists in North City.

To Billie Fenton, it also meant a great deal, for she was a writer whose first novel had been looked upon with favor by the critics. The reviews had been more than kind and glowing.

"You're a genius," Norma had said when she had read the book-reviews, and then she smiled a quaint smile that was like a gay hued butterfly's wing fluttering in the sunshine. "And so am I!" she announced proudly.

Norma turned her head and glanced about the studio. A faint glow came from the fading coals in the open fire-place. Upon a pillow tossed carelessly on the floor near the hearth, a stuffed toy camel not more than a foot high stood patiently and a bit deject-edly gazing at the brooding embers. Upon a stand near the door of the studio were pink roses in a black-and-silver vase. Soft, fresh little pink buds that seemed so brave and yet so helpless and so very much like Norma.

Upon the wall a short distance from the fire-place there hung a suit of ancient armor.

"That's for those who forget to wear it in real life," Norma always said. "You see I'm very kind."

The big room was filled with the things that the two girls loved. Jars and boxes of hammered brass with quaint Chinese designs upon them gleamed dully in unexpected corners. Drawings that Norma had made were scattered here and there upon the high walls. The lights about the room gleamed softly down upon things that were far more than just furniture, for about them all hung the comfort that was part of a place where one really lived.

In the center of the room stood a big table. Amid the jumble of books and magazines that were usually scattered about on it in delightful confusion, a strange wooden beast painted a sickly green and said to represent an ancient dinosaur ruled supreme. It was a quaint creature named Gerald, and was Norma's especial property.

On either side of the table were two comfortable arm-chairs. In a corner of the room directly beneath a sky-light there was a table piled with artist's materials, and beside it an easel. It was here that Norma did her work. Across the room was the worn oak desk now painted black, with its typewriter lost amid a mass of manuscripts. This was Billie's nook. Beyond this was a closed door leading into a tiny apartment consisting of bed-room, kitchenette, and bath.

Norma sat up in surprise as there came a soft rap on the studio door. She glanced at her wrist-watch and found it was just eleven-thirty. At first she thought it might be Billie returning from her engagement—still it was very unlike her to knock, and so gently at that.

"Wonder who's barging around here this time of night," murmured Norma as she went to the door.

As she opened it her eyes widened in surprise. She found herself gazing up at a tall good-looking young man who nervously ran his fingers through his thick blond hair when he observed the vision in the green silk lounging-pajamas standing in the doorway.

"I beg your pardon," he said, and Norma found that she liked his voice. "I was looking for someone—I must have knocked on the wrong door."

"That's quite all right." Norma spoke a bit more coldly than she intended. She rather regretted that this interesting-looking young man was seeking someone else. "Who is it, if I may ask? Perhaps I can help you."

Ted Ames looked at her. He did not quite know how to explain that an hour or so ago he had chanced upon Glynn Landor going into this building, and had followed him without knowing exactly why. Since then, Ames had made his way from floor to floor but had been unable to find any sign of The Lizard. This door was the first upon which he had knocked, and now he was glad of the sudden hunch that had made him do so.

"You can help me," he said finally, a mad desire to know more about this girl sweeping over him. "But it's rather a long story."

Norma hesitated a moment and then smiled.

"Won't you come in," she said softly. "We can talk better then."

"That's mighty fine of you, and I appreciate it," said Ames as he stepped into the big studio and the girl closed the door. "Most girls wouldn't take such a chance with a stranger."

"Oh, I'm not quite as daring as you think," Norma laughed. "I'm expecting my roommate almost any moment now." She looked at him, an amused expression upon her lovely face. "So you see, Mr.—" she hesitated.

"Ames—Ted Ames," he answered promptly.

"Mr. Ames, I'm not taking any chances—" again she smiled. "Please sit down." She looked up at him. "When a giant more or less enters a mouse's den, he should try to make himself more nearly her size."

"Such a delightful mouse," exclaimed Ames as he sank into one of the arm-chairs.

"And such a flattering giant on such very short acquaintance," said Norma, dropping into the other chair. "But I believe you said I might be able to help you. Please tell me how?"

"By doing just what you are doing now—talking to me." Ames' face grew dark and as the girl watched him she realized that he was evidently in some really serious difficulty.

Norma found herself extremely anxious to aid him as much as she could. In fact, she was rather surprised at herself for having developed such a deep interest in this young chap, whom she had seen for the first time in her life a moment before.

His words puzzled her. She did not quite see what good it would do for her merely to talk casually as she had been doing.

"I'm afraid I don't understand," she said, her eyes fixed upon his strong young face. "How can I help you by talking?"

"You don't need to understand." Ames waved away the idea of her doing so with an impetuous gesture of his hand. "Have you ever passed someone in a crowd, and something inside you made you wish you knew him?"

"Of course, often." Norma nodded her head. "Why?"

"Because that was the way I felt when I saw you standing there in the doorway." Ames laughed a bit ruefully. "I hope you won't think me silly—talking to you this way when I don't even know your name."

"I'm Norma Burton," she smiled. "And I don't think you're silly at all."

"Thank you," he said and she was glad he had not somehow made the statement seem impersonal by adding, Miss Burton. "Then you do understand what I mean—what I said about someone in a crowd?" he asked boyishly.

"Surely," she said, her voice very low. She found herself in a very confidential mood with this man, who after all was only a stranger. "I understand perfectly."

Ames looked at her for a moment without speaking. There was something about her voice that puzzled him. It seemed familiar, and yet he knew that if he had ever heard it before he would remember.

A question rose unexpectedly in his mind. A question that he suddenly realized he would have to ask—although he shrank from doing so.

"Did you ever hear of a man named Glynn Landor?" he blurted out abruptly, and hated himself for having asked the question.

Norma gazed at him in surprise. For a moment she hesitated before she spoke, and now he seemed to feel that she was nervous.

"Glynn Landor," she repeated. "Why yes—I have heard the name—why do you ask?"

Now it was Ames who hesitated. The calm matter of factness of her reply disappointed him. He had hoped that she had never heard of the strange, suave creature who was known as The Lizard. It seemed so incongruous that this lovely girl should even know the name of Landor.

"Then you *do* know him!" Ames could not suppress the regret in his voice as he spoke, though he tried to do so.

"I didn't say that," Norma spoke slowly, as though she were choosing her words very carefully. "I merely said that I had heard the name. But really, Mr. Ames, I'm quite at a loss to understand why you consider the subject so vital."

"The subject of Glynn Landor *is* vital." Ames' tone was hard as he spoke. "I have reason to wish that it weren't so important to me."

"Then you know Mr. Landor?"

"Yes, I know him," stated Ames grimly, an unconscious scowl on his handsome face. "I know him very well."

Norma started to speak, and then changed her mind as the door opened and a slender dark-haired girl dressed in evening clothes appeared.

"Hello," she exclaimed. She glanced from Norma to Ames, who had risen to his feet.

"This is Mr. Ames, Billie," said Norma. "Mr. Ames, this my long expected room-mate, Miss Fenton."

Ames bowed as Billie smiled at him. He saw that she was a very attractive girl, and there was something in her manner which indicated that she was very sure of herself.

"You must pardon me, Mr. Ames," said Billie. "But I'm not in the most agreeable of moods."

"Why, Billie?" Norma looked at her in surprise. "What happened?"

"Nothing, only I don't like being sent home alone on a stormy night like this."

Ames realized with the arrival of Billie Fenton that the atmosphere of the studio had changed. No longer did he feel that he might dare hope to find the understanding mood that Norma had shown him previously. The knowledge that he was a stranger to these girls swept over him and he desired to get away.

"I didn't realize it was so late," he said as he glanced at his watch. "I must be going."

He hoped that Norma would suggest that he stay a little longer, but he was disappointed. She merely smiled and held out her hand to him.

"Goodnight, Mr. Ames," she said. "Won't you drop in again. I'd like to finish that little discussion of ours."

"Thank you, I'll be delighted." Ames bowed over her hand, and then turned to Billie Fenton. "Goodnight, Miss Fenton."

"Goodnight, Mr. Ames. Sorry you have to run away so soon." Billie spoke casually and without interest.

Ted Ames moved toward the door. As he drew it open he heard Billie speak to Norma.

"The next time I have a date with Glynn Landor—he'll know it," Ames heard as he opened the door.

He was frowning as he stepped out into the hall. So the Fenton girl had had an engagement with Landor this evening. What was The Lizard's game?

8
A LOVELY SUSPECT

CHIEF KENNY GLANCED at the clock on the desk as he once more sat in his office. It was now a quarter to one. The chief smiled grimly as he observed the time. The past hour had brought some very startling developments in what he termed the Martin case.

The deputy coroner had gone after examining Grant Ellery and having the body removed to the morgue for the time being. Doctor Wilson had appeared quite upset over Ellery's death, and had performed his duties with all possible haste. Now Kenny found himself with a few minutes in which to think things over.

The murder of Grant Ellery had been a new and unexpected angle, following the stabbing of Fosdick Martin. Yet Kenny was positive that the connection between the two crimes was a close one. The chief was almost certain that the murderer had killed Ellery because he felt that the latter knew too much about the attempt to assassinate Martin. It was a series of wheels within wheels, and Kenny was grimly determined to stop those wheels from revolving by capturing the murderer.

The chief glanced up quickly as the door of the office opened and O'Shay entered the room. The big detective closed the door carefully behind him and then dropped into a chair. There was a serious expression on his face as he gazed at Kenny.

"What do you make of it, Chief?" he asked. "Ellery being murdered in his cell like that has got me up in the air. I can't figure it out." He shook his head. "Nope—I don't get it."

"It does seem we have a great many things to take into consideration," remarked Kenny. "Tim, I want you to find out all you can about those other three men who were locked up at the time that Ellery was murdered. Never mind about Perry Fulson, we'll come to him later."

"Think one of those birds may have done it, Chief?" asked the detective sergeant, looking at Kenny questioningly.

"Of course he might." The chief waved his hand impatiently. "Anyone might have done it, Tim." He shook his head. "But I'm not thinking now. I want facts—all the information you can dig up about each of those three men. You'd better send some of the boys out to get the low-down. See if Danny Lester has ever been connected with Grant Ellery in any way, and the same goes for Hogan, and Brown."

"O.K., Chief." O'Shay rose and started toward the door, but paused as the telephone rang.

Kenny motioned the detective sergeant back to his chair and picked up the receiver.

"Hello? Yes, Sergeant? A Miss Lily Lawton to see me. What does she want? Won't say, eh? All right, send her in." The chief hung up and then glanced at O'Shay. "Lily Lawton—ever hear of her, Tim?"

"Yes, she's an actress. Leading lady with the Troupers' Stock Company, here in town. They've been playing at the Globe Theatre for the past month."

"I see. Guess you'd better stay and make a few more shorthand notes while I talk to her, Tim. I suspect that she may know something about this case." Kenny smiled grimly. "If she does, she will tell me!"

"Uh huh!" the big detective laughed. "I'll bet that dame doesn't know what she's letting herself in for, coming to see you."

Kenny did not answer as there came a soft knock on the closed door. He rose from his desk and went to the door. Al he opened it, he found himself gazing at a slender, dark-haired woman. She was very smartly clad from head to foot and carried an umbrella in one gloved hand.

"Chief Kenny?" she asked, her voice low and musical. "I'm Miss Lily Lawton," she added as Kenny bowed.

"Won't you come in, Miss Lawton?" The chief stepped aside as the actress entered the room. "Please be seated." He indicated the chair facing the desk.

"Thank you." As she took the chair, Lily Lawton glanced casually at O'Shay, who was now standing some distance off.

"One of my men, Detective Sergeant O'Shay," said Kenny as he observed the direction of the actress' gaze. "A very valuable aid."

Lily smiled at O'Shay and then turned to the chief who had returned to his desk.

"I suppose you are wondering why I am here, Chief Kenny," she said. "Am I right?"

"Quite right, Miss Lawton." Kenny smiled. "I hardly expected such a charming visitor at this time of night."

"You flatter me." Lily glanced at her wrist-watch. "Dear me, it is rather late, isn't it? But you see I did not think of coming here until after the performance tonight." She hesitated.

"Perhaps I would not have come at all had I permitted myself to stop and think."

"I'm glad you acted upon the impulse. Ah, just why did you say you came, Miss Lawton?"

"I haven't said yet," she smiled nervously. "But I will." She paused as though she were choosing her words carefully. "It is because of Mr. Martin, Mr. Fosdick Martin."

"I see," said Kenny very softly.

"Yes, I—" the actress found difficulty in uttering the words. "I've heard that he has been—murdered!"

Kenny's expression remained placid as he gazed at Lily Lawton. His tone was quiet and unexcited as he spoke.

"May I ask where you heard that, Miss Lawton?"

The actress looked at him strangely, a queer expression in her large, grey eyes. His attitude of serenity was not quite what she had expected. For the moment it left her floundering and uncertain.

"Fosdick Martin is dead, isn't he?" she finally asked.

"The coroner's report to me was murder," answered Kenny, and the actress did not realize that he had evaded her question. "But may I ask how you heard of Mr. Martin's, ah, death?"

"Surely there is nothing mysterious about that." Lily laughed. "It is very simple. I phoned Mr. Martin's house a short while ago and one of the servants told me that he had been stabbed. That he had been taken to the hospital."

"So that was it?" Kenny leaned back in his chair. "Well, that does explain matters." He studied Lily as he spoke. "But how did you happen to call the house, if I may ask?"

Lily hesitated for an instant before she answered. She looked about the room casually. O'Shay had moved over to the window. He appeared to be staring out into the storm, but his note-book and pencil were in his hands.

"I phoned because, well, Mr. Martin and I were friends, quite close friends. It was something rather personal that I wished to speak to him about." Her voice broke. "I hope you'll understand when I tell you the news—has been a shock." Lily dabbed her eyes with a tiny handkerchief. "Talking about it now is rather difficult."

Kenny appeared to be very much interested in the little elephant paper-weight on the desk as he rolled it about in his fingers, but he was watching Lily Lawton closely. As he observed her costly jewels and smart, expensive clothes he felt that she had told the truth. It was quite clear in his mind that this woman and one of North City's wealthiest men had been—friends.

"Of course it must be difficult," agreed Kenny. "I can see now that the report of Mr. Martin's death must have proved quite a shock to you."

"Oh, it has, it has!" exclaimed Lily. "And it is because I want to see the murderer brought to justice that I am here now, Chief Kenny."

"Then you know who the murderer was?" The chief leaned forward eagerly as he asked the question.

"No—that is, at least I have no definite evidence. It's just a woman's intuition." The actress smiled. "And we are often right. Chief Kenny, I suspect Grant Ellery, Mr. Martin's partner!"

From the window O'Shay smothered a laugh by a sudden fit of coughing. Kenny frowned as he glanced toward the detective and then looked again at Lily.

"Why Grant Ellery?"

"Because Fosdick, that is, Mr. Martin, has told me about Ellery. Mr. Martin was afraid of him. I know that he hated Mr. Martin—" she paused.

"What makes you so sure of that?"

"I have been with them both and seen the vindictive look upon Grant Ellery's face when he watched Mr. Martin. Oh, he thought that no one was looking, but I have seen it just the same. He hated Fosdick, longed for his death—I am sure of that!"

"Then possibly it may interest you to know that we placed Grant Ellery in jail tonight, to be held as a material witness."

"Grant Ellery in jail!" There was a strange mixture of surprise and delight in Lily's tone. She was a clever actress. "Held as a material witness. Then you *do* suspect him?"

"That was only natural, when Mr. Martin's secretary, Perry Fulson insisted that Ellery stabbed Martin," said Kenny. He was playing his hand slowly for he realized that this woman was a vital element in the case. "We are also holding Fulson."

"But why, what has he done? Surely you don't suspect him of killing Mr. Martin?"

"No, Miss Lawton, I do not." The chief's face was expressionless as he spoke. "I don't suspect Perry Fulson for the simple reason that Fosdick Martin is not dead!"

"Not dead!" exclaimed Lily. "Why they told me that is—I was quite sure—" she paused, confused.

"Why were you so certain of Martin's death?" demanded Kenny, his voice growing stern. "I'm afraid there are a few things I must ask you to explain, Miss Lawton."

"What do you mean?" She was on the defense now. She sat holding her slender body tense and her vivid mouth was hard as she looked anxiously at the chief. "I don't understand?"

"I want to know how you learned that Mr. Martin had been, as you thought, murdered?"

"But I explained that. I telephoned his house and one of his servants said that Mr. Martin had been taken to the hospital."

"No, you didn't, Miss Lawton. Ever since Fosdick Martin was stabbed, two of my men have been stationed at the house. Their orders are to give out no information, and not to let the servants talk over the phone!"

Lily dropped back in her chair. For a few seconds she sat staring at the chief as the meaning of his words became clear. Kenny said nothing. The only sound in the room was the steady drumming of the rain upon the window panes. Finally, the actress smiled.

"You are very clever, Chief Kenny," she said. "I did not tell the truth because I did not wish to involve myself any more than was absolutely necessary." She shook her head. "I was wrong. I shall tell you everything now."

"Please do. It will make things easier," Kenny smiled grimly, "for us all!"

"Very well. I knew that Fosdick Martin had been stabbed and, as I thought, killed, because I was at his house this evening!"

"What?" exclaimed the chief excitedly. "You admit that?"

"Certainly. You said that it would make things easier for us all if I told the truth, didn't you?" She looked at Kenny, who nodded. "Well, that is what I am trying to do. I had tea with Mr. Martin this afternoon. He then left me to go to his office."

"What time was that?"

"A little after five, I should say."

"Wasn't that rather late for Mr. Martin to return to his office?"

"I really couldn't say."

"It is unimportant. Please go on with your story, Miss Lawton."

"After Mr. Martin had left I discovered he had taken my purse with him. It was one of those small affairs, and I distinctly remembered his placing it in the pocket of his coat, to save me the bother of carrying it."

"What did you do when you found it was gone?"

"I phoned Mr. Martin's office. He wasn't there, and he had not reached his residence as yet. So I had dinner in my apartment and then decided I would take a taxi out to Mr. Martin's house and get the purse. I felt that the drive would do me good, as I had not been feeling very well. Besides, there was something I wanted to talk to him about."

"Would you mind telling me what that was, Miss Lawton?"

"I'm afraid I would." Lily smiled. "It was a rather personal matter, Chief Kenny."

Kenny started to insist that she explain and then changed his mind. He merely nodded as the actress continued.

"I knew that Mr. Martin would be home, for he had told me Grant Ellery was arriving from the West this evening."

"Did Mr. Martin appear pleased at his partner's return?"

"Far from it. As I told you before, Mr. Martin was afraid of Grant Ellery."

"Why?"

"I don't know, except that Fosdick—Mr. Martin, might have sensed how much Ellery hated him. I am quite sure that he dreaded the interview."

"What did you do when you reached the house?"

"I dismissed my taxi at the entrance to the place."

The chief glanced toward the window where the rain poured steadily as it had been ever since morning. But he made no comment.

"As I walked along the gravel drive leading to the house, I saw a light in Mr. Martin's study on the first floor."

"Then you did not go directly to the front door?"

"How did you know that?" Lily looked at Kenny in surprise.

"Just a surmise on my part. What did you do?"

"It was such a terrible night. I had my umbrella with me but the rain was beating down so that my first thought was to get under cover. I went in the direction of the study when I saw the light. Just as I reached the top of the steps leading to the porch I heard voices. Two men talking in loud, angry tones."

"Did you recognize these voices?"

"Yes. It was Mr. Martin and Grant Ellery."

"Do you remember what was said?"

Lily sat thinking silently for a moment. She appeared to be striving to recall the words she had heard. At last she shook her head.

"No I'm sorry, but I don't. It seemed to me that Ellery was threatening Mr. Martin, and they both appeared very excited." She paused and glanced down at the floor.

"Then what happened?" asked Kenny.

"Suddenly the lights in the study went out. I remained standing right where I was at the steps of the porch. I was suddenly very frightened. The words, the expressions upon the faces of both Fosdick and Ellery—I saw them through the French windows, when the light was turned on, you know. Well, it cast a feeling of dread over me. I stood wondering what was happening in the darkness that had fallen over the study so quickly. I couldn't move though I wanted to run, to scream—but I just stood there." The actress touched her lips with her handkerchief. "It was dreadful—that moment of silence and darkness."

"No one passed you? You saw no one on the porch then?" demanded the chief.

"Not a soul. A few minutes later I saw the lights in the study go on again. From the distance I could see Mr. Martin on the floor—and then I heard the secretary phoning for the police. Grant Ellery stood nearby. I hurried away then, for I did not want to be mixed up in the affair unless it were absolutely necessary." The actress moved restlessly in her chair as she finished speaking. It was evident that she thought the interview should end now.

"Is that all?" asked Kenny.

"Why, yes." Lily looked surprised. "I've told you everything. Surely you see now that it was Grant Ellery who tried to murder Mr. Martin, don't you?"

"I might feel that such were the case, were it not for just one thing," said the chief slowly.

"What is that?"

"The fact that Grant Ellery has been found murdered in his cell!"

"Grant Ellery murdered!" Lily rose swiftly to her feet, her eyes glaring, her face hard and set. "How was it done?"

"He was stabbed to death, and probably by the same person who attempted to kill Fosdick Martin!"

"*Oh!*" Lily Lawton dropped weakly into her chair.

"Would you mind telling me where you were about an hour ago?" the chief demanded quietly.

"Why—why I was at the theatre removing my make-up after the performance."

"No you weren't." Kenny leaned forward. "You have forgotten one important detail in your story, Miss Lawton. This happens to be Sunday night. There was no performance. Isn't that true?"

The actress did not answer as she suddenly slumped limply in her chair.

"O'Shay," called Kenny calmly. "You'd better get a glass of water—the lady has fainted!"

9

SHADOWS IN THE NIGHT

WITH THE COMING OF MIDNIGHT, the rain which had poured down steadily for nearly twenty-four hours had finally ceased. Now the dense clouds which had hung over the Martin residence were gradually drifting away to the north. Here and there in the sky, dark patches of blue appeared and the stars twinkled in the clear spaces.

The big, white frame house was a blaze of light from top to bottom, though it was late; nearly two-thirty in the morning. The array of illumination had been created by detectives Voring and McDonald who now guarded the place. All during the night Voring had wandered about on the lower floor, while McDonald had made numerous expeditions about the grounds.

A few minutes before, McDonald had returned to the house without seeing the shadowy figure lurking beneath one of the oak trees near the winding gravel driveway that led in through the entrance cut in the hedge. Glynn Landor had been careful not to be observed. He stood beneath the tree for some time after he had made sure that the detectives had departed—and then he began to move cautiously toward the house. He went slowly, and as always, he was very much alert.

When he reached a tree some distance from that beneath which he had first stood, The Lizard paused and swung around. A soft snarl passed his lips as he caught sight of a bulky form moving toward him steadily. Landor's fingers clutched the automatic in his pocket and he was about to draw the weapon. The other man drew nearer.

"Careful with that gun!" The second man's voice was low but sharp as he came closer. "I have one of my own and have you covered from my pocket."

Landor realized that the other might be telling the truth. To shoot now would be a risk—the sound of the report might bring the detectives from the house.

"Who are you?" demanded Landor, staring into the round, fat face that gazed at him serenely.

"Stevens is the name," said the private investigator softly. "I am delighted to meet you, Mr. Landor."

The Lizard's eyes narrowed as the other called him by name. This fat individual did not appear to be the fool Landor had considered him at first glance. The Lizard realized that he had better act and think carefully.

"And just what are you doing here, Mr. Stevens?" he asked politely. "If I may ask?"

"Certainly, you may ask," Stevens chuckled. "But I'm afraid that you won't be answered correctly." He moved closer to Landor, his eyes fixed upon the other's face in the semidarkness. "Suppose I was seeking—a lizard?"

Landor drew back—his fingers tight about his automatic. That Stevens had known the name of Glynn Landor, had not been vital. The name had not been kept a secret since Landor had been in North City—but that the man should know that Landor was The Lizard—bespoke danger, and Landor was wary.

"I see the name means something to you," said Stevens casually. "I rather thought it would."

Landor cursed mentally as he realized the slip he had made. The sudden appearance of Stevens had confused him, and made him drop the suave cloak he usually wore at all times. He should have given no indication of the word 'lizard' meaning anything to him—but now it was too late.

"What name?" he asked, and his voice was soft, and without the slightest trace of emotion. "I'm afraid you don't make yourself quite clear."

"No?" Stevens smiled as he spoke. "Still, I don't feel that I need give you any elaborate explanations, Mr. Landor. I mentioned The Lizard, and you know whom I mean!"

"Really?" Landor appeared bored as he stood there in the shadow of the tree. "Are you suggesting that some, ah, reptile, you might say, is a personal friend of mine?"

"There is no one you like better," stated Stevens. "You would risk everything for The Lizard's safety."

Landor hesitated for an instant before he spoke. A feeling of elation stole over him. The stout man sounded as though he did not really know that Landor was The Lizard. Merely that he was a henchman of the individual who went by that name. It was a pleasing thought and The Lizard delighted in it.

"And if I am a friend of this Lizard?" he demanded finally. "Just what is it to you, Mr.—" he laughed. "I didn't catch the name, pardon."

"Stevens" said the private investigator tersely. "And if you are a friend of The Lizard's I suggest that you warn him to keep away from the Martin residence!"

"I'm sure The Lizard will be pleased when he hears your suggestion," said Landor calmly. "But I doubt whether he will act upon it."

"Quit bluffing, Landor!" Stevens' tone was sharp, and the other man found himself staring into the muzzle of an automatic. "I know you're The Lizard—and you are taking a long chance sneaking around here after what happened last night."

"You seem to know a bit too much!" Landor's tone was vicious. "I'm afraid it will prove very unfortunate for you!"

"Threats, eh? And do you think you can frighten me?" Stevens laughed. "I'm not built that way—I don't scare easily."

"That's very fortunate," said Landor slowly, and grimly. "But dead men tell no tales."

"No?" There was derision in Stevens' tone. "And you still believe that, after the clumsy murder of Grant Ellery in his cell tonight? You're more of a fool than I thought you were, Landor."

"What do you mean?" Landor seemed a little unnerved by the other's statement.

As Homer Stevens watched the other's face he was sure that The Lizard knew more about the murder in the cell than he was willing to admit. The fact interested the private investigator greatly. His remark about Grant Ellery had been a blind stab in the dark, and it had evidently struck home.

"Just what I said," replied Stevens. "That murder in the cell wasn't the careful job it is thought to be. Why, unless Chief Kenny is far less shrewd than I think he is, he has already found lots of things to indicate just who did it."

"Who are you?" demanded Landor tensely.

"I told you my name and I'm a private investigator."

"Oh, one of those amateur masterminds, eh?" Landor laughed, and for the moment he was the ruthless, hard-boiled individual known as The Lizard. "I get it now—the great private detective who steps in when the police are baffled."

"But the police may not be baffled," said Stevens calmly. "Now, you get out of here, Landor—and get quick." His tone was hard. "And I mean it."

Landor stood for an instant glaring at the other man. He was reluctant to go at Stevens' command, and yet he could not see how he would gain anything by staying. In fact, he was rather surprised that the private investigator dismissed him so readily.

"All right," he said shortly. "I'll go—but I'm warning you that you know too much."

"Thank you for the warning," Stevens chuckled. "Goodnight, Mr. Landor. Sorry you must go—but I really do want to see if the police are baffled."

Without another word Landor moved past the other man and went hastily across the grounds toward the hedged gateway.

Homer Stevens frowned as he stood watching the other man until he finally disappeared beyond the hedge. Then the private investigator ducked back behind the tree. He was not taking any chances of being shot from the distance.

"What a fitting name," he murmured softly. "The Lizard, ugh!"

For fully twenty minutes Stevens remained hidden in the shadows of the tree, as he watched for a reappearance of Landor, but The Lizard had evidently departed.

Finally Stevens glanced at the bright lights gleaming through the windows of the Martin residence. An idea struck him and he chuckled softly.

"Of course," he explained. "Probably just the sort of a dumb-bell that would fall for it. I'll try it."

Cautiously he made his way closer to the house. Then he stepped boldly forward so that he was clearly revealed in the light from the windows. Keeping in the light as much as possible, he paused once or twice and stood looking down at the ground as though searching for something.

Detective Jake McDonald stepped out onto the porch of the house. He had remained inside for quite some time talking to his companion on guard, Detective Voring. McDonald now paused abruptly and stood staring as he caught sight of the stout, moon-faced man who was going over the grounds so carefully.

A pleased expression passed over McDonald's rather stupid countenance as he watched. This man was a suspect, of course. He might even be the criminal himself. McDonald had often heard of the irresistible impulse that led murderers back to the scene of their crime. The fact that the stout man appeared to be looking for something made it all the more clear in the mind of the detective. It was the murderer, and he had come back because he had left some clue behind him. That was what he was looking for now.

As noiselessly as possible, McDonald moved down off the porch. The other man's back was toward him—and he did not hear the detective approach. McDonald drew his revolver as he came closer.

"I've got you covered," he barked. "Don't move."

Stevens swung around so that he faced the detective, and there was a look of surprise upon the face of the private investigator.

"What's the meaning of this?" he demanded nervously. "Who are you—and do be careful with that gun."

"I'm a detective," announced McDonald. "And you're under arrest."

"Under arrest," exclaimed Stevens, in tones of horror, but his eyes twinkled. "What for? What have I done?"

"Never mind about that—you're under arrest."

"But—but this is an outrage," stammered Stevens. "I can explain—"

"Not to me, you can't," said McDonald sharply. "You'll do all your explaining to the chief."

"You mean that you are going to take me to the chief of police?"

"I certainly am," growled McDonald. "And I don't want to hear any more out of you until we get there—see."

"You'll regret treating me like this." Stevens' tone was blustering now. He was enjoying himself immensely. I tell you that I can explain everything, if you will only let me talk—"

"Shut up," growled McDonald. "I've heard enough out of you." He drew a police whistle from his pocket and blew it sharply. "You are going into town."

A moment later Detective Voring appeared from the house very much excited. When he saw the two men standing in the light from the windows he came running toward them.

"What's the matter, Jake?" he demanded as he reached them.

"I caught this guy sneaking around outside here," McDonald nodded toward Stevens, who now appeared silent and crest-fallen. "I'm gonna take him in to the chief."

"Who is he?" asked Voring, looking at the stout man with interest.

"I don't know," said McDonald impatiently. "It doesn't matter. Put the cuffs on him, Jim."

Voring started to speak, and then shrugged his shoulders as he produced a pair of handcuffs and placed them on Stevens' wrists, while the latter protested violently. Voring felt that McDonald's actions were a bit high-handed, but as the other detective was the older he was more or less in command.

"I'll drive him into town in my car," said McDonald. "You stay here at the house, Jim—and see that you watch out for things while I'm gone."

"But Chief Kenny said for us both to stay right here on guard," said Voring. "Hadn't you better call him on the phone first?"

"Naw," said McDonald impatiently. "Why should I? I know that this guy is somebody the chief wants to see. I wouldn't be at all surprised if he is the one that stabbed Fosdick Martin."

"I tell you I can explain," broke in Stevens nervously, "if you will only let me talk!"

"Why don't you let him talk?" demanded Voring.

"How many times must I tell you I haven't time?" growled McDonald. "I'm running this, Voring." He grabbed Stevens roughly by the arm. "Come on, you!"

"Gently, gently!" said the private investigator, a sharp note in his tone that made Voring look at him intently. "And the name is Stevens!"

McDonald merely grunted as he led the stout man around the side of the house to where a touring-car was parked.

Voring frowned as he stood motionless, watching them. In a moment they had disappeared. A few seconds later there came the grinding of a self-starter and then the sound of a motor.

Voring was still standing in the same spot when the car passed him rolling along the gravel drive toward the gateway in the hedge.

"The fool," murmured Voring. "In the first place, he's taking a chance driving into town alone with that bird, and in the second place Kenny's gonna raise hell!" Still shaking his head Voring returned to the house. "The pigheaded idiot—" he muttered as he closed the door. "And he calls himself a detective!"

10

A NEW ANGLE

"The lady has fainted," repeated Chief Kenny as he sat calmly at his desk gazing at the limp form across from him. "I'm afraid the excitement has been too much for Miss Lawton."

Detective Sergeant O'Shay turned from the window as he heard Kenny's quietly spoken words. There had been something in the chief's tone that puzzled O'Shay, a note of mockery that O'Shay did not understand. He glanced at Kenny questioningly, but the latter did not catch the sergeant's expression.

The chief sat motionless, his eyes fixed upon the dark-haired woman, and a faint twinkle in his eyes indicated that he was amused.

Lily Lawton had fallen back in her chair, her hands hanging limply at her sides, her face white and her eyes closed. She was a charming picture of defenseless womanhood. A picture that was a bit too carefully posed in Kenny's estimation.

O'Shay started toward a water-cooler which stood in one corner of the office. The chief rose from his desk and went quickly to the stout detective's side. They both were behind the actress and some distance from her chair.

"Have her shadowed when she leaves, Tim," commanded Kenny in an undertone, watching Lily closely as he spoke. "Tell the man to be careful. He must not be seen, but get all the information he can, and stay on the job until you send someone to relieve him."

"O.K., Chief," whispered O'Shay as he filled a glass with water. "Think she really fainted?" There was doubt in his tone as he looked at the actress. "She doesn't strike me as that kind."

296

"Of course she didn't faint," Kenny said softly. "It's just a bluff. Try and see."

The detective sergeant nodded as he went to the actress. She still remained motionless, her eyes closed.

"What should I do now, Chief?" O'Shay asked loudly, as he stood in front of Lily with the glass in his hand.

"Dash the water in her face. That will bring her back to consciousness," commanded the chief sharply.

"Where—where am I?" demanded Lily, abruptly opening her eyes before O'Shay could move, and looking about her dazedly. "What happened?"

From his position behind the woman, Kenny smiled sardonically. He knew now that he had been right. Lily had revived just a bit too opportunely. It was extremely doubtful that she would have recovered from a real faint at such a propitious moment.

O'Shay coughed to hide a laugh and then handed Lily the glass of water. She took it languidly and raised it slowly to her lips.

The chief returned to his desk. His expression was serious as he sat gazing at the woman.

"Thank you." Lily handed the glass back to O'Shay, who took it and walked away. She looked at Kenny, a long, searching look. "I remember now—I must have fainted." A frown swept over her face. "Stupid of me, wasn't it?"

"Hardly that, Miss Lawton." The chief's tone was polite, so much so that his voice sounded cold. "Shall we say merely unfortunate?"

"Unfortunate?" Lily looked at Kenny and he returned her gaze calmly, but she thought she detected a mocking gleam in his eyes, and it worried her. "Why do you say that?"

"Merely because fainting rather confuses one."

"Oh, I see," Lily laughed nervously. Kenny frightened her; there always seemed to be a hidden meaning in his words. "And one really should be careful not to be confused when talking to the Chief of Police."

"I didn't say that." The chief turned to O'Shay, who was again standing near the window. "Oh, Sergeant, please tell Burns I want to see him the first thing in the morning about that Davis case. You'd better get him before he leaves for the night."

"Right, Chief." O'Shay nodded as he went toward the door. "I'll tell him now."

The detective sergeant left the room, closing the door gently after him. For a moment the actress and Kenny remained silent. The only sounds were the faint ticking of the clock on the desk, and the murmur of the wind. The rain had ceased.

"The news about Mr. Ellery—" said Lily finally as she found the silence unbearable. "It was so—so unexpected."

"Yes, it was." Kenny appeared to be considering the subject very carefully. He spoke slowly and thoughtfully. "Not only unexpected, but very unfortunate. Mr. Ellery had promised to talk to me about the affair which happened out at Mr. Martin's house this evening."

"Then you think that he was killed because he knew too much?" Lily asked the question hurriedly, and she seemed to be hiding some secret fear.

"It is always dangerous to know too much when a murderer is concerned," said the chief. He looked at her. "Sometimes one death may call for another, in the mind of a murderer." His tone changed. "Why did you hate Grant Ellery so bitterly, Miss Lawton?"

"Hate him?" She appeared surprised, but Kenny was sure that she was merely acting. "Why do you say that? I didn't hate him, Chief Kenny. He hated me as he did Mr. Martin. That was why I was so sure that he had tried to kill Fosdick—Mr. Martin."

"And now do you still think so, knowing that Grant Ellery is dead?"

"I don't know," Lily hesitated and then nodded. "Yes, I still think that perhaps he did."

"That's possible," agreed Kenny, silently drumming his fingers on the desk. "In a case like this anything is possible. There is just one thing that does not fit in with the probability of Ellery having tried to murder Mr. Martin."

"What's that?"

"The fact that at the time the attempt at murder took place, the Martin residence was robbed!"

"Robbed!"

"Yes, Mr. Martin's collection of unset diamonds were taken from a wall-safe in the room where he was stabbed!"

"The diamonds are gone!" exclaimed Lily excitedly. "And you are sure that," she seemed to be seeking wildly for a name, "that Perry Fulson did not take them?"

Kenny looked at her in surprised wonder. He had not thought of that possibility. It was well worth considering. The secretary might have stolen the diamonds. That he had mentioned them at all had merely slipped out in Fulson's nervous excitement.

"No, Miss Lawton," said Kenny. "I must admit that I had not considered that angle. But I shall do so, of course."

She hardly appeared to hear him. Her eyes were wandering about the room, a look of fear in their depths. The chief sensed that she wanted to get away, and found that he was right when she spoke.

"Please, Chief," she looked at Kenny appealingly. "I'm rather unnerved—" she was obviously striving to repress a sob. "I wonder if I might go now?"

"Certainly, Miss Lawton." The chief rose to his feet, satisfied that he could learn nothing more from her at present. "And thank you for coming to see me as you have." He leaned across the desk, his face serious as he looked at her. "I'm sure your visit will prove a great aid—to justice!"

"Oh, I hope so!" She shuddered as she got to her feet. "It is all so horrible." She extended one slender hand to him as he moved around the desk. "Thank you, Chief Kenny—you have been very kind."

"It is you who have been kind," said Kenny as he took her hand. "Miss Lawton, just one more thing." He spoke slowly. "I would not advise you to leave town at present. You understand?"

An expression of fear crept into Lily Lawton's eyes. There had been an ominous note of warning in the chief's tone. She felt that she had implicated herself in the case far more than she had realized. Finally she smiled, her hand upon the knob of the door.

"Yes, Chief Kenny," she said in a low voice. "I understand—perfectly. Goodnight."

Kenny did not speak. He merely bowed as the door closed behind her. As he heard the latch click he began to pace about the
office. He was like an old lion moving back and forth in his cage,
ever alert and ready to pounce.

After a few seconds he paused and stood for a time looking out
the window. The rain no longer fell but the night was still filled
with dark clouds, though they were rolling swiftly away from the
city. He noticed that there was little traffic passing along Eastern
Avenue. It mattered little—his thoughts were upon other things.

Ellery's death had complicated matters, there was no doubt
about that. The murder in the cell had been cleverly executed and
carefully planned. In Kenny's estimation it was far more of a premeditated crime than had been the attempt upon Fosdick Martin's
life. No doubt the murderer had unlocked Danny Lester's cell with
just what had followed in view. The murderer had guessed, or at least
hoped, that Lester would try to make his escape, and had timed it so
that Yeager would be forced to chase the dope-addict out of the building. During the possible ten minutes that the turn-key had been in
pursuit of Danny, the assailant had completed his task. Kenny felt
that he must have worked fast and been very sure of his ground.

The chief's gaze rested upon a tiny black spider that was busily
weaving a web in one corner of the window-sill. Kenny smiled to
himself. The events of the night were steadily weaving a web within
his own mind—a web of evidence. Yet so far that evidence was as
fragile as the spider's web. Still there were flies in the trap already.
Perry Fulson, the three other men now in jail, and within the last
half hour Lily Lawton. One of them might know the little detail
which would prove the key to the puzzle.

Kenny turned, half startled, so deeply had he been lost in his
thoughts. He had heard a knock upon the door of the office. He
frowned in surprise as the door opened at his command. A thin-
faced man with a dark mustache entered, holding a stout moon-
faced individual by one arm.

"McDonald!" exclaimed Kenny, glaring at the man with the
mustache. "What do you mean by disobeying orders? I told you to
remain at Fosdick Martin's house!"

"I know, Chief," said Detective McDonald, in what he tried to make a soothing tone. All the way into town he had been gradually realizing that he had acted hastily. "But this is important, and besides Voring is still at the house. I thought that you would want me to—"

"How do you know it's important enough to act against my orders?" The chief was angry. In his estimation Jake McDonald was one of the stupidest men in the police department. "Why didn't you phone me first?"

"But this man is a suspect," stammered the detective. "I caught him sneaking around the Martin place about half an hour ago. When I tried to question him he refused to talk."

"I'm afraid that Mr. er, McDonald rather distorts the truth," said Homer Stevens calmly. "I told him that I could explain, but he would not let me."

"Is that true, McDonald?"

"Well, he acted mighty suspicious," growled the detective. "I watched him for some time before I spoke to him."

"What was he doing?"

"He was searching the grounds outside Mr. Martin's study."

"Were you?" Kenny glanced at Stevens. "What for?"

"Certainly I was," the private investigator smiled. "I wanted to see if the police were baffled."

"Huh!" The chief glared at him. "Who are you?"

"Homer Stevens is my name. If this detective had not been so nasty I might have explained—" The stout man shook his head sadly. "In all my experience I don't believe I've ever come in contact with quite such a stupid individual." He laughed. "He put me right beside him when we drove into town. I could have knocked him out beautifully while he was using both hands to drive."

McDonald looked startled as he heard what Stevens said. The risk that he had run had not even entered the detective's head.

"If he hadn't been nasty I would have explained," said Stevens casually.

"He can't explain," interrupted McDonald. "I caught him when he didn't expect anyone would be watching."

DONALD BAYNE HOBART

"You see?" Stevens glanced at Kenny. "Rather a disagreeable attitude, don't you think?"

"Yes, I do," said the chief. "Suppose you let me talk for awhile, McDonald."

"But this guy is a suspect!" exclaimed the detective excitedly. "I thought I was doing right in bringing him in."

"You should never try to think, McDonald." Kenny was still angry. "It's beyond your ability."

"Perhaps these might interest you." Stevens produced some papers from his pocket and handed them to the chief. "Probably make things a bit clearer all around."

Kenny took the papers, glanced at them, then gave a start as he hurriedly read each one. When he had finished, he gave them back to Stevens. The chief glared at McDonald.

"One more break like this and you'll find yourself back pounding a beat," he said sharply. "This man is a private detective!"

"Huh?" McDonald was dumbfounded, and then he grinned. "Maybe—but I've arrested him as a material witness."

"I have something to say about that," shouted Kenny. "Take those handcuffs off Mr. Stevens—and hurry."

"Yes, sir," said the detective meekly, as he unlocked the handcuffs.

"That's much better," said Stevens, rubbing his wrists. "Very much so."

"Just what were you really doing at Fosdick Martin's house?" asked Kenny.

"I'm quite willing to explain in detail," replied Stevens. He paused and looked at McDonald. "But couldn't you send this man away? He rather annoys me."

"Careful, Chief," said McDonald. "This guy is dangerous. He might make trouble for you."

"I'll worry about that," stated Kenny grimly. "You get back to the Martin place at once, McDonald—and stay there, do you hear!" He glared at the man. "Phone me the next time you have anything to report."

"Yes, sir," said McDonald meekly, as he hurriedly left the room.

"Sit down please, Mr. Stevens." Kenny returned to his desk as he spoke and indicated the chair across from him. "I'm sorry that McDonald has made such a fool of himself."

"He did just as I expected, or rather hoped he would do." Stevens laughed as he settled himself comfortably in the chair facing the chief. "I stood out there in front of the house with the intention of being caught."

"What?" Kenny looked startled. "I don't understand?"

"I knew that one of your men was patrolling the grounds from time to time. If I had not wanted him to find me I'd hardly have stood in full view of the lights from the windows. McDonald finally discovered me."

"Oh," Kenny smiled. "Then I imagine you must have found being arrested very amusing!"

"I did," said Stevens. "By the way, the other man you have stationed out there is quite a sensible chap. He suggested that McDonald phone you first." The private investigator shook his head in mock sadness. "But McDonald wouldn't listen."

"Well, at least Voring showed some sense. I'm glad of that!"

Kenny produced a box of cigars and offered them to the stout man. Stevens took one with a word of thanks. He unbuttoned his raincoat and dropped his hat beside his chair. The chief placed the cigar-box back on the desk and then picked up his pipe and filled and lighted it.

"Rather an intriguing case, don't you think, Chief Kenny?" remarked Stevens when he had his cigar going to his satisfaction. "Things seem a bit tangled though."

"They are," said Kenny laconically. He had no intention of making any statements until he had some inkling of how much the other man knew. "And seem to grow more complicated all the time."

"Really? Then you probably know of some developments of which I am unaware."

"I wouldn't be surprised if I do." The chief's tone was placid as he puffed upon his pipe. "Would you mind telling me who retained you in this case? I must say it was quick work on his part."

"I'd prefer not to mention names, but it was someone very close to Mr. Martin. An individual who wished to see the guilty brought to justice."

Kenny puffed reflectively upon his pipe for a moment or two. He had not the slightest intention of taking Homer Stevens at his word. The latter might be a private investigator, and then again he might not. The man's papers had seemed real, but they might have been forged or stolen. The chief felt that the wisest plan would be to let Stevens talk, and not to indicate that he even thought of doubting the private investigator's statements.

"But Mr. Martin has no close relatives, none living as far as we have been able to learn." Kenny said finally. "Someone who desires justice, hum—justice!" A thought struck him. "Could it be a woman?"

From something in Kenny's tone, Stevens was sure that Lily Lawton had obeyed instructions and called on the chief. The private investigator wondered what had taken place during the interview.

"A woman, Mr. Stevens?" repeated Kenny.

"Yes, I see no reason to deny that. A woman acting as she feels Fosdick Martin would desire her to proceed in his behalf." Stevens puffed at his cigar, found that it had gone out, and lighted it again. "In coming here I thought we might work together to a certain extent." He smiled. "Otherwise I would not have given your man the opportunity to arrest me."

"I'm sure of that now. Perhaps cooperation is advisable, Mr. Stevens. Suppose you tell me what you know about this affair, then we'll see if I'm not able to shed a bit of light on the subject myself."

"With pleasure." Stevens leaned back in his chair, and then began thoughtfully. "First, we know that Fosdick Martin was stabbed. He was taken to the hospital very near death, but now there is a good chance of his recovery—"

"How did you know that?"

"It was quite simple. I phoned the hospital, informed them that I was a relative of Mr. Martin and asked for a report upon his condition. The nurse on duty was evidently new and inexperienced. She believed my claim to relationship and gave me the information I wanted."

"So that's it!" Kenny laughed, his respect for the other's mentality increasing. "I think we'll get along together, Mr. Stevens. Go on!"

"We know that you have arrested both Perry Fulson and Grant Ellery and are holding them here in jail as material witnesses."

"How did you gain that information?"

"McDonald mentioned the fact," Stevens shook his head sadly. "I'm afraid that he will never make a good detective."

"He's an idiot!" exclaimed Kenny impatiently. "And what else do you know, Mr. Stevens?"

"Well, both Fulson and Ellery might have attempted to kill Fosdick Martin."

"What makes you so sure of that?"

"Ellery had learned that Martin had virtually tricked him out of every penny he owned."

"Quite true, but what of Fulson? I fail to see his motive?"

"He has one, Chief. When Fosdick Martin dies, Perry Fulson is to receive fifty thousand dollars as a beneficiary in his will!"

"Oh, he is!" the chief smiled. "That's interesting. I felt that we'd be a help to each other, Mr. Stevens!"

"No doubt," agreed the private investigator. "And now, are there any further developments in the case?"

Kenny hesitated before he answered. He glanced at the clock in front of him. The hands pointed to two a.m.

"Yes," he said finally, looking intently at the other man. "One very important development. We found Grant Ellery murdered in his cell a little while ago."

"I know that," said Stevens calmly. "I was in the editorial room of the *News* tonight when Heath was talking to the City Editor. Clark is a friend of mine." He frowned. "You know, I rather expected that Ellery would be murdered."

11
A SHOT IN THE DARK

JED CLARK, City Editor of the North City *Morning News* yawned as he peered through a haze of blue tobacco-smoke at the man who sat pounding steadily at a typewriter a short distance away.

"What are you writing, Dave?" asked Clark, merely for the sake of conversation.

"A lead for tomorrow's story on the Martin case," answered Heath, without turning from his desk. "I'll be through in a minute or so."

The tall, lanky police reporter was in his shirt-sleeves and his soft hat was thrust far back on his thatch of red hair. A cigarette dangled from one corner of his mouth as he continued to bang away at the typewriter in front of him.

Clark glanced about him without interest. The editorial room was small and usually crowded when the entire staff of the paper was at work, but now it was nearly three a.m. The dead-line of the paper had been reached over an hour ago. Of the editorial staff only Clark and Heath still remained, the others had gone home some time before.

Somewhere in the distance the giant presses grumbled as they rolled back and forth, printing the morning news. Clark smiled to himself as he realized the sensation that the glaring headlines would create. The attempt to kill Fosdick Martin and the actual murder of Grant Ellery in his cell would be more of a local news bomb-shell than anything which had appeared in the paper for the past six months.

With the feeling that the morrow would bring the public real news, Clark began to examine some work which might just as well have been done the next day. He always worked as far ahead as possible, for he was an old newspaper veteran who had lived in harness the greater part of his life. His work was food and drink to him; nothing else mattered. He had no family, and his home was a hotel room. He delighted in lingering at the office as late as possible each morning. There was always the possibility that something might happen which would prove exciting. He sat now at his desk, a tall, thin man with grey hair and a grey mustache. His face was lined but his eyes were keen, and his brain remarkably active for a man of his years. His coat was off and the glaring pink of his shirt contrasted vividly with the somber blue of his coat and trousers.

Clark glanced up as the door of the editorial room opened and a stout man appeared. The latter was puffing a cigar and he beamed at the City Editor as he walked across the room to Clark's desk.

"Hello," he said, as he dropped down in a chair nearby. "How are you, Jed?"

"Fine, Steve." Clark looked at Homer Stevens in surprise. "But what are you doing wandering around in the cold, grey dawn like this?"

"Oh, I just happened to be passing and thought I'd drop in and see you," explained the private investigator casually. Anything exciting, Jed?"

"That's a nice question for a private investigator to ask," the City Editor laughed. "I suppose you haven't heard anything about Fosdick Martin—and what happened out at his place tonight?"

"Of course I have," Stevens grinned. "I just left Chief Kenny a little while ago. We had quite an interesting talk. I'd never met Kenny before. Certainly strikes me as a man who can think for himself."

"He can," agreed Clark. "And he usually does, too."

Heath ceased typewriting. He stretched, and then yawned as he gathered up the sheets of copy he had written, and wandered over to Clark's desk.

"Here's a man that may be able to give you a little more dope on that Martin affair," said the City Editor to the reporter, nodding toward Stevens. "Mr. Stevens, this is Mr. Heath. He has been covering the case for the *News*."

"Mighty glad to know you, Mr. Heath," said Stevens as he rose and shook hands with the reporter. "Police reporter, eh? Thought I had seen you around town quite often. And you're working on the Martin case?"

"I certainly am," said Heath eagerly. He looked at Stevens. "Do you happen to know anything about it, Mr. Stevens?"

"Well, yes," the private investigator nodded. "You might say that I do know a little. As I just told Mr. Clark, I only left Chief Kenny a short time ago."

"Any new developments?" asked the reporter.

"Nothing except my arrest," said Stevens calmly.

"Your arrest!" exclaimed Clark in startled tones. "What do you mean, Steve?"

"One of Kenny's men happened to find me out at the Martin place an hour or so ago. He arrested me and brought me in to the chief. Of course when I explained who I was, I'm afraid the man felt rather foolish."

"You clever devil," exclaimed Clark. "I know you—I'll bet you deliberately acted suspicious so you would be arrested."

"Well," Stevens grinned. "As I told you, I had never met Kenny— I rather thought I would like to do so."

"Did he have any more facts on the case?" asked Heath. "When I last saw him he wasn't very willing to talk."

"He still isn't particularly anxious to tell all he knows," said the private investigator thoughtfully. "He let me do most of the talking when I was with him."

"But how did you happen to know anything about the case?" demanded Clark. He shook his head sadly. "That's a foolish question, for I know you won't answer it."

"Quite right, I won't." Stevens smiled. "I never felt it wise to talk for publication. I know you newspaper men; everything I say will turn into headlines overnight. That is, if it proves important enough."

"You're not a resident of North City, are you, Mr. Stevens?" asked Heath. "I can't recall having seen you around town before."

"No, I've only been here about a week. Just taking a little vacation."

"A vacation!" Clark laughed. "That's a good one. And as you're on a holiday, the first thing you do is plant yourself so you will be arrested and taken to see the chief of police when a murder breaks."

"But you can hardly blame me for that," Stevens laughed. "It's such a nice case, and I already suspect it has a number of very interesting angles to it." He glanced at the City Editor. "How about having a little something to eat. I'm beginning to feel that I could stand a cup of coffee and a sandwich."

"So could I!" exclaimed Heath.

"Sorry," Clark glanced at the copy that the reporter had placed on his desk. "I'm not a bit hungry. But you two run along." He smiled. "Maybe Heath will get a little more news out of you for us."

"He's welcome to try," said Stevens as Heath put on his coat and raincoat. "Anyway I'll treat him to a cup of coffee."

"That's fair enough," said the reporter as they started to leave. "So long, Clark, I'll be back in a little while."

"I'm not making any promises, Jed," said Stevens. "I may drop back, but the chances are that I won't." He yawned. "Another half hour and it will be way past my bed time. But I'll see you again soon."

"Right, Steve." The City Editor called as the two men started for the door. "Drop in any time—glad to see you."

Clark sat staring into space very thoughtfully as the reporter and the private investigator disappeared. He knew Homer Stevens quite well, and the private investigator never did anything without good reason. That he had come to North City on a vacation was extremely doubtful. Stevens was not the type of man who went in for vacations. The City Editor was beginning to realize that there might be far more to the Fosdick Martin case than he had thought at first. Still, he considered it quite an interesting case, and one which might prove involved.

For half an hour Clark worked at his desk, and he became so engrossed in his task that he lost all track of time. He finally glanced up as the door opened suddenly and Heath stepped into the room.

The reporter's face was white and drawn and he was holding his right arm with his left hand. Clark leaped to his feet when he saw Heath's coat sleeve covered with blood.

"What happened?" demanded the City Editor excitedly.

"Nothing much," said Heath slowly. "I passed a dark alley on my way back here and somebody took a shot at me, that's all."

"Good Lord!" exclaimed Clark. "We'd better get you to a doctor at once. Shot, eh?" He stood looking at the other man's arm. "Hm, that's bad."

"Just a flesh-wound I guess," said the reporter. "But it sure bleeds like hell." He smiled weakly. "It's taught me that it's dangerous to know too much about the Martin case."

Clark hardly heard him; he was already carefully cutting away the reporter's sleeve with a pen-knife, and started to give first aid until he could get the man to a doctor.

"What happened to Stevens?" he asked as he worked.

"I don't know," answered Heath. "He left me some time ago. Haven't the faintest idea where he went." Suddenly the reporter staggered and then dropped weakly into a chair. "Sorry; I'm a little shaky, I guess."

12

THE WHITE HAND

CHIEF KENNY YAWNED WEARILY as he sat alone in his office. He was tired both mentally and physically, for the events of the night had proved a constant strain. Since early in the evening when he learned that Fosdick Martin had been stabbed, perhaps murdered, Kenny had realized that it was necessary to keep himself keenly alert.

He had found that so often it was the little things which were the revealing factors in a case of this kind. An excited and unguarded gesture—a word thoughtlessly spoken, either one might prove vital. These were the things for which one must keep constantly on guard, and he had done so. He had missed very little of the speech or actions of those with whom he had come in contact during the evening. The interviews that he had given to Grant Ellery, Perry Fulson, Lily Lawton, and Homer Stevens had all called for keen observation and guarded speech on his part, but each interview had proved of value, in his estimation.

Kenny glanced at the clock on the desk in front of him. It was just three a.m. For over an hour the head of the North City Police department and Homer Stevens had sat in Kenny's office discussing the case from various angles. Never had the chief been more wary of his speech, or more alert for some slip of the tongue on the part of his visitor.

Kenny was fully aware that Homer Stevens was a shrewd individual. He had told nothing about himself which would not have been a simple matter for the chief to learn through investigation. Nor had Kenny related all he knew regarding the events of the

311

night. It had been a battle of wits, a battle which terminated with
neither man feeling that he was the victor.

Stevens had refused to explain why he had expected the murder
of Grant Ellery. He had merely stated that he had suspected such a
thing would happen. Kenny had not pressed the question too
closely. He was not anxious to have Stevens realize that he found
the latter's casual statements important. He felt he would learn
more about the man in time, and by so doing would have a clearer
idea of the extent of the man's actual connection with the case.

The chief did not doubt that Homer Stevens was just what he
had represented himself to be, a private detective. The man had
been too ready and willing to present his credentials to have been
anything else. Still, that he was a private investigator meant very
little to Kenny. He could still prove a very vital and ominous factor in the case.

John Kenny was not inclined to trust any one too far; particularly when he himself was working on a murder case and the other
was a possible suspect. Homer Stevens might be all that he said he
was, and still have committed the crime.

Kenny had learned that murder was often the impulse of the
moment. In numerous instances it had been proved the chaotic
reaction of a person in a state of insane hysteria who, under normal circumstances, would have found the deed impossible. At other
times it might be instigated by cool and calculated thought; the
premeditated act of a person who had considered the situation from
all angles and come to the conclusion that murder would prove to
his or her advantage.

Kenny rose to his feet. He was a tall man, and his carefully tai-
lored grey business-suit covered a well-built muscular frame which
his twenty years of active duty had kept in fine condition. John
Kenny at fifty was a man to be reckoned with both mentally and
physically. He had proved the best chief of police North City had
ever possessed, and its citizens were proud of him both as an officer and as a man.

The chief began to pace up and down the office slowly. He felt
that he might relieve his weariness by a little activity. Finally, he

decided that he would take a walk through the jail. There might be some little thing he had overlooked that would have a bearing on the case.

Slowly he strolled down the corridor that led from his office to the main hallway in the center of the building. When he reached the spot where the two met he paused and gazed about him.

As he stood facing the jail, the closed door which led out into the police detention-room was behind him. It was through this door that one had to go to reach the room in which the Desk Sergeant was located, and where all those placed under arrest were brought first.

Every door in the building except the one which led past the Sergeant's desk was locked at six each evening. Kenny realized that had the murderer come from outside, it would have been necessary for him to have passed the Sergeant on duty or to have unlocked the door at the extreme end of the jail. This was the door leading out onto Eastern Avenue through which Yeager, the turn-key, had chased the dope-addict, Danny Lester.

The chief moved on toward the jail. It was his intention to question every one of the men who had been in the cells at the time of the murder of Grant Ellery, but he felt that could wait until morning. He hoped that his men would have brought him the facts about Danny Lester, Henry Brown, and Tom Hogan by then. It would make the cross-questioning much easier, were they able to do so. Kenny was glad he had decided to let it go until morning. He was tired now and he wanted to be at his best when he talked to those men. There was no hurry so far as they were concerned. They were all prisoners and the chief felt that there was little chance of their escaping.

Kenny realized that it was possible for one of the men to be murdered as Ellery had been, but he doubted that such a thing would happen. In his estimation, the murderer would not try to repeat the deed he had accomplished successfully once. It was far too risky. The chief knew that Yeager had found the cell-doors unlocked when they went to investigate Ellery's death, but he did not believe that would happen again. The turn-key would be constantly on guard now.

When Kenny reached the corridor of the jail he smiled. Ahead he could see the blue uniformed figure of the short, thick-set Irishman trying the cell doors as he patrolled grimly up and down.

The turn-key saluted as he saw the chief and hurried forward. Kenny awaited him, smiling pleasantly. The chief had the faculty of making his men feel that they were human beings—that he was interested in each and every man on the force, from the greenest rooky to the best detective. Yet they did not impose upon him; they did not dare. They knew that Chief Kenny had always carried out police regulations since he first joined the force as a patrolman, and he expected all of them to do the same.

"Everythin' is all right now, Chief," said Yeager as he reached Kenny's side. "All of them sleepin' exceptin' that Danny Lester. Poor divil, he's sittin' on his bunk down there talkin' to himself."

"What's he saying?" asked the chief casually. "Anything in particular?"

"That I don't know. But you can be sure it ain't worth listenin' to, I'm thinkin'." Yeager shook his head. "Just ravin' like them birds always does."

"Probably," said Kenny with a nod. "I'll go and have a look at him."

"Want me to come with you, Chief?" The turn-key was eager to be of service.

"No, just keep on watching the cells." The chief smiled. "We don't want anything else to happen you know."

"That we don't!" exclaimed Yeager fervently, as the chief walked away.

As Kenny reached the door of Danny Lester's cell he heard the dope-addict mumbling to himself. The chief went closer, but he was careful to keep out of Danny's sight.

The man, a wizen-faced little creature dressed in ragged and worn clothing, sat on the edge of his bunk staring vacantly at the stone floor of his cell.

"I seen it," he mumbled. "Sittin' here on me bunk just like I am now I seen it. A white hand reaching around the door—a white hand all kinda shiny like." He laughed inanely but he did not look up.

"They'd think I was nuts if I told them that. But it was a hand, I seen it, an' it unlocked th' door of me cell. Then I gets out an' th' guard chases me. Huh, that guy sure could run fast for a harness bull—but I nearly lost him in th' rain—nearly lost him." He laughed again. "Wonder what become of that hand? I didn't see nobody when I run, only the guard—a white hand—a white hand kinda shiny looking"—his voice dropped and the words became indistinct.

Kenny shrugged his shoulders and moved silently past the cell. Danny did not look up. He was still murmuring insanely to himself. The chief turned to his left and went along the short corridor that led to the door opening on Eastern Avenue.

The door was locked now, as it was supposed to be at all times. Yet it had been open when Yeager had chased Danny. Then it was possible that there had been someone in the jail, someone beside the four men in the cells. The murderer might have come from outside.

The chief studied the door. He observed that it opened inward and that there was about four feet between the frame on the left and the wall. An object on the floor caught the chief's eye. He reached down and picked it up. It was a woman's handkerchief rolled into a ball.

"Hm," Kenny said to himself softly as he examined it. "Just a bit too clever. I thought that would be the case."

The chief yawned as he placed the handkerchief in his pocket. He felt that there was little more that could be done before daylight. He decided that he was going home and get some sleep. He realized that he would need it, for there was still much work to be accomplished on the Martin case.

As he walked back to his office Kenny found himself puzzling over what Danny Lester had been mumbling. He did not quite see why he had dwelt upon the fact that the white hand he had seen had appeared shiny.

"Shiny?" Kenny stopped in front of his door. "Why of course it would be, of course. I should have thought of that before!"

The chief found O'Shay waiting as he entered the office. The detective turned from where he stood gazing out the window and smiled at the chief.

"Kinda thought you were still around," said the detective sergeant. "You and Thomas A. Edison are a couple of guys that don't need much sleep."

"Where have you been?" asked Kenny, wearily dropping into a chair. "You've been gone about three hours."

"Yea, I know. After I tipped Burns off to trail that Lily Lawton, I got an idea. I've been over to the Allen Hotel digging up a little information on this guy, Henry Brown. I didn't think he was in North City for his health."

"Well, why was he here?" asked Kenny as O'Shay paused.

"To try and blackmail Fosdick Martin!"

"What? How do you know that?"

"Found a guy that had the next room to Brown in the hotel. The walls are kinda thin there and he heard Brown and another guy talking—"

"Know who the other man was?"

"No, not yet. The feller I questioned didn't hear any names mentioned except Martin's. Brown called his visitor 'Bo' all the time."

The telephone on Kenny's desk rang, and he answered it.

"Hello . . . oh, Clark . . . what's on your mind? Good Lord, when did that happen? About a half an hour ago? Sent him to the hospital, eh? That's good. Was he badly wounded? Just through the arm? I see. All right, thanks for calling me."

Chief Kenny's expression was very thoughtful as he hung up the receiver. "That was Clark of the *News* calling. He says that Heath has been shot!"

"Heath?"

"Yes. I never expected that," said Kenny. "No, I never expected that. I wonder just where Homer Stevens went after he left me?"

"Who the devil is Homer Stevens?" demanded O'Shay.

"That's just what I'd like to know, remarked the chief.

13

A GOLDEN SNAKE

THE BRIGHT SUNLIGHT of early morning gleamed down upon North City.

Over countless breakfast tables the citizens of the town had read the glaring headlines in the *Morning News* that told of the Martin case. Everywhere the newspaper report had created excited comment; men and women had read and re-read the story of the attempt to murder Fosdick Martin, and the actual killing of Grant Ellery in his cell. The news was, as Jed Clark had felt it would be, a sensation.

North City only boasted a population of a little over fifty thousand, and the report of a murder was of interest to everyone, particularly as both Martin and Ellery were well known in the town.

Ted Ames had a copy of the paper thrust carelessly into the pocket of his topcoat as he wandered slowly in the direction of the entrance to the apartment house where Norma Burton and Billie Fenton had their studio. Quite some time ago Ames had carefully read the newspaper report of what had happened during the night. He had gone through the article carefully, hoping to find among the related facts those which would aid him to unravel the puzzling circumstances in which he found himself involved far more deeply than he had at first realized.

As he walked slowly along thinking the matter over, he found there were a great many pieces in the mental puzzle which he could not as yet fit into their proper grooves.

In the first place, someone had stabbed Fosdick Martin when Ames was in the banker's residence. The deed had been done in the dark, and might have been committed by Grant Ellery, Perry Fulson, or possibly Glynn Landor. The fact that Martin's collection of unset diamonds were in The Lizard's possession made Ames very much inclined to suspect the man. Yet Ames had not forgotten the telephone call which Landor had received the previous evening. At that time The Lizard announced that the real murderer was speaking over the wire. Ames had puzzled over that cryptic statement, and had been unable to quite understand it. However, it had proved one thing to his satisfaction, and that was that Glynn Landor knew the person who had committed the crime.

Ames had not seen The Lizard since his interview with the man the previous night. A quixotic desire to try and guard Norma Burton from harm had kept Ames lingering in the vicinity of her dwelling all night and on into the morning. He was tired now but he still remained in the block in which the big apartment house was located. Just how his constant vigil could prove of service he did not know. There were vague thoughts in his mind of confronting Landor, should the man appear in the vicinity, and warning him away from the two girls.

Now it was a little after nine o'clock and Ted Ames found himself sauntering by the door of the entrance to the apartment house for at least the twentieth time.

He halted abruptly and stood staring in delighted surprise as a trim slender figure stepped out into the bright sunshine. That Norma herself would appear had been beyond his faintest hopes, and yet it was the girl who had occupied his thoughts who started to brush past him and then smiled and hesitated as she recognized who was gazing at her so fixedly.

"Oh, good morning, Mr. Ames," she said. "I never expected to see you here."

"Good morning, Miss Burton," exclaimed Ames, as he swiftly removed his hat. "I just happened to be passing," he smiled. "And now I'm glad."

He was looking at her closely, noticing the smartness of her tweed suit, the perfect lines of her hat, and the lovely radiance of the girl herself.

"I've been wondering a lot about you since last night," she said, smiling at him. "After all, your visit was rather mysterious and unexpected, you know."

"Yes, I suppose it was." He nodded, his face sober. "I had hoped to try and explain more fully, but well, I just didn't find an opportunity after Miss Fenton arrived."

"I'm afraid I must apologize for Billie: you may have considered her a bit rude, but I assure you it wasn't intentional. She was just a bit keyed-up, that was all."

Ames merely nodded without making any attempt at speech. They had started walking along the street without either of them being particularly conscious of their actions. Ames felt that it was quite natural for Billie Fenton to have been a bit excited after having been out with Glynn Landor. The man was bound to prove a disturbing influence to anyone who came in contact with him.

Norma glanced at Ames from time to time as they walked. She found that he was even better-looking than she had realized the night before. There was an interesting hint of aggressiveness in the firm cast of his chin, and his eyes, though a bit weary now, possessed a nice clear frankness that she liked. It dawned upon her that Ted Ames might be much more of a man than she had previously guessed. During their talk in the studio there had been something in his manner which made her think he was a bit weak, for his mood had been rather a hopeless one.

"Hope you don't mind me walking along with you like this," said Ames finally. "I'm just out for a stroll myself."

"Not at all. I'm delighted." Norma's tone was gracious. "I'm only going over to Green Street to a jeweler's. I have a little trinket I want to have repaired. You may come right along if you wish."

"Thank you, I shall."

Ames laughed, for he was finding the morning much more glorious than he had at first realized. "I certainly was in a mournful mood last night. I guess you must have thought I was a bit crazy!"

"Not in the least. You were worried about something; just what it was, I don't know, of course." Norma smiled at him. "But I will admit I was flattered when you told me that I could help you by just talking to you."

"And you did help me," said Ames seriously. "You are still doing it by being nice to me this morning. But tell me about yourself; you're an artist, aren't you?"

"Yes, a poor, struggling free-lance who manages to gather a few pennies now and then doing fashion designs for the newspapers and the shops," she laughed. "Really I think it would be much more exciting to talk about you, Mr. Ames. You still remain an unknown quantity, you know."

"I'm not worth talking about," Ames said slowly, and there was a bitterness in his tone that surprised her. "Up till six months ago I was doing newspaper-work, but something snapped I guess, and ever since then I have just been drifting."

"Really?" She glanced at him curiously. "Somehow you don't seem the sort who would enjoy—just drifting."

"Enjoy it." Ames laughed grimly. "I don't."

He found that the conversation was treading upon dangerous ground. He could not explain his connection with The Lizard to this girl. An accomplice of a clever crook, there was nothing else he could say. When he thought of himself in that light Ames realized that he had no right to even speak to Norma Burton, much less seek her friendship as he found himself anxiously doing.

"I'm hoping that some day you will know me well enough to tell me all about it," she said softly, as they paused in front of a shop. "Here's the jeweler's. You may come in with me if you wish."

Ames drew open the door of the shop, and held it for her as she entered. He followed close behind her. He stood a short distance away as the clerk behind the counter stepped forward.

As Ames watched, Norma took a small white envelope from her purse. From this she drew out a gold bracelet designed to represent a snake. Ames gave a start of surprise as he saw it. It appeared exactly like the one on the arm of the woman he had encountered in the dark hallway of Fosdick Martin's house the previous evening.

"The clasp is broken," Norma said to the clerk. "I wonder if you will be able to fix it for me?"

"Certainly, Miss." The clerk had the bracelet in his hands as he spoke and was examining it carefully. "The catch is completely gone. We'll have to put on a new one for you. It will be a dollar."

"That's quite all right," said Norma. "When will it be ready?"

"Tomorrow morning about this time. The name and address, please."

Ames was not listening as Norma gave her name and address. He was worried. He did not want to believe that this girl was the woman he had met there in the house. She just couldn't be! A feeling of relief swept over him as he realized that there were doubtlessly countless other bracelets similar to the one she possessed.

"You know I'm terribly fond of that bracelet," she said to Ames as they started to leave the shop. "I don't believe I have ever seen another just like it anywhere. A friend of mine gave it to me a long time ago."

Ames did not speak. He knew he had to ask her a question, and he feared she might take it amiss. He realized it had been her voice that had warned him away from Fosdick Martin's house. Again he seemed to hear the whisper, "Go, oh, please, go at once." And now he was certain that it had been this lovely girl who had spoken, there in the grim darkness of that hallway where a man had just been stabbed.

"What's the matter, Mr. Ames?" Norma asked as they were once more on the street. "You look so serious and solemn."

"Did you see the paper this morning?" he questioned slowly.

"Why, yes." A look of surprise passed swiftly over her face, and he thought he detected a look of fear in her eyes as she glanced at him. "What makes you ask?"

"This Martin case," he said. "I wondered if you noticed the headlines."

"Of course I did." Her voice was low. "It all seems so terrible," she hesitated. "I wonder why such things have to happen?"

"Miss Burton," he ignored her question. "There is something I would like to ask you, but I don't know just how to say it. I don't want to offend you—" he stopped vaguely.

"Please ask it, Mr. Ames," she said quietly. "I'll try to understand."

"What were you doing at Fosdick Martin's house last night?" he blurted out abruptly.

She suddenly halted, for an instant she stood staring at him, her eyes flashing.

"So you have finally come out into the open, Mr. Ames," she said, her voice like ice. "I understand everything now. Your visit last night. Your deliberate effort to gain my confidence all part of the game. So that's what it all amounts to—no doubt you are a detective. I've been a fool!"

He started to speak but she stopped him with a wave of her hand.

"Please! Let me finish. I almost trusted you—was willing to consider you a friend. I'm glad I learned my mistake before it was too late. Fortunately, the men I know are not your type. They don't hide behind subterfuge." She laughed mockingly, a bit hysterically. "So you are a detective, Mr. Ames—well, you won't learn anything from me—not one damned thing!" She turned. "I never want to see you again!"

Before Ames could speak she had hurried away. He started to run after her and then suddenly grew conscious of the fact that there were a number of people on the street. He shrank from making either himself or the girl conspicuous. He just stood there staring after her. Finally she disappeared around the corner.

"A detective!" he exclaimed ruefully. "Lord, but Landor would find that amusing!"

Frowning, he began to walk slowly in the opposite direction from the one the girl had taken. Then she *had* been at Fosdick Martin's house, after all. Ted Ames suddenly found himself very tired and very much worried.

"If only she had told me why!" he exclaimed, as he walked along. Then abruptly he brightened up. "After all it doesn't matter so terribly—I know she can explain—and now it doesn't seem quite so hard for me to find my way out of all this—alone!" His chin went up. "No, never so quite alone after having met her!"

14

BLACKMAIL

THE CLOCK IN FRONT of him indicated nine a.m. as Chief John Kenny sat at his desk in his private office once more. He was keenly alert and greatly refreshed after sleeping soundly for five hours at his home. He had left the police station shortly after he received the telephone message from the City Editor of the *Morning News* informing him that Dave Heath had been shot. He had felt that everything connected with the Martin case could wait until morning, though he had left orders for someone at the station to phone him should there be any further startling developments. Now he found that he did not regret his decision.

A copy of the *Morning News* lay upon the desk. Kenny had just finished reading Heath's account of the Martin case. The chief saw it was obvious that the reporter had written his story before he had been shot. That was quite as Kenny had expected, for the City Editor had phoned some time after the hour the chief knew the paper was scheduled to go to press.

As he thought it over he realized he had been right. Dave Heath knew how to handle a good newspaper yarn, and his was a well-written account of the events of the night. Kenny picked up the paper again. He smiled as he read the last paragraph for the second time.

> Chief Kenny states that the police have discovered a number of clues, and the arrest of the murderer is expected to take place within the next twenty-four hours.

"He's right at that," murmured Kenny as he picked up the telephone. "Hello, Sergeant—has O'Shay come in yet? He has? Good! Send him in to me, please."

A few moments later the detective sergeant rapped on the chief's door and then entered. He was smiling and appeared in very good humor.

"Morning, Chief. Did you get some sleep?"

"Yes," Kenny nodded and smiled. "How about you, Tim?"

"Plenty. What do you want me to do this morning?"

"I think I'd like to talk to this Henry Brown."

"O.K. I'll go get him. He's a smooth bird—I don't think he will say much."

"I suspected that, but it won't do any harm to question him."

"Right," said O'Shay as he left the office.

Kenny studied the confidence man closely when the detective sergeant returned with Henry Brown. The latter was a thin-faced, suave individual with heavy brown hair and cold blue eyes. He was well dressed, and in spite of his night in a cell he appeared quite dapper.

"Sit down please, Mr. Brown," said Kenny indicating the chair in front of the desk.

Brown merely nodded as he took the chair. He sat there patiently waiting for Kenny to continue. His manner was casual and not the least bit excited.

"Did you know Grant Ellery?" asked the chief.

Brown hesitated for a moment before he spoke, as though debating the question in his own mind. Finally he shook his head.

"No, I don't recall the name."

"Ellery was the man in the cell across from yours. You saw him there, didn't you?"

"Naturally. But I did not notice him particularly." Brown smiled faintly. "I'm not very much interested in prisoners as a general rule. My having been thrown in jail like this will prove something that the North City police department may regret!"

"We'll worry about that," said Kenny grimly. "Just why did you intend to try to blackmail Fosdick Martin?"

"And who is Fosdick Martin?" asked Brown calmly. "I don't remember having heard of him before."

O'Shay uttered a growl of rage from where he sat. He glared at the confidence man. The latter looked at the stout detective serenely, then turned his attention to the chief as Kenny spoke.

"Oh, yes, you do, you know all about him. You were overheard plotting against Fosdick Martin in your room at the Allen Hotel!"

"Was I?" Brown appeared surprised. "Do you happen to know who I was talking to at the time?"

"Yes," stated Kenny decisively. "I do. We know a lot more than you think, Mr. er—. Brown!"

O'Shay looked at the chief. He was wondering if Kenny had discovered something which he had not previously mentioned. As far as the detective sergeant was concerned, he did not know who Brown had been talking to in the hotel. Kenny's face was expressionless. He did not appear to have noticed O'Shay's glance.

"Well, if you know so much," said Brown quietly, "there is little reason for my being questioned."

"I wouldn't say that." Kenny shook his head. "It's always possible to learn just a bit more." He leaned forward, watching Brown closely. "You know who murdered Grant Ellery in his cell last night?

"Grant Ellery?" The confidence man looked puzzled. "Oh, you mean the chap across the way from me, don't you?"

"Yes."

"And he was murdered last night!" Brown frowned. "I'm not so keen about being held in this jail—it's unsafe!"

"Very!" remarked Kenny drily. "Particularly for anyone who knows as much as you do." His tones grew stern. "Listen, Brown, you're going to talk before we get through with you, understand?"

"Third degree methods, eh? I'm not easily frightened, Chief."

"Maybe not, but you're going to talk. Perhaps not now, but you will later!"

"The usual police bluster!" Brown laughed. "All right, we'll see!"

"Who murdered Grant Ellery?" the chief roared, banging his fist down on the desk. "Tell me!"

"I don't know," said Brown calmly. He looked at Kenny's fist. "Aren't such gestures hard on the furniture?"

"A smooth guy, eh?" growled the chief, glaring at the confidence man. "You won't be so sure of yourself when we get through with you. Perhaps you'll talk when I tell you one thing."

"What is it?"

"At the time Ellery was murdered your cell door was unlocked! You killed him, Brown—killed him because he knew of your plot to blackmail Fosdick Martin!"

For an instant a worried expression swept over the face of the confidence man; then he smiled. His life was based upon bluff and he intended to carry one through now.

"Not guilty. I didn't even know my cell-door was unlocked. I wish I had. I seem to have missed an opportunity to leave North City."

"You killed him," repeated Kenny, paying not the slightest heed to the man's words. "You did it!" The chief glanced at O'Shay and nodded.

The detective sergeant moved close to Brown. He stood beside the chair, glaring down, a heavy menacing figure.

"You murdered Ellery!" he roared. "Killed him because he knew too much!"

"You are the murderer!" shouted the chief.

Over and over Kenny and O'Shay repeated the statement, one after the other. They gave Brown no chance to speak, or to deny the charge. Finally it began to get on his nerves. Their voices seemed to roar in his ears. A sensation of helplessness and fright swept over him, but still Brown said nothing, even when they paused to let him speak.

"You see," said Kenny as he observed the man's silence. "You don't deny it—you can't, because you know we are right. You murdered Grant Ellery in his cell! You did it, you killed him!"

"I *do* deny it!" exclaimed Brown excitedly. "I tell you I didn't do it—I didn't even know that he was murdered."

"Your cell was unlocked," stated O'Shay. "You're guilty!"

"I—" began the confidence man.

"Be quiet!" interrupted Kenny. "You had your chance and you would not talk. Now we know you're the one who murdered Grant Ellery." The chief waved his hand. "That's enough, Sergeant. Take him away. We'll talk to him later. Change the charge against him to first degree murder."

Brown started to speak, and then seemed to feel that anything he could say would be futile. He silently permitted O'Shay to lead him out of the office.

"I guess that guy has something to think about," remarked O'Shay as he returned to Kenny's office after locking Henry Brown in his cell. "Do you believe he really did it, Chief?"

"Of course not. But I think he knows who did. Tim, the same person that talked to Brown at the hotel was the one who murdered Ellery and tried to kill Fosdick Martin." The chief smiled. "And I'm almost certain I know who that was!"

"What?" There was a startled expression upon O'Shay's face. "Who was it?"

"I can't tell you yet, but I will before twenty-four hours have passed."

"Another of your hunches, Chief?"

"Not altogether this time. Just a nice little collection of facts that all point in one direction. Someone has been just a bit too clever, Tim."

"I guess you know something, all right," said the detective sergeant. "And I'll bet it's plenty." He thought for a moment. "Wonder if that drunk seen anything last night?"

"I doubt it. From what Yeager tells me, Hogan was sleeping it off most of the time. Did you have someone look up Hogan?"

"Yes, Ed Mooney is working on that. I sent him out early this morning before I went home. He should be back any time now. I don't think we'll have much trouble digging up the facts on a guy like Hogan."

"I guess not." The chief lapsed into silence.

O'Shay wandered about the office and then dropped into a chair. For a few minutes both men sat thinking, their minds centered upon the Martin case.

A strong suspicion on the part of Kenny which had formulated during the night was gradually evolving into a certainty in the chief's mind. Yet he did not possess all the proof he desired. He felt that would develop during the next twenty-four hours. Then in his estimation it would be a simple matter to arrest the murderer and close the case.

Kenny smiled. Arrest might not even be necessary. He had not forgotten the three men who were already locked in the cells.

The telephone rang and Kenny answered it. It was the Desk Sergeant asking permission for Detective Mooney to see the chief. A little later the detective entered the office. Both O'Shay and Kenny looked at him expectantly.

"I've the facts on Tom Hogan," Mooney announced. "He lives over on James Street, has a wife but no children. He's a hard drinker, and has been fired a number of times because of it. The last place he worked was the North City Sand and Gravel Company, and you know who owns that."

"Sure," remarked O'Shay. "That's one of Fosdick Martin's companies."

"Does Hogan know that?" asked the chief.

"Yes, and he hates Martin. He seems to think that there was something personal on the old man's part. Hogan figures that's why he has lost so many jobs. Martin is poison to him. Every time Hogan gets liquored up he raves about killing the old man. Just talk I guess—still there might be something to it."

"That's possible," agreed Kenny. "Hogan might not have been as drunk as everyone thought last night. Where was he picked up, Mooney?"

"About five blocks away from Martin's place. He was brought in just a little while before you went out to the house."

"Hm, then he could have stabbed Martin." The chief shook his head. "Still there doesn't seem any reason for the murder of Ellery as far as Hogan is concerned."

"No, from what I could learn, Hogan never mentioned Ellery. I doubt if he even knows who he was," said Mooney.

"But don't forget Hogan's cell was open," remarked O'Shay. "He might have killed Ellery, you know."

"Of course he might," said Kenny. "But I don't think he did." He looked at the detective. "All right, Mooney, that'll be all. But stay around awhile—I may need you later."

"Right, Chief," said Mooney as he left the room.

"Tim," said Kenny as the door closed. "I'm going out to Fosdick Martin's place now and I want you to come along. We'll take Perry Fulson with us. I'm curious to see how he will act. Get him and meet me at the entrance. We'll take my car."

"Sure, Chief," said O'Shay moving toward the door. "I'll get him."

As the detective sergeant departed, the phone rang. Kenny answered and found that Homer Stevens was waiting to see him.

"Send him in," said Kenny over the phone.

He had scarcely hung up when there came a knock on the door. At a word from the chief, the private investigator entered the office.

"Good morning, Chief Kenny," said Stevens, a smile on his round face. "How are you this morning?"

"Fine," stated Kenny. "How are you, Mr. Stevens?"

"All right, thank you." Stevens dropped into a chair. "Any new developments since I left you last night?"

"Very few," answered Kenny. He knew that the fact of Heath's having been shot had not been printed in the *Morning News*. He did not intend to say anything about it unless Stevens mentioned the subject. "How about you?"

"Nothing in particular except that I have advised the lady who engaged me that it's best for us to come out in the open."

"Oh, you did?"

"Yes, and I no longer see any reason for concealing her identity."

"Naturally not," said the chief smoothly. "When I already know it is Miss Lily Lawton."

"I rather suspected you did." Stevens did not appear in the least surprised. "You are quite right. By the way, I suppose you know that Fosdick Martin is resting comfortably this morning?"

"Certainly. I had one of my men telephone the hospital as soon as I arrived here about an hour ago. They seem to feel Martin has a fair chance of living."

"I don't believe there is much doubt of that."

Kenny hesitated for a moment and hen reached a decision.

"I was just about to drive out to Martin's house," he said. "I'm taking the secretary with me—I want to see how he acts when we get there. Would you like to come along, Mr. Stevens?"

"I'd be delighted. It's very kind of you to ask me. I suspect we may learn a lot from watching Fulson."

"So do I," remarked the chief. "We'd better start now."

A short drive in Kenny's sedan brought the four men swiftly to Fosdick Martin's residence.

McDonald was standing at the gate of the curving gravel drive that led up to the house. The detective appeared rather nervous when he recognized Kenny and Stevens. He was convinced that he had blundered badly in arresting the private investigator upon the previous night, and now seeing Stevens with the chief made him all the more certain of his error. He was very much relieved when Kenny halted the car and motioned him to get on the running board as they drove up to the house.

Perry Fulson glanced about nervously as he sat in the back of the car beside O'Shay. The secretary had passed a sleepless night and his whole bearing was one of utter dejection.

The chief brought the car to a halt at the steps leading to the front porch of the house. As the men got out of the car, Kenny turned to McDonald.

"Anything happen here during the night?" he asked.

"Not a thing, sir," answered McDonald. "All has been quiet."

"Where is Voring?" asked Kenny, as he thought of the other man he had left on guard.

"Somewhere in the house, I think."

"All right, McDonald. You'd better stay around the grounds. Keep out of sight and let me know if you see anyone."

"Yes, sir." The detective hurried off around the corner of the house.

Kenny looked at Stevens and smiled. The latter nodded. He had observed McDonald's meekness, and it amused him.

Instead of entering the house, Kenny led the way along the porch until they came to the French windows of Fosdick Martin's study. These were closed now, but unlatched, and the chief opened them. As he did so, Perry Fulson stared into the room beyond nervously. He seemed to fear that he might still see Martin lying upon the floor as he had been the previous evening.

Kenny and Stevens entered the room and Fulson and O'Shay followed. Martin's study was obviously the room of a very rich man. The furnishings—the whole atmosphere of the place spoke of wealth and luxury. Elaborate bookcases held row after row of rare editions, and the massive flat-topped desk that stood in one corner was built of an exceptionally fine-grained wood.

The chief and the private investigator appeared to have little interest in the actions of their companions as they moved about talking earnestly in low tones. O'Shay glanced about the room and then stepped to the French windows. Here he paused gazing out over the grounds as he lighted a heavy black cigar.

Perry Fulson moved about restlessly, casting furtive glances at the others from time to time. Finally the secretary edged close to Martin's desk. A half open drawer caught his eye and he glanced inside. As he did so his expression became frightened. He looked at Kenny and Stevens. They were standing some distance away talking earnestly.

Slowly and cautiously Fulson pushed the drawer shut and then moved away from the desk.

"Tim," called Kenny a few seconds later.

The detective sergeant stepped in through the window, and looked at the chief.

"Take Fulson in the other room, will you," he ordered. "There is something that Mr. Stevens and I want to discuss privately."

"Sure, Chief," said O'Shay as he left the study with Fulson and closed the door behind him.

"And now," remarked Stevens when the two men were alone. "Perhaps you had better see what was in that drawer that worried Fulson so much."

Kenny glanced at the private investigator and then smiled as he went to the desk. He drew the drawer open. He picked up a typewritten sheet of yellow paper and read it slowly.

"Listen," said the chief. "I'll read this aloud. 'If you don't leave fifty thousand dollars in cash on the sundial in the garden before midnight on October 13th you will die!'" Kenny handed the paper to Stevens. "It's unsigned, you see."

"Yes, I see," said Stevens slowly. "And yesterday was the fourteenth. I don't believe that Fosdick Martin obeyed instructions!"

"No, and that is why someone tried to murder him last night," stated the chief grimly. "I wonder if—"

He left the sentence unfinished as O'Shay burst into the room. The detective sergeant bore a look of chagrin upon his heavy face.

"Fulson got away," he exclaimed. "Beat it when my back was turned. I can't find him anywhere."

"The fool!" said Homer Stevens. "I'm afraid he was safer where he was!"

15
YOU KNOW TOO MUCH!

G LYNN L ANDOR had just returned to his apartment after a brisk walk to the little restaurant where he usually went for breakfast. It was his habit to become an established patron at various eating places, for in his estimation it was the customers who appeared frequently who were taken as a matter of course, while casual visitors were closely observed. Besides, he felt it in keeping with the part he had played since he had first come to North City; that of a rich and rather quiet individual.

As Landor put his hat and topcoat away carefully the doorbell of his apartment rang once, then twice, then once again. He smiled as he heard it.

"So early," he murmured softly. "I hardly expected him this soon."

With the strange, gliding gait that had earned him the name of The Lizard, the man moved to the door. A few seconds later he returned to the living-room of the apartment and Ted Ames was with him.

"Have a chair and cigarette," said Landor, with a wave of his hand toward a chair with a smoking-stand beside it. "Aren't you a little early this morning, Ames?"

The Lizard watched the other man as he spoke, but his voice was languid as he dropped into a chair. The bright morning sunlight streamed into the windows of the room but it was slightly diffused by the heavy silk curtains which were drawn across each. From the building across the street it was impossible to see into Glynn Landor's apartment. The Lizard was always careful.

Ted Ames produced a pipe from his pocket, filled and lit it slowly before he made any effort to answer Landor's question. Though the latter's face was expressionless, he was a bit puzzled as he watched the younger man. There was a quiet air of self-possession about Ames that he had never displayed before. He seemed in quite a contented mood.

"I suppose I am a bit early," said Ames finally, when the pipe was going to his satisfaction. "I hope you don't mind?"

"Not at all," said Landor politely. He picked up a cigar, clipped off the end with a silver cutter on the smoking-table, which was a duplicate of the one at Ames' elbow. "Something on your mind?"

"Naturally, after last night." Ames spoke very calmly. "Did you see the paper this morning?"

"Of course," The Lizard smiled. "It contained a very interesting account of what the police don't know."

"Possibly." Ames puffed reflectively. "Then again it may only contain just what the police want the public to know."

Landor frowned. Ames had changed overnight. Previously he had seemed a bit awed in the presence of The Lizard, but now he was much too calm and cool to suit that individual.

"I think you give Kenny and his men credit for more intelligence than they really possess," said Landor thoughtfully. "This is one case they will never figure out in a hurry."

"It has a few unusual angles, I'll admit," said Ames. "But I believe it was you who once told me that the man who underestimated his enemies was a fool."

"Meaning just what?"

"Well, you'd hardly consider the police your friends, would you?" Ames frowned. "Nor mine either for that matter, thanks to you."

"Still resenting the fact I got you into this, eh?" Landor leaned forward. "Listen, Ames, I don't like your attitude this morning. I'm afraid you don't realize how serious this Martin affair really is!"

"The more I think it over the more certain I am that you are the one who stabbed Martin and murdered Ellery," said Ames calmly. "You must have been at the house last night, for you got the diamonds."

"You're a bigger fool than I thought you were, Ames." The Lizard's voice was cold and hard. "It's dangerous to know too much right now. I said last night that I didn't do it, and I repeat it, but that's neither here nor there." His eyes were fixed intently upon Ames' face. "Grant Ellery knew too much and you read in the paper this morning what happened to him."

"So that's it?" There was not the slightest trace of excitement in Ames' tone. "If I don't keep my mouth shut I'll be next on the murderer's list!" He shook his head. "Suppose I told you that your threats don't scare me worth a damn, Landor?"

"Most people rather object to dying," said The Lizard grimly.

"Well, I'm not afraid of it," said Ames, his voice as cold as the other man's. "I've let you make a fool out of me—you've used me as your tool, and in a way I guess you have found me afraid—but I'm not afraid to die."

"Go on," said Landor with a laugh. "You're rather amusing with your heroic speeches. But death is a dangerous thing to play with, my dear boy."

"Maybe, but I've played with it before. I'm thirty years old, Landor. I'm one of the boys that went over during the war—and I saw action, plenty of it. Front line trenches, and all that. Death— we had it for breakfast, lunch and dinner. And you, I'll wager you were too clever to have any of that in your life. I guess there's more meaning to that nickname of yours than I realized. The Lizard! Sure—lizards usually creep away from danger."

"That's enough out of you!" growled Landor rising to his feet. "As long as you were willing to do as I say, we worked together— but now I'm going to let you get what's coming to you, Ames—and I won't have to even bother seeing that you get it. I merely have to mention what I haven't up to now—and that is the fact that you know too much!"

"The same threat—murder!" Ames laughed. "You'll have to do better than that, Landor. Last night I even let you frighten me by saying you would reveal the fact that I was at Fosdick Martin's house when he was stabbed. You sent me there so you would have something on me—but it's not enough!"

"No?" Landor suddenly grew calm. He sank back in his chair. "Then suppose I suggest something else that may disturb you slightly?"

"Go right ahead, I'm listening."

"All right, Ames. I know what you may not have quite realized yourself. You've fallen in love with Norma Burton—" The Lizard paused, and an amused smile passed over his face as he saw Ames give a start of surprise. "And that is very dangerous for her!"

"You—you know that I have met her?" Ames was nervous now, for there had been something ominous in The Lizard's tone when he said the situation was dangerous for the girl. "How did you learn that?"

"I have my way of learning things," said Landor. "The girl is pretty well mixed up in this Martin business." He smiled an evil smile. "I don't doubt that she would be pleased if the old man had died!"

"You rotten—" Ames leaped to his feet, glaring at Landor wildly.

"Sit down, Ames!" The Lizard's tone was sharp. "You don't know anything about either of those girls. I do!" he smiled. "As you may remember, I had an engagement with Miss Fenton last night." He shook his head mockingly. "I'm afraid you rather misunderstand me though. I'm not casting any reflections on their virtue. I never play the game that way, only they are rather deeply involved in this affair."

"Just what do you mean?" asked Ames in a calmer tone. "I don't quite understand."

"That's more like it," said Landor. "Now that you have decided to consider things a bit more calmly, perhaps I can make the situation clear." He paused and looked at his cigar. It had gone out and he lighted it again.

"Well," demanded Ames impatiently. "What were you going to tell me?"

"That it will be well for you to continue to work with me. I hardly think you would enjoy realizing you had sent Miss Burton to jail accused of murder!"

"Of murder!" exclaimed Ames. "Why, that's impossible! She couldn't have done it."

"No, not impossible," Landor smiled. "Women are such impulsive creatures. They have done such things. In Miss Burton's case, a bit improbable, but still I'm afraid rather damning evidence could be produced. Mind you, I don't say that it will be—merely that it could, if you, as I once heard a preacher say, do not see the light.'"

Ames stared at the other man for a moment and then frowned.

"You win, Landor," he said slowly. "I work with you until you find my services are no longer needed!"

"Good! That's the way I like to hear you talk, Ames." He looked at the younger man long and searchingly. "You know, I'm glad we've had this little talk. It has taught me something about you I did not realize before."

"What's that?"

"That it might be possible to respect you as a man." The Lizard smiled. "And I repeat, I never underestimate my enemies or my confederates." He grew serious. "One more thing, Ames. You may feel that with me out of the way things would be a bit easier for you. But permit me to remind you of that telephone call I received last night. I never work alone—and I did not kill Ellery, nor stab Martin. I hope I make myself clear."

"Perfectly," said Ames as he rose. "And now if you have no objection, I'm going back to my room at the hotel and get a little sleep."

"Vigils of, ah, devotion are rather wearying," Landor smiled. "I saw you doing patrol duty in front of Miss Burton's apartment house this morning—and later, on the street, when she left you so abruptly." He laughed. "Really, Ames, you are not a very observant watchdog."

"I'm afraid you're a little too clever for me, Mr. Landor," said Ames mournfully, as he turned to leave. "I'll see you later."

"Yes, I'll expect you to phone me this evening," said Landor as Ames disappeared into the hallway of the apartment.

The Lizard leaned back in his chair with a sigh of satisfaction. The interview had proved pleasing after all.

Had he seen the ironical smile upon Ted Ames' face as he departed, Glynn Landor's mood would have been far less amiable. The younger man had no intention of being as docile as he seemed.

16
DEATH STALKS AGAIN

"Perry Fulson got away," repeated O'Shay ruefully. "I'm just plain dumb, that's all, Chief!"

"Never mind, Tim," said Kenny. "He can't have gotten very far from here. We'll find him."

Chief Kenny took command of the situation at once. He doubted that the secretary had as yet succeeded in leaving the Martin estate. He was still sure of it a moment later when Detective Voring appeared. O'Shay had left Voring searching the house when the Sergeant came to tell Kenny the news.

"No sign of him anywhere inside the house," reported Voring. "I looked every place I could, and there wasn't a trace."

"We'd better spread out and search the grounds then," said Kenny. "I doubt whether he's managed to get off the place. I think he's hiding somewhere nearby. Voring, you go and tell McDonald what's happened." He turned to the private investigator who stood nearby. "Mr. Stevens, if you don't mind, will you see what you can find in the rear of the estate?"

"Certainly," Stevens smiled, pleased with the task Kenny had given him. "I'll go at once." He moved away as he spoke.

"Tim, you look for Fulson about the grounds on the right of the house," ordered the chief. "I'll take the left side of the place myself."

A few moments later Kenny found himself alone as he strolled over the well-kept lawn on the left side of the big white house. It was early in April and already the foliage of the trees was thick and green. There were many of them scattered about the Fosdick

Martin estate. Tall oaks held their branches out proudly to the bright morning sunlight, and here and there a weeping willow drooped as though the blue skies made them just a little sad.

Kenny walked on through the grounds, for the Martin place was built upon a six-acre tract of land. About forty feet from the hedge which surrounded the entire property the Chief found that the trees stood close together. Kenny felt that it might be possible for Fulson to be hiding behind one of the large trunks. He carefully circled those nearest to him, but found it was fruitless. He was just about to turn away when he glanced toward the grounds at the front of the house. As he spied the figure of a woman running swiftly toward a side-opening in the hedge Kenny dashed after her. Though he moved swiftly, he was just in time to see her reach the highway and enter a taxicab as he reached the hedge.

Kenny cursed softly as the machine sped away. He had not been close enough to see the woman's face. Nor had he any inkling as to who she might have been.

The taxi disappeared in a cloud of dust and Kenny again returned to the trees. For at least twenty minutes he wandered about, but did not find anything which interested him. Finally he started back to the house, certain that if the secretary had come in that direction he had not lingered long.

As he stepped out from the trees the chief caught sight of a lean figure strolling toward him. From the distance Kenny recognized Dave Heath. The chief frowned. He was not in the mood to give out newspaper interviews at the moment; he had more important things in mind.

"Morning, Chief," said the reporter as he reached Kenny. "I had a hunch I'd find you at Martin's place. That's why I came here as soon as they let me out of the hospital." He held up his right arm and the chief saw that it was carefully bandaged. "Somebody got me last night, you know."

"Yes, Clark phoned me and told me you had been shot," said Kenny, looking at the other man curiously. "What happened, Heath?"

"All I know is that somebody shot me. I worked at the office pretty late, and then Mr. Stevens dropped in—"

"Oh, he did, eh?"

"Yes," the reporter nodded. "He's an old friend of Clark's. We chatted for awhile and then Mr. Stevens suggested that we go out and have something to eat. Clark was busy, but as I was hungry I went along."

"And was Mr. Stevens with you when you were shot?"

"No, I left him a few blocks away from the office. I went on back and just as I passed an alley on Zone Street, someone winged me. He must have been using a gun with a silencer on it. I didn't even hear a report."

"Hm," said Kenny thoughtfully. "I wonder what they had against you?"

"That's what I have been trying to dope out," said Heath. "I can't think of any reason, unless somebody thought I knew too much about this Martin case." The reporter produced a package of cigarettes from his pocket. He used both hands to draw out one of the white cylinders. "Not much of a wound at that," he said as he lighted the cigarette. "Just through the fleshy part of my arm— bled a good bit at first. Kinda silly for Clark to have sent me to the hospital, I thought. They wouldn't let me leave until a little while ago."

Both men turned as Homer Stevens came toward them. The private investigator's round face was expressionless as he reached the two men.

"Mr. Stevens," said Kenny. "This is Mr. Heath, of the *Morning News.*"

"Oh, hello, Heath," exclaimed Stevens. "Sorry, I didn't recognize you at first." He glanced at the reporter's bandaged arm but made no comment.

"Did you find anything?" Kenny asked, looking at the private investigator.

"Yes," Stevens nodded solemnly. "I think you'd better come with me, Chief."

"Mind if I come along?" asked Heath eagerly.

Stevens glanced quickly at Kenny; thought that he caught a note of warning in the look, but merely smiled.

"I guess it doesn't matter," said Kenny. "Come ahead, Heath."

Without further words Stevens led the way back around the house. Here there was a formal garden enclosed in a high hedge. The private investigator pushed open a rustic gate and entered with the others close at his heels. Stevens continued along a flag-stone walk until he reached a little rustic summer house. He paused at the door of this and turned to the chief.

"I think you had better look inside," he said quietly.

Kenny stepped forward and opened the door of the summer house, and then stood frowning as he peered in. Upon the floor of the place lay the limp form of Perry Fulson. The secretary was sprawled face downward, a knife sticking in his back.

"What is it?" exclaimed Heath drawing closer, and then as he saw the figure. "Why it's the secretary, Perry Fulson, isn't it."

"It was," stated Stevens laconically.

Kenny had already entered the summer house, and now he knelt down and examined the secretary. Perry Fulson was dead. He had been stabbed through the back so that the knife had entered his heart. Stevens and Heath stood in the doorway staring in.

"You were right, Stevens," said Kenny grimly as he got to his feet. "Fulson was much safer with us."

The chief frowned as he looked about the summer house. The sunlight streamed in through the windows of the place and gleamed upon a shining silver object. Kenny grunted as he picked it up. It was a woman's vanity case.

"A clue, perhaps," said Stevens as he observed the chief's actions. "It may prove useful."

"Perhaps," said Kenny, as he walked to the door of the summer house. "One never knows."

As Kenny stepped outside O'Shay appeared from the garden. The detective sergeant hurried to them as he saw the others.

"I've been looking all over for you, Chief," he said, and then as he observed the serious expressions upon the faces of the three men, "Why, what's happened?"

"We found Fulson." Kenny waved his hand toward the summer house.

O'Shay stepped to the door and glanced in. He drew back, startled.

"Dead?" he asked in a low tone.

"Yes," the chief nodded. "You'd better run back to the house and telephone Doctor Wilson. Tell him to come out here right away."

"Right, Chief." O'Shay hurried away to carry out his instructions.

"Just how did you get out here this morning, Heath?" asked Kenny as the sergeant disappeared.

"Why, I came out in a taxi," answered the reporter. "It's waiting out in front of the house."

"No, I'm afraid it isn't." Kenny smiled. "Just a little while ago I saw a woman get in it. The taxi left rather hurriedly."

"A woman!" exclaimed Stevens.

"Yes. I guess she must have told the driver that he did not need to wait any longer." The chief looked at Heath. "I wonder if you will pardon me a moment, while I speak to Mr. Stevens." He laughed. "One of the penalties of being a reporter, Heath. I don't want to talk for publication, as it were."

"Sure, Chief, that's quite all right." The reporter smiled as Kenny drew Stevens aside.

"Was Fulson just like he is now when you found him?" asked Kenny, when he and the private investigator were out of earshot of Heath.

"Yes," answered Stevens slowly, his eyes fixed upon the chief's face. "I knew better than to touch the body before the deputy coroner arrived. That is why I came to you at once. As a matter of fact I wasn't certain that Perry Fulson was dead—but I considered it more than likely."

"Did you see anyone in the vicinity?"

"Yes, just as I approached the summer house I caught a glimpse of a woman running through the trees."

"The same woman I saw!" exclaimed Kenny. "Did you recognize her?"

Stevens hesitated for an instant, before he spoke.

"Yes," he said slowly. "I am almost positive that it was Miss Lily Lawton."

"Miss Lawton!"

"I'm afraid so." Stevens shook his head. "I wish I could have prevented her running away as she did. That was very unwise upon her part. I must admit that I don't understand her being out here this morning."

"Neither do I," said Kenny grimly. "After what we have just discovered in there," he nodded toward the summer house. "I'm afraid she is implicated rather deeply."

"I realize that," exclaimed Stevens. "I advised her to remain quietly in her apartment until all this had blown over—and the first thing she does is to disobey my orders." The private investigator smiled. "I know you have someone shadowing her, of course. It is the obvious thing for you to do. After all, I am sure you consider Miss Lawton an important factor in this case."

"I do, and you are quite right. I had one of my men follow her when she left the police-station last night."

"I thought you did."

"She must have managed to elude the man who has been shadowing her," the chief scowled. "That's the second mistake my men have made this morning. First O'Shay lets Fulson get away from him and then Burns loses Miss Lawton."

"Poor devil," remarked Stevens glancing toward the summer house. "It would have been much better for Fulson if he had not tried to escape. I thought that when we first heard the news at the house."

"Why did you think so?"

"Because I feel certain that the secretary must have seen Grant Ellery murdered in his cell last night. That's why Fulson is dead now, the murderer knew that the secretary saw him."

"I wonder if you are right?" said Kenny thoughtfully. "Yes, that might be it."

"Oh, Chief, just one more thing," said Stevens as Kenny started to move away. "I didn't shoot Heath last night, though you may suspect me of it. It was the murderer who did the shooting!"

17
A DIFFICULT MISSION

NORMA BURTON WAS ANGRY. She had liked Ted Ames—had hoped that she might consider him a friend, and now she was positive that he was a detective. When she told him what she thought of him and then left him so abruptly upon the street she had been rather surprised that he had not followed her. Surely he had some explanation for his actions, other than that which she had stated so decisively.

Norma did not stop to consider the fact that she had not given Ames the opportunity to say anything in his own behalf. She only knew that she hated him, and she was rather startled when she realized the bitterness of that hate. It made him much more important to her than she had thought.

When she reached the studio apartment Norma slammed the door viciously as she entered.

Billie Fenton swung around from her desk, where she had been sitting at her typewriter working on a short story.

"Why all the violence?" she demanded quietly. "What's wrong, Norma?"

"Nothing." Norma threw herself into a chair, and jerked the smart black hat off her blond head. "I'm just mad."

"So I judged," Billie laughed. "Who is it, that man who was here last night? Mr. Ames, I believe his name was."

"It still is Mr. Ames," said Norma crossly. "I wish I had never seen him and I hope that I never do see him again."

"Oh!" Billie picked up a cigarette and lighted it. "I didn't know it was that serious. Rather sudden wasn't it?"

"Wasn't what?" asked Norma in surprise.

Billie gazed at the ceiling as she sent a blue cloud of smoke soaring slowly upward. She knew how to tantalize Norma, and she was doing it now.

"What was rather sudden?" demanded Norma impatiently.

"Your falling in love with Mr. Ames," said Billie serenely.

Norma looked at her for a long time, and then her eyes dropped. Billie's words had startled her; in a way they frightened her. In love with Ted Ames! Why the idea was silly, and yet—suddenly Norma turned and buried her face in the soft cushioned back of the chair as she began to sob softly.

Billie placed her cigarette in an ash tray, and hurried across the room. Gently she put her arms around Norma.

"Come on, Babe," she said softly. "Snap out of it. Don't be an idiot. Why you don't know a thing about the man."

"I do, too," sobbed Norma. "He—he's a detective!"

"A detective!" exclaimed Billie. "How do you know?"

"Lend me your handkerchief," said Norma growing calmer. She took the gay-hued bit of silk that Billie handed her, and dried her eyes. "I'm sorry," she said smiling, as Billie perched upon the arm of the chair. "Your saying that I was in love sort of hit me all in a heap. I'm all right now."

"But how do you know that Ames is a detective?" repeated Billie, and it was quite evident that she considered the subject vital. "Tell me."

"Well, about an hour ago I met him outside the apartment." Norma frowned. "I'll bet that he was just hanging around to spy on us."

"I wonder," said Billie thoughtfully. "You know, I thought it was rather strange when you told me about meeting him outside our door last night. After all, he didn't mention the name of any-one he was looking for, did he?"

"No, he didn't. He did ask me if I knew Glynn Landor though."

"Oh, he did," said Billie. "You didn't tell me that before."

"I know," Norma nodded. "I forgot about it. Strange that I should when you were raving about Landor sending you home the way he did."

"Never mind that now," Billie said impatiently. "Tell me more about Ames."

"Well, when I first met him outside this morning he was very nice. I liked him. When I told him I was going to the jeweler's to get my bracelet fixed he asked if he might come along. I told him he could. We just talked until after we had left the jeweler's—and then he began to ask questions."

Norma paused and seemed reluctant to say anything further. Billie looked at her curiously. She felt that something had been worrying Norma ever since yesterday evening, but she did not know what it could be. Billie hadn't asked, for she felt that if Norma had wanted to tell her about it she would have done so. Even now Billie was rather reluctant to do any questioning, and yet she felt that in so doing she might be able to help Norma.

"What sort of questions, Norma?" she said finally.

Norma thought for a moment before she spoke, and then she smiled.

"I don't see any point in trying to keep it from you, Billie," she said slowly. "He asked me if I was at Fosdick Martin's house last night—and I was!"

"You! At Fosdick Martin's house!" exclaimed Billie. "Good Heavens, Norma, have you seen the morning paper?"

"Yes," Norma nodded. "That's why I was sure that Mr. Ames was a detective when he asked me that question." She shook her head. "I wonder how he knew I was there?"

"I don't know." Billie's tone was serious. "But what were you doing at Fosdick Martin's house?"

"I'd rather not tell you about that now," Norma said slowly. "It's a long story, and it really isn't very terrible. At least my part of it isn't!"

"Just as you wish," said Billie. "I know you will tell me when you feel like it." She glanced at her wrist-watch. "Good Lord, it's ten-thirty and I have an appointment at the hair-dresser's at eleven. I've got to go, Norma."

Hastily Billie rushed to her room to get her hat and coat. A few minutes later she reappeared, dressed for the street. Norma was sitting on the window-seat staring out into the bright sunlight of the morning.

"I'm on my way," said Billie starting toward the door, then she paused as a thought struck her. "Oh, Norma, if you go out leave a note for me telling me where you've gone, will you?"

"Of course, old darling." Norma smiled at her. "Better hurry if you don't want to be late."

"I go at your command," Billie laughed as she disappeared through the door of the studio.

Norma turned again to the window. She was thinking about Ted Ames. Was it possible that she really did love him? She found that she did not know. He interested her greatly, even though she resented the fact that he was doubtless a detective. In a way she felt he had imposed upon her. She had been nice to him both last night and this morning, had been willing to consider him a friend. But now she never wanted to see him again, she was sure of that—and yet she wished he had made some effort to explain.

Norma sat there lost in her thoughts for almost half an hour. She had just glanced at her watch and found it was almost eleven-thirty when the doorbell of the apartment rang. Norma hesitated a moment before she went to answer it.

"If that's Mr. Ames I shall refuse to have anything to say to him," thought Norma as she reached the door.

She opened the door to find an attractive dark-haired woman standing smiling at her.

"Miss Burton?" the woman asked. "I'm Miss Lawton—Lily Lawton of the Troupers' Stock Company here in town—you may have heard of me."

"Oh, yes, Miss Lawton." Norma smiled. "I have heard of you, in fact I have seen you in a number of plays, won't you come in?"

"Thank you." Lily looked about her with interest as she stepped into the big studio. "My, what a charming place you have here."

"I'm glad you like it," said Norma politely, as she wondered just why the actress happened to be calling upon her. "Do sit down, Miss Lawton."

"Perfectly delightful." Lily was still gazing about the room as she dropped into a chair.

"I think it's rather noble myself." Norma smiled as she took a chair near the actress. "Billie and I call it home, you see."

"Billie?"

"My room-mate, Billie Fenton. She's out now. I'm sorry, I'm sure she would have been quite thrilled over your being here. We both admire your work on the stage so much, you know."

"How kind of you to say that." Lily smiled. "I suppose you are wondering what on earth made me call like this—when I don't even know you."

"Really, I hadn't thought about it," said Norma. She could be quite urbane when she felt it necessary. "I have merely been flattered by your call, Miss Lawton."

"Graciously said, my dear." Lily laughed, and then suddenly she grew serious. "Miss Burton, I am here on a rather difficult mission."

"A difficult mission? I'm afraid I don't quite follow you, Miss Lawton."

"That's just it. I find my mission a hard one because I am afraid you will not understand. It concerns Ted Ames."

"Really?" Norma's tone was cool. So Ted Ames was a friend of this woman? Without realizing it the girl found that she was a bit jealous. "And why do you feel that I would be interested in Mr. Ames?"

"I don't feel that," said Lily slowly. "I merely came to you because I hoped you would be kind." She shook her head. "The poor boy is so deeply interested in you," she laughed. "If Ted and I weren't such old and platonic friends, I'm afraid I should be terribly jealous of you, Miss Burton. But I have known him ever since he was a boy, and frankly, after seeing you I must admit that he shows good taste."

"So sweet of you," said Norma in a warmer tone. "But I have told Mr. Ames that I never want to see him again—and I mean it."

"But surely you wouldn't be that cruel!" exclaimed Lily. "Why, just an hour or so ago he came to my apartment. He was so white and haggard that he frightened me. Of course I asked him what was wrong. At first he wouldn't tell me—merely said that his life was a mess and that he thought seriously of killing himself—"

"Killing himself!" broke in Norma tensely. "He didn't really mean that?"

"I don't know." Lily shook her head, her expression serious. "I have never seen him in such a desperate mood before in all the years I've known him. He's in trouble, Miss Burton, serious trouble and he needs you."

"But how is that possible? Why he only saw me for the first time last night."

"How can one ever explain such things, my dear?" Lily shrugged her shoulders in an expressive gesture. They just happen. The boy loves you, I am sure of that." Her voice was pleading. "I made him promise that he would wait at my apartment until I returned. He needs you, Miss Burton; won't you come with me now? I'm afraid that he may do something desperate!"

"But what can I do?" demanded Norma nervously, impressed by the sincerity in the actress' manner. "How could I help any?"

"Just by talking to him, by letting him realize that you are still his friend." Lily smiled. "Surely, my dear, you can do that much for him—it hasn't been easy for me to come here like this and ask it of you—but I do ask it—won't you come with me, please? Ted Ames needs you!"

Norma hesitated before she answered. After all, Ted Ames might not be a detective—she had no real proof that such was the case. This woman had said that he was in trouble, serious trouble, and that he needed her friendship. The least she could do was offer him that friendship—and then perhaps he would explain.

"I'll go, Miss Lawton," she said finally, as she rose from her chair. "I must leave a note to Billie telling her where I have gone. She went to Billie's desk, picked up a pencil and wrote hastily. When she had finished she placed the note in an envelope and then stuck it on the typewriter. "I'll be with you in a minute," she said as she picked up her hat and went into the next room to put it on before a mirror.

Lily Lawton smiled sardonically as the girl disappeared. Swiftly the actress went to the typewriter. She tore open the note which Norma had just written. Hurriedly she put it in her purse and then placed the empty envelope back on the typewriter. She was sitting in the chair in which Norma had left her when the girl reappeared.

"I'm ready, Miss Lawton," said Norma. She glanced at the typewriter and saw that her note apparently was still where Billie would find it readily. "Shall we go now?"

"At once," said Lily as she rose and moved to the door with the girl. "I think you will understand everything when you have seen Mr. Ames."

"I hope so," said Norma as the door of the studio closed behind them.

18

THE LOCKED DOOR

CHIEF KENNY STARED at Homer Stevens intently as he heard the latter's calm and matter-of-fact statement. The stout man returned the gaze serenely as they stood in the bright sunshine which gleamed down upon the formal garden of the Martin estate. The chief had found Stevens' words rather unexpected. Kenny had suspected that something had happened during the interval Heath and Stevens had been together in the early hours of the morning, yet to now hear the private investigator quietly announce that he had not shot the reporter was surprising.

"Heath was shot by the real murderer," Kenny echoed Stevens' words. "How do you know that?"

"Purely deduction," the private investigator smiled. "I simply have been carefully considering the facts in the case as I know them." He shook his head, his expression serious. "Unfortunately, what proof I have is not as positive as it might be."

"Still you seem to feel that you have some proof," said Kenny thoughtfully. "I wonder just how much, Mr. Stevens?"

"Enough to make me feel that I may be able to aid you when the proper time arrives."

Kenny started to say something further, and then changed his mind when he saw O'Shay hurrying through the garden with a short, stockily built man wearing shell-rimmed glasses beside him.

"Here comes Doctor Wilson," remarked the chief, with a nod in the direction of the two men approaching. "I guess we will have to abandon our little talk for the present, Mr. Stevens." He glanced

351

at the private investigator. "But there are a number of things I'd like to discuss with you later."

"Of course, that's to be expected," said Stevens, gazing at the new arrivals. "Doctor Wilson, the deputy coroner, eh?" he observed, as he noticed the petulant expression on the face of the man with the glasses. "He doesn't appear very pleased at your having sent for him."

"He never is pleased," said Kenny drily. "In fact he has a damn disagreeable disposition. I'd much rather work with Coroner Blake."

Kenny and Stevens lapsed into silence as they strolled back to the spot where Heath was standing patiently in front of the summer house. The reporter looked at the chief expectantly, as though hoping he would make a statement which could be used from a news angle, but Kenny did not even glance at him. The chief's interest was centered upon Doctor Wilson as he hurried to them.

"More trouble for me, this detective says," growled Doctor Wilson as he reached the chief.

"Not only for you but for all of us, Doctor," said Kenny calmly.

"Huh! Who is it this time?"

"Perry Fulson, the secretary of Fosdick Martin," answered the chief. He swung around and faced the door of the summer house. "You will find him in there, Doctor."

"Dead, I suppose," remarked the physician as he went toward the door. "You don't need a doctor for a deputy coroner in this case, Chief; an undertaker would do!"

"What a nice pleasant manner," murmured Stevens softly as Doctor Wilson disappeared inside the summer house. "I suspect that I would also prefer to work with Coroner Blake and I have never even seen him."

"Any statements, Chief?" asked Heath, edging forward eagerly.

"Not now, Heath." There was a hint of impatience in Kenny's voice. "Haven't you enough news this morning with what we found in there?"

"I'll say I have!" the reporter grinned. "I'm going to grab a phone and give Clark an earful just as soon as I hear what the deputy coroner has to say."

"Maybe he did it," remarked O'Shay glancing toward the door of the summer house. "That's an idea."

"Another of your suspects, eh, Tim?" Kenny laughed. "But why pick on coroners all the time, first Blake and now Wilson. You'll have to do better than that."

"I agree perfectly." There was a smile upon Homer Stevens' round face as he spoke. "I'm afraid that the Sergeant's judgment isn't what I would consider perfect in the line of suspects."

"Oh, is that so?" O'Shay glared at him. "Well, maybe I ain't leaving you out, Mr. Stevens!"

"I rather hoped you wouldn't," said the private investigator. "After all, it is a logical thought!"

Kenny looked at him. The more he saw of Stevens the more he was impressed by the man's cleverness. The private investigator had a keen brain. He had spiked the chief's guns to an extent by agreeing with O'Shay's statement that he might be a suspect. It was a possibility, and one which Kenny still seriously considered. He felt that Stevens would be just shrewd enough to stress the fact that he should be suspected if he were the real murderer, and by so doing make it seem improbable.

Doctor Wilson remained in the summer house for a little over five minutes before he finally reappeared. He glared about him through his glasses as he stepped out into the sunshine and then went to Kenny.

"He's dead all right," Doctor Wilson announced. "Murdered just as Grant Ellery was in his cell last night—a clean knife thrust, through the back and into the heart. Fatal, of course. Been dead a little over half an hour, I should say."

"Then your report is murder?" asked Kenny, more or less as a matter of form.

"Of course!" snorted Doctor Wilson. "What the devil did you think it would be—suicide?" He frowned at the chief. "It seems to me it was about time your police department made an arrest before the whole town is murdered one by one!"

"I'll make my arrests when I'm good and ready!" said Kenny angrily. "I'm capable of attending to my department without advice from you, Doctor."

"Oh, are you?" snarled Wilson. "Then why don't you show some action?"

"I will!" stated the chief, glaring at the deputy coroner. "And I shall certainly report your lack of cooperation to Blake when he returns."

"I'm sorry," said Doctor Wilson hastily. "I had no intention of offending you, Chief Kenny. I was merely expressing my opinion. I offer my apologies." And then as the chief continued to glare at him. "Oh, very well then, you'll find me at my office—the Inquest upon both Ellery and Fulson's death will be held about five this afternoon." He swung around. "Good day, gentlemen."

No one spoke as the little doctor marched stiffly through the garden and disappeared. Finally Stevens sighed softly.

"Such a delightful gentleman," said the private investigator. "He seems to have an ingrown disposition."

"I must phone Clark," exclaimed Heath as the chief remained silent. "This thing gets better all the time—what a story! I'm getting the breaks, all right."

"Oh, Heath!" called Kenny as the reporter started to hurry away. "As a favor to me don't mention the little argument with Doctor Wilson you just heard."

"All right, Chief, I won't," said the reporter. "Fulson's murder is all I need for a wow of a news story."

Heath started on a run through the garden and in a moment he had disappeared beyond the hedge. Kenny, Stevens, and O'Shay stood watching him. When the reporter was out of sight the chief turned to the detective sergeant.

"Better stay here, Tim," he said. "I suppose that Doctor Wilson will make the necessary arrangements regarding taking Fulson's body to one of the undertaking parlors." Kenny glanced at Stevens. "Any suggestions, Mr. Stevens?"

"Yes," the stout man nodded. "What about Fosdick Martin's two servants? Have they been questioned?"

"Only casually, by Voring last night, I believe," answered the chief. "Perhaps it wouldn't do any harm to talk to them again."

"I suspect it would be worthwhile," said Stevens. "Just a hunch on my part, but I would like to be positive that they only left Martin, Ellery, and Fulson at the house last night."

"What do you mean?"

"It has just occurred to me that there might be some other woman involved in this case besides Miss Lawton."

"Another woman," said Kenny thoughtfully, remembering the handkerchief he had found in the space behind the door at the jail, and the silver vanity case that he now had in his pocket. "I must admit that is a possibility, Mr. Stevens," he smiled. "I'm glad you suggested it. Come on, we'll question the servants."

A few minutes later Kenny and Stevens sat in Fosdick Martin's study patiently waiting while Detective Voring went to bring the two servants. They appeared after a short wait.

They were an elderly couple by the name of Dale. The man was a sullen-looking individual with a hard face and a furtive manner. The woman, who proved to be his wife, seemed to be the elder of the two, and it was noticeable that her husband glanced at her before answering any questions addressed to him.

"Since Detective Voring interviewed you last night," began the chief, "we won't bother going into the full details now—there are just one or two things I would like to know and I think you can help me."

Both the man and the woman watched him closely but they said nothing.

"You are Mr. Martin's butler, aren't you?" Kenny looked at Tom Dale as he asked the question.

"Yes, sir."

"And your wife is the cook?"

"Yes, sir." Dale answered each question in a toneless voice.

"Doesn't a house of this size require a lot of work from only two servants?"

"It does, sir, but we manage all right," said Dale. "Mr. Martin pays us well, so we have no complaint."

"I see. When Mr. Ellery arrived last night was there anyone else in the house besides Mr. Martin, Mr. Fulson, and yourselves?"

"There might have been." Dale seemed puzzled by the question. He glanced at his wife who shook her head swiftly. "No, sir, I don't believe there was."

"There seemed to be some doubt in your mind," said Kenny slowly. "Why is that?"

"I think Tom was remembering the girl who has been painting the pictures," said Mrs. Dale hastily.

"What girl?"

"The young artist-lady. I don't know her name, sir." It was Dale who answered. "I believe Mr. Martin engaged her to retouch some of his paintings—cracking they was, or something."

"Hm," said Kenny thoughtfully, and then he glanced at Stevens, who had been listening intently. "And you think that this young lady might have been here last night?"

"She might have, sir." Dale bore a dumb expression upon his face. "I didn't see her though, but then it was hardly likely I would. She always works in the room across the hall from this—and with the door shut mostly."

"Any paintings in the room across the hall?" Kenny turned to Voring as he spoke.

"Yes, sir." The detective nodded. "Quite a gallery."

"Can you describe the young lady?"

"Describe her?" The word appeared to puzzle Dale.

"He means, tell what she looked like," said Mrs. Dale. "She's a blond, tall and kinda thin to my way of thinking. You might say as she was pretty."

"A tall, thin blond. What color were her eyes?"

"I can't say as I ever noticed," answered Mrs. Dale after thinking a moment.

"Did Mr. Martin act as though he were interested in her?"

"I don't know, sir." Mrs. Dale glanced at her husband. "Did he, Tom?"

"Not as I noticed," the butler shook his head. "He just talked to her all the time about the pictures."

"And you don't remember her name?"

"No, sir. I don't think I ever heard it," answered Dale.

"Would you recognize her if you saw her again?"

"Yes, sir. I believe I would."

"Good!" Kenny smiled at Stevens. "I don't imagine there are a great many artists in North City, who are tall blond girls."

"I wonder," said the private investigator. "The one we are looking for may have left town by now."

"That's true." A thought struck the chief. "Did you notice anything strange last night after Mr. Ellery arrived?"

Dale hesitated before he answered. He glanced at his wife. She nodded as she caught his look.

"Tell them about it," she said. "Maybe it don't mean anything, but it sounded strange when you told me."

"It was Mr. Fulson, sir," said Dale. "Last night, just after dinner I was passing through the hall and I heard him telephoning."

"What was strange about that?"

"Nothing, sir, only I heard him say, 'But The Lizard insists.'"

"Ah!" said Homer Stevens softly.

"The Lizard insists?" repeated Kenny in puzzled tones. "What did he mean by that?"

"I don't know, sir—but it seemed strange him talking like a lizard was something that was giving orders."

"Very!" said Stevens. He looked at Kenny. "But it is just what I hoped for!" He smiled. "I don't think you need question them any further, Chief. I can tell you much more than they can."

"All right, you may go," said Kenny. "That's all—thank you!"

The servants hurriedly left the room, glad to be through with the ordeal so easily.

"Better see that they don't leave the place, Voring," commanded the chief.

"Yes, sir," said the detective as he departed, closing the door of the study behind him.

"Now what is this lizard business?" asked Kenny.

"I'll try and tell you all I know about it," Stevens rose and began to pace up and down the room. "The Lizard—" he broke off abruptly as a bullet whistled by his head and lodged into the wall across the room.

Kenny leaped to his feet, drawing the automatic which he always carried, from his pocket. In a moment he was at the French windows peering out. There was no one in sight. Carefully, his eyes searched the grounds.

"I can't find anyone," he said without turning. "Who the devil fired that shot?"

He swung around when there was no answer to his words. The door of the study was still closed but Homer Stevens was no longer in the room. The private investigator had disappeared. With an oath, Kenny rushed to the door—it was locked on the outside.

"Damn him!" growled the chief. "What's his game anyway?"

19
SHE MAY BE IN DANGER

TED AMES HAD FOUND HIMSELF far more satisfied with the world when he left Glynn Landor's apartment. While The Lizard had made it clear that he would not shirk from implicating Norma Burton if he felt it necessary, he evidently did not intend to do so unless Ames proved too difficult to handle. It was this fact that pleased the younger man. Since he had met the girl, he had changed. It almost seemed as though he had matured overnight.

Thinking over the interview with The Lizard carefully, Ames was certain that his attitude and calm matter-of-factness had at least increased Landor's respect for him. That in itself was a victory, for no doubt The Lizard had considered him a spineless individual. But now he at least knew that Ames was not afraid of him, that the younger man did not fear death, and that the only reason he still remained submissive to Landor was because of the girl.

After leaving Landor's apartment Ames had gone directly to his hotel. Upon reaching his room he had dropped wearily upon his bed and slept soundly for nearly three hours.

It was one-thirty in the afternoon when he finally awoke. After having shaved and bathed and put on clean linen he ate a hearty meal which was really a combination of breakfast and lunch so far as he was concerned.

During the course of the meal his thoughts dwelt upon Norma Burton a great deal. He realized that he should make some effort to explain. He liked the girl, in fact when he paused to consider the question seriously, Landor had not been far wrong when he

359

said that Ames was in love with Norma. Ames knew it to be true. It left him with a feeling of exaltation. In spite of the cloud which hung over both the girl and himself, a cloud which had steadily grown darker since Fosdick Martin was stabbed the previous evening, Ted Ames was in a rather happy frame of mind. He was beginning to be more sure of himself than he had been in some weeks. There had been a complete realization of what he was doing when he first met Glynn Landor in the speakeasy, but with the passing days he had found himself more and more under the ruling spell of The Lizard. He had feared the man and in so doing had found himself weak.

But in talking to Landor as he had this morning, Ames had regained the moral courage which, after all, had not been lacking, but merely lying dormant. And it had been because of the girl. He had spoken more truly than he realized when he told Norma Burton the night before in her studio that she could help him by just talking to him. She had done so; she had made a man of him, when before he had been a boy lacking in the valor which made the game of living worthwhile.

After he finished his meal Ames decided he would go to Norma's apartment. He wanted to talk to her. He was confident that if she would give him the opportunity to explain, he could convince her that he was not what she thought. He would prove to her that the idea of his being a detective was in itself ridiculous.

As he stepped out onto the street, Ames heard a newsboy shouting an extra. He bought a paper, and then stood frowning as he read the headline MARTIN'S SECRETARY MURDERED. Swiftly Ames moved back against a building as he read the newspaper story of the gruesome discovery which had been made on the Martin estate that morning. First Martin stabbed, then Ellery killed in his cell, and now Perry Fulson found murdered.

Ames' expression was very thoughtful.

Glynn Landor had been quite right when he intimated that it was dangerous to be connected with the Martin case. Death hovered in the air, ready to swoop down upon the next victim—and there was no way of telling who that might be.

Ames found himself worrying about Norma. The Lizard had seemed to consider that the girl was deeply involved—and in that there was danger. If the murderer felt that the pretty little blond artist knew too much, there was no telling what might happen.

Ted Ames' one thought was to warn Norma of her danger as he hurried through the streets in the direction of her apartment house. He wanted to know that she was safe—that she was not in the power of The Lizard.

The conviction that Glynn Landor was the real murderer had become more and more certain in Ames' mind. That The Lizard denied the fact meant nothing. There was much to lose and little for him to gain by admitting his guilt, even to Ames. The statement that the telephone-call the previous evening had been from the real assailant might merely have been a clever lie on Landor's part.

At last Ames found himself at the apartment house. A few minutes later he was ringing the door of the studio. It was Billie Fenton who opened the door. She stared at Ames without speaking, her manner cold and forbidding.

"Is Miss Burton in?" asked Ames.

"No, she isn't." Billie seemed about to slam the door in his face as she answered.

"Please, Miss Fenton," exclaimed Ames excitedly. "I must see her—it's vital!"

"I really don't think she is at all interested in seeing a detective," said Billie.

"But I'm not a detective—it's all a mistake. I can explain everything if she will only see me."

Ames was convinced that Norma was really in the studio, and that Billie was merely saving the other girl the trouble of dismissing him.

"Really, Mr. Ames, she isn't here." Billie spoke in a more friendly tone. She had sensed something sincere in his agitation. "I don't know where she is."

"Then won't you let me talk to you?" asked Ames. "Perhaps you can explain to her later—make her understand that I had no intention of offending her by my questions this morning." He looked at her pleadingly. "Please, Miss Fenton, at least grant me that favor!"

Billie hesitated, her eyes looking into his. He faced her gaze unflinchingly. Finally she smiled.

"All right, Mr. Ames, come in please."

Ames glanced about him as he stepped into the studio. A sense of disappointment swept over him when he realized that Billie had been telling the truth. Norma was not in the big studio, though she might be in the girls' apartment beyond.

"You see," said Billie, as she observed his expression. "She isn't here. But do sit down, Mr. Ames." She dropped in a chair as she spoke.

"Thank you," Ames murmured automatically as he sat opposite her. "But Miss Burton will be back won't she?"

"I don't know," Billie said reluctantly. "You really are not a detective, Mr. Ames?"

"No, of course not. I can't quite understand how Miss Burton gathered that impression. I'm just a former newspaper reporter out of a job."

"Oh, so that's it? Then you were asking Norma all these questions from a news angle?"

Ames gazed at the pretty dark-haired girl who sat across from him. He found that he liked Billie Fenton far better now than he had when they first met the night before. There was a sincerity in her manner that told him she would prove a loyal friend. Ames realized that he wanted her friendship as much as he wanted Norma Burton's love. Both seemed so worthwhile.

"Not from a news angle at all," he said slowly. "But in the hope of being able to aid Miss Burton." He stared at her seriously. "I don't quite know how to explain, but ever since we first met last night, helping her has seemed so vital to me—she—" he hesitated, unable to put his thoughts into words. "Well, I just wanted to aid her, that was all."

Billie slowly picked up a cigarette. She had scarcely done so before he was on his feet, holding a lighted match for her.

"Thank you," she smiled at him. "I think I'm beginning to understand, Mr. Ames."

Billie did understand. It was so obvious that he was in love with Norma. He had said far more than he realized, for Billie had not judged him merely by his words, but by the way he had said them. The tone of his voice when he spoke of Miss Burton, the earnest way in which he looked at her as he spoke of the other girl, all indicated the depth of his feelings.

Billie remembered Norma sitting in the same chair that Ames now sat in. Norma crying and showing that this man really meant something to her. In her way Billie was devoted to Norma, and so it pleased her to find that Ted Ames was so sincere.

"I'm going to be frank with you, Mr. Ames." Billie said finally. "For the last hour or so I have been worried."

"Worried?" He looked at her in surprise.

"Yes, about Norma. I left her a little before eleven this morning. I went to keep an appointment with my hair-dresser. Before I left, I made Norma promise that she would leave a note for me if she went out, telling me where she was going."

"And did she?" asked Ames eagerly.

"I don't know," Billie rose and went to her desk. She returned with an envelope in her hand. "This was all I found." She handed it to Ames. "It is addressed in Norma's handwriting."

"I see," said Ames, glancing at the envelope. On it was written simply, 'Billie.' He looked inside and found it was empty. "But there's nothing in this," he exclaimed.

"That's what worries me," said Billie. "I found the envelope on top of my typewriter where Norma knew I would be sure to see it. It had been torn open and the message evidently removed. I looked everywhere but I couldn't find anything else."

"Then someone must have stolen the note when Norma wasn't looking." Billie smiled as she noticed Ames' unconscious use of the other girl's first name. "Perhaps he left the envelope so she would think the note was still there."

"But who could it have been?" asked Billie nervously. "Can you think of anyone?"

"Only one person," replied Ames thoughtfully, his eyes upon the girl as he spoke. "And that is Glynn Landor!"

"Glynn Landor!" exclaimed Billie. "Oh, no, no! That just couldn't be!"

"What makes you so sure of that?" asked Ames. "You know Landor, don't you?" Billie stared at him wildly. She seemed badly frightened.

"Yes," she said in a low tone. "I know Mr. Landor."

"Then you must help me; must help Norma, by telling me all that you know about him," said Ames earnestly. "And I need your aid so much."

"When you talk like that you make me think you are what Norma said you were." Billie looked at him nervously. "A detective!"

"A detective! Because I ask you to tell me what you know about Glynn Landor? Miss Fenton, don't you see how strange that sounds?"

"It's all so strange." Billie was almost tearful. "And it's my own fault!"

"Your fault—what do you mean?"

"Mr. Landor, Norma, oh, everything," said Billie. "She warned me about him, but I wouldn't listen—oh, I'm—I don't know what to say!"

"Tell me, please," Ames' voice was gentle. "What is Glynn Landor to you?"

"How can I answer that?" Billie looked at him appealingly. "You will consider me such an idiot if I do."

"Not at all—it's the only way you can help Norma. By telling me everything."

"Help Norma? Oh, I want to do that so much. Something tells me that she may be in danger—terrible danger right now." Billie laughed brokenly. "I know it's probably just a silly fear on my part, but I can't help feeling it might be true!"

"You are right," said Ames grimly. "I feel it more than you do—" he hesitated, and then reached a decision. "And that danger may come from Landor! Because I want you to trust me I am going to tell you something that no one else knows." He looked at her, a grim smile upon his face. "I've heard it said that a woman can't keep a secret, but in telling you what I do I am trusting you—and if what I say is repeated it may cost me my life!"

"Your life!" Billie looked at him in startled wonder.

"Yes. I know Glynn Landor, know him for what he really is—a very clever criminal who is known in the New York underworld by the sinister title of The Lizard."

"The Lizard—what a repulsive name!" exclaimed Billie. "Glynn Landor, a criminal!" She shuddered. "Oh, I was afraid of this. There was something about him that I did not understand. Norma sensed it the first time she saw him. She disliked him intensely." She paused and stared at Ames. "But how do you know all this about him?"

"I'm going to tell you everything," said Ames slowly. "I realize the risk is great; for all I know, you may repeat every word I say to Landor. But I have gone too far to stop now." He frowned and glanced at his watch. "We don't know how many hours Norma has been missing, but I judge that at least two hours have elapsed since you returned from your hair-dresser's and found that empty envelope."

"At least that," said Billie. She looked at him. "You can tell me what you wish, Mr. Ames—and you may be sure that I will try to prove worthy of your confidence." She paused and then went on swiftly. "And I will tell you everything I know. There is no danger of my ever repeating anything to Mr. Landor."

"Very well then," said Ames slowly. "But I must ask you not to judge me too harshly." He smiled. "Perhaps I may prove not to be as weak as I seem!"

"Why should you feel that I would want to judge you? I only want to try and understand. Tell me, Mr. Ames, please."

"Six weeks ago I first met Glynn Landor. Where and how does not matter. I want to speak as briefly as possible. Perhaps you may have read in the newspapers of a large number of daring jewel robberies which have been going on not only in North City but in other towns nearby—"

"Yes, I do remember something about them." Billie nodded. "And Glynn Landor—"

"Was the one who committed those robberies!" Ames smiled grimly. "And I aided him, by acting as a sort of lookout."

"You—a criminal!" There was a note of disappointment in Billie's tone that stung Ames as he heard it. "I can't believe it!"

"I asked you not to judge me too harshly," he said quietly. "Last night Landor sent me to Fosdick Martin's house to steal a very valuable collection of unset diamonds—"

"Then you were there when—" Billie hesitated, unable to finish the thought in her mind.

"When Fosdick Martin was stabbed? Yes. I was standing in the dark in the hallway—I heard a thud and a groan. Then a woman's voice whispered to me. She told me to leave at once. I switched on my flashlight but I only caught a glimpse of her arm as she disappeared, closing a door behind her."

"And that woman? Who was she?"

"I don't know," said Ames. "At least, I am not sure. I noticed an odd-looking gold snake bracelet on her arm when she disappeared. This morning when I met Norma she was going to the jeweler's to have her bracelet repaired—it was exactly like the one I saw last night—and she said she did not believe there was another just the same design anywhere!"

"Then—then it was Norma?" demanded Billie, gazing at him fearfully.

"I don't know." Ames shook his head. "But if it wasn't, why did she think I was a detective?" He looked at Billie intently. "And why did you think so?"

"I only thought so because Norma suggested it. She insisted that you were—and seemed so worried about it that I thought it best to agree with her. It seemed probable after the way you appeared at the door last night. She told me all about it." Billie smiled. "She even told me that she was at Fosdick Martin's house last night."

"Then it was she who warned me!" exclaimed Ames. "Did she tell you why she was there?"

"No, but she said it really wasn't very terrible, and that she would tell me about it later." Billie looked at Ames. "And now I will try to tell you what I know about Glynn Landor. I'm afraid you will find it so little compared to your knowledge of the man."

"That doesn't matter—tell me."

"I first met him about two weeks ago. Some friends of mine here in town introduced me to him. He interested me, he was quite charming, and very different from most of the men I know. I took him for just what he said he was, a man from New York spending a little time in North City. He rather conveyed the idea that he was looking about with the intention of establishing some sort of a business here.

"He took me to the theatre two or three times. Twice we went to see plays that were presented by the Troupers' Stock Company. I teased him about being interested in Miss Lily Lawton, the leading lady with the Troupers. He admitted that he knew her, and thought she was a splendid actress."

"Lily Lawton," said Ames. "I must remember that name. Go on, please!"

"Well, I hadn't heard from him in some time, but about a quarter to ten last night he phoned me. He asked me to be ready a little after ten, and he would promise me an unusual evening." Billie smiled. "I was just in the mood for adventure so I agreed to go out with him. He took me to a café run by some negroes on the south side of town. I didn't like it much, but I tried to pretend that I was enjoying myself. I don't believe we had been there more than an hour when he was called away by a telephone-call. When he returned, he appeared excited, though he made no attempt to explain. In fact he was rather curt and rude and bundled me into a cab and sent me home without any apologies."

"And is that all you know about him?" asked Ames as Billie paused.

"Yes, and I hope I never see him again! It was silly of me to play around with him anyway—though I must say he never tried to make love to me. He just seemed to enjoy my company."

"I'm afraid that Glynn Landor never does anything without a good reason," said Ames thoughtfully. "I'd advise you to continue to keep away from him, Miss Fenton."

"Don't worry, I shall." Billie smiled. "And you may be sure that I'll never mention anything you have told me, Mr. Ames—thank you for trusting me." She looked at him anxiously. "But what shall we do about Norma? I'm so worried about her."

"You just stay here; she might return," said Ames as he rose. "I think that Glynn Landor may know where she is." His tone grew harsh. "And if he does, I'll make him tell me! I'll phone you just as soon as I learn anything."

"Thank you," Billie went with him to the door. "Perhaps it may interest you to know that Norma seems to like you." She smiled.

"Interest me!" he exclaimed as he departed. "That's scarcely the word. But I must try to tell her about it."

Billie's smile was a little sad as the door closed.

"It must be nice to be in love," she murmured softly.

20
THE POLICE ACT

CHIEF KENNY WAS IN FAR from a pleasant humor. For over an hour he and his three men had searched the Martin estate for some sign of Homer Stevens, or the person who had fired the shot which had narrowly missed the private investigator, but their efforts were futile. Stevens had disappeared completely. There was no trace of him having even been at the house. When he had found the door of the study locked it had been a simple matter for the Chief to step out through the French windows and re-enter the Martin residence through the open front door.

Kenny realized that the possibility of the stout man escaping without being seen was not as difficult as it had seemed at first. O'Shay had remained on guard at the summer house, and he had not seen Stevens pass in his vicinity. Voring had been in the house with the servants, while McDonald had been patiently standing by the hedge gateway at the foot of the drive. It was possible for the private investigator to have run through the trees either to the right or the left of the house without being seen and then break through the hedge.

The fact that Stevens had run away puzzled the Chief. He had seemed quite willing to work with Kenny, had insisted upon it himself, and yet, why had he run away? And why had he locked the door? Homer Stevens did not strike the Chief as the type of man who would be frightened by a shot, even if the bullet had come dangerously close. Fear had not instigated Stevens' flight, if his disappearance could be considered that.

Kenny realized that it was barely possible Stevens had recognized the person who had fired at him and had gone in pursuit without stopping to explain. Still if that was the case, the Chief could not understand why the private investigator had not returned. Nor why the door had been locked.

After a search of an hour or more Kenny gave it up as hopeless and returned to the house. Now he was strolling about in the little picture gallery opposite Fosdick Martin's study. He found that quite an interesting collection of paintings were grouped upon the walls. Near a window was an easel on which stood a canvas whose frame had been removed. Kenny examined this painting carefully and found that it had been very carefully retouched here and there.

This was enough to convince the chief that the blond artist whom the servants had mentioned had really been at work.

Kenny swung around as the door opened and O'Shay entered the room. There was a frown on the face of the detective sergeant, and he dropped wearily into a chair.

"This is the damnedest case I've ever seen," he said crossly. "Just when we get ready to start working on something another guy gets bumped off."

"Yes, and it's up to us to see that it doesn't happen again," said Kenny. "Two murders, almost three, if you want to count Martin, since last night. Well, it's bad, that's all."

"Your friend Doctor Wilson was just here a few minutes ago," announced O'Shay. "He came out with the undertakers to arrange about bringing Fulson's body into town."

"Why didn't you call me? Did Wilson ask for me?"

"I didn't think you'd want to bother talking to him, and he didn't say anything about you anyway. He only stayed a few seconds. All he does is march up to the door of the summer house with the other guys and say, 'There it is,' and then march away again. He didn't even say hello, or go to — to me, though he sure seen me standing there."

"I wish Blake would get back!" said Kenny, walking up and down impatiently. "I don't believe Doctor Wilson has the faintest idea of the real scope of a coroner's duties in a case like this."

"He sure ain't putting himself out any." O'Shay grinned. "Well, Chief, I don't know about you, but as far as I'm concerned we've got a red hot suspect in this guy Stevens."

"I'm beginning to feel that way myself," said the chief. "Still for a time he had me pretty well convinced that he was a private detective. His papers were all right—and he certainly knows a lot about this affair."

"Sure, that's just the point. He knows too blooming much about it." A thought struck the sergeant. "Say, Chief, who was it found Fulson?"

"Why, Stevens found him and then came and told me about it."

"Oh, he did, eh! Now ain't that nice! Nothing to prove he didn't knife the secretary, is there?"

"No," Kenny shook his head. "And there's nothing to prove that he did." He glanced at his watch. "Hm, two o'clock—we'd better get back to town. I've given both Voring and McDonald their instructions. They are to arrest Stevens or anyone else they catch on these grounds, and then report to me. The servants are not to leave the place. I guess that's all."

"Sure," said O'Shay. "I'm all for getting back to the station. I'm hungry—haven't had anything to eat since breakfast."

A few minutes later O'Shay sat beside Kenny on the front seat of the chief's car as they drove back into North City.

"There's one thing I want you to do when we get to town," said the chief as they rolled along. "And that's see what you can learn about any tall, blond girls who are artists."

"I don't think there are many of them in town," said O'Shay. "It ought not to be hard to look them up."

"You'd better spend the afternoon on it, and don't forget that this girl is said to be pretty."

"Don't worry—I won't forget that," the detective sergeant laughed as the car drew up in front of the police station. "I'm not so old that I can't still enjoy looking at a pretty girl."

"Forget it, Tim." The chief looked at the short stocky sergeant. "You're not the build for a Don Juan."

"Don who?" demanded O'Shay as they left the car, and started inside. "I didn't get you."

"Never mind," said the chief. "I was merely telling you that you are not the flame in flaming youth."

"Sure, I know it," said O'Shay. "And if you didn't tell me, Mrs. O'Shay would!"

When they were inside the police station Kenny left O'Shay and went directly to his office. He found that there were a number of routine matters to be attended to which had developed during the morning. When he had finished these tasks, the chief leaned back in his chair.

For about twenty minutes he sat thinking. Finally he decided to follow a hunch that he had. He put on his hat, and left the station house bound for Lily Lawton's apartment.

Homer Stevens had claimed he had been engaged by the actress. In that case, there was a remote possibility that the private investigator might be found at Lily's apartment. At any rate Kenny wanted to talk to the woman. He was almost certain that she knew a great deal more than she had admitted the previous evening.

Besides, she had been out at the Martin place that morning, and Kenny wanted to know what had brought her there and how much she knew about the murder of Perry Fulson. He was sure that she had been the woman he had chased through the trees. Homer Stevens had admitted seeing her on the grounds. As he walked toward the street on which Lily's apartment was located, which was but five blocks from the police station, the chief became more and more convinced that his hunch was a good one.

When he finally reached the apartment house he found Detective Burns standing patiently across the street. Kenny went to him, at the same time observing a cigar store a little further along the street.

"See me in the cigar store," said Kenny without looking at the other man as he sauntered casually by.

The chief went on and entered the cigar store. He bought a package of cigarettes from the listless clerk, and then walked over to the magazine rack. He was standing gazing at the covers when Burns entered.

Kenny glanced at him, and then nodded. "Oh, hello, Mike," he said. "How are you?"

"Why, hello," said Burns taking the hint from the chief. "It's been a long time since I've seen you."

The clerk, not in the least interested in a chance meeting between two old friends, picked up a magazine and began to read.

"Well, what do you know?" said Kenny in a low tone.

"All is quiet," replied Burns. "She is still in the apartment."

"How'd she happen to get away from you this morning?"

"Huh?" Burns looked startled.

"She was out at Martin's place. Early in the morning. I saw her, but she got away."

"I'm sorry, Chief." Burns looked crestfallen. "I guess she put one over on me—must have gone out when I was getting a cup of coffee down the street. I thought she appeared for the first time at eleven this morning."

"Where did she go then?"

"I trailed her to an apartment house over on Grand Street. She went up to an apartment on the fourth floor. I couldn't find out the name of the people who lived there. About fifteen minutes later she came down again. A tall blond girl was with her. They came back here."

"A tall blond girl. Was she pretty?"

"I'll say." Burns rather fancied the ladies. "She was swell!"

"That's the best news I've heard in some time," said the chief. "We're looking for that girl. Listen, Burns, I'm going up to see Miss Lawton. Have a hunch I may learn something. You stay down here in the street. If you hear me blow my whistle, you arrest the first person who appears. You understand?"

"Sure, Chief." The detective nodded. "I'll be on the job. Sorry I let the dame pull a fast one on me this morning. It won't happen again!"

"Good, see that it doesn't." Kenny started to walk out of the store as he spoke.

Burns paused to buy a paper. When the detective reached the street Kenny had already entered the apartment house.

The chief went directly up to Lily Lawton's apartment. He had brushed the boy at the switchboard aside with a curt, 'I live here,' when the attendant asked him whom he wanted to see. The boy had been impressed by the chief's manner and he said nothing further.

Kenny rang the door of the actress' apartment. In a moment it opened and Lily Lawton herself stood gazing at him. She stepped back as though startled when she saw the chief and then she smiled.

"Why, Chief Kenny," she exclaimed. "This *is* a surprise. Won't you come in?"

"Thank you." Kenny stepped into the living-room of the apartment as he spoke.

Lily closed the door, and then turned to the chief.

"Do sit down," she said. "I rather felt it was your turn to pay me a visit."

"Just one question first," said Kenny. "Is there anyone else in this apartment?"

"Why, of course not." Lily's eyes turned toward a closed door on her right as she spoke. "What makes you think there might be?"

"I know there is someone else here," said Kenny moving toward the door. "And I want to talk to her."

Lily did not move. She merely stood watching as the chief tried the door and found it locked.

"Unlock this door," he commanded as he faced her.

"Why should I?" demanded Lily. "I don't recall your showing me any warrant to search the premises."

"No?" Kenny glared at her. "But you may have forgotten that I have the power to arrest you as a material witness in a murder case!"

An expression of fright swept swiftly over the actress' face. It was gone in an instant. But without further words she walked over to a table in the center of the room, picked up a key and handed it to Kenny.

"Here you are, Chief Kenny," she said.

Kenny took the key and swiftly unlocked the door. As he opened it he saw a blond girl sitting in a chair. A gag was in her mouth and her hands and feet were tightly bound. As the chief stepped into the room he heard a slight sound behind him. He turned just in time to see the figure of a man disappear through the doorway leading out into the hall of the apartment house. Kenny rushed to the open window of the room in which Norma was a prisoner. He put his whistle to his lips and the blast echoed shrilly upon the still afternoon air.

This done the chief rushed past Lily and out of the apartment, hoping to catch the man who had disappeared: As he reached the elevator he found that it had just descended. He pushed the bell, realized that it was wasted effort and dashed for the stairs. He leaped down them two at a time. When he reached the lobby of the apartment house, he passed the colored attendant with a rush that left the boy staring after him in wide-eyed amazement.

"My!" murmured the bellboy. "That gentleman shore is goin' some place!"

When Kenny reached the street he saw that Burns and the patrolman on the beat, who had evidently appeared at the sound of the chief's whistle, were both holding a stout man. Kenny uttered an exclamation of delight as he recognized the latter. It was Homer Stevens.

"We got him, Chief," said Burns with a nod in Stevens' direction as Kenny reached them. "You told me to arrest the first person who came out of the house when you blew your whistle—and this is the man."

"Greetings, Chief," said the private investigator. "If I had known you were calling on Miss Lawton I certainly would have gone on up to her apartment instead of remaining in the lobby."

"Oh, is that so!" Kenny glared at him. "Well, as a matter of fact I know you were in Miss Lawton's apartment. You tried to sneak out when you thought I wasn't looking!"

"I tried to sneak out?" Stevens seemed surprised. "Then you saw me?"

"Yes, I saw you, or at least I caught a glimpse of a man just as he disappeared through the hall door." The chief continued to glare. "And I know now that it was you!"

"But I am sure you are mistaken," stated Stevens.

"Never mind!" interrupted Kenny. "I'm through listening to your smooth explanations. You're under arrest, Stevens, charged with being a murder suspect!"

"You really mean that?" For the first time the private investigator appeared perturbed. "And you won't give me a chance to explain?"

"No, I won't," exclaimed the chief impatiently. "Perhaps later I'll let you talk, but not now." He turned to the policeman. "Take him to the station house, Creagan, and have him locked up—and see that he gets there safely!"

"Yes, sir." The patrolman produced a pair of handcuffs. He hooked one of the steel bracelets around Stevens' right wrist, and then fastened the other about his own left wrist. "I'll get him there all right."

Burns ran his hands swiftly over the private investigator, searching for a weapon. Finally he stepped back, satisfied that the stout man was not armed.

"All right, Creagan," he said. "Take him away."

"You stay here, Burns," said Kenny to the detective as Creagan and his prisoner started to march down the street. "I'm going upstairs again. And I expect to make an arrest. Don't let anyone pass you, particularly Miss Lawton!"

"Right, Chief," said Burns, but he found himself speaking to thin air, for the chief had again disappeared into the apartment building.

"'Scuse me, boss," said the colored attendant nervously. "But is something done happened?"

"Not yet," said Kenny throwing back his coat and revealing the shield pinned on his vest. "But it will happen if you don't get me up to the third floor in a hurry."

"Lawdy, a policeman. Yes, sir, we're moving." The bellboy started the elevator as he spoke.

"Wait here," commanded Kenny as they reached the third floor. "I'll be going back down again in a minute."

The chief rushed to the door of Lily Lawton's apartment. To his surprise he found it standing open. Hastily he entered, his hand upon the automatic in his pocket. There was no sign of the actress in the living-room. The chief went at once to the room in which he had seen the blond girl tied to the chair. This, too, was unoccupied. The chair still stood as he had last seen it, but bits of cut rope were tossed heedlessly about on the floor.

Kenny tore through the entire apartment, looking in closets and under beds, searching in every possible place that a human being might hide. Finally he realized that his efforts were futile. Both Lily Lawton and the blond girl had completely disappeared.

The chief returned to the living-room and stood there for an instant cursing vehemently. He realized that he had given the actress a perfect opportunity to escape completely when he had run downstairs in pursuit of Homer Stevens.

As he grew calmer Kenny let his gaze travel around the room. A silver cigarette case lying on a stand near the door caught his eye. He went to it and picked it up. Frowning he observed that the initials engraved upon it were G. L.

"G. L." murmured Kenny. "Hm, I guess I had better have a little talk with Homer Stevens!"

21
CONFLICT

Ted Ames left Billie Fenton in a grimly determined mood. He had but one object in view, and that was to find Glynn Landor at once and force him to tell what had become of Norma Burton.

Ames realized that his mission was a dangerous one. When one stopped to consider the ruthless character of The Lizard it was scarcely likely that he would let anyone interfere with his plans. If Landor were the real murderer, and Ames still considered it more than likely, then he would not even shirk at death if he thought it to his advantage.

As Ames hurried through the streets in the direction of The Lizard's apartment he gradually grew calmer. It had dawned upon him that the only way he could even hope to cope with Landor would be by clear-headed, carefully thought-out action. It would gain him little to face the man with an openly defiant attitude. Landor would not be inclined to receive blustering threats with any degree of meekness. He was by no means afraid of Ted Ames. Far from it, in fact. It was doubtful that The Lizard really feared anyone. That was not the way he lived.

When Ames found himself at the corner of the street upon which Landor's apartment house was located he slowed his pace. He was a little uncertain as to his next move. He knew that it would be difficult for him to even talk to the man without giving some indication of his anxiety regarding Norma. He did not want to do that, for he felt that in doing so he might ruin his chances of finding the girl.

Ames stood at the corner staring at the big greystone apartment house further along the street. It was with a sense of relief that he saw a tall, well-dressed man step out of the entrance. Ames ducked back out of sight in a doorway as Landor strolled down the street, idly swinging his cane as though he were enjoying a walk in the bright afternoon sunshine.

The Lizard passed without apparently seeing Ames as the latter crouched back in the doorway. The younger man breathed a sigh of relief. His problem had been solved for him. He would follow The Lizard, though he had not the faintest idea as to Landor's destination. Still Ames hoped that The Lizard might lead him to Norma. At any rate he intended to trail Landor and see what happened.

Ames waited until the other man had turned the corner and then he stepped out of the doorway and started in pursuit. He moved swiftly. He did not run, but merely walked along at a fast pace.

When he reached the corner Ames rounded it cautiously for he did not wish to be seen by Landor, should the latter glance back. Ahead of him, half-way down the block Ames spied The Lizard sauntering along. For at least twenty blocks they went on in this fashion, and not once did Landor glance over his shoulder or give any indication that he sensed he was being followed.

Ames found that the other man evidently had a definite destination in view for they went across the city to the railroad terminal. Landor circled around the station and then started down a long avenue in the poorer section of the town. Ames followed at a safe distance. Finally The Lizard swung into a dingy little street that was scarcely more than an alleyway. For the first time he glanced back, but Ames stood beneath the shadow of an awning gazing at the display in a shop window.

Apparently satisfied that he was not being followed Landor went on. When he reached a dilapidated two-story house at the far end of the street he paused at the door. He disappeared inside the house a moment later.

Ames continued to remain under the awning gazing down the street. He was almost certain that Norma was being held a captive in the house The Lizard had just entered. If such were the case it was up to Ames to rescue her and do so as promptly as possible.

But there was another detail to be considered. The street appeared seldom used and anyone passing the house could be easily detected from the windows by those watching inside. It was more than likely that Landor would recognize Ames if he saw him in the neighborhood, and know just what had brought him there. In that event he might endanger the safety of the girl, if she were in the house.

Ames found himself wishing it were night, but it was only a little after two-thirty in the afternoon. He realized that he had to act at once. It would avail him nothing to wait. The feeling that Norma was in danger was the dominating factor in his mind and he wanted to do everything in his power to aid her.

He seriously considered telephoning the police and requesting them to come to the old house on Larkin Street. The only thing which stood in the way of his doing so, was the realization that he would involve Norma. She had been at Fosdick Martin's house the previous evening. Just how much she knew of what had actually occurred there Ames did not know, but he was sure that if the police learned she had any possible connection with the Martin case they would make things difficult for her.

Finally Ames made up his mind to a bold plan. He intended to go directly to the house and demand that Glynn Landor let him in. Once inside he could at least learn if Norma were being held a prisoner. What would happen after that he did not know, but he was sure that he would do his best to aid the girl.

Having made up his mind to his course of action Ted Ames walked boldly down the street in the direction of the house. When he reached it, he climbed the three low steps which led to the front door. He pushed the doorbell. Somewhere in the distance he heard the bell ring.

For a few moments he stood there waiting, not at all certain that anyone would answer his ring. To his surprise the door finally opened and Glynn Landor stood gazing at him, an ironical smile upon his face.

"So it's you, Ames," said The Lizard. "Come in, I've been expecting you."

Ames did not move as he stared at Landor in surprise. The other man's words startled him. What did The Lizard mean?

"I hope you're not surprised," Landor laughed. "I'm afraid you have rather misjudged my powers of observation. I know quite well that you followed me all the way across town. Surely you must realize that I have been trailed by some of the cleverest men on the police force of various cities—and I must admit that their work has been a bit more expert in that line than yours was this afternoon. But come in, please."

Reluctantly Ames stepped into a dark hallway. Landor closed the door and bolted it. An instant later Ames felt something jab him in the ribs.

"That's a gun that I just poked you with," said Landor calmly. "I'm afraid that I'm not taking any more chances with you, Ames. You seem a bit too inclined to kick over the traces."

"Where's Miss Burton?" demanded Ames abruptly.

"So that's it," Landor laughed. "I thought as much. You don't mean to say she is missing."

"You know damn well she's missing," said Ames angrily. "And if any harm has come to her—I'll—I'll kill you."

"Rather a silly threat, don't you think? When I happen to have you covered with a gun at the moment."

"What of it?" demanded Ames. "I'm not afraid! You can't do any more than kill me and when the police catch you they will have one more murder to blame you for!"

"But I have not the slightest intention of killing you," said the Lizard quietly. "At least not yet—you are much more useful to me alive."

As he spoke, Landor took Ames by the arm and led him along the hall. When they reached a door at the far end The Lizard opened it and the two men entered the room beyond.

Ames blinked when he found himself in the brightly lighted room, for the shades were carefully drawn and the electric fixtures had been turned on.

A dark-haired woman whom Ames had never seen before sat on a chair in one corner of the room. She puffed upon a cigarette as she slowly examined Ames from head to foot.

"We seem to have a visitor, Glynn," she remarked finally looking at Landor. "You must introduce me."

"I'll be delighted," The Lizard smiled. "Miss Lawton, may I present Mr. Ted Ames."

"Mr. Ames!" Lily smiled. "This is a surprise—and I have heard so much about you." She laughed mockingly.

Ames bowed but said nothing. He was looking about the room seeking some indication that Norma was in the house. He knew that this woman was the leading lady with the Troupers' Stock Company, the woman that Billie Fenton had mentioned as having evidently interested Glynn Landor. It was quite obvious that the two were good friends, though just what Lily Lawton might be doing in this old house Ames did not know.

"If you are looking for Miss Burton by any chance," said Lily as she observed Ames' searching gaze, "you'll find her in the next room!" She nodded toward a closed door at her left.

Landor stood watching Ames, a faint smile upon his face. His hands were thrust into the pockets of his topcoat, for The Lizard still wore his coat and hat, and Ames realized that one of those hands held an automatic.

"Then Miss Burton is in there?" asked Ames looking at the door the actress had indicated.

"Why don't you see for yourself, Ames?" demanded The Lizard with a quick glance at Lily.

Ames caught the glance. From the first he had felt there was some trick to the whole thing. Both Landor and the woman were far too willing to have him investigate the next room. He was sure it was a trap, though just what it might be he did not know.

He glanced about and saw that there was another door on the opposite side of the room. As he looked in that direction he heard the muffled sound of a sob. The others did not appear to have heard it.

"What's the matter, Ames?" Landor moved closer as he spoke. He smiled mockingly as he drew a package of cigarettes from his pocket and placed one in his mouth. "Not afraid of what you might find in there are you? I told you this business was dangerous—for Miss Burton!"

"No!" said Ames sharply, and as he spoke his right arm swung upward in a smashing uppercut that caught The Lizard squarely on the point of the chin. "Not a bit!"

As Landor staggered back Ames' left arm followed the course of his right with a blow that jarred Landor from head to heels. Lily screamed and rose from her chair as Ames struck again. This time The Lizard fell to the floor. Ames dived on top of him, anxious to get the automatic before the other could use it. Landor was fighting now, punching wildly at Ames. The latter's fists pounded at The Lizard, and then as the man tried to rise, Ames' right fist caught him on the chin for the third time. Landor's head struck the hard wooden floor with a thud, and he suddenly went limp.

Ames went hastily through the man's pockets, and found the automatic. He leaped to his feet, the weapon in his hand, just in time to duck the wooden chair that Lily Lawton had swung in his direction. The chair fell to the floor with a crash.

Roughly Ames pushed the woman aside as she drew near him again. She stumbled back and then sat down suddenly in the chair she had just vacated a few moments ago. She sat there staring at him dazedly.

"Sit there or I'll shoot!" warned Ames grimly as he went to the door at the right of the room. He found it was locked on the outside by a heavy bolt. He drew this back and flung the door open.

"Norma!" he called. "Norma!"

As he spoke the girl appeared in the doorway. She stared at him wildly, and then as she realized who he was, she gave a cry of joy.

"Ted!" she exclaimed. "Oh it's you!" With a sob of relief she rushed to him and flung her arms around his neck, hardly realizing what she was doing. "I hoped you would come!"

For the moment Ames forgot everything but the fact that the girl was in his arms.

He did not hear The Lizard as the latter got slowly to his feet.

Lily watched tensely, her arms gripping the arms of her chair.

Silently Landor picked up a chair. As he raised it above his head to bring it crashing down upon Ames, the door on the left opened.

"Put that chair down!" commanded Detective Sergeant O'Shay tersely, as he stood in the doorway covering Landor with a revolver. "Drop it I say!"

Ames released Norma and swung around as he heard the words. He was covering Landor with his own weapon as he glanced at the sergeant.

"I thought something was up when I seen you trailing that guy." O'Shay nodded toward The Lizard. "So I did a little shadowing on my own hook. Looks like I stumbled into something sweet."

"Who are you?" demanded Ames.

"Detective Sergeant O'Shay," said that individual with a grin. "And very much at your service, young feller." He looked at Norma. "Are you by any chance an artist, Miss?"

"Yes," Norma nodded. "Why?"

"That makes it perfect," said O'Shay. "Chief Kenny is gonna be pleased!" He produced his whistle from his pocket and blew it shrilly. "The whole bunch of you are under arrest."

Ames looked at Norma regretfully, but she only smiled.

"I'm glad!" she said softly, and then a thought struck her. "Are you a detective, Ted?"

"Him a detective!" O'Shay laughed. "No, I'll bet he ain't—he's not the type," he grinned, the memory of what Kenny had said to him still in his mind. "But maybe he's Don Juan—whoever that is."

"Maybe he is," said Norma softly, looking at Ames.

22

FOUR PRISONERS

CHIEF KENNY GLANCED at the clock on his desk. It was just four p.m. It startled him when he realized that less than twenty-four hours had elapsed since he received the report that something had occurred at the residence of Fosdick Martin. The subsequent events had developed with a rapidity which might have left a man with a less phlegmatic disposition than Kenny in a state of mental turmoil. The Martin case had proved an octopus whose long arms had reached out to entwine a number of people in a grip of suspicion and death.

In the interval that had passed two men had died, cruelly murdered because they had known too much. At the moment, Homer Stevens was lodged in the cell in which Grant Ellery had been found the night before. The private investigator had refused to talk when Kenny had attempted to question him earlier in the afternoon. He had merely smiled and announced that he would have a lot to say later. The chief had let him return to his cell reluctantly for he felt that in what Homer Stevens might say he would find the solution to the mystery. Yet Kenny was adverse to attempting drastic methods to force the private investigator to speak. If that were necessary it would come later, when Stevens indicated that he intended to actually remain silent for any length of time.

Kenny found that he liked Stevens in spite of the man's erratic actions. There was something sincere about him which impressed the chief. He was still more than half inclined to believe that Stevens was just what he represented himself to be, a private detective. Still Kenny had gone beyond the point where he could permit his personal likes or dislikes to sway his good judgment. Stevens had acted suspiciously, and therefore the chief deemed it advisable for the man to be locked up. Stevens seemed to realize Kenny's attitude in the matter and he had displayed very little resentment at his arrest.

Kenny glanced at the door of his office as it opened abruptly and O'Shay stepped into the room. There was a satisfied grin upon the heavy face of the detective sergeant as he closed the door behind him carefully and then turned to the chief.

"Well, Tim," remarked Kenny. "Did you find the blond girl?"

"I'll tell the world I did!" exclaimed O'Shay. "Say Chief, I sure stumbled into something sweet this afternoon!"

"What do you mean?"

"I just brought in four prisoners, and believe me they know something."

"Four prisoners!" Kenny stared at the detective sergeant. "Who are they?"

"Two men, a woman and a girl. The girl is the blond you told me to look for and the woman is Lily Lawton."

"Fine!" exclaimed the chief delightedly. "Miss Lawton and the girl got away from me this afternoon. Where did you find them?"

"I spotted a young fellow, Ted Ames, he says is his name. Anyway he was trailing another guy, a man named Landor."

"Glynn Landor?" broke in the chief.

"Yes. Do you know him?"

"I've seen him around town, and know him by sight and name. He has a record."

"Well, when I seen this Ames trailing Landor I followed them. Landor goes into a house over on Larkin Street. Ames hangs around a few minutes and then goes in, too."

"But I thought you said that Ames was trailing Landor?"

"He was, but I guess Ames sort of figured on making a grandstand play. Steppin' in and doing a little noble hero stuff."

"What did you do then?"

"I sneaked around the house and when I found a window that was open I climbed in. That part of it was easy. Soon as I get inside I hear a grand fight going on in the next room, rough and tumble stuff it sounds like. So I opened the door a little bit when no one was looking and takes it in. I was just in time to see this Ames give Landor a beautiful sock in the jaw. He finally knocks him out, too. A damn good fighter, that boy."

O'Shay laughed as he dropped into a chair. Kenny glared at him.

"Then what happened?" he demanded impatiently.

"The Lawton woman picks up a chair and starts to hit Ames with it when she sees that Landor is out. He stops her, Ames I mean, and gives her a shove. She lands in a chair and just sits there watching him kinda dazed. Ames has a gun that he frisked from this Landor. He covers the actress while he opens the door to the next room and the blond girl, Norma Burton, steps out."

"Norma Burton!" exclaimed Kenny. "Why, I knew her father well. She comes from a fine family. What the devil is she doing mixed up in this?"

"How do I know?" said O'Shay with a grin. "I'm leaving all that part of it to you. Anyway the girl and this Ames go into a romantic clinch. Just about then Landor comes to, and gets up. He grabs the chair and is just about to put Ames out when I step in and arrest the whole bunch. I blew my whistle and Cassidy, who is on the beat, hears it and comes a runnin'. So Cassidy and I brought all four of them in. They're outside making faces at the Desk Sergeant."

"Good work!" exclaimed Kenny. He thought for a moment. "Bring the girl to me at once, Tim. I'll talk to her alone first. Then I'll see what the others have to say."

"Right." The detective sergeant rose and moved toward the door. Then he turned, his face serious. "Treat her gently, Chief, she's a nice kid, and I guess she's scared."

"Go on!" barked Kenny, but he smiled as he spoke. "She's a suspect."

"Not with me," said O'Shay. "She's a wow!"

Kenny laughed softly as the detective sergeant left the room. He quite agreed. He was not really inclined to consider James Burton's daughter a suspect in a murder case.

A few moments later O'Shay reappeared and Norma Burton was with him. The girl looked at the chief nervously as he rose from his desk and bowed.

"Please be seated, Miss Burton," Kenny said with a friendly smile, as he waved his hand in the direction of the chair that faced the desk.

"You are Chief Kenny?" asked Norma, gazing at the grey-haired man who had resumed his seat at the desk. "The chief of police?"

"Yes, Miss Burton," said Kenny, and he continued to smile. "But please don't let the fact alarm you."

"It doesn't now," said Norma with a note of relief. "You see I rather thought you would be different. Hard and stern and all that sort of thing, and I really don't believe you are!"

"I'm not—at least I hope such is not the case." The chief's expression grew serious. "Still I'm afraid that there are a few questions I must ask you, Miss Burton."

"I—I rather expected that." A hint of nervousness had returned to Norma's voice. "It's about Mr. Martin I suppose?"

"Yes, that and what has happened today."

"I'll try to explain as best I can, Chief Kenny. Though I really know so little." She looked at him appealingly. "I guess first I had better tell you that I was at Mr. Martin's house last night."

"You were? At the time he was stabbed?"

"Yes." Norma nodded. "But I didn't see anything. I only knew that something had happened."

"Just what, Miss Burton?"

"Please, may I try and tell it all in my own way?" Norma looked at the chief anxiously. "Questions seem to confuse me. You don't mind if I just—just sort of talk, do you, Chief Kenny?"

"Of course not," said Kenny soothingly. "Go right ahead."

"Thank you." Norma paused to gather her thoughts. "I guess I will have to go back a little. I have known Mr. Martin ever since I was a tiny kid. Daddy and he used to be friends before my father died. I know there are lots of people in North City who hate Mr. Martin—" she broke off as a thought struck her. "Mr. Martin will live, won't he, Chief Kenny?"

"Yes, I had a report from the hospital at noon. He is still a very sick man—too weak to talk as yet, but slowly gaining."

"Oh, I'm glad." Norma smiled. "I must try and tell you my story. As I was saying, lots of people dislike Mr. Martin and say nasty things about him, but he has always been mighty sweet to me. He always treated me just as though I were his daughter—and I was welcome to come out to his house any time.

"Yesterday evening about seven I decided that I would go out there. I had been working on a miniature of Mr. Martin's grandmother, and also cleaning up some of the paintings in his gallery. It was raining when I started but I didn't mind, and besides I took a taxi. When I reached the house, I remembered that Mr. Martin had said something about having an important business engagement last night. I decided not to disturb him, so I unlocked the front door and went directly to the gallery where the pictures are. I worked a little on one of the old paintings, but after a while I became sleepy. I curled up in a big chair, and finally did fall asleep. I must have been very tired for I slept for some time.

"When I woke the house seemed very quiet. Yet I had the strangest feeling, just as though something awful had happened, and I didn't know what. I thought it might have been some half-remembered part of a dream." She shook her head. "It's hard to explain."

"I know just what you mean," said Kenny as the girl paused. "I've had the same feeling often."

"But I guess it wasn't all a dream," said Norma. "Something did happen while I was asleep, for that was when—when Mr. Martin was stabbed."

"But you neither saw nor heard anything?"

"Not then. When I was wide awake I went to the closed door of the gallery, and opened it. The hall outside was dark. As I opened the door I heard a voice in the room across the hall say, 'You'd better phone for the police, Fulson.'"

"You're sure of that?" interrupted Kenny.

"Quite sure." Norma nodded her blond head. "I heard the words distinctly, even though the door of the room across the hall was closed. They frightened me. A moment later I realized that there was a man standing in the hallway. I was sure he was a burglar, and I didn't know what to do. I was afraid that if I screamed he would grab me—I didn't know what might happen. I wanted him to go away, for I was afraid. So I told him to please go—and then when he didn't seem to realize what I was saying I told him that they had sent for the police." She smiled nervously. "I know it sounds rather silly, but I wanted to get rid of him at once, and that was all I could think of doing. He turned his flashlight on me, but I was so frightened then that I stepped back into the gallery and locked the door."

"Did you recognize the man?" asked Kenny.

"No, it was too dark in the hall for that. After I locked the door I decided to leave the house at once. So I stepped out through a window of the gallery onto the back porch. It wasn't very hard to do as the room is on the ground floor. Then I ran through the grounds until I reached the highway. I went along this for some little distance and then a bus came along and I took it back into town. I had the miniature with me."

"I see," said Kenny, "but why didn't you tell us about all this before, Miss Burton? Surely you read what happened in the morning papers?"

"Yes, I did read about it in the morning paper. But after I realized how terrible it all was—I was afraid. I wouldn't even tell my roommate, Miss Fenton, about it. We share an apartment and I usually tell her everything."

"It doesn't matter," Kenny smiled. "Now that you have told me all about it, I think I understand just how you felt. But what happened today, Miss Burton?"

"Must I tell about that, too?" Norma looked at the chief questioningly. "I really can't quite explain all of it myself."

"Yes, I'm afraid it is best that you do," said Kenny. "And perhaps we may be able to understand the things you can't explain."

"But if I do, will you promise not to—to be too hard on Mr. Ames?"

"Is Mr. Ames a friend of yours?" asked Kenny, and O'Shay grinned as the chief spoke.

"Oh, yes, a very good friend," said Norma, her eyes shining.

"I won't be hard on him then, I assure you."

"Then I'll tell you all I know."

Swiftly Norma related how she had first met Ames the previous night at her studio, though she went into little detail. She then told of having met him this morning and thought that he was a detective.

Kenny questioned her on this point and learned far more than the girl realized, but he finally asked her to continue her narrative. She told of Lily Lawton having called on her and pleaded with her to come to the actress' apartment, to aid Ames.

"And then when we got there Mr. Ames wasn't there at all," said Norma. "I thought it strange. But when I asked Miss Lawton about it she said he might have stepped out, but she was sure he would be back and I must wait. I finally agreed to stay. While I was waiting Miss Lawton stepped into the next room. I thought I heard her talking to someone, but I couldn't be sure.

"She came back in a few moments and said, 'My dear, I have had a wonderful new perfume made up, do smell it—it's glorious.' She held a handkerchief to my nose and I don't remember what happened for quite a while after that. It must have been chloroform or something—anyhow, the next thing I knew I found myself tied to a chair and all alone in a room."

"That was where I found you," said Kenny.

"Yes. It was you," Norma nodded. "I remember now—I didn't recognize you then. You blew a police whistle and then went away. Right afterwards Miss Lawton rushed in and cut my ropes. She made me leave the apartment house by the back stairs. She frightened me, and I was afraid to disobey her orders. Finally we got into a taxi and were driven to that old house where Mr. Ames and this gentleman here," Norma smiled at O'Shay, "found us—and I certainly was glad to see him."

"That seems to be all, Miss Burton," said Kenny as Norma finished. "I believe every word you have told me—and just to show you that I really do trust you I am going to let you go home."

"Oh, thank you, Chief!" exclaimed Norma as she rose. "You have been very kind," she hesitated. "But there is one favor I would like to ask you."

"I'll be delighted to grant it if I can. What is it, Miss Burton?"

"Could you please let Mr. Ames go, too? I'm sure that he had nothing to do with what happened out at Mr. Martin's house."

"I'm sorry, Miss Burton, but I can't grant that yet." Kenny smiled as he walked to the door with her. "But I may be able to do so after I have talked to him. We'll hope so anyway."

"I shall hope so!" said Norma softly. "There is so much that I want to talk to him about!"

"Then perhaps we had better speed things up a bit," said Kenny. "Sergeant, see that Miss Burton gets a taxi, please, and then bring Mr. Ames to me."

"Yes, sir," said O'Shay as he left the room with the girl.

Kenny smiled as the door closed, and he returned to his desk. He had a hunch that the Martin case would be solved before many more hours had passed.

23
A MAN DIES

CHIEF KENNY PACED UP and down his office impatiently. He was in far from an amiable frame of mind. The past two hours had been far less productive of results than he had hoped. The solution of the Martin case still seemed to be a remote possibility. Kenny found himself groping in the dark, and yet he had by no means lost hope of solving the puzzle soon. He was sure it would be accomplished and it was merely the delay that annoyed him.

In his estimation the three interviews he had had with Ted Ames, Lily Lawton, and Glynn Landor had in each case proved futile. None of the three had been willing to make any definite statements, and Kenny had been working under difficulties. When he had tried to question Lily Lawton she had gone into a fit of nervous hysteria that the chief secretly considered a remarkable display of histrionics. In Kenny's estimation Lily Lawton was a very excellent actress. When he had found that he could do nothing with her, he had permitted her to return to her apartment under the double guard of a detective and a police matron, both of whom had been instructed to remain on constant guard over the actress until Kenny sent for her to be brought back to the police station.

Ames had refused to say anything, for he did not know how much Norma had revealed to the chief, and he had no desire to implicate her any more deeply than she might be at present. Besides, Ames felt that it was not advisable for him to admit his former connection with Landor. Kenny finally had reluctantly

393

ordered Ames to be placed in a cell and held there for the time being as a material witness.

As for Glynn Landor, the chief had found him the most unperturbed of the three questioned. Landor had quietly stated that he could explain everything when the proper moment arose. He had been very suave and sure of himself. So much so that he had annoyed Kenny greatly. While the chief could not quite place the man, he was sure that Landor was a criminal with a record. After nearly an hour of questioning which had proved futile Kenny had ordered Landor placed in the cell next to Tom Hogan, the drunken laborer who was still being held, as were Danny Lester, Brown the confidence man, and Homer Stevens.

Kenny walked over to his desk and looked at the clock. It was just six p.m. Frowning, he again paced the floor. He was still moving restlessly up and down when O'Shay knocked on the door and then entered the room.

"Them newspaper men give me a pain," said the detective sergeant as he dropped into a chair. "Always asking questions—questions!"

"What's wrong now?" demanded Kenny returning to his desk.

"Aw, Heath, and Davis from the *Evening Banner* were just here. They wanted to see you, but I wouldn't let them. They got wind of our having some new prisoners, and wanted to know what there was to it. Of course, I didn't tell them anything. But you know those guys, they'd already talked the Desk Sergeant into letting them see the blotter. He shouldn't have done it, but they got the names of Landor and Ames."

"Don't worry about it," said Kenny. "They'd probably get that anyway. It doesn't matter. Are they still hanging around?"

"Nope, they left when I told them they couldn't see you. But they'll be back. They always come back."

"Hm." The chief thought for a moment. "Listen, Tim, where did you put Landor—what cell, I mean?"

"In number two, next to that guy Hogan. Nobody on the other side of Landor—that's an empty."

"And Homer Stevens is in the cell in which Ellery was murdered."

"Yes." O'Shay looked at Kenny. "What of it?"

"Nothing, only it might be bad from a psychological angle."

"Oh, yea?" The detective sergeant was puzzled. "I don't get you."

"Well, it seems to be barely possible that Glynn Landor may be the murderer, and if he is, it might have an interesting mental effect upon him should he find himself locked up in the same cell in which Grant Ellery was killed."

"I'll bet it would if he's the guy," said O'Shay. "Do you think he is, Chief?"

"I don't know, Tim. It's a possibility, and yet I've had something else in the back of my mind ever since last night." The chief played with the ivory elephant paper-weight on his desk. "I think we'd better try it anyway. Put Landor in Ellery's cell."

"Right, but what will I do with Stevens?"

"Stevens, hm." The chief thought for a moment. "Bring him in here to me, I want to talk to him."

"O.K.," said O'Shay as he left the room.

The detective sergeant returned in a little less than ten minutes and now the private investigator was with him. Stevens smiled as Kenny motioned him to the chair which faced the desk.

"I rather hoped you would send for me," he said as he sat down. "If you hadn't done so I probably would have asked someone to tell you that I wanted an interview with you."

"Then you are going to talk?" Kenny smiled as he looked at the stout man. His hunch was proving even better than he had expected.

"Yes, I'm going to talk," said the private investigator. "In fact, Chief Kenny, I realize that the time has come when it is best that I tell you all that I know about this case."

"Good!" The chief waved O'Shay toward a chair. "Sit down, Tim, I want you to hear this."

"So do I!" Stevens laughed. "I feel that the sergeant should hear all that I have to say." He grew serious. "I'm afraid I have let you draw one or two false conclusions, Chief."

"In what way?"

"When we first met I intimated that I had been retained on this case by somebody very close to Fosdick Martin—"

"And that was Miss Lawton?"

"No, when I said that a person who was very close to Mr. Martin had retained me, I'm afraid I misled you by letting you think it was a woman. It wasn't at all."

"No?" Kenny looked puzzled. "Who then?"

"Four days ago I was retained by Mr. Fosdick Martin himself, through his New York attorneys."

"What?"

"Just so." Stevens smiled. "You may recall that threatening blackmail letter which we found in Mr. Martin's desk this morning. Well, Mr. Martin apparently considered the threat quite serious. The letter we found was the third that Mr. Martin had received. He had had two others within the past week or so."

"Blackmail, eh?"

"Of course, but with a real menace in the threat of murder if Mr. Martin did not comply with the demand. I didn't realize how serious it was myself until I first saw The Lizard sneaking around the grounds of the Martin estate about nine o'clock last night."

"The Lizard!" exclaimed Kenny impatiently. "Who or what the devil is that?"

"The Lizard is one of the most ruthless and cold-blooded criminals that ever came out of the underworld. A lone wolf type of man, who has had his hands in all sorts of crooked deals, and one who does not shirk at burglary if he thinks it worth his while. Those jewel robberies which have been going on around this section can doubtless be credited to him."

"But who is he?" demanded the chief. "The Lizard means nothing to me."

"His real name—" Homer Stevens paused deliberately, and smiled, "is Glynn Landor!"

"Glynn Landor!" shouted Kenny. "The man O'Shay brought in this afternoon!"

"Yes," the private investigator nodded. "The man O'Shay just placed in my cell a few minutes ago." He looked at the chief. "A nice bit of psychology on your part, Chief. Particularly if Landor is the murderer—and I'm convinced he is."

"Can you prove it?" asked Kenny eagerly.

"I'll state all the facts I know and let you decide," said Stevens. "First, we know that Landor is a criminal. Second, I am sure that he instigated the blackmail plot against Fosdick Martin."

"But he was not alone in that," said the chief. "The man in the cell opposite the one you were in is mixed up in it. A confidence man, going under the name of Brown."

"All right. We'll leave Brown aside for a moment." Stevens dismissed the confidence man from his mind with a wave of his hand. "Let's stick to Landor. Last night shortly after nine I was hidden behind a tree near the Martin house. I had followed Landor in from the grounds, or rather the entrance to them. I watched Landor go up on the porch and disappear in the shadows to the right of the French windows of Martin's study."

"Was it dark enough for a man to hide in the shadows of the porch?" asked Kenny.

"Yes, it was- a black night, as you remember. I remained where I was. Suddenly from a tree not far from where I stood, a masked figure dashed toward the porch. Then abruptly the lights in the study went out." Stevens paused impressively. "Do you see it now, Chief. Martin was stabbed in that interval of darkness—and it was either Landor or the masked man who did it." The private investigator frowned. "And I think it was Landor."

"Why?" asked Kenny softly.

"Because he is the most logical person to have done it. He had been standing there on the porch long enough to overhear the quarrel between Ellery and Martin."

"But if that was the case, why did Landor spoil his own blackmail scheme? Martin was no use to him dead. No use at all."

"Of course not, but it gave Landor a chance to kill Martin, or at least try to, and also get the collection of diamonds."

"The diamonds!" exclaimed the chief. "You know about them?"

"Of course," Stevens smiled. "I told you Mr. Martin retained me—he told me everything." He thought for a second. "But we are not sure that it was Landor yet. Let me continue to state what I know. As I stood there, a woman ran down off the porch."

"Who was she?" asked Kenny, thinking of Norma Burton's story.

"Lily Lawton. I recognized her when she passed me, for she was not five feet away from the tree behind which I stood. I had seen her with Mr. Martin, so I knew her face."

"Just what is the connection between the actress and Martin?" asked Kenny.

"Rather a novelty," Stevens laughed. "I suspected a bit of sordid romance myself at first, but I was wrong. Lily Lawton happens to be Fosdick Martin's first cousin. Her father and Martin's father were brothers. The old man has never wanted his relationship with Lily Lawton known, merely because she was on the stage and he was afraid his name would be used for publicity purposes. I strongly suspect that it has rather amused Martin to let the dear public think whatever they chose about himself and Miss Lawton."

"Hm," said Kenny. "That explains a little bit about her, but why did she hate Grant Ellery?"

"Possibly because Ellery wasn't interested in her." Stevens smiled. "Women are that way sometimes, you know."

"But what was her connection with Landor?"

"Oh, that. It took me some time to figure that out, but it is all clear now. Do you happen to know whose money is backing the Troupers' Stock Company here in town?"

"Why, a man named Frank Raleigh appears to be the head of it."

"Raleigh is only the local manager. Glynn Landor owns the troupe, and Lily Lawton knows it—that's why she had to do what he said at all times."

"But why did she come here to see me last night?" asked Kenny.

"I sent her," answered Stevens calmly. "I went around to her apartment—bluffed her into thinking that I knew more than I did— and sent her to you in the hope that she might more or less spill the beans as far as Landor was concerned. When I was at her apartment I saw a cigarette case with the initials G. L. on it, and knew that Landor had been there."

"But Landor must have had a very powerful influence over her to make her kidnap—" Kenny paused and stared at the private investigator as he realized that the latter probably did not know what he was talking about. "It doesn't matter."

"Landor is in himself a powerful influence, said Stevens. "Later last night I met him out at the Martin estate and warned him away."

"Why didn't you arrest him?"

"I hadn't enough on him. I decided that if I gave him plenty of rope he might hang himself. He did, for he is in jail now."

"And you think he is the murderer?" asked Kenny slowly.

"I'm positive," replied Stevens. "Why, I—"

Abruptly the lights in Kenny's office went out, leaving the room in darkness.

"Good God!" came Kenny's voice. "I knew it! Come on, the jail—quick!"

Already the chief had made his way to the door; as he tore it open the lights in the office came on again. But Kenny did not pause. He started on a run toward the cells with Stevens and O'Shay close behind him as they dashed through the corridors.

When they reached the corridor between the cells Kenny gave a shout. A blue uniformed figure lay in a limp heap near the door of the first cell on the right.

"It's Yeager," said Kenny, and he leaned over the still form. "Just knocked out." He stood up frowning. "I wonder which one," he said looking about him.

"What do you mean?" demanded Stevens.

Kenny did not answer. He had gone to the door of the cell in which Glynn Landor had been placed.

"We don't need to look any further," said the chief, staring in.

The Lizard lay upon the floor of the cell, sprawled face downward, a knife sticking in his back. The cell door was unlocked.

Kenny stepped inside quickly, and examined the man on the floor.

"Still warm," said the chief. "But he's dead." He rose to his feet, his face grim, as he turned to Stevens. "That was meant to be you," he said nodding toward the still figure. "The murderer made a big mistake when he switched off the lights!"

"For me?" asked Stevens hoarsely, his face white. "You mean?"

"That the murderer thought you knew too much," said Kenny slowly. "O'Shay," he said, turning to the detective sergeant. "See if Yeager's keys aren't missing. Also if the Eastern Avenue door isn't open again!"

It took O'Shay but a few moments to report that the chief was right in both guesses.

"I thought so," said Kenny. He smiled grimly.

"You know the murderer?" demanded Stevens eagerly. "Is that it, Chief?"

"I have some grave suspicions," said Kenny. "Oh, Tim, you had better phone our dear friend Doctor Wilson—have him come right away—and if any of the newspaper men show up I'm ready to talk for publication!"

24
YOU ARE GUILTY!

THE CLOCK IN FRONT OF HIM pointed to nine-fifteen as Chief Kenny again sat in his office. Grouped about him now were four men. On his left was Homer Stevens, watching everyone alertly. In front of Kenny, in the chair in which he always placed those whom he questioned, sat Deputy Coroner Samuel Wilson. He stared at the chief viciously through his heavy, shell-rimmed glasses. The doctor was still in a disagreeable humor. On Kenny's right sat Dave Heath, of the *Morning News*, a cigarette in one corner of his mouth, his hat thrust back on his shock of red hair, a pencil in his left hand, a bit of paper on his knee. Beyond him sat Detective Sergeant O'Shay— there was a satisfied expression upon his face, for he was sure Chief Kenny knew exactly what he was doing.

Kenny had not brought the four men to his office until the coroner had completed the necessary arrangements in regard to Glynn Landor. The sinister individual known as The Lizard had gone on his last journey when he was taken away from the police station.

"Before making any direct accusations," said Kenny and he glanced at Doctor Wilson as he spoke, "I shall try to give you all a few further details of the case. Three men have died because they were suspected of knowing who it was that stabbed Fosdick Martin just twenty-four hours ago. Two of those men did know—the third did not. That third man was Grant Ellery.

"To begin with, the murderer was instigated by three motives, and the first and most important of these was greed, and there was also hate, and last, but not least, insanity. These three things

401

caused his attempt to murder Fosdick Martin last night." Kenny paused.

The four men remained silent, but Doctor Wilson drummed his fingers nervously upon the arm of his chair.

"The murderer knew the confidence man, Harry Brown, and between them they planned to intimidate Fosdick Martin. They hoped to frighten him to such an extent that he would leave fifty thousand dollars in cash on the sun-dial in his garden." The chief paused. "You may wonder how I know all this, and the explanation is that within the past hour Brown, the confidence man has talked. Glynn Landor's death frightened him, for he feared he would be next. And he might have been!"

The chief's eyes swept the faces of the men gathered about him. Stevens was leaning forward drinking in every word. Heath was making little notes upon the paper on his knee, while O'Shay was all attention.

"The plot between the murderer and Brown was overheard by Glynn Landor. It suited his plans perfectly. He doubtless felt that the blackmailing would not be carried through successfully, but to him that did not matter. For his silence, he demanded the collection of unset diamonds which Fosdick Martin possessed. He did not say how or when he would get them. I am beginning to have a great deal of respect for The Lizard's rather warped mentality.

"Unfortunately, Mr. Martin refused to be frightened by the threatening letters he received." Kenny glanced at Stevens. "Perhaps his courage may have been increased a bit by the presence of this gentleman here."

The private investigator said nothing but he smiled grimly.

"The murderer went to Mr. Mart's residence last night. He was masked. He lurked outside in the shadows of the porch and overheard Martin and Ellery quarreling. The murderer did not know that Glynn Landor was also on the porch watching him. The quarrel provided an opportunity for which the murderer had not even hoped. He realized that if he could kill Martin then and there, the blame would doubtless be cast upon Ellery.

"This morning in looking over the study I discovered that the electric switch that turns on the lights in that room is a double one. There is one at the door as you enter the room, and a second in the wall close to the French windows.

"The murderer awaited his opportunity. When Ellery threatened Martin and then lapsed into silence to carry through his bluff, the murderer pushed the switch near the windows. In the darkness the murderer stabbed Fosdick Martin and then stepped back onto the porch. But when he struck he spoke—and doubtless he may have felt that Ellery would remember his voice. I suspect that Ellery grabbed him anyway, but the murderer broke away.

"Fulson, who had been listening to Martin and Ellery quarreling stepped into the room, closed the door and then switched on the lights. He lied about it for he was afraid of being implicated deeper, and he was sure he would be if he admitted entering the room.

"Fulson was mixed up in the whole thing pretty deeply. It was he who made sure that Fosdick Martin actually received the blackmail notes. Brown and the murderer had sized the secretary up as a little sneak and decided he would be useful." The chief paused.

"So that was why he tried to hide the note this morning," said Stevens.

"Yes, Fulson knew he would receive fifty thousand dollars in Martin's will if the old man died—and he had no objection to someone else trying to blackmail him for a similar sum, as he had been promised a share of that. If Martin was actually killed, all the better for Fulson." Again the chief paused.

The others waited patiently for him to continue.

"I'm afraid I may have created a wrong impression," said Kenny slowly. "There may be one or two of you here who think that I have been implicating Doctor Wilson. But one man knows I am not."

"Implicating me?" exclaimed the deputy coroner excitedly. "What the devil do you mean?"

"Nothing to alarm you, Doctor," said Kenny. "There is only one man who could have murdered Grant Ellery, and murdered the secretary and Landor because they knew too much, and there he sits!" The chief swung around so that he faced Dave Heath. "He is the murderer!" he said pointing to the police reporter.

"You're crazy, Chief," Heath laughed. "I didn't do it."

"Oh, yes, you did," said Kenny coldly. "And you gave yourself away all the way through by being just a bit too clever!"

"It's a lie!" shouted Heath rising from his chair as he observed the expression on the faces of the others—the four countenances that stared at him were hard and stern. "If I did it, prove it, damn you!"

O'Shay had moved with startling rapidity for a man of his bulk. He was now standing close beside the police reporter, waiting for any move upon Heath's part.

"I can prove it!" said Kenny. "I can prove that you are guilty!"

"I'll get you for this!" shouted the reporter as he lunged toward the chief. "I'll kill you!"

O'Shay went into action abruptly. His big arms circled the reporter in a bear-like grip—and a moment later a pair of handcuffs clicked about the struggling man's wrists. The detective sergeant thrust Heath roughly back in his chair.

"I'll tell the rest of it now," said Kenny calmly. "I think Heath will listen more quietly. He has been, as I have said before, a bit too clever. I believe that I have just about covered everything up to the murder of Grant Ellery in his cell. As soon as he left Fosdick Martin's house last night Heath went directly to the hospital. He must have felt that he had not really killed Martin and gone to the hospital to be there in case the old man was brought in. Which, of course, he was.

"That was a mistake upon Heath's part. He doesn't usually cover the hospital for his paper. When I looked the matter up and found that he had arrived there first—it made me wonder when I connected it with the other things I have learned.

"Coroner Blake played right into Heath's hands when he gave him that report to bring to me. Heath knew that Martin had a chance to live, and doubtless as time passed he became more and more convinced that Grant Ellery had recognized his voice, for Heath had interviewed him often.

"The next thought which must have entered Heath's mind was to get rid of Ellery because he knew too much. I suspect that he planned the murder in the cell on the way down from the hospital. I made it easy for him myself, though I did not realize it until later."

"You made it easy?" demanded Doctor Wilson as the Chief paused. "How was that?"

"The night before last Heath dropped in to see if there was any news. He had been doing that for some time. I have always kept a set of keys which unlock the cells and the doors of the station house here in my desk. While Heath was here a few nights ago I left the room for a short time. I didn't even notice that the keys were missing until the next day, for I very seldom use them. When I did discover they were gone I thought I might have left them home in some other suit. Last night I was rather surprised to find them back in my desk."

"Then Heath put them there?" asked Stevens.

"Yes, last night," said Kenny.

"I didn't see him do it," exclaimed O'Shay, "and I was here all the time."

"He put them back last night as he answered the telephone for me," said Kenny, looking at the detective sergeant. "Remember when we left the room to see what had happened to Ellery and Heath called me back, Tim? The hospital was calling me about Fosdick Martin."

"Yes, I remember." O'Shay nodded.

"Well, Heath put the keys back then. He had used them to unlock the door leading in through Eastern Avenue to the cells. After he was inside he reached around the corner and unlocked the cell of Danny Lester. Heath's hands must have been wet—that was why Danny raved about seeing a shiny white hand as I heard him do last night.

"As soon as Heath unlocked Danny's cell he hurried back along the corridor and hid behind the door leading out to the street. I measured it last night and a man could hide behind it all right.

"Yeager chased Danny outside just as Heath hoped he would do. Heath worked fast. He unlocked the cells silently as he went along, probably to cast suspicion upon the others. Fulson did not hear him, nor did Brown, but when Heath went into Ellery's cell and murdered him both of those men saw him do it."

Kenny paused and glanced at the reporter. Since O'Shay had placed the handcuffs on his wrists Heath had sat motionless staring at the floor. He did not look up now.

"And knowing what we do about them," remarked Stevens, "it is quite easy to see why they would not talk."

"What's he mean?" barked Doctor Wilson.

"I'll tell you about that later, Doctor," said Kenny. "Now I want to present my facts against Heath. He left a handkerchief behind the door in the jail and also a vanity case in the summer house when Fulson was murdered to make us think that a woman was mixed up in the case. I am sure that he left the knife after committing each murder, for the simple reason that he had no chance to dispose of such weapons, for he has always remained at the scene of his crime. Or at least appeared after a very brief interval. There was always the possibility of his being searched in his mind, I suppose." A thought struck the chief and he turned to Stevens. "This morning when you said that the real murderer had shot Heath just what did you mean?"

"I thought that Glynn Landor had done it," replied the private investigator. "But I realize now that I was wrong."

"You were," said Kenny dryly. "Heath shot himself in the hand last night after he left you, and he did it for two reasons. First, to try to throw suspicion upon you, Mr. Stevens. Second, to be sent to the hospital. I have talked to Clark of the *News* and he told me that Heath appeared to be suffering from something more serious than the shot. Clark put a first aid dressing on Heath's hand and knew just how bad the wound was. So Clark did send him to the hospital. That was what Heath wanted. He hoped to be near Fosdick Martin, doubtless with the thought of finishing the old man," the chief smiled. "I thought of that and phoned the hospital last night, after Clark told me Heath had been shot. That was why the ward in which Heath was placed happened to be on another floor from that of Martin's private room, as Heath doubtless discovered."

"But why did he want to kill Martin in the first place?" demanded Doctor Wilson. "That's not quite clear in my mind."

"I'll tell you why!" exclaimed Heath, suddenly lifting his head and gazing about him wildly. "Because he had all the money—what right had he to have everything when I had nothing? He has always had everything and I nothing. I hated him, I planned the murder, yes, I planned it." He laughed hysterically. "He wouldn't meet our demand for fifty thousand—and he had millions. When I heard him there in his study talking money, money, to Ellery I only had one thought and that was to kill." Heath grinned weirdly, the light of insanity in his eyes. "To kill him with a knife—I liked that." He laughed again. "I like to use a knife!"

"The man is insane!" exclaimed Doctor Wilson watching the reporter closely. "Not the least doubt of it."

"Of course he is," said Kenny. "A madman with a lust for murder. Motives have been secondary to him, and yet those he has killed have died because he felt that they knew too much."

"I never would have suspected him," said O'Shay staring at Heath, who had again lapsed into silence and now sat staring at the floor. "How did you happen to do it, Chief?"

"Heath was just a bit too clever, and it was the cleverness of an insane mind. He overlooked a few little things which I have remembered. The most important of these was that there is usually only one way to get to my office from outside at night. That is by passing the desk sergeant on duty. Last night Heath *did not* pass the desk sergeant, nor was he announced by telephone as everyone who comes in to see me is—except my own men. Heath came in last night unannounced."

"But how did you know something had happened in the jail when we found Landor murdered earlier this evening?" asked Stevens.

"By the fact that the lights went out in my office," said Kenny. "Today I had my lights and those of the jail connected to the same switch. It is in the corridor and controls the lights in the cells. Heath switched off the lights and murdered Landor in the dark, thinking it was Stevens. Heath was not thinking as carefully that time as he was last night. For tonight he did pass the desk sergeant.

He turned out the lights, knocked out Yeager, got his keys, murdered Landor and then left by the Eastern Avenue door which he left open."

"Just a bit too clever seems to be right," said Stevens. "Then it was Heath who shot at me at Martin's house this noon. I saw someone but the man got away before I could get out of the house." The private investigator smiled at the chief. "I rather hoped you would rush out on the ground when I locked the door of the study, Chief, for then we would have come after him from two directions."

"So that's why the door was locked." Kenny smiled. "I understand now, Mr. Stevens." His face grew serious as he turned to the deputy coroner. "You asked for action in this case, Doctor Wilson. I think you have it."

"There is no doubt about it." Doctor Wilson looked at Heath. "The man is a homicidal maniac."

"I think I would like to kill you," said Heath lifting his head and staring at the deputy coroner. "With a knife!"

"Lock him up," said Kenny, and then shook his head as he reached for the phone. "No, wait a minute. Hello, Sergeant," he said over the wire. "Send two men in here right away."

A few minutes later Heath was led away by two broad-shouldered policemen.

"And now I think that about settles the Martin case," said Kenny. "I'm glad I phoned you and asked you to postpone that Coroner's Inquest you were going to have this afternoon, Doctor."

"So am I," said the deputy coroner. "Chief Kenny, I hope you will accept my apologies this time." He smiled. "I have a rotten disposition—I'm sorry."

"That's quite all right," the chief said. "And now, Doctor, if you wish any more details, Mr. Stevens and I will be glad to give them to you."

"Please do," said Doctor Wilson.

"In that case," remarked Kenny, "I think I had better pass the cigars, for we have quite a bit to tell you."

"And that ain't one of your hunches, Chief," said O'Shay with a grin. "Doctor, I've been listening in for some time, and they sure found out plenty!"

"And we haven't forgotten that you made some very vital arrests," said Stevens, smiling at the detective sergeant. "You've done your share in clearing things up, O'Shay."

25
HAPPINESS

NORMA BURTON WALKED NERVOUSLY about the big studio. From time to time she glanced at her wrist-watch, and then continued to walk up and down.

"Norma," exclaimed Billie, from the big chair in which she had been reading. "Sit down, child, you'll tire yourself out wandering around like that."

"Let me alone," said Norma crossly. "And besides I'm not a child—I'm as old as you are." She dropped into a chair near Billie as she spoke. "I don't understand it," she said half to herself. "Chief Kenny seemed so nice."

"Still worrying about Ted Ames?" asked Billie softly. "Don't you know that he may be held as a material witness or something?"

"Yes, I know." Norma nodded her pretty blond head. "But I don't want to think about that. Chief Kenny promised me that he would let Ted go after he had questioned him."

"But now that you have told me all that happened I can see how the chief might wish to detain Mr. Ames a while longer," said Billie thoughtfully, then she looked at the other girl. "Norma, has it occurred to you that Ted Ames might be the man you saw in the hall at Martin's house last night?"

"Ted, that man!" exclaimed Norma. "Why—why, that couldn't be. I'm sure that it was a burglar that I saw."

"Well, if it wasn't Ted Ames then how did he know that you had been there and question you about it enough to make you think he was a detective?" Billie knew that Ames had been the man in the hall, but she wanted to see if Norma knew it also—in spite of her denials.

"Oh, I don't know," said Norma nervously. "Honestly, Billie, sometimes you can ask as many questions as a detective yourself!"

Both girls glanced at each other as the doorbell rang.

"It's Ted," whispered Norma, as she rose to go to the door. "I'm sure of it."

"I hope you're right," said Billie. Norma opened the door. Ted Ames stood there smiling at her.

"Norma!" he exclaimed. "It's all over! The Martin case has been solved!"

"Oh, I'm so glad!" said Norma. "Come in. I've been worried about you. What happened?"

"Plenty!" said Ames smiling as he entered the studio. "Hello, Miss Fenton," he said as he saw Billie.

"Greetings, Ted," Billie smiled at him. "And don't you think it had better be Billie from now on?"

"Suits me fine," said Ames. "I'm all for it." He glanced at Norma. "Besides, you're going to see me around a lot from this moment hence!"

"Strange," said Billie dryly. "But I rather suspected that."

"Don't listen to her," commanded Norma. "Give me your hat and coat, Ted. And do tell us all that has happened."

"Well, something rather terrible happened," said Ames as he removed his topcoat and placed it on a chair with his hat. "I'm afraid you will find it a shock." He looked at Billie. "Glynn Landor was murdered tonight in his cell!"

"Glynn Landor murdered!" exclaimed Billie dazedly. "I can't believe it!"

"It's true, all right," said Ames. "In a way I'm sorry. I had disliked the man but I did not desire his death." He looked at Billie. "Did you tell Norma what I told you about myself this afternoon?"

"Of course not," said Billie. "I told you that I would never tell anyone."

"Um, secrets," remarked Norma. "I don't crave that so much."

"I will tell you about it," said Ames. "I can now—that it is all over."

"But who was the murderer?" asked Billie. "Did they catch him?"

"Yes, it was Dave Heath, a reporter on the *Morning News*. He did it all, but Glynn Landor worked with him to an extent. It's a long story. Chief Kenny wouldn't tell me all the details. But I learned the important facts." Ames smiled. "The vital thing is that Heath was the murderer. It will all be in the papers in the morning."

"Dave Heath," said Norma. "I never even heard of him. I wonder if he was the man I saw standing out in the hall at Mr. Martin's house last night?"

"No," Ames shook his head. "I was that man."

"Then you were there!"

"Of course he was," Billie smiled. "He told me about it early this afternoon."

"I had gone there to rob the place," said Ames quietly, watching Norma as he spoke.

"If you did you must have had a very good reason," said Norma softly.

"I did, but how fine of you to say so," exclaimed Ames. "And I'm so glad I can explain. I met Glynn Landor sometime ago in a speakeasy—I had gone there deliberately in the hope of making friends with the man. A man in the New York Detective Bureau had pointed Landor out to me at one time. Said that he was a famous criminal, but they had not been able to get very much on him. As I happen to be a free-lance newspaper feature writer I decided that I might get a wonderful series of articles if I could get in with the man they called The Lizard. I did, and I guess Billie can tell you the rest, Norma. What little of it you don't know."

"Then you are a reporter after all!" exclaimed Billie.

"Yes, I am," said Ames, his face lighting up. "And what a series of articles my adventures with Glynn Landor are going to make! I explained everything to Chief Kenny, and he assured me that no trouble would develop through my having worked with The Lizard, for when I had the opportunity I intended to call in the police."

"I think you had better tell everything you told me, to Norma," said Billie, "and Ted, explain how foolish I was to associate with that Landor." She rose. "I have a bit of a headache—so if you don't mind I'll leave you two to yourselves." She smiled. "I think you'll have a lot to talk about. Goodnight."

"Goodnight, Billie." Ames smiled. "You're right. It seems that I have been saving things to say to Norma all my life."

"Reckon I've been rather thrifty that way myself," said Norma with a happy laugh. "Night, Billie, you're a sweet child."

Smiling, Billie left them, closing the door leading into the other part of the studio apartment.

"I think I'd like to hear those words you've been saving," said Norma softly as Ames gathered her into his arms.

COACHWHIP PUBLICATIONS

COACHWHIPBOOKS.COM

THE MUMMY
CASE MYSTERY

DERMOT
MORRAH

ISBN 978-1-61646-250-7

THE PHILOSOPHER'S
MURDER CASE

JACK R. CRAWFORD

ISBN 978-1-61646-251-5

COACHWHIP PUBLICATIONS

COACHWHIPBOOKS.COM

THE
MUSEUM MURDER
JOHN T. McINTYRE

ISBN 978-1-61646-252-9

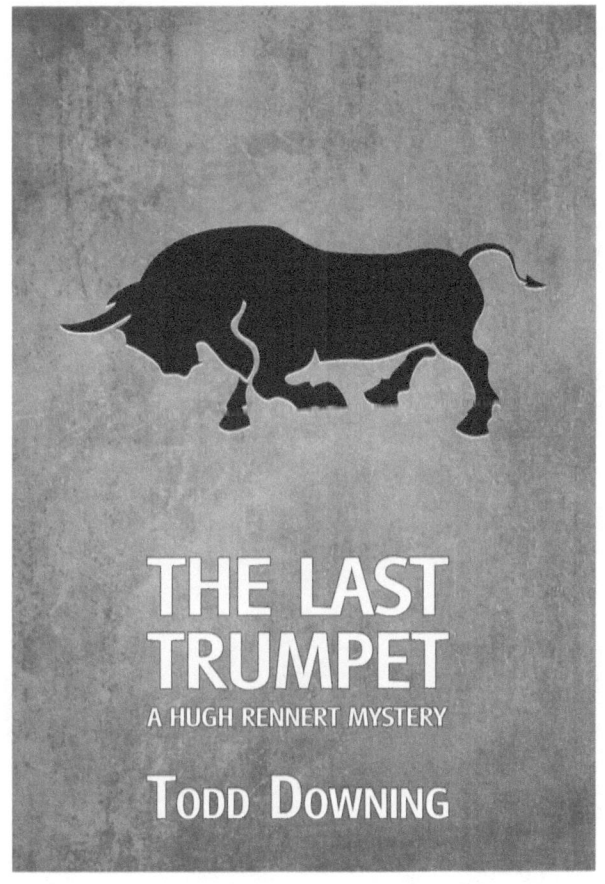

THE LAST
TRUMPET
A HUGH RENNERT MYSTERY

TODD DOWNING

ISBN 978-1-61646-152-2

COACHWHIP PUBLICATIONS

COACHWHIPBOOKS.COM

MURDER OF
THE HONEST BROKER

WILLOUGHBY SHARP

ISBN 978-1-61646-211-6

COACHWHIP PUBLICATIONS

COACHWHIPBOOKS.COM

ISBN 978-1-61646-232-1

COACHWHIP PUBLICATIONS

COACHWHIPBOOKS.COM

MURDER
À LA RICHELIEU
THE ADELAIDE ADAMS MYSTERIES
ANITA BLACKMON

ISBN 978-1-61646-222-2

www.ingramcontent.com/pod-product-compliance
Lightning Source LLC
Chambersburg PA
CBHW021845010726
47493CB00005B/1559